Evelyn Ashley

The Life of Henry John Temple

viscount Palmerston 1846-1865 - Vol. 2

Evelyn Ashley

The Life of Henry John Temple
viscount Palmerston 1846-1865 - Vol. 2

ISBN/EAN: 9783337095765

Printed in Europe, USA, Canada, Australia, Japan

Cover: Foto ©Raphael Reischuk / pixelio.de

More available books at **www.hansebooks.com**

OF

HENRY JOHN TEMPLE,

VISCOUNT PALMERSTON:

1846–1865.

WITH SELECTIONS FROM

His Speeches and Correspondence.

BY

THE HON. EVELYN ASHLEY, M.P

VOLUME II.

LONDON:

RICHARD BENTLEY & SON, NEW BURLINGTON STREET,

Publishers in Ordinary to Her Majesty.

1876.

CONTENTS OF VOLUME II.

CHAPTER I.

CHAPTER II.

CHAPTER III.

CHAPTER IV.

CHAPTER V.

CHAPTER VI.

CHAPTER VII.

CHAPTER VIII.

CHAPTER IX.

CHAPTER X.

APPENDIX.

LIFE OF HENRY JOHN TEMPLE,

THIRD VISCOUNT PALMERSTON, K.G.. G.C.B.

CHAPTER I.

Goes to the Home Office in the Aberdeen Administration—Work
at Home Office—Temporary Resignation.

LORD ABERDEEN was charged with the formation of
a new Government.   He at once sought the co-operation of Lord Palmerston, who, at first, withheld it,
being unwilling to share the responsibility of a
Cabinet whose foreign policy, he anticipated, would
be of a character to merit his disapproval.   But he
was indispensable.   A general though undefined
feeling among the public had already marked him
out as the coming man.   Lord Lansdowne therefore
renewed Lord Aberdeen's solicitations, and induced
Lord Palmerston to reconsider his decision.   He
selected the Home Office as his department, and gives
to his brother the following account of his feelings
and motives :—

"C. G., December 22, 1852.

" MY DEAR WILLIAM,

     " I have accepted the Home Office in the new

Government.   When first Lansdowne and Aberdeen
asked me to join the new Government I declined,
giving as my reason that Aberdeen and I had differed
so widely for twenty-five years on all questions of
foreign policy that my joining an administration
of which he was to be the head would be liable
to misconstruction both at home and abroad.   But
the next day Lansdowne came again and urged me
strongly, and I found that the Foreign Office, which
I had determined not myself in any case to take,
would be held either by Clarendon or John Russell, whose well-established reputations for liberality
would give a security in regard to our foreign relations.

" Lansdowne's representations of the great importance, in the present state of things at home and abroad,
that the new Government should be as strong in its
fabric as the materials available for the purpose can
make it, determined me to yield to his advice and to
accept the Home Office ; and the more I have thought
the matter over, the better satisfied I have felt that I
have acted right.   The Foreign Office will be taken
by John Russell, but if he finds the business too much
for him, in addition to his employment as leader in
the House of Commons, he will then give it up to
Clarendon.   The Home Office was my own choice ;
I had long settled in my own mind that I would not
go back to the Foreign Office, and that if I ever took
any office it should be the Home.   It does not do
for a man to pass his whole life in one department,

and the Home Office deals with the concerns of the country internally, and brings one in contact with one's fellow-countrymen, besides which it gives one more influence in regard to the militia and the defences of the country.

" This Government will combine almost all the men of talent and experience in the House of Commons except Disraeli; but the Opposition will be numerically strong, as they reckon about three hundred and ten. A good many of these, however, will probably be disposed to give the new Government a fair trial.

" Yours affectionately,

" PALMERSTON."

And to Mr. Sulivan, his brother-in-law, he writes :—

" Carlton Gardens, December 24, 1852.

" On Tuesday I positively declined joining the new Government, first to Lansdowne, who was nearly an hour talking to me, and afterwards to Aberdeen, who came and offered me *carte blanche* as to departments; but on Wednesday morning Clarendon came to tell me he had had the Foreign Office offered him, and that he was disposed to accept it. That removed much of the objection which I had felt. When he left me, Lansdowne came again earnestly to press me to take office; and I at last consented to take the Home Office, the department which I had mentioned as the one I should have preferred if I had been willing to join the new regiment. Reflection has satisfied me I have acted rightly. The state of the country in all its interests, foreign and domestic, requires a Government as strong as there are elements for making it; and if my aid is thought by Lansdowne and others likely to be useful, I ought not to let personal feelings stand in the way. As regards myself individually, it must be borne in mind that when the Whigs and Peelites unite to form a Government and to support it, I should, if I had persisted in standing aloof, have been left in a little agreeable political solitude. I am glad, therefore, that I have not adhered to my first determination; and I am sure that the course which, on second thoughts, I have pursued is the best for the public interest and for my own comfort."

There was a large body of men, however, who would have been only too glad to relieve Lord Palmerston from the " political solitude " which he here mentions as the alternative to joining Lord Aberdeen's Government.

The Tories were discontented with their House of Commons leader. They further had been so demoralised by recent party circumstances as to have come to doubt all political morality, and to regard statesmen as mere party swordsmen; when, therefore, at the outset of the year they saw the Foreign Secretary summarily turned adrift by the Whig leader they began looking towards him with the same anxiety and yearning with which an Italian little state in the Middle Ages would have looked for some *condottiere* of good repute who was about to be out of employment. They would gladly have hailed him as their new chief had he been minded to join them. But between these three hundred and odd gentlemen and Lord Palmerston there was little common political creed; and the members of the Opposition who indulged in such a dream as this only showed thereby how completely they misunderstood his position, his character, and his political principles.

On the 27th of December the new Government appeared in their places in Parliament, when Lord Aberdeen, in the House of Lords, gave a sketch of its intended policy. With regard to foreign affairs, he said that it would " adhere to the principles which had been pursued for the last thirty years, and which consisted in respecting the rights of all independent states, while, at the same time, we asserted our own rights and interests; and, above all, in an earnest desire to secure the general peace of Europe."

Considering that Lord Palmerston had been at the Foreign Office during more than half the period named, Lord Aberdeen was paying an indirect tribute to his policy. As for Lord Palmerston himself, he quickly settled down to his new duties, and writes thus to his brother :—

"Carlton Gardens, January 31, 1853.

" MY DEAR WILLIAM,

"We (the Government) are now preparing for the renewal of the session on the 10th of this next month. We shall be strong on the Treasury bench, and I hope not weak in the division lobby. It is clear that if we were to be turned out, the only Government that could be put in our stead would be Derby's, and experience has proved that his Government could not stand. We may therefore expect that the moderate men who supported him will not be disinclined to give us a fair support, and it will be our business to deserve it. Though the Cabinet consists of men of various parties and shades of opinion, all having agreed to unite, will, I doubt not, unite to agree, and in that case we shall go on very well.

" We are labouring to place the country in a state of defence, and our only limit is the purse of the Chancellor of the Exchequer; but whatever may be at the bottom of the secret thoughts of the French Emperor, into whose bosom no man can dive, yet I see no reason to apprehend an immediate or even an early rupture with France; and if we have two years more of preparation allowed us, we shall be in a good defensive position. In the meantime we do not allow that we are even now defenceless. The increase of navy, artillery, marines, and the or-ganisation of the militia, have placed us in a very different condition from that in which we stood two or three years ago.

" Napoleon's marriage seems to me a most sensible one. He had no chance of a political alliance of any value, or of sufficient importance to counter-balance the annoyance of an ugly or epileptic wife whom he had never seen till she was presented to him as a bride; and he was quite right to take a wife whom he knew and liked. I admire the frank-ness with which he declares himself a *parvenu*, and the assertion of that truth, however it may shock the prejudices of Vienna and Petersburg, will endear him to the bulk of the French nation.

" Yours affectionately,

" PALMERSTON."

As Home Secretary Lord Palmerston astonished everybody except those who knew him well, by the vigilance, care, intelligence, and originality with which he discharged his duties. No details were too small if only they were important to those con-cerned. He paid a visit to Parkhurst Prison, and wrote a memorandum on the ventilation of the cells with just as much zeal and thoroughness as if he were conducting a Government measure in full view of the country. A standing monument of this period of his career is the system of granting tickets of leave to convicts. Hazardous as the experiment was at that time considered, it proved successful, and solved the difficulty which stared us in the face when the Colonies declined any longer to allow us to shoot our refuse on their shores. It devolved on him to find a substitute for transportation, which had become no longer available, and he carried through the House of Commons a Bill constituting the new system of secondary punishment, which, in its main features, is still in force.

Many other useful measures owed their birth to his activity during the two years that he was at the Home Office. The abatement of the smoke nuisance in the metropolis, whereby to a great extent its atmosphere was purified—the cessation of intramural interments, of which people could only have been induced to tolerate the evils by the influence of long custom—the extension of the Factory Acts,* and the more general holding of winter assizes for the trial of prisoners awaiting gaol delivery, were among the most prominent of the undoubted boons which his practical mind devised for the benefit of the country.

He was especially happy in his manner of receiving those numerous deputations which always converge towards the Home Office. Deputation has

---

* The 10½ hours of work were by existing Acts to be between 6 A.M. and 6 P.M. This was a great guarantee against evasion of the law. It was found, however, that the wording of the Acts did not extend this limitation to children, but only to young persons. Lord Palmerston warmly took up the cause of the children when this was brought to his notice, and rectified the law.

been wittily defined as " a noun of multitude which signifies many, but does not signify much." However accurate this may be as a definition, it would be a grave error to undervalue the importance to a minister of possessing the art of listening patiently, and giving a straightforward though civil " No." Lord Palmerston had it in a notable degree. His prompt but cordial refusal was often more palatable than another man's cold and doubtful acquiescence.

He alludes to some of his work in the following letters :—

"C. G., April 3, 1853.

" My dear William,

" It is now a long while, I fear, since I last wrote to you, but ever since the meeting of Parliament I have been living as people do during a contested election, talked to from morning till night, and with no time to do anything. The mere routine business of the Home Office, as far as that consists in daily correspondence, is very far lighter than that of the Foreign Office, but, during a session of Parliament, the whole day of the Secretary of State, up to the time when he must go to the House of Commons, is taken up by deputations of all kinds and interviews with members of Parliament, militia colonels, &c. But on the whole it is a much easier office than the Foreign, and, in truth, I really would not, on any consideration, undertake again an office so unceasingly laborious every day of the year as that of Foreign Affairs. I shall be able to do some good in the Home Office. I am shutting up all the graveyards in London, a measure authorized by an Act of last session, and absolutely required for preservation of the health of the town. There is a company who are going to make two great tunnels under London, fifty feet below the surface, one north, the other south, of the Thames, running nearly alongside the river, beginning some way above the town, and ending some way below it. These tunnels are to be the receptacles into which all the sewers and drains of London are to be discharged, so that nothing is to go into the Thames, and the contents of these tunnels are, at the point of termination, to be dried and converted into manure to be sold to agriculturists as home-made guano. I shall try to compel, at least, the tall chimneys to burn their own smoke, and I should like to put down beershops, and to let shopkeepers sell beer like oil, and vinegar, and treacle, to be carried home and drunk with wives and children.

"Our session will be long but not dangerous. We shall have to renew the income tax and the East India Charter. These and other matters will take time, but I do not see that any other Government is, at present, possible. The last Cabinet has been too much discredited to be put back again, and Derby, having failed in his experiment to make a Cabinet out of men who knew nothing of public business, would scarcely like to make another trial with a new lot equally ignorant and incapable. Besides, if we were beat by mere numbers, there would be the resource of a dissolution, to which I conclude we should have recourse rather than at once give up our posts. We may have some difficulty next year about Parliamentary Reform, but enough for the year are the troubles thereof. As yet, nothing can be more harmonious than our Coalition Cabinet.

" I daresay you have heard at Naples much about our harbouring conspiring refugees. The answer I make to those who complain of those matters here is, that a handful of refugees in London cannot arrange a revolution in a foreign country, and send out the plan to be executed off-hand. They must, in the first place, have associates and instruments many thousand in number in the country to which the plan is to be applied, because a revolution cannot be acted by a handful of men. They must have much local know-ledge to make their arrangements, and this knowledge, bearing upon circumstances which vary from day to day, is not possessed by men in London, and can only be furnished by men on the spot. Therefore these London conspirators can do nothing without the co-operation of a great number of people in the foreign country, with whom they must have long and detailed communication either by letters or by messengers. But what are the Governments of the foreign countries about if they cannot, by their police and their passport system, find out the proceedings of the large mass of these conspirators who are in their own country, and if they cannot intercept the letters or discover and arrest the messengers? It is plain that the real and practical conspiracy is worked out in the foreign country and not in England ; and these foreign Governments try to throw upon us a blame which really belongs to them, and if arms and ammunition are sent or provided, it is the foreign Government that ought to be able to find that out.

" The country generally is highly prosperous, trade flourishing, the revenue good, and the emigration having gone just far enough to raise wages to a proper amount without making labour inconveniently scarce. The Irish emigration will, I hope, go on, and it would be a good thing if a larger number would go off to America. The priests are, of course, furious, every emigrant is so much out of their pocket.*

" We have a plan in prospect for a general system of drainage of the whole of the valley of the Test, from Whitchurch to Redbridge. I think it will be carried into execution, and, if so, it will improve the climate as well as the soil.

" I am very glad that Clarendon† has got the Foreign Office. He will do the business well and keep up the character and dignity of the country. Good-bye.

" Yours affectionately,

" PALMERSTON."

---

* Lord Palmerston for many years spent a large portion of his Irish income in enabling those of his tenants to emigrate who wished to do so.

† He had succeeded Lord John Russell.

The cholera appeared this year in the United Kingdom, and in the autumn the Presbytery of Edinburgh wrote, through their Moderator, to Lord Palmerston, asking whether, under the circumstances, a national fast would be appointed on Royal authority. The Home Secretary, like Cromwell, who supplemented his exhortation to his men to put their trust in God by a caution to keep their powder dry, sent the following answer :—

"Whitehall, Oct. 19, 1853.

"Sir,—I am directed by Viscount Palmerston to acknowledge the receipt of your letter of the 15th inst., requesting, on behalf of the Presbytery of Edinburgh, to be informed whether it is proposed to appoint a day of national fast on account of the visitation of the cholera, and to state that there can be no doubt that manifestations of humble resignation to the Divine Will, and sincere acknowledgments of human unworthiness, are never more appropriate than when it has pleased Providence to afflict mankind with some severe visitation; but it does not appear to Lord Palmerston that a national fast would be suitable to the circumstances of the present moment.

"The Maker of the Universe has established certain laws of nature for the planet in which we live, and the weal or woe of mankind depends upon the observance or the neglect of those laws. One of those laws connects health with the absence of those gaseous exhalations which proceed from over-crowded human beings, or from decomposing substances, whether animal or vegetable; and those same laws render sickness the almost inevitable consequence of exposure to those noxious influences. But it has at the same time pleased Providence to place it within the power of man to make such arrangements as will prevent or disperse such exhalations so as to render them harmless, and it is the duty of man to attend to those laws of nature, and to exert the faculties which Providence has thus given to man for his own welfare.

"The recent visitation of cholera, which has for the moment been mercifully checked, is an awful warning given to the people of this realm that they have too much neglected their duty in this respect, and that those persons with whom it rested to purify towns and cities, and to prevent or remove the causes of disease, have not been sufficiently active in regard to such matters. Lord Palmerston would, therefore, suggest that the best course which the people of this country can pursue to deserve that the further progress of the cholera should be stayed, will be to employ the interval that will elapse between the present time and the beginning of next spring in planning and executing measures by which those portions of their towns and cities which are inhabited by the poorest classes, and which, from the nature of things, must most need purification and improvement, may be freed from those causes and sources of contagion which, if allowed to remain, will infallibly breed pestilence and be fruitful in death, in spite of all the prayers and fastings of a united but inactive nation. When man has done his utmost for his own safety, then is the time to invoke the blessing of Heaven to give effect to his exertions.

"I am, sir, your obedient servant,

"HENRY FITZROY."

This letter created a great stir, and some indignation among certain sections of the community; but it was, after all, the embodiment of common sense. It reminded those in authority that it was their bounden duty not to neglect the teachings of science or the spirit of practical Christianity. It suggested that until they had fulfilled their duty to their neighbour, they could not lift up clean hands in prayer and fasting. The lesson which it thus sought to inculcate on the municipal authorities of Scotland was greatly needed. Sanitary laws were at that time even less known and less cared for than now; and in the terror excited by the mysterious appearance of this terrible disease the fact was overlooked that the conditions under which it was developed and diffused were under human control, and grew out of the negligence and folly of individuals and local authorities. To substitute a national fast for the paramount duty of cleansing the drains and purifying the streets· would have been a strange misunderstanding of the Divine will, as revealed in the operations of natural causes.

The free wits of the day averred that Lord Palmerston had brought into his new office the proclivities of his former department, and that in his answer to the Presbytery he treated Heaven as a " foreign power." The joke was, however, wide of the mark, if it meant to insinuate any irreverence for sacred things on his part, as he never either showed such a feeling himself, or encouraged its manifestation in others.

There was yet another occasion, about this time, when he found himself become a theological target, owing to a speech. In the winter of 1854, presiding at a labourers' meeting at Romsey, he told them that they would find that all children were born good, and that only bad education and bad associations corrupted the mind.　There might be exceptions, as there are men born physically defective; but that the heart of man was naturally good, and that it depended upon training whether that goodness, implanted at birth, should continue to display itself. This apparent piece of heresy as to the doctrine of "original sin" stirred up the clerical world at the dull season.　One leading organ had an amusing but reproachful article, saying that if Lord Palmerston had been a nurse, he would have known better.　" If anybody," it continued, "could teach a child to smile away its tears, to bear abstinence with fortitude, rebukes with patience, and inward commotions with grace, Lord Palmerston is the man to do it; nevertheless we feel sure that he would soon find he had as difficult subjects to deal with as he ever found in perverse princes and the evil associations of Courts."　But others were not disposed to deal with it so lightly, and discussed it very gravely.　The truth being all the time that the Premier had not the remotest idea of touching upon such an abstruse topic as "original sin," but was talking to labouring men about those ordinary features of generally good or generally bad conduct which could be evident to every one of them.

One of the provisions of the Act forbidding intramural interment gave power to the Home Secretary to make exceptions in cases which he might deem fit.　Lord Palmerston, however, appears to have deemed none fit, as may be gathered from the following answer to a request for a special permission in the case of a deceased dignitary of the Church :—

"Broadlands, January 3, 1855.

" MY DEAR STANLEY,*

" I am sorry to say that I have already felt myself obliged to decline compliance with the request contained in the enclosed letter. The practice of burying dead bodies under buildings in which living people assemble in large numbers is a barbarous one, and ought to be at once and for ever put an end to, and I have made this a general rule in all cases. But a rule is no rule if partial exceptions are made; the rule then degenerates into an invidious selection of particular persons for its application, and other particular persons for its relaxation.

" And why, pray, should archbishops and bishops, and deans and canons, be buried under churches if other persons are not to be so? What special connection is there between church dignities and the privilege of being decomposed under the feet of survivors? Do you seriously mean to imply that a soul is more likely to go to heaven because the body which it inhabited lies decomposing under the pavement of a church instead of being placed in a churchyard?

" If commemoration is what is wanted, a monument may be placed in a church though the body is in the burial-ground; but why cannot the monument

* Lord Stanley of Alderley.

be equally well erected in the consecrated burial-ground?

"As to what you say about pain to feelings by shutting up of burial-grounds, that is perfectly true. I am quite aware that the measure is necessarily attended with pain to feelings which excite respect, as well as to pressure upon pecuniary interests which are not undeserving of consideration. But no great measure of social improvement can be effected without some such temporary inconvenience to individuals, and the necessity of the case justifies the demand for such sacrifices. To have attempted to make the application of the new system gradual would have reduced it to a nullity. England is, I believe, the only country in which, in these days, people accumulate putrifying dead bodies amid the dwellings of the living; and as to burying bodies under thronged churches, you might as well put them under libraries, drawing-rooms, and dining-rooms.

"Yours sincerely,

"PALMERSTON."

During the first year of his renewed tenure of office he very nearly parted from his colleagues. In the ' Annual Register' for 1853 occurs this passage: —"On the 16th of December an important ministerial crisis was occasioned by the announcement that Viscount Palmerston had resigned his office. His resignation, however, was not accepted, and, after an interval of some days' suspense, the noble lord was prevailed upon to withdraw it. The opponents of the Government asserted that Lord Palmerston's secession from office was occasioned by a difference of opinion on his part as to the policy of the Cabinet upon the Eastern question. On the other hand, it was strenuously contradicted by the adherents of the Ministry; but as all explanation upon the subject was declined in Parliament, the motive for a step so dangerous to the stability of the Earl of Aberdeen's Cabinet must remain matter for conjecture."

I quote a letter to his brother-in-law, the Right Hon. Laurence Sulivan, which states the case :—

" C. G., December 19, 1853.

" MY DEAR SULIVAN,

"The state of the matter is plain and simple. I told Aberdeen and Lansdowne last year, when I joined the Government, that I felt great doubts as to my being able to concur in the plan of parliamentary reform which John Russell might propose this year.

"The other day I was put on the Committee of Cabinet to prepare the plan. John Russell stated his scheme. I wrote to him next day to state my objections. I re-stated them verbally in the Committee, and stated them again to the Cabinet when John Russell explained his scheme to the Cabinet. I stated them in a private interview afterwards, on two occasions, to Aberdeen. I stated them afterwards to him in writing. In reply to that communication, I was first told by him that he would communicate with the Queen and his colleagues. He then afterwards wrote me word that he had communicated with John Russell and Graham ; that they said my objections were inadmissible ; and that he concurred in their decision. I had then nothing left for it but to resign. My office is too closely connected with parliamentary changes to allow me to sit silent during the whole progress of a Reform Bill through Parliament ; and I could not take up a Bill which contained material things of which I disapproved, and assist to fight it through the House of Commons, to force it on the Lords, and to stand upon it at the hustings. I am sorry to leave an office in which I took interest, and political associates whom I like ; but I could not do otherwise.

" The ' Times ' says there has been no difference in the Cabinet about Eastern affairs. This is an untruth ; but I felt that it would have been silly to have gone out because I could not have my own way about Turkish affairs, seeing that my presence in the Cabinet did good, by modifying the views of those whose policy I thought bad.

" Yours affectionately,

" PALMERSTON."

What were the " differences " on Turkish affairs will be seen later on, when we come to the Eastern question ; but they concerned the moving of our fleet up to the scene of conflict. However, Lord Palmerston withdrew his resignation, as is shown by the next letter :—

" C. G., December 25, 1853.

" My dear Sulivan,

" I was prevented from calling on you to-day to tell you that I remain in the Government. I was much and strongly pressed to do so for several days by many of the members of the Government, who declared that they were no parties to Aberdeen's answer to me, and that they considered all the details of the intended Reform measure as still open to discussion. Their earnest representations, and the. knowledge that the Cabinet had on Thursday taken a decision on Turkish affairs in entire accordance with opinions which I had long unsuccessfully pressed upon them, decided me to withdraw my resignation, which I did yesterday.

" Of course what I say to you about the Cabinet decision on Turkish affairs is entirely for yourself, and not to be mentioned to anybody. But it is very important, and will give the allied squadrons the command of the Black Sea.

" Yours affectionately,
" Palmerston."

The French ambassador rejoiced at the return of the Home Secretary to the Cabinet. As soon as he heard that the resignation was withdrawn, he wrote to him :—" Au début de la campagne que nous allons faire ensemble, c'est un grand comfort pour moi et une grande garantie pour l'Empereur que de vous savoir l'âme des conseils de notre allié. Votre concours d'ailleurs pèse d'un poids très-réel dans la balance, et on sait à Paris en apprécier toute la valeur."

Abroad as well as at home Lord Palmerston was regarded as the backbone of the ministry.

CHAPTER II.

IT can hardly be doubted that the prospects of peace were darkened during the eventful preliminaries of 1853 by the fact of Lord Palmerston's absence from the Foreign Office. He had won a character in Europe for being resolute, and was regarded as the embodiment of English pugnacity. That a statesman of his undoubted prestige should at this crisis in foreign affairs be relegated to the Home Office meant, in the opinion of the adversaries of England, that his policy was at a discount, and that the tide of national spirit was ebbing which had formerly floated him through so many foreign difficulties. Lord Palmerston, all the same, was not so thoroughly engrossed by questions of health, police, and local administration as to view with any indifference the dispute between Russia and Turkey. On the contrary, he watched every turn with the keenest interest, and held himself not only entitled but bound to evince his active concern in the progress of the negotiations.

Many a man, ousted from his old post, would have shown, or at any rate would have felt, some slight jealousy towards the person who had been preferred to him. Lord Palmerston, so far from being influenced by any such feeling or indulging in any carping criticism, frankly acknowledged that Lord Clarendon was the more fit minister to be at the Foreign Office at this moment. His reasons for saying so may be gleaned from the following extract of a letter to the Foreign Secretary :—" I admired greatly your writhing letter, but I did not like to say too much in its praise at the Cabinet, for fear that by so doing I might lead others to think that it was too strong. I can assure you that it is a great comfort and satisfaction to me to know the conduct of our foreign relations is in such able hands as yours, and your administration of your important department is attended with this great advantage to the country, that, from a variety of circumstances, you can say and do things which could not so easily have been said or done by me."*

He hated war as much as any man; but he hated humiliation more ; and he thoroughly understood the character of the adversary against whom England and France were entering the diplomatic lists in a struggle which he very soon saw involved far more than the mere questions immediately at issue. He

* To Lord Clarendon, July 31, 1853.

thus describes the usual tactics adopted by Russia in any acts of aggression :—

"The policy and practice of the Russian Government has always been to push forward its encroachments as fast and as far as the apathy or want of firmness of other Governments would allow it to go, but always to stop and retire when it was met with decided resistance, and then to wait for the next favourable opportunity to make another spring on its intended victim. In furtherance of this policy, the Russian Government has always had two strings to its bow—moderate language and disinterested professions at Petersburg and at London; active aggression by its agents on the scene of operations. If the aggressions succeed locally, the Petersburg Government adopts them as a ' fait accompli ' which it did not intend, but cannot, in honour, recede from. If the local agents fail, they are disavowed and recalled, and the language previously held is appealed to as a proof that the agents have overstepped their instructions. This was exemplified in the Treaty of Unkiar-Skelessi, and in the exploits of Simonivitch and Vikovitch in Persia. Orloff succeeded in extorting the Treaty of Unkiar-Skelessi from the Turks, and it was represented as a sudden thought, suggested by the circumstances of the time and place, and not the result of any previous instructions; but having been done, it could not be undone. On the other hand, Simonivitch and Vikovitch failed in 'getting possession of Herat, in consequence of our vigorous measures of resistance; and as they failed, and *when* they had failed, they were disavowed and recalled, and the language previously held at Petersburg was appealed to as a proof of the sincerity of the disavowal, although no human being with two ideas in his head could for a moment doubt that they had acted under specific instructions."*

As soon as the question of the " Holy Places " had been settled, through the intervention of Sir Stratford Canning, Russia had put forward her claim to a Protectorate over the Greek Church in Turkey. On the refusal of this demand by the Sultan, Prince Menschikoff left Constantinople, and, on the 2nd of July, the Russian army crossed the Pruth and occupied the Danubian Principalities. The combined English and French fleets were at Besika Bay, at the entrance to the Dardanelles. Lord Palmerston was meanwhile writing to the Premier as follows :—

" C. G., July 4, 1853.

" MY DEAR ABERDEEN,

"I quite agree with you that we ought to try whether we can devise any proposal which, without involving any departure by the Sultan from the ground of independence on which he has taken his

---

* To Lord Clarendon, May 22, 1853.

stand, might satisfy every just claim which the Emperor can put forward. In the meantime, however, I hope you will allow the squadrons to be ordered to go up to the Bosphorus as soon as it is known at Constantinople that the Russians have entered the Principalities, and to be further at liberty to go into the Black Sea, if necessary or useful for the protection of Turkish Territory.

" The advantages of such a course seem to be—

" 1st. That it would encourage and assist the Turks in those defensive arrangements and organizations which the present crisis may give the Turkish Government facilities for making, and the benefit of which, in strengthening Turkey against attack, will continue after the crisis is over.

" 2ndly. It would essentially tend to prevent any further inroad on Turkish territory in Europe or in Asia, and it is manifest that any such further inroad would much increase the difficulties of a settlement.

" 3rdly. It would act as a wholesome check upon the Emperor and his advisers, and would stimulate Austria and Prussia to increased exertions to bring the Russian Government to reason.

" 4thly. It would relieve England and France from the disagreeable, and not very creditable, position of waiting without venturing to enter the back door as friends, while the Russians have taken forcible possession of the front hall as enemies.

"If these orders are to be given, I would suggest that it is very important that they should be given without delay, so that we may be able, when these matters are discussed this week in Parliament, to say that such orders have been sent off; of course they would at the same time be communicated to the Russian Government.

"I am confident that this country expects that we should pursue such a course, and I cannot believe that we should receive anything but support in pursuing it from the party now in Opposition.

"Yours sincerely,

"Palmerston."

Lord Aberdeen replied, that although the invasion of the Principalities was an indefensible act, and one that gave to every European Power a right of interference, still, as the Emperor had made no declaration of war, but, on the contrary, notified that he would not make war, it became very doubtful how far it would be justifiable for our fleet to violate the treaty of 1841 by passing the Dardanelles. As to Lord Palmerston's assertion of the general approval which a bold course would receive, Lord Aberdeen concluded his letter by a characteristic paragraph: "In a case of this kind I dread popular support. On some occasion, when the Athenian assembly vehemently applauded Alcibiades, he asked if he had said anything particularly foolish."

Meanwhile the representatives of the four Powers, England, France, Austria, and Prussia, were conferring in the Austrian capital and drawing up a document, which soon became known to Europe under the name of the " Vienna Note." It was an abortive attempt to reconcile conflicting views. The English Cabinet were busy on a similar hopeless task :—

" C. G., July 7, 1853.

" My dear John Russell,

" The Cabinet yesterday agreed provisionally to an amended draft of Convention to be proposed for Russia and Turkey, simply renewing the engagements of Kainardjy and Adrianople without any extension. This was to be communicated first for approval to the French Government, and, if finally agreed to, it was proposed that it should be sent by Vienna to Constantinople, and, if not strongly objected to by the Porte, to be returned to Vienna, and to be sent on thence to Petersburg with any recommendation which the Austrian Government might be inclined to give. This Convention made no mention of the Holy Places, because the French would not agree to a Convention between Russia and Turkey on that matter. All this is very well for effect and for a Blue Book, but, in my opinion, the course which the Emperor has pursued on these matters from his first overtures for a partition of Turkey, and especially the violent, abusive, and menacing language of his last manifesto, seem to show that he has taken his line, and that nothing will satisfy him but complete submission on the part of Turkey; and we ought, therefore, not to disguise from ourselves that he is bent upon a stand-up fight.

" I tried again to persuade the Cabinet to send the squadrons up to the Bosphorus, but failed; I was told that Stratford and La Cour have powers to call for them. This is, no doubt, stated in public despatches, but we all know that he has been privately desired not to do so. I think our position, waiting timidly and submissively at the back door while Russia is violently, threateningly, and arrogantly forcing her way into the house, is unwise with a view to a peaceful settlement, and derogatory to the character, and standing, and dignity of the two Powers. I think that when pressed on this point, as of course we shall be in both Houses, we shall have no good answer or explanation to give. We cannot say that the provinces are not parts of the Turkish empire, because treaties have made them so, and it is as such that Nicholas seizes them, as a way of compelling the Porte to submit to his demands.

" We cannot say that Turkey is at peace, because no country is at peace when important parts of its territory are invaded as a means of coercion, with a threat of further advance if stubbornness and blindness should make such a step, in the opinion of the invader, necessary. We cannot deny that the presence of our squadrons in the Bosphorus would greatly encourage the Porte, greatly discourage insurrections in any part of Turkey, and greatly tend to make the Emperor pause. The only reason we can give for our inactivity must be a yielding to Brunnow's advice and a fear of displeasing the Emperor. But these motives ought to have led us to leave Turkey to her fate. Words may properly be answered by words, but acts should be replied to by acts; and the entrance of the Russians as invaders into the Turkish territory ought to be followed and replied to by the entrance of the squadrons into the Bosphorus as protectors. Much, however, of the effect of such a measure must depend on the promptitude of its execution, and it would have this advantage that, while it indicated spirit and determination on the part of England and France, it could not by any perversion be represented as an act of hostility against Russia. We should be relieved from much embarrassment in the approaching debate if we could say that orders for this purpose had actually been sent, and the actual advance of the squadrons ought surely to accompany any overtures made to Russia.

" Yours sincerely,

" PALMERSTON."

The Russian Government now addressed a despatch to its diplomatic agents, the burden of which was to the effect that the occupation of the Principalities was in answer to the presence of the British and French fleets outside the Dardanelles, and would only cease when they retired.

In the following memorandum, sent round by Lord Palmerston to the members of the Cabinet, he states how he would wish to meet this declaration :—

"C. G., July 12, 1853.

" The circular of Count Nesselrode, dated the 2nd of July, and published in the newspapers of this morning, shows how imperfectly we have understood the character of the Russian Government, and how entirely thrown away upon that Government has been the excessive forbearance with which England and France have acted. But the result might have been foreseen. It is in the nature of men whose influence over events and whose power over others are founded on intimidation, and kept up by arrogant assumptions and pretensions, to mistake forbearance for irresolution, and to look upon inaction and hesitation as symptoms of fear, and forerunners of submission.

" Thus it has been with Russia on the one hand and England and France on the other. If the two Powers had acted with that energy, decision, and promptitude which the occasion required; if when Menschikoff began to threaten the two squadrons had been sent to the neighbourhood of the Dardanelles, and if the Russian Government had been plainly told that the moment a Russian soldier set foot on Turkish territory, or as soon as a Russian ship-of-war approached with hostile intentions the Turkish coast, the combined squadrons would move up to the Bosphorus, and, if necessary, operate in the Black Sea, there can be little doubt that the Russian Government would have paused in its course, and things would not have come to the pass at which they have now arrived. But the Russian Government has been led on step by step by the apparent timidity of the Government of England, and reports artfully propagated that the British Cabinet had declared that it would have *la paix a tout prix* have not been sufficiently contradicted by any overt acts. The result has now been that the Cabinet of St. Petersburg, not content with bullying Turkey, threatens and insults England and France, and arrogantly pretends to forbid the ships-of-war of those Powers from frequenting the waters of another Power over whose waters Russia has no authority whatever, and who has invited those ships into those waters specifically to protect it against Russian aggression.

" It is the robber who declares that he will not leave the house until the policeman shall have first retired from the courtyard.

" The position of England and France was already sufficiently humiliating, but this insolent pretension, published to all Europe even before it was communicated to us, seems to me to make that position no longer tenable consistently with a due regard to the honour and character of this country.

" I would therefore beg to submit, and to place my opinion thus on record, that orders should forthwith be sent to the two squadrons to go up to the Bosphorus, and that the Russian Government should be informed that, although we had not intended that this move should have taken place without some fresh incident, or some more urgent request from the Porte, yet after the inadmissible pretension put forward in Count Nesselrode's note, to dictate to us as to the movements of our fleet, we had no alternative left but to station that fleet at the heart of that empire whose integrity and independence have been unwarrantably threatened by a Russian invasion of its territory.

" PALMERSTON."

Lord Aberdeen, on the other hand, hoping and believing that the form of Convention between Russia and Turkey, which had been prepared by France and England, would be accepted, and that peace would thus be maintained, considered that Count Nesselrode's circular should only be met by a grave expostulation. " When," he added, " the four Powers simultaneously advised the Porte not to regard the entrance of the Russian troops into the Principalities as a *casus belli*, it was not that they attached any weight to the declaration of the Emperor that he did not intend to make war upon Turkey, or that they entertained any doubt of an act of real hostility having been committed, but they wished to accept his declaration so far as to preserve in their own hands the means of negotiating with greater hopes of success than if the utmost extremity of war had been proclaimed." Lord Clarendon also shared Lord Aberdeen's views.

Lord Palmerston acquiesced, with reservations, in the Premier's decision. He said :—

"I do not think that we advised the Porte not to consider the invasion of the Principalities a *casus belli*. A *casus belli*, if I understand the term, means a case which would justify war. Now we have told the Porte that the invasion of the Principalities would justify war on the part of Turkey against Russia, but we advised the Sultan, on grounds of prudence and as a question of strategy, not to exercise his right and to send an army to fight at a disadvantage beyond the Danube. It seems to me, therefore, that we have told the Sultan that the invasion of his territory is a *casus belli*, but that he would do best by standing on the defensive. As to the fleet, I acquiesce in your reasoning, and, on consideration, I admit that, as we have launched proposals for a peaceful arrangement, it would be better not to endanger the negotiation by throwing into it any fresh element of difficulty; and I am, therefore, prepared to share the responsibility of submitting even to insult rather than afford to the quibbling and pettifogging Government with which we have to deal any pretext arising out of our course for refusing terms of accommodation unobjectionable in themselves."*

Parliament was prorogued, with an expression of hope, in the Speech from the Throne, that the dispute would yet be arranged without recourse to arms. Lord Palmerston, as soon as he was released from the House of Commons, went down to Derbyshire to open the Melbourne Athenæum, on which occasion he gave an address on the educational facilities provided by such institutions. This was very proper for a Home Secretary, although, in his character of ex-Foreign Secretary, it was abroad that his eyes were fixed, while he was in close correspondence with his colleagues, stimulating each in turn to adopt a bold tone as to the events then taking place. To Mr. Sidney Herbert, Secretary at War, he writes, in September, from Balmoral, whither he had gone in attendance on the Queen :—

"Balmoral, September 21, 1853.

" MY DEAR SIDNEY HERBERT,

"The question between Russia and Turkey seems, as you say, to be in an unsatisfactory and unpromising state, and yet it lies in a nutshell, and its solution depends upon honest intentions and plain dealing on the part of Russia. What is it the

* To Lord Aberdeen, July 15, 1853.

Emperor wants? Why will he not plainly tell us what it is? Does he want merely what all of us want, namely, that the Christians in the Turkish empire shall be safe from oppression, vexation, and injury? If that is what he wants, let him begin by himself setting the example, and let him, by evacuating the Principalities, relieve the Christian inhabitants of that part of the Turkish empire from the complicated and various miseries which the occupation of their country by a Russian army inflicts upon them. Beyond that, let him be satisfied, as we all are, with the progressively liberal system of Turkey, and let him keep his remonstrances till some case and occasion arises which calls for them. At present he has not been able even to allege any oppression of the Christians, except that which he himself practises in the Principalities. I believe the real fact at the bottom of all these unintelligible pretences is that what he really wants is that the Sultan should not, by liberal measures and progressive improvement, interfere with the arbitrary and tyrannical powers which the Greek clergy now too often exercise, whether by right or by assumption, to the cruel oppression of the Greek communities. But if the Emperor wants no more than what I have said, he ought to be satisfied with the declarations which the Sultan is ready to make. If, on the other hand, the Emperor wants to become acknowledged protector of the Greek subjects of the Sultan, and to be allowed to interfere between the Sultan and the

Sultan's subjects, why, then I say let him manfully avow this pretension, and let us manfully assist Turkey in manfully resisting it, and let the fortune of war decide between the Emperor's wrong and the Sultan's rightful cause. In my opinion Russia ought to be required to give a categorical answer and to be driven from the discreditable subterfuges behind which she has so long sheltered her aggressive intentions. I believe that what I have last stated is what the Emperor really means and wants, and therefore I am coming reluctantly to the conclusion that war between him and Turkey is becoming inevitable. If such war shall happen, upon his head be the responsibility of the consequences.

"I by no means think with you that he will have an easy victory over the Turks. On the contrary, if the betting is not even, I would lay the odds on the Turks. All that the Turkish army wants are directory officers, and it would be strange indeed if England, France, Poland, and Hungary could not amply supply that deficiency. I do not believe in the disaffection of the Turkish provinces; this is an oft-repeated tale got up by the Russians. The best refutation is, that for many months past the Russian agents have been trying *per fas et nefas* to provoke insurrection in Turkey, and have failed. The fact is, that the Christian subjects in Turkey know too well what Russian *régime* is not to be aware that it is of all things the most to be dreaded, and the oftener Russian troops enter Turkish territory the stronger this conviction is impressed upon the people. Russia ought not to forget that she has weak points —Poland, Circassia, Georgia. My wish is that England should be on friendly terms with Russia; it is desirable that this should be, for the sake of both countries and for the sake of Europe. Neither country would gain anything by war with the other; and Russia, if her Government understood properly her position, has important and useful functions to perform in the system of Europe. The Emperor has, since 1848, and till this last affair, performed those functions to the admiration of all thinking men. He seems latterly to have lost his reasoning faculties.

" Brunnow has often said to me that, however different the internal organisation of England and Russia, and however opposite their respective views as to the theory of government, they have, nevertheless, so many great interests in common, that there is nothing to prevent them from working well together *so long as no difference arises between them in regard to the affairs of Turkey or of Persia.* Brunnow is a *wise* man, but matters seem to have been lately managed at Petersburg by men who are *otherwise.*

" All I can say is that, as far as I am concerned, I am desirous that England should be well with Russia as long as the Emperor allows us to be so; but if he is determined to break a lance with us, why, then

have at him, say I, and perhaps he may have enough
of it before we have done with him.

> "Yours sincerely,
>
> "PALMERSTON."

On the 4th of October he wrote to Lord Aberdeen, suggesting that it would be advantageous
in all communications with Baron Brunnow, the
Russian ambassador, to maintain a mysterious in-
definiteness and uncertainty as to the degree and the
manner of assistance which England would give to
Turkey against Russia, and pointing out that the
Russian Government must greatly dread an open
rupture with England and France. He knew that
private and verbal communications, given in all
honesty, but tinctured by the personal bias of the
Prime Minister, were doing irreparable mischief, and
that the Russian minister was determined not to
take them at their true value, but persisted in giving
them the interpretation which he desired for them,
namely, an insuperable dislike on the part of the
English Government to any active measures against
his country.   Lord Aberdeen replied, with a view
to reassure Lord Palmerston : "It is very true that
I may formerly have regarded the possibility of
war between England and Russia with the utmost
incredulity; but for some time past I have seen the
desire for war increase so much as to lead me to
think that it is but too probable. At present, therefore, *vous prêchez le converti.* As for Brunnow, he is

already frightened out of his wits at the prospect, and most assuredly he hears nothing from me to diminish his alarm."

The crisis was now rapidly culminating. On the 5th of October the Porte issued a declaration making the further continuation of peace depend upon the evacuation of the Principalities within fifteen days; and on the 14th of October the English and French fleets passed up to Constantinople, at the request of the Sultan. Lord Palmerston wanted something even more decisive on our part.

" C. G., October 7, 1853.

" MY DEAR ABERDEEN,

"The state of Russo-Turkish affairs seems to require some statement on the part of England and France, assuming, of course, that war has been declared by Turkey, and that hostilities between Russia and Turkey are about to commence. I should, therefore, wish to propose to the Cabinet to-day—

" ' First, that instructions should be sent to Constantinople that, in the event of war having been declared, the two squadrons should enter the Black Sea, and should send word to the Russian admiral at Sebastopol that, in the existing state of things, any Russian ship-of-war found cruising in the Black Sea would be detained, and be given over to the Turkish Government.

" ' Secondly, that England and France should propose to the Sultan to conclude a convention to the effect that, whereas war has, unfortunately, broken out between Russia and Turkey, in consequence of differences created by unjust demands made upon Turkey by Russia, and by an unwarrantable invasion of the Turkish territory by a Russian army; and whereas it is deemed by England and France to be an object of general European interest, and of special importance to them that the political independence and the territorial integrity of the Ottoman empire should be maintained inviolate against Russian aggression, the two Powers engage to furnish to the Sultan such naval assistance as may be necessary in existing circumstances for the defence of his empire; and they moreover engage to permit any of their respective subjects who may be willing to do so to enter the military or naval service of the Sultan. In return, the Sultan to engage that he will consult with England and France as to the terms and conditions of the new treaty which is to determine, on the conclusion of hostilities, the future relations of Russia and Turkey.'

" Such a convention would unquestionably have a great and useful effect on the course to be pursued by the three Eastern Powers.

" Yours sincerely,

" PALMERSTON."

Lord Aberdeen, in reply, said: " I cannot say that I think the present state of the Russo-Turkish question would authorize such a proceeding on our part as that which you intend to propose." Indeed, as the rupture of peace appeared more and more likely, more and more hesitation was developed in high quarters. Representations were made that the fanatical party at Constantinople had become so clamorous for war, for their own purposes, that the Turk was thwarting instead of assisting English efforts to come to a satisfactory understanding with Russia. It began to be feared that England was about to be dragged behind the Ottoman chariot in a campaign the real object of which was to obtain more power for two millions of Mussulmen to rule oppressively twelve millions of Christians. Suggestions were thrown out that if, setting aside all Turkish considerations, it was thought that England and Europe had such a strong interest in keeping Turkish territory out of the hands of Russia as to be justified in going to war for that purpose, such a war ought to be carried on unshackled by any obligations to the Porte, and ought to lead to such a peace as would provide other and better arrangements for the future than the " recomposition of the ignorant, barbarian, and despotic rule of the Mussulman over the most favoured and fertile portion of Europe."

Lord Aberdeen had forwarded to Lord Palmerston a memorandum which he had received drawn up in this sense. Lord Palmerston returned it, with the following remarks :—

" Broadlands, November 1, 1853.

" MY DEAR ABERDEEN,

      " I return you the memorandum, which states very clearly the course of past events, but which, towards its conclusion, points to future objects not consistent with the policy laid down in its beginning, and not easy to be carried into execution.

" According to my view of the matters in question the case is simple and our course is clear. The five great Powers have, in a formal document, recorded their opinion that it is for the general interest of Europe that the integrity and independence of the Ottoman empire should be maintained; and it would be easy to show that strong reasons, political and commercial, make it especially the interest of England that this integrity and independence should be maintained. But Russia has attacked the independence and has violated the integrity of the Ottoman empire; and Russia must, by fair means or foul, be brought to give up her pretensions and withdraw her aggression. England and France, urged by common interests to defend Turkey against Russia, have given Turkey physical assistance and political and diplomatic support. They undertook to obtain for Turkey, by negotiation, a satisfactory and honourable settlement of her differences with Russia, and, failing that, to support Turkey in her defensive war.

" Hitherto, our efforts at negotiation have failed, because the arrangement which we proposed was declared, both by Turkey and by Russia, to be such as Turkey could not honourably nor safely adopt. The Turkish Government, seeing no apparent prospect of better results from negotiation, and aware that lapse of time was running to the disadvantage of Turkey, at length, after having for some considerable time yielded to our advice to remain passive, came to a determination not unnatural, and not unwise, and issued that declaration of war which we had officially and publicly said that the Sultan would have been justified in issuing the moment the Russians invaded his territory.

"This declaration of war makes no change in the position of England and France in relation to Turkey. We may still try to persuade Russia to do what she ought to do, but we are still bound, by a regard for our own interests, to defend Turkey. Peace is an excellent thing, and war is a great misfortune; but there are many things more valuable than peace, and many things much worse than war.

"We passed the Rubicon when we first took part with Turkey and sent our squadrons to support her; and when England and France have once taken a third Power by the hand, that third Power *must* be carried in safety through the difficulties in which it may be involved. England and France cannot afford to be baffled, and whatever measures may be necessary on their part to baffle their opponent, those measures must be adopted; and the Governments of the two most powerful countries on the face of the earth must not be frightened, either by words or things, either by the name or by the reality of war.

" No doubt when we put forth our whole strength in defence of Turkey, we shall be entitled to direct in a great measure the course and character of the war, and to exercise a deciding influence on the negotiations which may afterwards lead to peace. And it was with that view that, some time ago, I proposed to the Cabinet that, negotiation failing, England and France should conclude a convention with Turkey, by which, on the one hand, the two Powers should engage to afford Turkey naval assistance, and to permit their respective subjects to enter the Sultan's service, naval and military; and by which the Sultan, on the other hand, should engage to consult with the two Powers as to the terms and conditions of peace. But the only grounds on which we can claim influence in these matters is our determination to give hearty and effectual support. We support Turkey for our own sake and for our own interests, and to withdraw our support, or to cripple it, so as to render it ineffectual, merely because the Turkish Government did not show as much deference to our advice as our advice deserved, would be to place our national interests at the mercy of other persons. If Lord Liverpool's Government had so acted in regard to the Provisional Government of Spain, we never should have driven the French out of the Peninsula.

" But, it is said, the Turks seem to wish for war, while we wish for peace. I apprehend that both parties wish for one and the same thing, namely, the relinquishment by Russia of inadmissible pretensions and her retirement from the Turkish territory; both parties would rather gain these ends by the pen than by the sword: we only differ in our belief as to the efficacy of these two methods. It is indeed possible that the Turks may think that a successful conflict would enable them to make a treaty of peace which should free them from the thraldom of some of their old engagements; and if this were possible, it would certainly place future peace on a firmer foundation.

"It is said, also, that the Turks are reawakening the dormant fanaticism of the Mussulman race, and that we ought not to be the helping instruments to gratify such bad passions. I believe these stories about awakened fanaticism to be fables invented at Vienna and Petersburg; we have had no facts stated in support of them. I take the fanaticism which has been thus aroused to be the fanaticism which consists in burning indignation at a national insult, and a daring impatience to endeavour to expel an invading enemy. This spirit may be reviled by the Russians, whose schemes it disconcerts, and may be cried down by the Austrians, who had hoped to settle matters by persuading the Turks to yield, but it will not diminish the goodwill of the people of England, and it is a good foundation on which to build our hopes of success.

"The concluding part of the memorandum points to the expulsion of the Turks from Europe, and the establishment of a Greek empire in European Turkey. But such a scheme would be diametrically opposed to the principles of the policy on which we have hitherto acted.   To carry such a system into execution, we ought to join the Russians against the Turks, instead of helping the Turks against the Russians; for how could such a reconstruction of Turkey become the result of a successful contest by England and France in defence of Turkey?   I have no partiality for the Turks as Mahometans, and should be very glad if they could be turned into Christians; but as to the character of the Turkish Government in regard to its treatment of Christians, I am well convinced that there are a vast number of Christians under the Governments of Russia, Austria, Rome, and Naples who would be rejoiced to be as well treated, and to enjoy as much security for person and property as the Christian subjects of the Sultan.

" To expel from Europe the Sultan and his two million of Mussulman subjects, including the army and the bulk of the landowners, might not be an easy task; still, the five Powers might effect it, and play the Polish drama over again.   But they would find the building up still more difficult than the pulling down.   There are no sufficient Christian elements as yet for a Christian state in European Turkey capable of performing its functions as a component part of the European system.   The Greeks are a small minority, and could not be the governing race.   The Sclavonians, who are the majority, do not possess the conditions necessary for becoming the bones and sinews of a new state.   A reconstruction of Turkey means neither more nor less than its subjection to Russia, direct or indirect, immediate or for a time delayed.

" It seems to me, then, that our course is plain, simple, and straight. That we must help Turkey out of her difficulties by negotiation, if possible ; and that if negotiation fails, we must, by force of arms, carry her safely through her dangers.

" Yours sincerely,

" PALMERSTON."

Lord Palmerston was not confining his suggestions to proposals for mere acts of force. He enters, in the next letter, on a discussion as to the best way of presenting a form of arrangement to the two contending parties so as to secure its favourable consideration. He agreed with Lord John Russell in thinking it unadvisable to present the note to the Turks without leaving them any discretion as to alterations which they might desire.

" Broadlands, October 24, 1853.

" MY DEAR JOHN RUSSELL,

" I have received your letter of yesterday, and entirely agree with you in regard to the two points you mention.

" If we wish to prevail on the Porte to sign a note for presentation to the Emperor, we must leave the Turkish Government the power of proposing alterations in the draft we send them. We may hope that our draft may be accepted by them without alteration; but they may have good reasons which have not occurred to us for desiring some changes, or they may have even bad reasons which, if the changes they propose would not increase our difficulties at Petersburg, might, in spite of their badness, be allowed to prevail. If we send them a draft which they must either take as it is or reject, we may have a rejection, and we may lose by our pertinacity an invaluable chance of a peaceful arrangement.

"But further, if we are prepared to impose our form of words on Turkey, we should thereby incur an honourable engagement to impose them equally on Russia; and are we, or are the French, or is Austria, or is Prussia prepared to declare war against Russia, not for the defence of the Turkish empire and the preservation of the balance of power in Europe, but in order to compel the Emperor of Russia to accept a particular form of words put together in Downing Street. This would surely be carrying the parental affection of authorship beyond reasonable extent. Then as to the way in which the draft of note should be sent to Constantinople. I agree with you that it would be inexpedient to revive the Vienna conference for such a purpose, or, indeed, for any other. That conference is dead—peace to its remains. No good can come out of a conference at Vienna on these matters, and at the present time. A Vienna conference means Buol, and Buol means Meyendorf, and Meyendorf means Nicholas; and the Turks know this, and so does all Europe.

" Westmoreland and Bourqueney are good men in their way, but neither of them up to the mark for conference functions.

" Moreover, the very atmosphere of Vienna is unhealthy.* I doubt whether even you or I should not find ourselves paralysed by the political miasma of the place. If the machinery of a conference is to be set up again, and it may be very useful to reorganise it, we ought to make a *sine quâ non* of its being held in London.

" Still, there would be an advantage in getting the concurrence of Austria and Prussia to the step we propose to take, and those Governments might usefully be asked to instruct their diplomatic agents at Constantinople to support and co-operate with Stratford and Lacour. Such a joint action would increase the chances of success both at Constantinople and afterwards at Petersburg; and, as the draft would come from London, the co-operation of Austria and Prussia would not be liable to the objections which would apply to a measure coming from a Vienna conference.

" It is, indeed, doubtful whether the gold and silver age of notes has not gone by, and whether, when the 'Fury' gets to Constantinople, she will not find the age of brass and iron already begun; but we are quite right to make the attempt.

" Yours sincerely,

" PALMERSTON."

* " Vienna is a sad place for humbug, and X. suffered from the atmosphere, as does the liveliest and sturdiest dog in the Grotto del Cane."—*Lord Palmerston to Lord Clarendon.*

Indeed it was so. The two armies were already in conflict; and, on the 30th of November, the navies also met in deadly fight, when the Turkish fleet was destroyed at Sinope. The feeling now roused in England was very strong; and Lord Palmerston, on the 10th of December, wrote to Lord Aberdeen :—

"Will you allow me to take this opportunity of repeating in writing what I have more than once said verbally, on the state of things between Russia and Turkey? It appears to me that we have two objects in view : the one to put an end to the present war between these two Powers; the other to prevent, as far as diplomatic arrangements can do so, a recurrence of similar differences, and, through those differences, renewed dangers to the peace of Europe.

" Now, it seems to me that, unless Turkey shall be laid prostrate at the feet of Russia by disasters and war, an event which England and France could not without dishonour permit, no peace can be concluded between the contending parties unless the Emperor consents to evacuate the Principalities, to abandon his demands, and to renounce some of the embarrassing stipulations of former treaties upon which he has founded the pretensions which have been the cause of existing difficulties.

" To bring the Emperor to agree to this, it is necessary to exert a considerable pressure upon him; and the quarter in which that pressure can at present be most easily brought to bear is the Black Sea and the countries bordering upon it. In the Black Sea, the combined English, French, and Turkish squadrons are indisputably superior to the Russian fleet, and are able to give the law to that fleet. What I would strongly recommend, therefore, is that which I proposed some months ago to the Cabinet, namely, that the Russian Government and the Russian admiral at Sebastopol should be informed that so long as Russian troops occupy the Principalities, or hold a position in any other part of the Turkish territory, no Russian ships-of-war can be allowed to show themselves out of port in the Black Sea.

" You will say that this would be an act of hostility towards Russia ; but so is the declaration already made, that no Russian ships shall be permitted to make any landing or attack on any part of the Turkish territory. The only difference between the two declarations is, that the one already made is incomplete and insufficient for its purpose, and that the one which I propose would be complete and sufficient. If the Russian fleet were shut up in Sebastopol, it is probable that the Turks would be able to make in Asia an impression that would tend to facilitate the conclusion of peace.

" With regard to the conditions of peace, it seems to me that the only arrangement which could afford to Europe a fair security against future dangers arising out of the encroachments of Russia on Turkey, and the attempts of the Russian Government to interfere in the internal affairs of the Turkish empire, would be that arrangement which I have often suggested, namely, that the treaty to be concluded between Russia and Turkey should be an ordinary treaty of peace and friendship, of boundaries, commerce, and mutual protection of the subjects of the one party within the territories of the other; and that all the stipulations which might be required for the privileges of the Principalities and of Servia, and for the protection of the Christian religion and its churches in the Ottoman dominions by the Sultan, should be contained in a treaty between the Sultan and the five Powers. By such a treaty Russia would be prevented from dealing single-handed with Turkey in regard to those matters on which she has, from time to time, endeavoured to fasten a quarrel on the Sultan.

"Yours sincerely,
" PALMERSTON."

Lord Aberdeen replied on the 13th: " I confess I am not prepared to adopt the mode which you think most likely to restore peace." He went on to say that he should prefer an open declaration of war to the " pressure " which Lord Palmerston proposed; but as the union of the four Powers had just been effected, with a declaration that the integrity of the Turkish empire was an object of general interest, it was to be presumed that they would take measures to secure it. Recourse, therefore, to direct hostility would be out of place, although it might eventually come.

Lord Palmerston resigned on the 15th. We have seen in the last chapter what was the immediate reason which he assigned ; but the fact is that, as Mr. Kinglake says, he was gifted with the instinct which enables a man to read the heart of a nation, and he felt that the English people would never forgive the Ministry if nothing decisive was done after the disaster at Sinope. During his short absence of about ten days, the Cabinet resolved to send the fleet into the Black Sea, with instructions to the admiral to prevent any Russian vessels of war from leaving port. Lord Aberdeen, in acknowledging the withdrawal of Lord Palmerston's resignation, says: "I am glad to find that you approve of a recent decision of the Cabinet with respect to the British and French fleets adopted in your absence. I feel sure you will have learnt with pleasure that, whether you are absent or present, the Government are duly careful to preserve from all injury the interests and dignity of the country."

The session of 1854 began on the 31st of January. On the 7th of February the Russian ambassador was recalled, and shortly after the British Government sent a final ultimatum to the Russian Emperor, calling upon him to evacuate the Principalities by the 30th of April. Meanwhile troops were despatched to the East, and active preparations were carried on at home. On the 7th of March Lord Palmerston presided over a banquet given at the Reform Club to Sir Charles Napier, previous to his departure with the fleet for the Baltic. I give an extract from Lord

Palmerston's speech on this occasion, both as illustrating the temper of the time, and as a specimen of
the spirited ease and humour with which he could
stir up an after-dinner audience. His enjoyment was
contagious, and the company laughed sympathetically
even before they heard the joke.

After the formal toasts had been duly drunk, Lord
Palmerston rose and said :—

"There was a very remarkable entertainer of dinner company, called Sir R. Preston, who lived in the city, and who,
when he gave dinners at Greenwich, after gorging his guests
with turtle, used to turn round to the waiters and say, ' Now
bring dinner.' Gentlemen, we have had the toasts which
correspond with the turtle, and now let's go to dinner.
(Laughter.) Now let us drink the toast which belongs to
the real occasion of our assembling here. I give you ' The
health of my gallant friend Sir Charles Napier,' who sits
beside me. If, gentlemen, I were addressing a Hampshire
audience, consisting of country gentlemen residing in that
county, to which my gallant friend and myself belong, I
should introduce him to your notice as an eminent agricul-
turist. (Laughter.) It has been my good fortune, when
enjoying his hospitality at Merchistoun Hall, to receive most
valuable instructions from him while walking over his farm
about stall-feeding, growing turnips, wire fencing, under-
draining, and the like. (Laughter.) My gallant friend is a
match for everything, and whatever he turns his hand to he
generally succeeds in it. (Cheers and laughter.) However,
gentlemen, he now, like Cincinnatus, leaves his plough, puts
on his armour, and is prepared to do that good service to his
country which he will always perform whenever an opportunity is afforded to him. I pass over those earlier exploits
of his younger days, which are well known to the members
of his profession ; but, perhaps, one of the most remarkable

exploits of his life is that which he performed in the same cause of liberty and justice in which he is now about to be engaged. In the year 1833, when gallantly volunteering to serve the cause of the Queen of Portugal against the encroachments and the usurpations of Don Miguel—to defend constitutional rights and liberties against arbitrary power—he took the command of a modest fleet of frigates and corvettes, and, at the head of that little squadron, he captured a squadron far superior in force, including two line-of-battle ships, one of which my gallant friend was the first to board. But on that occasion my gallant friend exhibited a characteristic trait. When he had scrambled upon the deck of this great line-of-battle ship, and was clearing the deck of those who had possession of it, a Portuguese officer ran at him full dart with his drawn sword to run him through. My gallant friend quietly parried the thrust, and, not giving himself the trouble to deal in any other way with his Portuguese assailant, merely gave him a hearty kick, and sent him down the hatchway. (Roars of laughter.) Well, gentlemen, that victory was a great event—(much laughter)—I don't mean the victory over the officer who went down (renewed laughter), but the victory over the fleet, which my gallant friend took into port; for that victory decided a great cause then pending. It decided the liberties of Portugal; it decided the question between constitutional and arbitrary power—a contest which began in Portugal, and which went on afterwards in Spain, when my gallant friend Sir De Lacy Evans lent his powerful aid in the same cause, and with the same success. My gallant friend Sir Charles Napier, however, got the first turn of fortune, and it was mainly owing to that victory of his that the Queen of Portugal afterwards occupied the throne to which she was rightfully entitled, and the Portuguese nation obtained that Constitution which they have ever since enjoyed. (Cheers.) A noble friend of mine, now no more, whose loss I greatly lament, for he was equally distinguished as a man, as a soldier, and as a diplomatist, the late

Lord William Russell—an honour to his country, as to his family—told me that one day he heard that my gallant friend Sir Charles Napier was in the neighbourhood of the fortress of Valenza, a Portuguese fortress some considerable distance from the squadron which he commanded. Lord W. Russell and Colonel Hare went to see my gallant friend, and Lord W. Russell told me that they met a man dressed in a very easy way (great laughter), followed by a fellow with two muskets on his shoulders. (Renewed laughter.) They took him at first for Robinson Crusoe (roars of laughter); but who should these men prove to be but the gallant admiral on my right and a marine behind him. (Laughter.) 'Well, Napier,' said Lord W. Russell, 'what are you doing here?' 'Why,' said my gallant friend, 'I am waiting to take Valenza.' 'But,' said Lord William, 'Valenza is a fortified town, and you must know that we soldiers understand how fortified towns are taken. You must open trenches; you must make approaches; you must establish a battery in breach; and all this takes a good deal of time, and must be done according to rule.' 'Oh,' said my gallant friend, 'I have no time for all that. (Cheers and laughter.) I have got some of my blue-jackets up here and a few of my ship's guns, and I mean to take the town with a letter.' (Laughter.) And so he did. He sent the governor a letter to tell him he had much better surrender at discretion. The governor was a very sensible man (cheers and laughter); and so surrender he did. So the trenches and the approaches, the battery, breach, and all that were saved, and the town of Valenza was handed over to the Queen of Portugal. Well, the next great occasion in which my gallant friend took a prominent and distinguished part— a part for which I can assure you that I personally, in my official capacity, and the Government to which I had the honour to belong. felt deeply indebted and obliged to him— was the occasion of the war in Syria. There my gallant friend distinguished himself, as usual, at sea and on shore. All was one to him, wherever an enemy was to be found;

and I feel sure that when the enemy was found, the enemy wished to Heaven he had not been found. (Great laughter and cheering.) Well, my gallant friend landed with his marines, headed a Turkish detachment, defeated the Egyptian troops, gained a very important victory, stormed the town of Sidon, captured three or four thousand Egyptian prisoners, and afterwards took a prominent part in the attack and capture of the important fortress of Acre. I am bound to say that the Government to which I belonged, in sending those instructions which led to the attack upon Acre, were very much guided by the opinions which we had received of the practicability of that achievement in letters from my gallant friend."

Mr. Bright, a few days later in the House of Commons, took Lord Palmerston to task for the tone of this speech. Such apparent levity and *gaîté de cœur* in a minister of the Crown must have grated on the sentiment of one who abhorred the war, and thought it unnecessary. But surely when the conflict was inevitable and imminent, it was the common-sense view of patriotism to neglect no means, however trifling, of keeping up the heart and spirit of the nation. Lord Palmerston, however, was so stung by the manner of the attack, that he replied with a bitterness and severity quite unusual for him, and which, perhaps, was excessive—the House for the moment showing by the exclamations of some of its members that this was the impression made upon it. At the same time it must be allowed that it was very galling to a man of Lord Palmerston's character to be held up to public reprobation as one who was inciting people to fight as if they were cocks in a pit.

The war had now fairly begun, and as early as June Lord Palmerston proposed to the Cabinet a descent on the Crimea. He urged that the siege of Sebastopol was the object on which the allied armies should be directed. The occupation of the Principalities by the Russian forces he regarded as a pledge for the neutrality of Austria, her active alliance with the enemy being quite possible should all fear be removed of Russia's permanent hold upon the Danube. He was, therefore, a strong advocate for leaving the Russians in undisturbed enjoyment of the pestilent air of the Dobrudscha, and for crossing over from Varna to the great Russian arsenal on the Black Sea.

The Cabinet unanimously acknowledged the force of his arguments, though there were some few who wished for a postponement of such an expedition until the second year of the campaign. The difficulty was the unprepared state of the French army, which was still deficient both in men and material.

The following memorandum on the measures to be adopted against Russia was sent round to the Cabinet :—

"C. G., June 15, 1854.

" Some conversation having passed on Wednesday evening at Sir Charles Wood's between some members of the Cabinet, about the objects to which our operations ought to be directed in the war against

Russia, I wish to submit the following observations to the Cabinet.

"England and France have entered into war with a great Power, have made great exertions, at a great expense, and for a great purpose. They would lose caste in the world if they concluded the war with only a small result. The particular overt act by which Russia broke the peace was the invasion of the Danube Principalities, but the purpose for which we took up arms would be very imperfectly accomplished if the only result of the war was to be the evacuation of those provinces by the Russian army, even if that evacuation were accompanied by a waiver on the part of Russia of the demands she has made upon Turkey. Such a result would be a triumph rather than a defeat for Russia.

"She would say that she had defied and withstood the naval and military strength of two of the greatest Powers of the world, that these Powers had been unable to hurt her, and that she had substantially gained all that she had set out by demanding, inasmuch as the Sultan had done by his own act for his Christian subjects that which she had required. We should then have no security for the future, and whenever a more favourable opportunity might present itself, whenever England and France were disunited, she would again make her spring upon Turkey, and with a better chance of success.

"It seems absolutely necessary that some heavy blow should be struck at the naval power and territorial dimensions of Russia, and unless this be done in the present year, the accomplishment of it will become more difficult, and the reputation of England and France will materially suffer.

" The points where such blows could best be struck are evidently the Russian possessions in Georgia, and Circassia, and the Crimea.

" The expulsion of the Russians from Georgia and Circassia must probably be left to the Turks and the Circassians, and no effort should be left untried to re-organise the Turkish army in Asia, by placing it under European officers, so as to put it into a condition to drive the Russians out of Georgia before the season for military operations is over, and to co-operate with the Circassians.

" The British and French troops are now, to a certain degree, pledged to co-operate with Omar Pasha in raising the siege of Silistria.

" If that can be accomplished easily enough to leave time for operations afterwards in the Crimea, well and good; and of course the British and French troops would be ordered in no case to cross the Danube, and entangle themselves in the unhealthy plains of Wallachia.

" But I confess that it seems to me, that if the combined army had been ready to undertake the reduction of the Crimea and Sebastopol, that object is so infinitely more important than the temporary defence of the Danube fortresses, that I would have preferred that Silistria and the line of the Danube should have been abandoned, and that Omar Pasha should have fallen back upon Schoumla, and Varna, and Adrianople, and that the allied army should have gone at once to the Crimea.

" The Russians could not retain permanently the Danube fortresses, and if they moved on to the southward they must have left garrisons in them. The further they advanced southward the greater would be their difficulties of all kinds, and the more the effective strength of their army would dwindle away, and the more easily, therefore, they would afterwards be defeated. But the further south the point at which they might be defeated, the more fatal a defeat would be.

" The occupation of the Danube fortresses by Russia would be only a temporary and precarious advantage for her. The capture of Sebastopol and of the Russian Black Sea fleet would be a lasting and important advantage to us. Such a success would act with great weight upon the fortunes of the war, and would tell essentially upon the negotiations for peace. We should be able materially and at once to reduce our naval expenditure if the Russian Black Sea fleet were destroyed or in our possession; and, holding the Crimea and Sebastopol, we could dictate the conditions of peace in regard to the naval position of Russia in the Black Sea.

" There does not seem good reason to believe that the Russians have at present more than 40,000 men in the Crimea, if they have so many; and if 25,000

English and 35,000 French could be landed some-where in the large bay to the north of Sebastopol, there can be little doubt that they would be able to take the fort on the hill on the north side of the harbour of Sebastopol, and they would then command the harbour, fleet and town.

" This enterprise need not prevent the capture of Anapa and Poti this year, but even if it did there can surely be no comparison between the value of the capture of Sebastopol and the taking of the forts on the coast of Circassia.   The capture of Sebastopol and the capture or destruction of the Russian fleet would of course imply the surrender of the Russian troops which form the garrison of the place, or their evacua-tion of the Crimea by capitulation, and either of these results would be a brilliant feat of arms for the allied forces.   Anapa and Poti might be taken at leisure afterwards, and with greater ease if Sebastopol had been mastered.

" But if the attack on the Crimea is put off till next year the Russian Government will have time to strengthen the defences of the place, and to increase the garrison to any amount which the peninsula can hold, and we may find the undertaking far more diffi-cult then than it would have been this year.

" The Emperor will, during the autumn, winter, and spring, raise and train recruits enough to make good his losses during this campaign, and next year we should have to deal with a reinforced and re-organised army, instead of with one worn down and dispirited by the unsuccessful operations of this summer. On the other hand, the allied troops are now fresh, eager, and ready for enterprise. If they are to remain inactive till next spring, their health may give way, their spirit may flag, their mutual cordiality and good understanding may be cooled down by intrigues, jealousies, and disputes, and public opinion, which in England and France now stands by the two Governments, and bears up the people of the two countries to make the sacrifices necessary for the war, may take another turn, and people may grow tired of burthens which have produced no sufficient and satisfactory result.

" It seems to me, then, that the French Government ought to be urged to press forward the complete formation of their co-operating army in Turkey, and that we ought to endeavour to make arrangements with them for an attack on Sebastopol as soon as the combined army is in a state to undertake it.

" We do not seem likely to accomplish anything of much importance in the Baltic, and on that account it is the more desirable that we should gain some real and signal advantage in the Black Sea.

" PALMERSTON."

And to the Minister of War he writes on the same subject.

" Brocket, June 16, 1854.

" MY DEAR DUKE OF NEWCASTLE,

" You said yesterday at the Cabinet that you wished to talk over what was to be written to Raglan by the mail which would go before our next Cabinet, and as I was obliged to leave the Cabinet early to save my railway train to this place, I send you my vote in writing.

"It seems to me that to keep the allied army in Bulgaria, and to carry on operations on the banks of the Danube, would be to throw away time, money, men, official and national reputation.

"Nothing that we could do there would have any decisive effect on the war, nor could it help us one step towards the attainment of that future security which our convention with France specifies as one of the main conditions of peace. Even if we were to drive the Russians across the Pruth, it would be what the French call a *coup d'epée dans l'eau*—a temporary advantage which would cease the moment we withdrew. I should, indeed, doubt the wisdom of an advance of the Turks to the north of the Danube, nor ought they to attach too much importance to the line of the Danube. Omar Pasha was quite right to defend the Danube and Silistria as long as he could, but I should not have thought less well of ultimate results if he had retired at length to Schumla and Varna, or even to Adrianople. The Russian difficulties would increase with every day's march to the southward, and the dangers of their position would become more and more serious.

"Our only chance of bringing Russia to terms is by offensive and not by defensive operations. We and the French ought to go to the Crimea and take

Sebastopol and the Russian fleet the moment our two armies are in a condition to go thither. Sixty thousand English and French troops, with the fleets cooperating, would accomplish the object in six weeks after landing, and if this blow were accompanied by successful operations in Georgia and Circassia, we might have a merry Christmas and a happy New Year.

" There is not the slightest danger of the Russians getting to Constantinople. The Turks are able to prevent that; but even if they could not, the Austrians would be compelled, by the force of circumstances, to do so. Austria has, as usual, been playing a shabby game. When she thought the Russians likely to get on, and while she fancied England and France needed hastening, she bragged of her determination to be active against Russia. As soon as she found our troops at Varna, she changed her tone, and, according to a despatch which Clarendon had in his hand yesterday, she now says she shall not enter the Principalities, and the Russians must be driven out by the Turks and the English and French. She can hardly think us simple enough to do her work for her; but the best way to force her to act would be to send our troops off to the Crimea. This is my vote.

" Yours sincerely,

" PALMERSTON."

On the 29th of June the Duke of Newcastle sent out instructions to Lord Raglan to make an immediate advance on Sebastopol. On the 14th of September the allied forces of France and England landed in the Crimea, and a few days later they·won the battle of the Alma. On the 3rd of October the news of the fall of Sebastopol arrived. It was believed by most people for nearly twenty-four hours. Indeed, the Emperor of the French himself announced it to his troops at the camp of Helfaut.

These reported successes drew from no less an authority than Mr. Gladstone a recognition of Lord Palmerston's initiative in designating the Crimea as the proper field for the allied armies. In a letter of the 4th October, he says :—

"My purpose is to offer you a congratulation which I feel to be especially due to you upon the great events which are taking place in the Crimea. Much as we must all rejoice on public grounds at these signal successes, and thankful as the whole nation may justly feel to a Higher Power, yet in looking back upon the instruments through which such results have come about, I for one cannot help repeating to you the thanks I offered at an earlier period for the manner in which you urged—when we were amidst many temptations to far more embarrassing and less effective proceedings —the duty of concentrating our strokes upon the true heart and centre of the war at Sebastopol."

In the month of November, 1854, Lord Palmerston went over to Paris with Lady Palmerston, mainly with the view of having an interview with the Emperor. He writes to his brother :—

"Yesterday Emily and I dined at St. Cloud. The dinner was very handsome, and our hosts very agreeable. The Empress was full of life, animation, and talk, and the more one looks at her the prettier one thinks her. I have found the Emperor and Drouyn de Lhuys in very good opinions on the subject of the war, and acting towards us with perfect fairness, openness, and good faith."

Meanwhile in the Crimea all was not prospering, and the disappointment of the public when they learnt that Sebastopol had not been taken, as reported, increased their impatience. A sort of Nemesis hung over Lord John Russell, and compelled him to become the spokesman of the general feeling, and to indicate Lord Palmerston, his rejected lieutenant, as the man of the hour. In a letter to the Prime Minister Lord John urged the necessity of a change in the War Department, and pointed out the " necessity of having in that office a man who, from experience of military details, from inherent vigour of mind, and from weight with the House of Commons, can be expected to guide the great operations of war with authority and success. There is only one person," he continued, " belonging to the Government who combines these advantages. My conclusion is, that before Parliament meets Lord Palmerston should be entrusted with the seals of the War Department." Lord Aberdeen, however, declined to recommend the change to the Queen, alleging, with great fairness, that although on the first constitution of the office such an arrangement might have been best, yet that the Duke of Newcastle had discharged his duties too ably and honourably to afford any justification for his removal.

After a short winter session, in which the Foreign Enlistment Bill was passed, Parliament reassembled on the 23rd of January, 1855. Mr. Roebuck, on the first night, gave notice that he intended to move for the appointment of a select committee "to inquire into the condition of our army before Sebastopol, and into the conduct of those departments of the Government whose duty it has been to minister to the wants of that army." Lord John Russell immediately resigned. Writing to Lord Aberdeen, he said : "I do not see how the motion is to be resisted ; but as it involves a censure upon the War Department, with which some of my colleagues are connected, my only course is to tender my resignation." Lord Palmerston's opinion on this event is contained in the following letter :—

" Piccadilly, January 24, 1855.

"MY DEAR JOHN RUSSELL,

"I received your letter of this morning with much regret, and I feel bound in candour to say that I think your decision ill-timed. Everybody foresaw that on the meeting of Parliament after Christmas some such motion as that given notice of by Roebuck was likely to be made; and if you had determined not to face such a motion, your announcement of such a decision a fortnight ago would have rendered it more easy for your colleagues to have taken whatever

course such an announcement might have led to,
either to have met your views by a new arrangement
of offices, or to have given up the Government in a
manner creditable to all parties concerned. As it is,
you will have the appearance of having remained in
office, aiding in carrying on a system of which you
disapproved until driven out by Roebuck's announced
notice, and the Government will have the appearance
of self-condemnation by flying from a discussion
which they dare not face ; while as regards the
country, the action of the executive will be paralysed
for a time in a critical moment of a great war, with
an impending negotiation, and we shall exhibit to
the world a melancholy spectacle of disorganisation
among our political men at home similar to that
which has prevailed among our military men abroad.
My opinion is that, if you had simply renewed the
proposal which you made before Christmas, such an
arrangement might have been made ; and there are
constitutional and practical grounds on which such a
motion as Roebuck's might have been resisted without violence to any opinions which you may entertain
as to the past period.

" Yours sincerely,
" PALMERSTON."

The ministerial explanations which took place in
the House of Commons were immediately followed
by the Roebuck motion for a select committee.
Left in the lurch by their recognised leader, the

Aberdeen cabinet found their best defender in the man for whom many of them had felt distrust. Lord Palmerston, coming gallantly forward to take upon himself the invidious duty of supporting an administration over which he had little control, and which, before disaster came, had neglected his advice, said that he fully concurred that the responsibility for the conduct of the war fell not on the Duke of Newcastle alone, but on the whole Cabinet. He did not deny that there had been something calamitous in the condition of our army, but he traced it to the inexperience arising from a long peace. If the House thought the Government not deserving of confidence, the direct and manly course would have been to affirm that proposition. The course about to be pursued would be dangerous and inconvenient in its results abroad. He hoped that when the House had determined what set of men should be entrusted with public affairs, they would give their support to that Government, and not show to Europe that a nation could only meet a great crisis when it was deprived of representative institutions.

When the House divided there appeared for Mr. Roebuck's motion, 305; against it, 148. Majority against the Government, 157. This startling result so amazed the House that they forgot to cheer, but laughed derisively.

On the 1st of February Lord Palmerston formally announced in the Commons the resignation of the Ministry. Thus fell the Coalition Cabinet of 1852, the victim of the war which it had itself declared.

CHAPTER III.

LORD DERBY was sent for to form a Government,
and immediately sought the co-operation of Lord
Palmerston, offering him the leadership of the House
of Commons, which Mr. Disraeli was willing to waive
in his favour. Offers were also made, through him,
to Mr. Gladstone and Mr. Sidney Herbert. Lord
Palmerston, however, in the following letter, declined the proposals, having also expressed his great
unwillingness, under existing circumstances, to belong to any Government in which the management
of foreign affairs did not remain in Lord Clarendon's
hands :—

"144, Piccadilly, January 31, 1855.

"MY DEAR DERBY,

"Having well reflected upon the proposition
which you made to me this morning, I have come to
the conclusion that if I were to join your Government, as proposed by you, I should not give to that
Government that strength which you are good

H 2

enough to think would accrue to you from my acceptance of office.

" I shall, however, deem it my duty, in the present critical state of affairs, to give, out of office, my support to any Government that shall carry on the war with energy and vigour, and will, in the management of our foreign relations, sustain the dignity and interests of the country, and maintain unimpaired the alliances which have been formed.

" I have conveyed to Gladstone and Sidney Herbert the communication which you wished me to make to them; but it seemed to me to be best that they should write to you themselves.

" My dear Derby,

" Yours sincerely,

" PALMERSTON."

Lord Derby at once retired, and Lord John Russell was the next person sent for by the Queen, who signified that it would give her particular satisfaction if Lord Palmerston could join in the formation. He expressed his willingness to do so; but many of the Whigs positively declined, and notably Lord Clarendon. Lord John Russell therefore resigned the commission which the Queen had entrusted to him; and in his letter announcing this to Lord Palmerston, he said: " I have only to thank you for the readiness with which you consented to aid me in the formation of a Government. Should the

Queen intrust you with this difficult but honourable task, I hope you may succeed; and if you form a Ministry, I shall be prepared to give you every support in my power." Lord Palmerston replied :—

" February 4, 1855.

" MY DEAR JOHN RUSSELL,

" Thank you for your letter, which I have just received. I think the course which you have adopted was, under all circumstances, the best. The events which led to the present state of things were too recent to have allowed personal feelings to subside sufficiently to have enabled you to succeed in the task which the Queen had asked you to undertake; and to have made an imperfect arrangement would not have been advantageous either to yourself or to the country.

" I feel very thankful to you for what you say with reference to the possibility that the Queen might desire me to try to form a Government; and if this should be, I should, of course, lose no time in communicating with you.

" Yours sincerely,

" PALMERSTON."

The " possibility" was what every one, during these " stage" negotiations, foresaw to be a necessity. Lord Palmerston was requested to take up the abandoned task, and he successfully performed it.

He thus writes to his brother to announce the event :—

" Downing Street, February 15, 1855.

" My dear William,

. . . . . . ' Quod nemo promittere Divum
Auderet volvenda dies en attulit ultro.'

" A month ago if any man had asked me to say what was one of the most improbable events, I should have said my being Prime Minister. Aberdeen was there, Derby was head of one great party, John Russell of the other, and yet, in about ten days' time they all gave way like straws before the wind, and so here am I, writing to you from Downing Street, as First Lord of the Treasury.

" The fact was that Aberdeen and Newcastle had become discredited in public estimation as statesmen equal to the emergency. Derby felt conscious of the incapacity of the greater portion of his party, and their unfitness to govern the country, and John Russell, by the way in which he suddenly abandoned the Government, had so lost caste for the moment that I was the only one of his political friends who was willing to serve under him. I could not refuse to do so, because he told me that upon my answer depended his undertaking to form a Government, and if I had refused, and he had declined the task, and the Queen had then sent for me, people would have ascribed my refusal to personal ambition. Besides, he broke with the late Government because the War

Department was not given to me, and it would have been ungrateful of me to have refused to assist him. It is, however, curious that the same man who summarily dismissed me three years ago, as unfit to be Minister for Foreign Affairs, should now have broken up a Government because I was not placed in what he conceived to be the most important post in the present state of things.

"I think our Government will do very well. I am backed by the general opinion of the whole country, and I have no reason to complain of the least want of cordiality or confidence on the part of the Court.

"As Aberdeen has become an impossibility, I am, for the moment *l'inévitable.* We are sending John Russell to negotiate at Vienna. This will serve as a proof to show we are in earnest in our wish for peace, and in our determination to have sufficiently satisfactory terms. I have no great faith in the sincerity of Russia, though it is said that the Emperor Nicholas is much pressed by many around him to make peace as soon as he can. But we must insist upon his having a very small number of ships-of-war in the Black Sea, probably not more than four, and it will be a great gulp for him to swallow such a condition, especially seeing that we have not been able as yet to take his fleet. We must also *ask* for the destruction of the works at Sebastopol, although we should not make that a *sine quâ non,* unless we had taken the place and had destroyed the works ourselves. However, a short time will show whether we are to have peace or war, and, in the meanwhile, we are making our preparations for war as if peace was out of the question.

"You may assure the King of Naples, if you see him, that I am anxious to renew with Naples that friendly footing of mutual relations which existed in the time of some of his ancestors, but that such a state of things is impossible unless he changes his system of policy, foreign and domestic.

"We do not presume to dictate to him on either of these branches, but we are entitled to say on what conditions our goodwill is to be obtained, and the course of events seems to show that the good-will of England is a matter of some importance even to states as far removed from our shores as Naples is.

"I expect to be tolerably strong in Parliament for some little time to come, and I think that when the session is over it will be advisable to dissolve.

"We shall have many discontented men behind us, because the body of the Whigs are angry that the Peelites joined me, and have occupied places which the Whigs hoped to have themselves; but if the Peelites had not joined me, we should have had an equally numerous band of discontented, only with this difference, that they would have consisted of more able men. Aberdeen and Newcastle behaved in the most friendly and honourable manner possible in persuading their friends to remain in the Government, but I see that the Peelite section still continues to endeavour to make itself a little separate section.   Good-bye.

"Yours affectionately,

"PALMERSTON."

When one of the leading Peelites hesitated to accept the offer made to him, Lord Palmerston, divining his thoughts, wrote openly to him as follows :—

" To speak plainly and frankly, you distrust my views and intentions, and you think that I should be disposed to continue the war without necessity, for the attainment of objects either unreasonable in themselves or unattainable by the means at our command, or not worth the efforts necessary for their attainment.   In this you misjudge me.   If by a stroke of the wand I could effect in the map of the world the changes which I could wish, I am quite sure that I could make arrangements far more conducive than some of the present ones to the peace of nations, to the progress of civilisation, to the happiness and welfare of mankind; but I am not so destitute of common sense as not to be able to compare ends with means, and to see that the former must be given up when the latter are wanting; and when the means to be brought to bear for the attainment of any ends consist in the blood and treasure of a great nation, those who are answerable to that nation for the expenditure of that blood and treasure must well weigh the value of the objects which they pursue, and must remember that, if they should forget the just proportion between ends and means, the good sense of the people whose affairs they manage will soon step in to correct their errors, and to call them to a severe account for the evils of which they would have been the cause." *

I here quote a letter to Lord Aberdeen, which is a testimony to his patriotic conduct under circumstances which must have been galling to him :—

"Piccadilly, February 12, 1855.

" My dear Aberdeen,

"I called at your door yesterday, and was sorry not to have found you at home. I wanted to say how much I have to thank you for your handsome conduct and for your friendly and energetic exertions, in removing the difficulties which I at first experienced in my endeavour to reconstitute the Government in such a manner as to combine in it all the strength which, in the circumstances of the moment, it was possible to bring together. I well know that without your assistance that most desirable and important combination could not have been effected.

" Yours sincerely,

" Palmerston."

No time was lost by the reorganised Cabinet in

* February 6, 1855.

remedying some of the most pressing evils which had borne down our army in the Crimea. Lord Palmerston, in announcing to the House of Commons the formation of his Government, detailed also some of his new administrative measures. The office of Secretary at War was to be amalgamated with that of the Secretary of State in the person of Lord Panmure; a Bill was immediately to be introduced for the enlistment of older men on short service; the Admiralty was to establish a special Board to superintend the transport service; lastly, a sanitary commission was to be sent to the Crimea, and another, under Sir John M'Neil, to superintend the commissariat. I append Lord Palmerston's letter to Lord Raglan accompanying the sanitary commission :—

" Downing Street, February 22, 1855.

" MY DEAR LORD RAGLAN,

    " This will be given to you by Dr. Sutherland, Chief of the Sanitary Commission, consisting of himself, Dr. Gavin, and Mr. Rawlinson, whom we have sent out to put the hospitals, the port, and the camp into a less unhealthy condition than has hitherto existed, and I request that you will give them every assistance and support in your power. They will, of course, be opposed and thwarted by the medical officers, by the men who have charge of the port arrangements, and by those who have the cleaning of the camp. Their mission will be ridiculed, and their recommendations and directions set aside, unless enforced by the peremptory exercise of your authority.

" But that authority I must request you to exert in the most peremptory manner for the immediate and exact carrying into execution whatever changes of arrangement they may recommend; for these are matters on which depend the health and lives of many hundreds of men, I may indeed say of thousands. It is scarcely to be expected that officers, whether military or medical, whose time is wholly occupied by the pressing business of each day, should be able to give their attention or their time to the matters to which these commissioners have for many years devoted their action and their thoughts.

" But the interposition of men skilled in this way is urgently required. The hospital at Scutari is become a hotbed of pestilence, and if no proper precautions are taken before the sun's rays begin to be felt, your camp will become one vast seat of the most virulent plague. I hope this commission will arrive in time to prevent much evil, but I am very sure that not one hour should be lost after their arrival in carrying into effect the precautionary and remedial measures which they may recommend.

" My dear Lord Raglan,

" Yours sincerely,

" PALMERSTON."

The patriotic impatience, however, of a certain section of ambitious politicians was so great that they could not wait. Before five days had elapsed Mr. Layard again drew attention to the state of the army, and, in a speech decidedly hostile to Lord Palmerston's Administration, recommended that, in imitation of the French revolutionary Convention, the House should send out some of its own members to sit in judgment on the guilty. In reply to this, Lord Palmerston, amid general laughter, suggested that it might be satisfactory to the House to take the honourable member at his word, and to add to the direction that he and his colleagues should proceed instantly to the Crimea, the further instruction that they should remain there during the rest of the session.

As to Mr. Roebuck's committee, Lord Palmerston still retained his objection to it, as not in accordance with the Constitution or efficient for its purpose. He told the House that, as an English king once rode up to an insurrection and offered to be its leader, so the Government offered to the House of Commons to be its committee, and would do of itself all that it was possible to do. As, however, Mr. Roebuck still persisted, " aiming," as he said, to " assist the noble Lord in infusing new vigour into the Constitution of the country," Lord Palmerston yielded, giving as his reason for so doing that the country asked for an inquiry, and that, whatever inconvenience there might be in such a course, there would be greater inconvenience and danger if the Government of the country were again to be in abeyance. This concession, however, produced another ministerial crisis, which was, however, of short duration. Sir James Graham, Mr. Gladstone, and Mr. Sidney Herbert retired because the renewed motion was not to be resisted; and Sir Charles Wood, Sir George Lewis, and Lord-John Russell took the vacant places.

The death of the Emperor Nicholas and the active alliance of Sardinia with the Western Powers were both events which appeared likely to affect favourably for peace the negotiations which had now been renewed at Vienna. Lord John Russell, who went to the Conference as English representative, was instructed that the end to be held in view was the admission of Turkey into the great European family, and that there were certain points which must be insisted on as necessary fully to attain this object. They lay under four principal heads, namely, the Principalities, the free navigation of the Danube, Russian supremacy in the Black Sea, and the independence of the Porte. Lord Palmerston writes to Lord John Russell private instructions:—

" Piccadilly, March 28, 1855.

" MY DEAR JOHN RUSSELL,

" I fear from all you have said to Clarendon, public and private, that there is no chance of the new Emperor of Russia agreeing to the only conditions which would afford us security for the future, and though some few people here would applaud us for making peace on almost any conditions, yet the bulk of the nation would soon see through the flimsy veil with which we should have endeavoured to disguise entire failure in attaining the objects for which we undertook the war, and we should receive the general condemnation which we should rightly deserve.

" The Austrians, the Prussians, and the Russian agents of course trumpet forth the vast value of the concessions made by Russia by her acceptance of the four points as a basis of negotiation; but the whole value and practical effect of those points must depend upon the manner in which they are worked out, and, according to the schemes of Gortschakoff and Prokesh, the vaunted concessions would be reduced to absolute nullity. The two important points of the four are the first and the third; the second lays down a principle not new, but always admitted even by Russia herself, though in practice she contrived to evade the carrying of it out. The fourth point Russia felt to be only the relinquishment of a pretension which could not be enforced by arms when England and France resolved to back Turkey, and the admission involved in the Russian acceptance of this fourth point does not take from her one particle of her power of future aggression against Turkey, though it saves Turkey from a source of great internal weakness. But the pretension was one which Russia had yet to make good, and she could not make it good against Turkey supported by England and France.

" The first point is very important, because the

object the allies had in view to be attained by it is to emancipate the Principalities from foreign interference and to tie them more closely to the Sultan, while, at the same time, security should be given them for the maintenance of local self-government, and for those privileges of religion, internal administration, and commerce which are essential to their welfare and prosperity. For these purposes it is plain that their Constitution should be improved and liberalised, that their Prince should be appointed by the Sultan, with the only condition that he should be one of the Sultan's Christian subjects. That the Constitution, which ought to include a representative system, should be granted (*octroyé*) by the Sovereign, confirmed by him by the most solemn sanction, and communicated by him to the contracting Powers. Such an arrangement would seem to be a sufficient guarantee, considering that there has been no complaint by the two provinces that the Sultan has endeavoured to infringe on their privileges or to curtail their liberties. The only evil to be guarded against is the recurrence of that intermeddling in the internal affairs of the provinces by a foreign Power, and those military occupations of those two provinces by foreign troops, which have led to the conflicts between the Powers of Europe.

" Now, the scheme of Gortschakoff and Prokesh so far from attaining the objects we have in view, would have the effect of riveting the foreign shackles which Russia has sought to fasten on the Principalities, adding to their tightness and their weight, and fixing them down by the assistance and co-operation of Austria, with the formal sanction and approval of England and France.

" The treacherous game of Austria and Russia is manifest and palpable. They propose to England and France the most objectionable arrangements on the first, second, and fourth points. They tell England and France, or, at least, Austria suggests to England and France, that it would be necessary for those two Powers to agree to these objectionable conditions, in order to secure the co-operation of Austria on the third point, the most important to the Western Powers. And what would be the result? Why that which follows all such bargains with his sable majesty: we should have paid the price without obtaining the thing we wanted to buy. Austria evidently means to throw us over on the third point; and if that is to happen, the sooner we are undeceived as to her intentions the better.

" Her substitutes for a narrow limitation of the Russian Black Sea fleet are, as you say, futile. The opening of the straits would be a standing danger to the Sultan, with no compensating advantage, but, on the contrary, with probable inconvenience to England and France. The maintenance by us and the French of permanent fleets in the Black Sea to counterbalance the fleet of Russia, is simply a *mauvaise plaisanterie*. The stipulation that Russia should not have a larger fleet than she now has, even assuming that the sunken ships are not to count, would still leave her with too powerful a naval force ; and it must be remembered that it is easy to build steamers which, though unarmed at first, may easily be strengthened and turned into ships-of-war. The neutrality scheme of Drouyn might do, if confined to the Black Sea and the Sea of Azoff, but it would probably be as distasteful to Russia as our own proposals. The truth is we are in the middle of a battle, and our adversary seems determined to try the fate of arms, though it is clearly for his interest not to do so. Possibly this Czar might find more difficulty in yielding than his father might have done. However, I presume a few days will now give a turn to affairs. Drouyn comes here to-morrow on his way to Vienna, whither he is going to stiffen Bourqueney.

" We are getting on very fairly in the House of Commons, and people there are behaving very well towards the Government.

" I am taking charge of the current business of the Colonial Office, in order to know a little about it, and because I thought it began to press a little too much on George Grey's health. I did not, however, state that latter reason to him, but put it upon the first, my proposal to take charge.

" Yours sincerely,
" Palmerston."

Whilst there was a chance of peace issuing out of the doings at Vienna, Lord Palmerston was con-

sidering what were the reforms which would have to
be demanded from the Sultan. Letters have been
already quoted to show how constantly he urged
upon the Turks that complete equality between
Christians and Mahommedans was the only means
whereby the Ottoman empire could be permanently
strengthened; and in the following letter he sum-
marises what he was prepared to press upon the
Porte. He also advocated the establishment of
primary schools in which Christian and Mussulman children should receive elementary instruction
together:—

"May 14, 1855.

" MY DEAR CLARENDON,

"What remains to be done for the *nonconformists* in Turkey would be, I apprehend, speaking
generally:—

" *a.* Capacity for military service by voluntary enlistment and eligibility to rise to any rank in
the army.

" *b.* Admission of non-Mussulman evidence in civil
as well as criminal cases.

" *c.* Establishment of mixed courts of justice (with
an equal number of Christian and Mussulman
judges) for all cases in which Mahommedans
and non-Mahommedans are parties.

" *d.* Appointment of a Christian officer as assessor
to every governor of a province when that
governor is a Mussulman; such assessor to
be of suitable rank and to have full liberty to

I 2

appeal to Constantinople against any act of the governor unjust, oppressive, or corrupt.

" *e.* Eligibility of Christians to all places in the administration, whether at Constantinople or in the provinces, and a practical application of this rule by the appointment of Christians at once to some places of trust, civil and military.

" *f.* The total abolition of the present system by which offices at Constantinople and in the provinces are bought and sold and given to unfit and unworthy men for money paid or promised. Such men become tyrants in their offices, either from incapacity or bad passions, or from a desire to repay themselves the money paid for their appointments.

" There ought not only to be complete toleration of non-Mussulman religion, but all punishment on converts from Islam, whether natives or foreigners, ought to be abolished.

" Yours sincerely,
" PALMERSTON."

This would have been a very complete programme of civil and religious emancipation, could only the instruments have been found to carry it out thoroughly and honestly. But thorough and honest instruments can never be found under such a blighting and corrupt despotism as that of the Sultan of Turkey. The depths of criminal recklessness and indifference to which it habitually descends is illustrated by the following memorandum of Lord Palmerston's, from which it appears that the very first loan the Turkish Government ever raised—a loan paid to them at the very height of war, and for the purposes of their struggle for national existence, was being deliberately squandered by their sovereign on favourites and on personal luxuries, while the fortress of Kars and its gallant defenders were being abandoned to their fate :—

" Should we not be justified in saying to the Turkish Government that we will not advance any more of the loan which we have guaranteed until these extravagant prodigalities have been put an end to? We shall not be able to justify to Parliament our having incurred pecuniary responsibility to assist the Turkish Government in carrying on the war if it turns out that our guarantee has thus been made subservient to wasteful expenditure for personal and private purposes. The Turkish troops are in arrear of their pay. We are told that commissariat supplies are stopped for want of money. Kars and its brave army are lost because the Turkish Government has not supplied pay, provisions, and munitions of war to them ; and at this crisis, when a proper sense of duty would have led the Sultan to stint himself, in order to find money for the defence of his throne and empire, he launches into extravagance in repairing and building palaces, and he nearly doubles the amount of money applied to his personal expenses and to the allowances to members of his family. This is scandalous.

"P. 16/12. 55."

The Conference, however, broke up without any result being arrived at, Russia declining to accede to the fixed limitations sought to be imposed on her naval forces in the Black Sea. Lord Palmerston had some difficulty during these Conferences in keeping our ally staunch. The war had never been so popular in France as it was in England, and the French appeared too ready to accept terms which the English Government thought insufficient. In the following letter the Emperor of the French is urged not to allow a subtle diplomacy to rob him of the fruits of victory. The English Ministry had just obtained a large majority in the House of Commons on Mr. Disraeli's resolution expressing "dissatisfaction with the ambiguous language and uncertain conduct of Her Majesty's Government."

"Londres, 28 Mai 1855.

"Sire,

"Votre Majesté a daigné me permettre de vous exprimer ma pensée de temps en temps dans des occasions importantes. J'ose donc vous soumettre que la proposition que nous fait l'Autriche de prononcer dans la Conférence de Vienne le mot 'Limitation,' n'est qu'un piége qu'on nous tend.

Le Principe de Limitation n'a aucune valeur pour nous, tout dépend du Chiffre. La Russie pourrait bien accepter le principe sans que nous fussions pour cela plus près d'une paix sûre et honorable. Mais par une telle acceptation, la Russie nous entraînerait dans un dédale de négociations qui amolliraient les esprits en France, en Angleterre, en Allemagne, partout, et même en Crimée ; car ces négociations oisives et illusoires empêcheraient de conduire énergiquement la guerre, et ne nous aideraient pas à faire la paix. La position de la France et de l'Angleterre n'est-elle pas simple et claire ? Nous avons fait à la Russie des propositions qu'on ne peut critiquer qu'en les prononçant trop libérales envers notre ennemi ; ces propositions, la Russie les a rejetées avec fièreté, on pourrait même le dire, avec insolence. Qu'avons-nous à faire donc, excepté de nous mettre à obtenir des succès par la guerre ; pourquoi nous humilier en faisant de nouvelles propositions à la Russie, et en quittant le terrain où nous nous étions placés ? Ce terrain n'est pas le principe de Limitation, mais une Limitation définie et suffisante à nos yeux pour parer aux dangers de l'avenir.

" Je sens bien que nous n'avons pas le droit de soumettre à V. M. des considérations puisées dans notre situation intérieure, mais peut-être V. M. me permettra de remarquer que le Gouvernement anglais vient de remporter une grande victoire Parlementaire : nous avons eu à la Chambre des Communes, vendredi soir, une majorité de 100 voix, et contre quelle attaque ? Contre une accusation que nous nous occupions d'une négociation inutile et peu honorable, tandis que nous devions nous occuper uniquement de remporter des succès dans la guerre. La Chambre a compris, d'après les explications que nous lui avons données, que les négociations étaient suspendues 'sine die,' et que la guerre se poursuivait avec vigueur. Si après cela nous nous trouvions replongés dans le Labyrinthe de Vienne, seulement et uniquement pour faciliter à l'Autriche le moyen de faire une communication à Frankfort, j'en craindrais les suites chez nous. On nous dit chaque semaine, 'il ne faut pas que l'Autriche nous échappe,' mais nous ne la tenons pas encore ; et jamais nous ne la tiendrons, tant que nous ne nous soyons montrés les plus forts.

"Victorieux en Crimée nous commanderons l'amitié, peut-être même l'épée, de l'Autriche ; manquant de succès en Crimée nous n'aurons pas même sa plume. Voici le Poste important de Jenikalé qui est tombé entre nos mains, voilà Anapa qui va suivre la même destinée, en peu de semaines nous serons maîtres de Sevastopol et de la force flottante des Russes ; ne permettons donc pas à la Diplomatie de nous ravir les grands et importants avantages que nous sommes sur le point de recueillir.

"J'ai l'honneur, &c.,

"Palmerston."

Napoleon's court and ministers were much mixed up in speculations and affairs on the Bourse, and it was by the Bourse-mongers at Paris that the cry for peace at any price was stimulated. Count Persigny told Lord Palmerston that as often as the Emperor received the English answers differing from his pacific proposals, he always smiled and said, " After all, the English are right."

The last formal sitting of the Conference was held on the 26th of April. Lord John Russell, who, at Vienna, had favoured the Austrian propositions of peace, returned to England to find the Cabinet indisposed to accept them. His first impulse was to resign, therein following the example of Monsieur Drouyn de Lhuys, the French minister, who had also expressed his assent to Count Buol's proposals. Yielding, however, to the representations of his colleagues, he remained a member of the Government till July, when Sir E. Lytton having given notice of a motion in the House of Commons directly aimed at him and his conduct at Vienna, he relieved the Government of the embarrassment natural to such an attack by retiring from the administration. Not only all the supporters of the Government, but nearly all its members out of the Cabinet had come to the opinion that this step was necessary.

During the whole of this session the Opposition and the Radicals poured an incessant fire on the Treasury Bench, discharging their artillery from very different quarters, though concentrating it in the same direction. The Opposition wished the country to believe that the Government were careless of the honour and prestige of England, and were too ready to make peace at any price; while the Manchester school, on the other hand, taking Lord John Russell's attitude at Vienna as their text, enlarged on the folly and wickedness of the war. Lord Palmerston, although almost single-handed, met these attacks with success. He had the confidence of the country, who saw in his character that mixture of moderation and firmness which the circumstances required. He struck the keynote of the public tone when, in a debate on the 7th of August, he referred to what had been alleged as to the assent of the Turkish ambassador to those proposals of the Vienna Conference which the English and French Cabinets had subsequently rejected, and asserted that the objects of the war were wider than could depend upon the decision of the Turkish Government. The protection of Turkey was a means to an end; behind the protection of Turkey was the greater question of repressing the grasping ambition of Russia, and preventing the extinction of political and commercial liberty. The Governments of France and England had as great, or even greater, interest than Turkey in the conditions of the future peace of Europe.

Parliament was prorogued on the 14th of August, the message from the Lords interrupting Lord Palmerston as he was speaking in acquiescence with Sir De Lacy Evans's exhortations for the vigorous prosecution of military measures.

The Prime Minister was indeed indefatigable in his attention to all the details of the campaign. The following letter, only one among many, illustrates the care and knowledge which he showed :—

" Piccadilly, June 10, 1855.

" MY DEAR PANMURE,

" This is capital news from the Sea of Azoff, and the extensive destruction of magazines and supplies in the towns attached must greatly cripple the Russian army in the Crimea. I am very sorry, however, to see so sad an account of the health of the Sardinians, and I strongly recommend you to urge Raglan, by telegraph to-day, to move the Sardinian camp to some other and healthier situation.

" Such prevalence of disease as the telegraphic message mentions *must* be the effect of some local cause; and I am as sure as if I was on the spot that these Sardinians are put down in some unhealthy place, from which they ought without the loss of a day to be removed. Our quartermaster-generals never bestow a thought about healthiness of situations, and, indeed, they are in general wholly ignorant of the sanitary principles upon which any given situation should be chosen or avoided; but if Raglan were to consult Dr. Sutherland on the subject, I am confident he would get a good opinion. At all events, these men ought to be removed from where they are without loss of a day ; and no excuse of military arrangements ought to be accepted as a pretence for delay.

" As the cholera seems to be increasing among the troops, I should advise you to send for the doctor I mentioned, and who would give you useful suggestions as to the treatment of the disease, and as to the best way of administering sulphuric acid, which seems now to be the most effectual remedy, and which, if taken in time, seldom fails in stopping the attack.

"We are 40,000 men short of the number voted by Parliament, and we shall be without the shadow of an excuse if we do not resort to every possible means and every possible quarter to complete our force to the number which Parliament has authorized. Let us get as many Germans and Swiss as we can; let us get men from Halifax; let us enlist Italians; and let us forthwith increase our bounty at home without raising the standard. Do not let departmental, or official, or professional prejudices and habits stand in our way. We must override all such obstacles and difficulties. The only answer to give to objectors on such grounds is, the thing *must* be done; we *must* have troops. War cannot be carried on without troops. We have asked Parliament for a certain amount of force, and have thereby pledged ourselves to the opinion that such a number is necessary; and we shall disgrace ourselves if we do not make every effort to raise that amount. We are now getting on in the month of June, and no time is to be lost.

"I wish you would send General Ashburton to me before he goes to Paris, that I may talk over with him the matters he will have from time to time to discuss, according to his instructions, with the French Government.

" Do not forget to suggest to our commissariat people in the Black Sea that large supplies of oxen to be eaten, and of horses to be ridden or to draw, may be derived from the country on the eastern shore of the Sea of Azoff, from whence these animals might be brought down to the port of Taman, near the Straits of Kertch, and be from thence carried coastwise to Balaclava; and it would be well also to point their attention to the projecting neck of land or island called Krassnoi, in the Bay of Penekop, which is said to abound in sheep and hay. It lies north-west of the coast of the Crimea.

" Yours sincerely,

" PALMERSTON."

The good results of the new energy infused into the military authorities were soon evident. In a speech at Melbourne during the autumn, Lord Palmerston was enabled to say that the hospitals in the Crimea were, at length, " in an admirable condition, and might, in fact, almost be regarded as models for the hospitals of London. The troops enjoyed every comfort compatible with a military campaign, and were in as good a condition as if they were on a peace establishment at home.

Thus was England, as is her wont, profiting by bitter experience, gradually strengthening through the conflict itself, and slowly, but surely, outstripping her allies in the development of her latent resources.

Lord Palmerston now foresaw with the daily decrease of the dangers which accompany war, the near approach of dangers from diplomacy. He writes to his brother :—

"Piccadilly, August 25, 1855.

" MY DEAR WILLIAM,

"I am kept in town for the present, but hope to go down to Broadlands in the first week of September, subject to weekly attendances here in London on matters connected with the conduct of the war. Things in that matter are looking well. Our bombardment of Sweabourg and our successes in repulsing the Russians in the Crimea will, I hope, be followed by the capture of Sebastopol and the expulsion of the Russians from the Crimea. Our danger will then begin—a danger of peace, and not a danger of war. Austria will try to draw us again into negotiations for an insufficient peace, and we shall not yet have obtained those decisive successes which would entitle us to insist on such terms as will effectually curb the ambition of Russia for the future.

"I must try to fight the battle of negotiation as well as the battle of war, and, fortunately, the spirit of the British nation will support us. I wish I could reckon with equal confidence on the steady determination of the French.

"King Bomba's insult to England, through the British mission at Naples, must be properly atoned for. Clarendon being at Paris, nothing can be decided till he returns and the Cabinet can be assembled ; but I have written to Clarendon to say that my opinion is that we ought to insist upon the immediate dismissal of Massa,* and upon a promise that he shall never again be employed in any public capacity. I would not make this demand till our reserve squadron—now in attendance on the Queen, but which will return with her on Tuesday, and which consists of three line-of-battle ships—shall have anchored in the Bay of Naples, opposite the King's palace, and shall have taken on board the mission and the consul, and then I would have a boat sent on shore with a demand that in two hours an answer should be sent by the King saying that Massa was dismissed, allowing half an hour for the letter to go, half an hour for the answer to come back, and a whole hour for writing the answer. If the time passed without a satisfactory reply, the palace should share the fate of Sweabourg; *e poi dopo*, if that should not be sufficient. However, we shall see what resolution may be come to when the Cabinet meets on the question.

" Yours affectionately,

" PALMERSTON."

The King of Naples had acted a very unfriendly part during our war with Russia. He had forbidden, within his territory, the sale of horses, mules, or other supplies to English agents. He gave way in this matter of the Minister of Police as soon as he heard of our success at Sebastopol, which happened very shortly after the date of this letter.

* Minister of Police at Naples.

CHAPTER IV.

In September came the news of the fall of Sebastopol.
Austria, who had never relaxed her efforts to bring
about an accommodation, now renewed her endeavours, and found in France a much more pliable
subject to deal with than England. The French
Emperor was assailed on all sides by a " feu d'enfer "
of Russian and Austrian intrigue trying to shake his
constancy and to drive him to some act of weakness.
One such act that he meditated at this moment, and
that it required all the weight of English persuasion
to arrest, was the recall of a considerable number
of his troops home from the Crimea.

The Austrian and French Cabinets, however,
very much mistook the intention of this country
if they imagined that we were going to surrender
ourselves blindly into the hands of our allies without fully exercising our own rights and judgment.
On the 21st of November, Lord Palmerston thus

writes to the Comte de Persigny, French ambassador in London :—

"Piccadilly, 21 Novembre 1855.

"MON CHER COMTE,

"D'après notre Constitution et notre Régime Parlementaire, le pouvoir exécutif ne doit jamais faire une démarche aussi importante que celle dont il s'agit, sans avoir des pièces officielles à produire au Parlement, afin d'être à même d'expliquer claire-ment ce qui a été proposé à l'Angleterre, par quels motifs la proposition a été appuyée, et quelles ont été les raisons qui ont conseillé son adoption.

"Mais, jusqu'à présent, nous n'avons rien de tout cela. Il y a eu à Vienne une négociation à laquelle nous n'avons pas pris part ; on a signé, du moins paraphé, un protocole pour nous, mais sans nous ; on nous communique confidentiellement ce protocole paraphé, à prendre ou à laisser, en nous disant qu'il faut ou le rejeter ou l'accepter immédiatement, bon ou mauvais, sans en discuter la rédaction et les détails.

"Cette manière d'agir dans une affaire tellement grave ne nous convient pas. Nous souhaitons nous conformer aux désirs de l'Empereur, mais il faut que nous soyons en règle vis-à-vis de notre Parlement ; et nous ne pouvons pas souscrire à une proposition de paix à être faite en notre nom, à la Russie, sans que nous soyons entièrement d'accord et sur la forme et sur la substance d'une telle proposition. Il est donc indispensable que nous ayons une proposition par écrit, dont nous puissions bien examiner la rédaction, avant de pouvoir donner à l'Autriche l'autorisation qu'elle nous demande, de parler à la Russie en notre nom.

" Je dis parler en notre nom, parce que, malgré que l'Autriche doit s'approprier la démarche qu'elle voudrait faire à Pétersbourg, elle se propose de dire qu'elle sait d'avance que sa proposition serait adoptée par la France et l'Angleterre, si elle venait à être acceptée par la Russie.

" La nation anglaise serait enchantée d'une bonne paix qui assurât les objets de la guerre ; mais plutôt que d'être entraînée à signer une paix à des condition insuffisantes, elle préférerait continuer la guerre sans d'autres alliés que la Turquie, et elle se sent tout-à-fait en état d'en soutenir le fardeau, et de se tirer ainsi d'affaire. Soumettez, je vous prie, ces observations à Walewsky.

" Mille amitiés,

" PALMERSTON."

These observations were not unnecessary, because Count Buol had already persuaded France to favour his proposal that the Black Sea arrangements should be contained in a separate treaty between Russia and Turkey. Four days after this letter, Count Persigny came to urge, at Downing Street, acquiescence in this arrangement, but he met with a distinct refusal. " We ought to stand firm," said Lord Palmerston, " as to having all the stipulations about the Black Sea made parts of the treaty between Russia and all the belligerents. I can fancy how I should be hooted in the House of Commons if I were to get up and say that we had agreed to an imperfect and unsatisfactory arrangement about one of the most important parts of the whole matter, as a personal favour to Count Buol, or to save the *amour-propre* of Russia. I had better beforehand take the Chiltern Hundreds."*

Towards the end of the year, when winter had caused hostilities to cease, Count Buol put forward, in the name of Austria, four new points, which in substance were nearly the same as the four old points. The third, on which the former negotiations had broken off, proposed that no fleet and no naval station of any country should be permitted in the Black Sea. The Czar, on the 16th of January, 1856, accepted these proposals as a basis for negotiating a treaty of peace; although, of course, there were other points, many and difficult, to be settled by subsequent negotiation. Sir Hamilton Seymour was now our ambassador at Vienna. He was one of the ablest members of our diplomacy, and Lord Palmerston felt that he could speak proudly to him in reply to Austrian pressure without leading him into imprudences.

" 94, Piccadilly, January 24, 1856.

" My dear Seymour,

        " Buol's statement to you the night before last was what in plain English we should call im-

---

* To Lord Clarendon, November 26, 1855.

K 2

pertinent. We are happily not yet in such a condition that an Austrian minister should bid us sign a treaty without hesitation or conditions. The Cabinet of Vienna, forsooth, must insist upon our doing so! Why, really our friend Buol must have had his head turned by his success at St. Petersburg, and quite forgot whom he was addressing such language to. He should remember that he is a self-constituted mediator, but that nobody has made him umpire, arbiter, or dictator. He may depend upon it we shall do no such thing. We shall not sign without knowing what it is that we are signing. We shall not sign unless we are satisfied with that which we may be asked to put our names to. Pray tell him so, and say to him privately from me, with my best regards and compliments, that we feel very sincerely obliged to him for his friendly and firm conduct in these recent transactions, that we accepted, with the addition of our own supplementary conditions, the arrangement which he proposed to us, because we felt that it contained all that, in the present state of things, we were entitled to exact from Russia, subject, of course, to any further demands which the fifth article provides for and authorizes us to make.

" But it is Russia rather than the allies who ought to feel grateful to him for his good offices in these matters, because we are confident that if the war goes on, the results of another campaign will enable us this time twelvemonth to obtain from Russia much better conditions than those which we are now willing to accept.

" We know the exhaustion, the internal pressure, difficulties, and distress of Russia quite as well as Buol does; but we know better than he does our own resources and strength. He may rest assured, however, that we have no wish to continue the war for the prospect of what we may accomplish another year, if we can now obtain peace upon the conditions which we deem absolutely necessary and essential; but we are quite prepared to go on if such conditions cannot be obtained. The British nation is unanimous in this matter. I say unanimous, for I cannot reckon Cobden, Bright, and Co. for anything; and even if the Government were not kept straight by a sense of our public duty, the strong feeling which prevails throughout the country would make it impossible for us to swerve. So pray let Count Buol keep his *threats* for elsewhere, and not send them over here.

" Yours sincerely,
" PALMERSTON."

On the 1st of February a protocol was signed at Vienna by the representatives of the five Powers, and the congress for the final settlement of the terms of peace was appointed to meet in Paris.

To this Congress Lord Clarendon went as British plenipotentiary, in concert with Lord Cowley. During its sittings Lord Palmerston was in constant correspondence with him, and entered, with indefatigable industry, into the smallest details. They had, however, a difficult task in the negotiations. The Russians, although beaten, were not inclined to yield one inch, save to absolute necessity, and the French were too eager for peace to be depended upon for much assistance. The Emperor himself was swayed by Count Walewski's many Russian affinities; he was horrified by the daily accounts of the privations endured by his army in the Crimea, and he was absorbed in a domestic event which had given him an heir, whom he was anxious to christen amid the rejoicings for peace. He was, therefore, only thinking of how to " faire le généreux" towards the Czar, whom he would gladly have conciliated now that his position in Europe was secured. Amid all such secret motives and tortuous actions the British Government had to hold on its way, now and then yielding on minor matters, but adhering firmly to the principal conditions of peace. In this it succeeded; and on the 30th of March the Treaty of Paris was signed.

A few days later, the plenipotentiaries also subscribed a declaration about maritime war.

At the beginning of hostilities Great Britain had tacitly abandoned her ancient doctrines respecting neutrals, which she could only have attempted to enforce under pain of having all mankind against her. It was evident that they could never be revived, and that the concessions which she had once made to neutral rights could never be withdrawn. When, therefore, the President of the Congress, in the name of his Government, suggested to the English plenipotentiary that it would be a "benevolent" act for the Congress to proclaim as permanent the principles upon which the war had been carried on, with the addition that privateering should be abolished,* Lord Clarendon referred the matter home, and, with the approval of the Queen and of the entire Cabinet, conveyed the assent of the British plenipotentiaries to the proposal, pointing out at the same time, as a necessary proviso, " that the declaration should not be binding except between those Powers who have acceded or shall accede to it."   This clause was added, and certain other modifications made in the declaration before it was finally settled.   Its policy is not a matter

* *Original Draft of Resolution handed to Lord Clarendon.*—"Le congrès de Westphalie a consacré la liberté des cultes, le congrès de Vienne l'abolition de la traite des noirs et la liberté de la navigation des fleuves; il appartiendrait au congrès de Paris de consacrer l'abolition de la course et la franchise du commerce des neutres, conformément aux principes appliqués dans la guerre actuelle.

"Ces principes sont, d'après les déclarations émanées de la France et de l'Angleterre au début de la guerre:

"Que le pavillon neutre couvre la marchandise ennemie, excepté la contrebande de guerre.

"Que la marchandise neutre, excepté la contrebande de guerre, n'est pas saisissable sous pavillon ennemi.

"Et que les blocus doivent être effectifs, c'est-à-dire maintenus par une force navale suffisante."

The Americans had previously, by a circular, asked the assent of the maritime Powers to the doctrine of "free ships, free goods." Most of the Powers consulted England as to the answer they should give, and, in accordance with our views, answered that they should not agree unless the United States at the same time gave up the system of privateers. This they declined to do; but by the Declaration of Paris they are left to stand alone in their anachronism.

for discussion here ; but the fact of its having been deliberately adopted by the English Cabinet, for what they considered good and sufficient reasons, is the point which it is desirable to record, as many absurd tales have been from time to time current about it : as though the English plenipotentiary had agreed to it without any authority from home or consultation with the rest of the Ministry.

On the 5th of May an animated and prolonged debate took place in the House of Commons on the treaty of peace. Lord Palmerston spoke on the second night of the discussion from twelve o'clock till half-past two, and exhaustively defended the acts of the Government. The following day he moved a vote of thanks to the navy and army.

Thus ended the Crimean war—a war which, however some men may look back to it with regret, on account of the incapacity since shown by the Turks for profiting by the breathing-time afforded to them, was certainly just, and probably necessary. Russian overbearance and greed of dominion received a wholesome, if only temporary, check, and, had the war continued a little longer, would have been still more severely punished. The plans proposed to the Allies for the ensuing campaign embraced operations in Circassia and Finland ; the English to have chief command in the South, and the French in the North. It is not impossible that the result might have been the restoration of Finland to Sweden, of her lost provinces to Persia, and the independence of Circassia.

Difficulties shortly arose respecting the execution
of some of the articles of the treaty of peace. A
Turkish officer had been sent to take possession of
Serpent's Island, at the mouth of the Danube, and
the Turkish flag was hoisted. Soon afterwards a
party of seven Russian marines, with a lieutenant,
landed and occupied the island. The Russian Government declined to remove them, on the ground
that the question of its occupation was to be settled
by a Conference at Paris. The English admiral then
stationed a vessel off the island, with orders to prevent, by force if necessary, all attempts to increase
the Russian force on the island. So matters remained
till the end of the year.

Another point in dispute was as to the identifica-
tion of a place marked Bolgrad on the map. The
treaty said that the new frontier was to run "south
of Bolgrad." When the commissioners met to mark
it out, they discovered that the real Bolgrad was
much more to the south than the Bolgrad of the
Conference maps. They were unable, therefore, to
agree, and the matter, together with the question of
Serpent's Island, was referred to a new Conference.

Lord Palmerston, in the following memorandum,
recounts his first interview with the new Russian
ambassador in London, and records what he said to
him about these two disputed points:—

" Piccadilly, August 12, 1856.

"Count Chreptovitch came to me this morning at half-
past eleven by appointment. He began by civil expressions

of pleasure at renewal of old acquaintance, to which I replied in similar terms. After some preliminary talk of this kind, I said I was sorry that, at our first interview on the renewal of diplomatic relations between the two Governments, I should have to enter upon a string of grievances. 'Well,' said he, 'let us hear them: what are they?' I said I was sorry to have to say that, ever since the conclusion of the treaty of peace, the Russian Government has been acting in a manner inconsistent with its engagements, and has in some instances broken them, in others tried to evade them. That the treaty distinctly says that the fortress and district of Kars are to be restored to Turkey; in violation of which engagement the fortress had been demolished, and the Russian occupying force increased. The treaty says that a portion of Bessarabia is to be restored to Turkey, and from the ratification of the treaty that territory belonged of right to Turkey; but in disregard of this, the Russians have destroyed the fortifications of Ismail and Reni. Here Count Chreptovitch interrupted me with much impatience. He said these things were done, whether right or wrong, and there was no use in going back to past events, and that we must look only to the future. I said I entirely differed from him; I thought there was great use in going back to past events, and that they had, as I would presently explain, a great bearing on the future. That I must be allowed to tell him fully and plainly all I think on these matters; that it was for the purpose of doing so that I had asked him to call upon me; and that if he did not choose to listen to me, he had better go back to Petersburg. I then resumed. I said that these acts were not only at variance with the treaty, but quite unworthy of a great Power like Russia. If Russia had been able at the Congress of Paris to obtain stipulations that there should be no defensive works at Kars, and no fortifications at Ismail and Reni, and that both those frontiers should be left open to the future attacks of Russia—meditated attacks, her conduct would lead us to think, though I did not ask him to admit that—if such stipulations could have been obtained, I could have understood the value which Russia would have attached to them, and they would have been worth a struggle in the negotiation; but as no such stipulations were made, the only effect of demolishing Kars and Ismail and Reni would be to put the Turks to some expense and trouble in reconstructing these works, and the probable result would be that they would be rebuilt upon a better plan. This, therefore, was an ebullition of ill-humour and revenge that might be called childish. I said, however, that we were glad to find that one part of this grievance is about to cease, and that Kars and its district is to be immediately evacuated by the Russians. The next point I had to complain of was the attempt to take possession of Serpent's Island. When the east and west boundary between Russia and Turkey in Europe ran south of this island, the island naturally belonged to Russia; but now that the east and west boundary line will run a good way to the north of that island, the island must naturally belong to Turkey. I said that the island has no intrinsic value as territory; that its only value is that it is, by means of its lighthouse, a guiding point to ships making the mouths of the Danube, and on that account it must belong to the Powers to which the mouths of the Danube belong. Count Chreptovitch said that the island is also important for ships going to Odessa, because when they happen, as is frequently the case, to be blown to the southward and out of their course by adverse winds, the light on this island tells them where they are. I said that the light kept for the Danube would do equally well for Odessa; and that, being on this point, I would observe, in passing, that we have been informed that the Russian detachment which landed to take possession of the island, finding a superior force of Turks there, endeavoured to induce the Turks to violate their duty, and either to go away and give up the island to the Russians, or to desert over to the Russian service. Count Chreptovitch seemed to admit the force of the reasoning that the change of the boundary line in those quarters must throw this island into the Turkish limits.

"I then went on to Bessarabia. I said that the Emperor of Russia had formally accepted the Vienna proposal, which drew the new boundary between Russia and Moldavia by a line starting from a point north of the Pruth, and going southward along a chain of hills to Lake Salyick; that at Paris, out of pure deference to the wishes of the Emperor of Russia, and from a desire to insist on nothing that had not a real political value, the allies had agreed to a great modification of this line in favour of Russia; that the new line was, however, very plainly and clearly described by the treaty; that it is to start from a point on the sea-coast beyond Lake Bourna Sola, to run up to the Ackerman Road, and to follow along that road to the River Yalpouk, leaving the town of Bolgrad to the north of the boundary; that at the Congress a map had been produced, on which a town had been pointed out bearing the name of Tabor, or of Bolgrad, and which was designated as the town to the south of which the boundary line is to run, and between that town and Lake Yalpouk there is space enough for the line to be drawn. But, I said, when the commissioners came to the ground, the Russians started a new Bolgrad on the allies; and this new Bolgrad is much to the south of the Bolgrad of the Conference, and so close to Lake Yalpouk that there is no space for a boundary line between the town and the lake. I said this was an unworthy deception which cannot be acquiesced in, and that the old Bolgrad, which was the town meant by the Congress, must be the Bolgrad to the south of which the boundary is to run. Count Chreptovitch said that in fact the new Bolgrad is the real town, the old Bolgrad being only a ruined and deserted village; but nevertheless he admitted that the old Bolgrad, and not the new one, must be deemed the Bolgrad of the treaty.

"I said that we had to complain of another proceeding of the Russian commissioners. That the commission had agreed to make a general survey of the whole line in the first instance, and then to go over it regularly, putting up landmarks as they went. That upon a great part of the line all are agreed ; and our commissioners proposed that upon those parts the landmarks should be fixed, leaving the other parts, as to which differences had arisen, to be landmarked afterwards, when the disputed points should have been settled. That to this the Russians have objected, and want to delay the whole till the whole is agreed upon. I said that in this way the season for operations will be lost; winter will come on before the boundary is laid down; and what will be the consequence? The Russians will not go out of the district to be ceded, because the boundary line is not settled and drawn ; the Austrians will not go out of the Principalities because the Russians are not out of ceded Bessarabia; and our fleet may probably not leave the Black Sea because the treaty is not executed. All this state of things will be contrary to the treaty ; but the fault will be with Russia, and with her also the responsibility; and this we shall have to say when Parliament meets. Count Chreptovitch said that these delays were the fault of subordinate agents, and not of the Russian Government, who are anxious for a final settlement. I said that might be ; but we cannot give orders to these subordinate Russian agents, and the Russian Government can ; and as that Government is despotic, it can make its orders to be obeyed, and we must therefore hold the Government answerable for the conduct of its agents. However, the Count assured me, in the most positive terms, that these matters shall be speedily and satisfactorily settled. I said I hoped they would, and that thus all difficulties would be got over. That the information that Kars is immediately to be restored to the Turks, had relieved us from an embarrassment we had felt as to whether Lord Granville should be allowed to go on to Moscow; and if those other points were well settled, we should resume with Russia our former habits of cordial friendship. That we are plain and simple people, and look

-to things and not to words; and that the sort of small attentions and flattery which we understand they are lavishing on the French—though with what success may be doubted —would be altogether thrown away upon us. That Prince Gortschakoff seems to have expressed to Lord Granville some surprise that England should have taken singly, in the Black Sea, a step with reference to a treaty to which England is only one of several contracting parties; but that Prince Gortschakoff must not be surprised if we continue to act in the same manner, whenever any occasion for doing so should arise, inasmuch as we consider that we have a right to do so, and we know that we have the power to do so.

"I said that Baron Brunnow had often said to me that England and Russia hold to different principles of Government. Russia is for despotic power; England for constitutions; but nevertheless the two countries have great interests in common, upon which abstract and theoretical differences of opinion have no direct bearing; and that, as long as Russia and England do not come into collision about the affairs of Turkey or the affairs of Persia, there is no reason why they should not act in concert on many important matters. I said I hoped that Russia would stick to her engagements about Turkey, and then there could be no differences on that subject. That as to Persia, Russia had, during the war, done in Persia what she had done in America, and what she had a perfect right to do, that is to say, create for England as much embarrassment and hostility as she could. That her instruments, however, had become, or will become her victims. That Russia had lost for President Pierce all chance of re-election by the course she urged him to take towards England; and that as to Persia, though we have hitherto shown great forbearance, the time is fast approaching when the Persian Government will see cause to repent its conduct towards us, unless in the interval that conduct shall be entirely changed, and fully atoned for. I observed that Count Chreptovitch did not very much deny what I said as

to the action of Russia in America and in Persia. I said—
and he with great warmth of manner joined in the wish—that
our sincere desire is to forget the recent past, and to remember only our former good relations. I said that, with
regard to himself personally, it is unfortunate that so long a
delay has taken place between his nomination and his arrival,
because it cannot be considered otherwise than as a mark of
want of respect to the Queen—not perhaps on his part, but
on the part of his Government. That in general, when a
foreign minister arrives while the Queen is at Osborne, such
minister is taken down by the Secretary of State for Foreign
Affairs, to have as early as possible his audience of Her
Majesty at Osborne ; but that in his case this practice will
not be observed; and that, as he has shown so little *empressement* to pay his respects to the Queen, Her Majesty
cannot be advised to show any *empressement* to receive him ;
and that he cannot have his audience till the Queen shall
return to London.

"We parted with much mutual cordiality, and tender
inquiries about mutual friends, English and Russian."

France did not show herself so ready to support
England at the council table as she had proved herself in the field. Lord Palmerston speaks frankly to
the French ambassador :—

" 94, Piccadilly, 10 Septembre 1856.

" MON CHER WALEWSKY,

" L'amitié sincère qui a depuis longtemps
existé entre nous, et la franchise qui a toujours carac-
térisé nos relations, m'encouragent à vous écrire ces
quelques lignes sur les questions très-importantes
qui se discutent maintenant entre nos deux Gouvernements, et je vous engage à y donner votre sérieuse

attention et de ne pas croire que ce sont des choses dont on peut disposer légèrement. Ce n'est qu'une nécessité absolue qui a amené la Russie à accepter l'ultimatum que l'Autriche lui a proposé comme base de traité de Paix. La ruse est toujours la ressource de la faiblesse, et depuis le jour où la Russie a accepté l'ultimatum *purement et simplement*, elle n'a fait que mettre en œuvre toutes les ruses imaginables pour se soustraire à l'exécution de l'engagement qu'elle avait pris. Vous savez mieux que moi tout ce qu'elle a fait dans ce but au congrès de Paris. Sur certains points elle n'a pas réussi, sur d'autres points, grâces au soutien qu'elle a reçu de la part de la France, elle n'a réussi que trop bien, et elle a obtenu une grande diminution de la cession que l'Empereur de Russie s'était engagé à faire en Bessarabie.

"Malgré, cependant, tous les efforts des Plénipotentiaires russes, nous avons conclu un Traité de Paix qui nous assure suffisamment les objets de la guerre, pourvu toujours que ce Traité soit fidèlement exécuté et loyalement observé. Mais ce Traité, la Russie l'exécute-t-elle avec fidélité? Pas du tout. Depuis l'échange des ratifications elle a montré partout et en tout une insigne mauvaise foi. Elle a violé la lettre même du Traité en détruisant la forteresse de Kars. Elle a agi de la manière la plus déloyale, pour ne pas me servir d'une expression plus forte, en démolissant les fortifications d'Ismail et de Kilia, et je suis fâché de le dire, elle s'est appuyée en ce sujet sur une sanction secrète qu'elle prétend avoir reçu de la part du Gouvernement français. Mais tout ceci c'est du passé, un passé cependant que nous ne devons jamais oublier, parce que le passé sert de clef à l'avenir. Maintenant elle nous suscite deux questions d'une importance grande et pratique. Elle a voulu saisir l'Ile des Serpents qui commande les Bouches du Danube, et elle voudrait conserver la nouvelle ville de Bolgrad qui lui donnerait les moyens de commander la Navigation de ce fleuve.

Quant à la première prétention, c'est purement et simplement une tentative d'agression contre la Turquie, qui nous montre que la Russie n'a pas changé le système—qu'elle n'a aucunement abandonné la politique envahissante contre la Turquie, et que ce n'était pas sans de bonnes raisons que nous avons conclu le Traité du 15 Avril. Cette prétention est inadmissible, et tant que l'Angleterre a un bâtiment de guerre la Russie n'y réussira jamais. La seconde prétention de substituer au Bolgrad de la Carte, dont le Congrès s'est servi pour tracer la frontière entre la Russie et la Turquie, cette nouvelle ville de Bolgrad dont le Congrès n'a jamais eu connaissance, est également inadmissible. D'abord cette prétention de la part de la Russie est une supercherie, c'est un tour de passe-passe qui est déshonorant pour la Russie, et qui rendrait ridicules ceux qui en seraient les dupes, et si nous n'avions d'autre motif pour ne pas y consentir que de ne pas vouloir nous laisser attraper par une ruse si grossière, nous pourrions pleinement justifier notre refus. Mais nous avons des raisons plus fortes à donner.

Le Congrès en réglant la frontière en Bessarabie a voulu deux choses—assurer à la partie cédée par la Russie communication libre et suffisante avec la Moldavie, et empêcher toute communication par eau entre le territoire russe et le Danube; la rétrocession à la Russie de l'ancienne Bolgrad, la seule qui se trouvait marquée sur la Carte du Congrès, n'était pas incompatible avec l'accomplissement de ces deux buts.

" Mais du moment que l'on substitue à cette vraie Bolgrad du Congrès la fausse Bolgrad nouvellement découverte par les Commissaires russes, aucune de ces conditions ne se trouve satisfaite. La partie cédée de Bessarabie devient une enclave dans le territoire russe, toute communication libre et assurée entre ce district et la Moldavie cesse, et la possession d'un point stratégique telle que la nouvelle Bolgrad par la Russie donnerait à cette Puissance les moyens faciles de commander et d'entraver la navigation du Danube.

" Pour toutes ces raisons il est absolument impossible pour l'Angleterre de consentir à admettre cette prétention de la Russie. Le Gouvernement anglais est responsable au Parlement et à la Nation. Personne dans ce pays-ci n'a été très-content des conditions de la Paix; on aurait voulu plusieurs choses qui ne s'y trouvaient pas. Mais on s'y est résigné plutôt que de voir continuer le fléau de la guerre. Mais la

Nation anglaise est résolue d'obtenir l'exécution pleine et entière des conditions du Traité, et je n'oserais pas me présenter au Parlement la session prochaine, et avoir à dire que j'avais consenti à un sacrifice quelconque des conditions du Traité.

"L'Autriche et la Turquie, comme de raison, sont entièrement avec l'Angleterre ; la France paraît vouloir changer de bord et s'associer en tout avec la Russie. Si cet état de choses continue, le Traité ne s'exécutera pas, et lorsque le Parlement se réunit nous aurons à expliquer le pourquoi. Réfléchissez un peu, je vous en prie, sur l'effet que tout cela doit nécessairement produire sur cette alliance entre nos deux pays, si honorable pour tous les deux et si utile aux intérêts de toute l'Europe. Il ne dépend que de vous de mettre fin à tous ces embarras. Nous n'avons pas besoin d'un nouveau Congrès. Conseillez aux Russes de se contenter de la Bolgrad du Congrès et de retirer de l'île des Serpents leurs sept matelots et leur lieutenant malade, et comme vous avez eu une grande part à la conclusion de la Paix, vous aurez aussi la satisfaction de savoir que vous avez contribué efficacement à en amener la fidèle et honorable exécution. Rappelez-moi et Lady Palmerston au bon souvenir de la Comtesse Walewska, et croyez-moi très-sincèrement à vous,

"PALMERSTON."

Count Walewski's answer was of a nature to draw from Lord Palmerston a very decided hint that England would take her own line, whether France went back or forward.

"24 Sept., 1856.

"Mon cher Walewsky,

"C'est avec bien des regrets que j'ai reçu votre lettre du 20 de ce mois, mais je ne veux pas continuer une discussion sans effet, ni reproduire des arguments qui n'ont pas eu de succès. Je suis bien fâché que vous décliniez le rôle de pacificateur que j'ai pris la liberté de vous proposer, mais puisque vous préférez laisser aux événements de décider de l'avenir, nous ne pouvons qu'accepter cette alternative, quoiqu'avec bien des regrets, dont la responsabilité ne pèsera pas sur nous.

"Mille amitiés,

"Palmerston."

Lord Palmerston's firmness eventually carried the day.

During the session a resolution was introduced in the House of Commons alleging that "the conduct of Her Majesty's Government in the differences with the United States on the question of enlistment has not entitled them to the approbation of the House." We had been charged with violating the neutrality of the United States, by enlisting recruits for the British service. No doubt the laws of the States had in some respects been infringed, but not intentionally, nor by any authorized English officials. However, Mr. Crampton, our minister at Washington, received

his passports from the President and left the country.
Our Government did not retaliate for this act of
diplomatic censure, but continued to receive Mr.
Dallas in London. Both their original offence and
their subsequent apologetic conduct formed the
grounds of Parliamentary attack on the Government.
Lord Palmerston, when the resolution was discussed,
successfully pointed out the inconsistencies of its
supporters. While with one accord they joined in
aspirations for peace and goodwill between the two
countries, they were doing all they could to create
illwill. " These gentlemen, so anxious for peace, tell
you that England has been insulted, treated with
contempt, contumely, and indignity. What is the
effect likely to be produced ? Why, to excite a spirit
of resentment towards our neighbours and kindred in
the United States. Others, again, tell the Americans
that their Government has been deluded, and persuaded to accept an apology they ought not to have
accepted, and that their laws have been intentionally violated by a foreign Government. Is that
the way to create good feeling ? Is that the way to
persuade the American people to cultivate the most
friendly relations with England ?" Thus he met his
critics.

Towards the end of the year Lord Palmerston
visited Manchester and Liverpool, and received, amid
much enthusiasm, addresses from the corporations
and other public bodies.

Any record of his life would be incomplete that

did not notice the death of his only brother, Sir William Temple, which occurred in London, in August of this year. Although Lord Palmerston was the older by not more than two years, he always treated his younger brother with the affectionate care which might rather be expected from a father. Many of the most interesting of his letters are those to his brother, who, being in the diplomatic service, lived much abroad, and whom Lord Palmerston therefore endeavoured, in spite of all his work, to keep informed as to what was going on at home. A strong affection subsisted between them, although their temperaments were very different; and during William Temple's last illness in London, Lord Palmerston passed a considerable time with him every day.

The future of Egypt must, for a long time to come, have a special interest for Englishmen. The following letter to Lord Clarendon sufficiently explains itself, and is interesting as showing the head of the British Cabinet declining proposals coming from an unexpected quarter, which were to lead to the possession of Egypt by England. Lord Palmerston's opinions on this matter were frequently repeated. He saw the paramount importance of its being kept open for transit, but never encouraged any idea of annexation. On one occasion, to Lord Cowley, he used a homely but apt illustration : " We do not want Egypt," he said, " or wish it for ourselves any more than any rational man with an estate in the north of England and a residence in the south, would have wished to possess the inns on the north road. All he could want would have been that the inns should be well kept, always accessible, and furnishing him, when he came, with mutton chops and post-horses.*

"Piccadilly, March 1, 1857.

" MY DEAR CLARENDON,

"As to the Emperor's schemes about Africa, the sooner Cowley sends in his grounds of objection the better. It is very possible that many parts of the world would be better governed by France, England, and Sardinia than they are now; and we need not go beyond Italy, Sicily, and Spain for examples. But the alliance of England and France has derived its strength not merely from the military and naval power of the two states, but from the force of the moral principle upon which that union has been founded. Our union has for its foundation resistance to unjust aggression, the defence of the weak against the strong, and the maintenance of the existing balance of power. How, then, could we combine to become unprovoked aggressors, to imitate, in Africa, the partition of Poland by the conquest of Morocco for France, of Tunis and some other state for Sardinia, and of Egypt for England? and, more especially, how could England and France, who have guaranteed the integrity of the Turkish Empire, turn round and wrest Egypt from the Sultan? A coalition for such a purpose would revolt the moral feelings of mankind, and would certainly be fatal to

---

* To Lord Cowley, November 25, 1859.

any English Government that was a party to it. Then, as to the balance of power to be maintained by giving us Egypt.   In the first place, we don't want to have Egypt.   What we wish about Egypt is that it should continue attached to the Turkish empire, which is a security against its belonging to any European Power.   We want to trade with Egypt, and to travel through Egypt, but we do not want the burthen of governing Egypt, and its possession would not, as a political, military, and naval question, be considered, in this country, as a set-off against the possession of Morocco by France.   Let us try to improve all these countries by the general influence of our commerce, but let us all abstain from a crusade of conquest which would call down upon us the condemnation of all the other civilised nations.

"This conquest of Morocco was the secret aim of Louis Philippe, and is one of the plans deposited for use, as occasion may offer, in the archives of the French Government.

"Yours sincerely,
. "PALMERSTON."

Lord Palmerston's character must have been quite a puzzle to the French Emperor, who found that he could neither intimidate nor cajole him, nor yet shake him off.   No wonder that he sometimes showed a little temper.   "I am rather surprised," says Lord Palmerston,* "that the Emperor should have spoken

* To Lord Clarendon, September 29, 1857.

with so much bitterness about me, for nothing could be more personally friendly than his manner at Osborne.   But the fact, no doubt, is that he is much annoyed at finding that we did not give in to his notions about driving the Mahomedans away from the southern shores of the Mediterranean, and about giving an extension to French occupation in Africa. The fact is that, in our alliance with France, we are riding a runaway horse, and must always be on our guard; but a runaway horse is best kept in by a light hand and an easy snaffle.   It is fortunate for us that we are thus mounted, instead of being on foot, to be kicked at by this same steed; and as our ally finds the alliance useful to himself, it will probably go on for a good time to come.   The danger is, and always has been, that France and Russia should unite to carry into effect some great scheme of mutual ambition.   England and Germany would then have to stand out against them; and Germany is too much broken up and disjointed to be an efficient ally."

We had this year a little war with Persia, owing to her occupation of Herat, contrary to the solemn engagements made with England in 1853.   Although the dispute did not attract much public attention, Lord Palmerston was fully alive to the importance of the issues involved.   He foresaw that Khiva and Bokhara would shortly be occupied by Russia, and that Cabul and Candahar might, before very long, be deemed the advanced outposts of British India. Whether it would be better that Herat should remain

a weak, independent Government, or that it should
be in the hands of a ruler able to defend it, like the
ruler of Cabul, and who, by geographical position,
must attach himself to an English alliance, might be a
moot point; but at any rate it was clear that it must
not be allowed to fall to Persia.   About the general
question he says to Lord Clarendon :—

" February 17, 1857.

" It is quite true, as you say, that people in general are disposed to think lightly of our Persian war;
that is to say, not enough to see the importance
of the question at issue.   Ellenborough is right : we
are beginning to repel the first opening of trenches
against India by Russia;* and whatever difficulties
Ferokh† may make about Affghanistan, we may be
sure that Russia is his prompter and secret backer.
But that makes it the more essential that we should
carry our point on that subject.   What, however,
are our important points ?   The renunciation by
Persia of all claim over Herat and of all future design or attempt to invade Herat.   This is a *sine quâ
non*, and, of course, includes an acknowledgment of
the independence of Herat, and includes it so completely that a distinct acknowledgment of that independence seems hardly necessary.   Any engagement
on our part towards Persia about our own relations
with Affghanistan should be peremptorily refused.

" As to our mediation, as there is in most men's

* Lord Ellenborough had just made a speech in the House of Lords
in this sense.

† Ferokh Khan, ambassador from Persia.

minds a confusion of ideas between mediation and arbitration, we might, if driven to it, substitute for mediation, a condition that if any difference should arise between Persia and any of the Affghan states, including Herat, Persia would, in the first place, ask our good offices to arrange the matter in dispute ; and we might promise to use our good offices to obtain a settlement just and honourable to both parties."

The treaty of peace between the Queen of England and " His Majesty whose standard is the sun" was signed at Paris on the 4th of March. Persia renounced all claim or dominion over Herat and Affghanistan, and engaged (in such terms as were suggested in the above letter) to refer any future differences she might have with the Affghan states to the friendly offices of the British Government.

The opportunity of this war was also taken to obtain the abolition of slave trade in the Persian Gulf—an act consistent with the many former efforts of Lord Palmerston to put an end to traffic in human beings.

I append a letter which, on the conclusion of peace, he wrote to the Sadr Azim* in reply to a flowery communication from that minister. It is a specimen both of the skill with which he could read as well as write between the lines and of candid irony in expressing his sentiments. Behind the diplomatic effusion of the Persian minister he discerned the true character and motives of his

* The " Prime Minister" of Persia.

correspondent, who had secretly been a bitter enemy of England. His courteous reply conveys very clearly that he knew it all, but that the "least said, soonest mended; only don't let it occur again": —

"London, September 8, 1857.

" Excellency,

"I have received with much pleasure the letter dated the 5th of June last, which you were so good as to address to me; and I have been much gratified by the friendly sentiments which it contains. I rejoice, as your Excellency does, at the treaty of peace, which has happily put an end to the war between England and Persia; and I hope that the peace which has thus been established may long continue for the mutual advantage of both countries. I can truly assure your Excellency that it is the wish of the English Government and of the English nation that Persia should be a happy, a prosperous, a strong, and an independent state, and that the most perfect friendship and the fullest confidence should prevail between the Governments of England and of Persia.

"I am rejoiced to find, from your Excellency's letter, that it is your desire and intention to cultivate in future the friendship of England. But I should not be deserving of your good opinion if I were to disguise from you the truth of my thoughts, and there are parts of your Excellency's letter which compel me to speak frankly in reply.

" Your Excellency says that, until now, out of various considerations, you have looked upon yourself as alone and without assistance in your endeavours to preserve the friendship of the two Governments from injury. And you further say that you request me, and you entertain the firm hope that I shall henceforward give my full attention to the observance of the rules of friendship and unity between the two Governments.

" Now upon this I feel myself obliged to say that the war which took place between our two countries was not owing to any neglect on the part of the English Government of the rules of friendship and equity, but was occasioned solely and entirely by your Excellency's own unfriendly conduct, and by the violent hostility which your Excellency displayed towards England, both in word and deed; and, therefore, so far from your Excellency having been alone in endeavours to preserve friendship between the two Governments, your Excellency was the main and principal cause of the cessation of that friendship.

" I have no doubt that your Excellency, in seeking a quarrel with England, believed that you were promoting the interests of Persia, and I am bound to suppose that your Excellency considered yourself as performing on that occasion the part of a true patriot; and this belief on my part strengthens my confidence in the future maintenance of friendship between the two Governments and countries, because the events of the war, and the decisive victories obtained by the British troops over superior numbers of Persian troops, must have shown and have proved to the sagacious mind and powerful understanding of your Excellency that the true interests of Persia are best promoted by peace and friendship with England, and that the sure results to Persia of war with England must be defeat and disaster. With this conviction strongly impressed upon your mind, your Excellency will, I am sure, like a good patriot, clearly see in what direction the welfare of your country lies, and you will direct your policy as minister of your Sovereign so as to secure that welfare. Therefore it is that, knowing the high statesmanlike qualities which so eminently distinguish your Excellency, I feel satisfied that the alliance between our two countries will rest henceforward upon the basis of national interest, which is a firmer foundation than the sentiments of individual ministers, however friendly and sincere those sentiments may be. With every wish for the health and happiness of your Excellency, and with a fervent hope that the reign of your illustrious master and Sovereign the Shah of Persia may be long and prosperous,

> " I have the honour to remain,
>> " Your Excellency's most obedient
>>> " and faithful Servant,
>>>> " PALMERSTON.

"His Excellency The SADR AZIM, &c."

CHAPTER V.

" HER Majesty commands us to inform you that acts of violence, insults to the British flag, and infraction of treaty rights committed by the local Chinese authorities at Canton, and a pertinacious refusal of redress, have rendered it necessary for Her Majesty's officers in China to have recourse to measures of force to obtain satisfaction."

So ran the Speech from the Throne at the opening of Parliament in February, 1857.

This was the affair of the lorcha ' Arrow,' destined to attain some celebrity. It happened thus. Under treaties with China, British vessels were to be subject to consular jurisdiction only. The ' Arrow,' having a British register, was boarded by Chinese from a war junk and the crew carried off, on a charge of piracy. Sir John Bowring, Governor of Hong-Kong, demanded satisfaction from the Chinese Commissioner Yeh, and, failing to obtain it, proceeded to use force with the fleet under Admiral Sir Michael Seymour. He also added to his former demands one for the admission of foreigners to the port and city of Canton under treaty engagements which had never been carried out. Yeh retaliated by proclamations offering rewards for the heads of the barbarians.

Such was the position of affairs when Mr. Cobden brought forward in the House of Commons a resolution to the effect that "the papers laid on the table failed to establish satisfactory grounds for the violent measures resorted to." The discussion lasted four nights, and was marked by great ability. Mr. Gladstone, Sir James Graham, Lord John Russell, Mr. Disraeli, and Mr. Roebuck all joined Mr. Cobden in his attack upon the Government. As the debate proceeded it became evident that the fate of the Government was involved. Meetings were held, on the one hand by the Opposition, and on the other by the friends of the Government, at which resolutions to put forward all their respective strength were adopted. The ministerial phalanx had been lately weakened, many Liberals having grown apathetic, owing to the coldness shown towards the cause of Reform. The issue was up to the last doubtful. Lord Palmerston spoke vigorously, and concluded with some pointed strictures upon the combination of parties confederated against him, warning the House that it had in its keeping not only the interests and lives of many of their fellow-countrymen, but also the honour and reputation of the country.

The resolution was, however, carried against the Government by a majority of sixteen.

" Let the noble Lord," Mr. Disraeli had said in his speech, " who complained that he was the victim of a conspiracy, not only complain to the country, but let him appeal to it." Perhaps he little thought that he would be taken at his word. Anyhow, the next day but one, Lord Palmerston announced to the House that, as soon as the necessary business could be completed, Parliament would be dissolved.

There never, perhaps, was a general election which turned more completely than this one of 1857 on the personal prestige of a minister and the national confidence in one man. Lord Palmerston—after declining overtures from the City of London and other places—put forth his address to the country through the electors of Tiverton, the Devonshire borough to which he was wedded, both by ties of gratitude and of inclination. In it he distinctly challenged the verdict of the constituencies as one of confidence or no confidence in his administration. But in a very short time there was no doubt as to what the answer would be. Personally, he was in the heyday of his popularity. The country remembered that when others had shrunk from the responsibility of conducting the war with Russia, he had come forward and carried it to a successful issue in the face of great difficulties at home, in the field, and at the congress table. It appreciated his talent and versatility. It admired his good-humour and gallant bearing in the face of opposition, and was proud of his marvellous energy and boisterous fun in despite of advancing years. The news of a happy conclusion to the Persian war came in time to aid his supporters. " Palmerston !" became a rallying cry on every hustings. The " fortuitous concourse of atoms," as he apologetically termed his opponents when they denied having *combined* against him, was scattered to the winds. Many of the leading Peelites lost their seats. Mr. Bright and Mr. Milner Gibson were displaced at Manchester ; Cobden himself was ousted from Huddersfield, and Mr. Layard from Aylesbury. The Opposition was discomfited, and a triumphant majority was returned to support Lord Palmerston's Government.

The new Parliament met on the 30th of April ; and almost immediately after the commencement of business Lord Palmerston moved the Army Estimates, Sir John Ramsden, the Under-Secretary for War, not having had time to make himself acquainted with the details of his office. This short session was naturally not very productive of legislation. One of the principal measures carried was the Divorce Court Bill, which encountered pertinacious opposition. Lord Palmerston met the charge of hurrying the Bill through Parliament by a laughing rejoinder that, on the contrary, he was quite ready to sit through September if it was desired to have a full discussion of all the details, and added, amid laughter and cheers, " One prominent opponent of the Bill said to me on one occasion, ' You never shall pass the Bill.' I replied, 'Won't we!'" The question had indeed occupied the attention of the Legislature for so many years, that it seemed likely to do so for many years longer. It was only the firmness and determination of the Premier that carried it to a settlement.

Lord Palmerston varied his labours during the session by a visit to Manchester, for the opening of the Fine Art Exhibition, and by interviews at Osborne with the Emperor of the French and the Grand Duke Constantine, who both visited England this summer. He availed himself of his conversation with the latter to tell him that the English Government could not consent to the proposal which had been made to them by the Russian Government, namely, to limit British consuls to the southern districts of Persia, and to leave the Russian consuls in undisturbed possession of the northern.

About the middle of June the news of the Indian mutiny burst upon the Government. The tidings of the death of General Anson arrived on a Saturday. That same night Lord Palmerston had an interview with Sir Colin Campbell, who started on the Sunday, to take the command in India. The first vessel sailed from our shores with troops on the 1st of July, and she was followed by others in continuous succession, so that by the end of September about eighty ships had left for India, with upwards of 30,000 troops on board. This rapidity and vigour was but the fitting counterpart to the heroic efforts of our fellow-countrymen in the East, who preserved for us our empire in Hindostan.   Lord Palmerston, at the Lord Mayor's banquet on the 9th of November, paid a tribute to the national spirit.

"It is impossible for any Englishman to allude to that which has been achieved in India—not by soldiers only, but by civilians, by individuals, and by knots of men scattered over the whole surface of a great empire—without feeling prouder than ever of the nation to which we have the happiness to belong.   There never was an instance in the history of the world of such splendid examples of bravery, of intrepidity, of resource, and self-reliance accomplishing such results as those which we have lately witnessed.   The Government at home, on the other hand, may justly pride themselves on not having been unequal to the magnitude of the occasion. We took the earliest opportunity of despatching to India a great army—an army which had not yet arrived when those great victories were accomplished, but which, when it shall arrive, will render that which remains to be done comparatively easy of accomplishment, and will, I cannot entertain the slightest doubt, re-establish the power and authority of England upon an unshakable basis throughout the whole of our Indian empire.   My noble friend Lord Panmure has alluded to the spirit which has been displayed in this country, and I am proud to say, that although we have despatched from these shores the largest army that I believe ever at one time left them, we have now under arms in the United Kingdom as many fighting men as we had before the news of the mutiny reached us ; and, therefore, if any foreign nation ever dreamed in its visions that the exertions which we had been compelled to make in India had lessened our strength at home, and that the time had arrived when a different bearing might be exhibited towards us from that which was safe in the moment of our strength, the manner in which the spirit of the country has burst forth, the manner in which our ranks have been filled, the manner in which our whole force has been replenished, will teach the world that it would not be a safe game to play to attempt to take advantage of that which was erroneously imagined to be the moment of our weakness. (Loud and prolonged cheering.) It has been the fashion among the people of the Continent to say that the English nation is not a military nation. In one sense, indeed —in their sense—that assertion may be said to be true. An Englishman is not so fond as the people of some other countries are of uniforms, of steel scabbards, and of iron heels; but no nation can excel the English, either as officers or soldiers, in a knowledge of the duties of the military profession, and in the zeal and ability with which those duties are performed; and wherever desperate deeds are to be accomplished—wherever superior numbers are to be boldly encountered and triumphantly overcome—wherever privations are to be encountered—wherever that which a soldier has to confront is individually or collectively to be faced, there, I will venture to say, there is no nation on the face of the globe which can surpass—I might, without too much national vanity, say, I believe that there is no nation which can equal—the people of the British islands. But, my Lord Mayor and gentlemen, while we all admire the bravery, the constancy, and the intrepidity of our countrymen in India, we must not forget to do justice also to our countrywomen. In the ordinary course of life the functions of woman are to cheer the days of adversity, to soothe the hours of suffering, and to give additional brilliancy to the sunshine of prosperity; but our countrywomen in India have had occasion to show qualities of a higher and nobler kind, and when they have had either to sustain the perils of the siege, to endure the privations of a difficult escape, to forget their own sufferings in endeavouring to minister to the wants of others, the women of the United Kingdom have, wherever they have been found in India, displayed qualities of the noblest kind, such as never have been surpassed in the history of the world. Henceforth the bravest soldier may think it no disparagement to be told that his courage and his power of endurance are equal to those of an Englishwoman."

In Lord Palmerston's pocket-book I find a note about this speech: "Gave much offence at Compiègne—can't be helped—il n'y a que la verité qui blesse." The allusion to the "foreign nation which might dream that we had lessened our strength at home" had been appropriated by the French Court, which was just then showing, in concert with certain noisy bodies in France, considerable umbrage at the protection England afforded to foreign refugees, although Lord Palmerston, writing to Lord Clarendon, says, "My speech was pointed, not at France particularly, but at the whole Continent, where, for the last six months, we have been talked of, and written of, and printed of as a second-rate power. I hear that at Paris, since the fall of Delhi, no Frenchman in the clubs ever mentions India."*

The fact was, that not only our Indian empire, but our place among nations was at stake during this crisis. So sensible of this was Lord Palmerston that he steadily declined pressing offers of foreign assistance which were made to the British Government, feeling that, from the tone adopted abroad, it became necessary that England should triumph entirely "off her own bat," as he jauntily expressed it. Not only did Prussian officers individually volunteer their services, but an offer was made of two Belgian regiments, to be taken bodily into our pay. The object

---

* To Lord Lord Clarendon, November 16, 1857.

in either case was, no doubt, the experience to be gained by active operations in the field on a large scale, rather than any quixotic devotion to the English cause. But, whatever the motives, Lord Palmerston steadily set his face against the proposals, although some in places of authority appeared inclined to favour the idea of a Belgian contingent.

Parliament was called together for the next session on the 4th of December, to pass a Bill of Indemnity for the Government for having suspended the Bank Charter Act during the financial panic of the autumn. Lord Palmerston has a pithy note about the debate : " Geo. Lewis and J. Russell made good speeches. The others, not having a clear idea, conveyed none." The two Houses adjourned for Christmas, and met again at the usual time in February. On the first evening the Premier moved an address of congratulation to the Queen on the marriage of the Princess Royal and the Crown Prince of Prussia. With his usual instinct as to what would be most pleasing to the people of England, he put into the foreground that this was not a marriage of mere political convenience, but one of mutual affection. The illustrious parties chiefly concerned, he added, " have been more fortunate than many royal personages. They, indeed, have belonged to that class whom it is said—

> . . . . " Gentle stars unite, and in one fate
> Their hearts, their fortunes, and their feelings blend."

A few days later he introduced the Government Bill which was to transfer the rule over India from the old Company to the Crown. Many vested interests were involved, and, under a plea of delay, a strong opposition was offered; but on a division the Ministry, contrary to general expectation, obtained the large majority of 145. Walking home with Lord Palmerston after this victorious result, Sir Richard Bethell, then Attorney-General, remarked to him that he ought, like the Roman consuls in a triumph, to have somebody to remind him that he was, as a minister, mortal.

That day week showed that no such reminder was needed. But we must go back to recall the circumstances which had prepared the ground for the catastrophe which was now imminent.

On the 14th of January a most determined attempt had been made to assassinate the Emperor Napoleon as he was being driven with the Empress to the Opera. Bombs had been thrown under his carriage, shattering the framework when they exploded and killing some twenty bystanders. Fortunately, the Imperial party escaped with only trifling injuries. The gang who had perpetrated this outrage, of whom the leader was one Orsini, had come from London, where they had made their preparations for this atrocious attempt. Much indignation was felt by the French that men should be able to contrive such a diabolical deed under the protection of English hospitality. It was felt to be unjust that shelter should be afforded by a Government—and still more by a friendly Government—to the assassins of a friendly

Sovereign. This very natural feeling found expression in a despatch from the Minister of Foreign
Affairs at Paris, to Count Persigny, the French
ambassador in London. Count Walewski, after de-
precating any intention to find fault with the right
of asylum which England extended to political refugees, pointed out that men such as Pianori and
Orsini were not mere fugitives, but were assassins.
" Ought the English legislation," he proceeded, " to
contribute to their designs and continue to shelter
persons who place themselves beyond the pale of
common right and under the ban of humanity ? Her
Britannic Majesty's Government can assist us in
averting a repetition of such guilty enterprises by
affording us a guarantee of security which no state
can refuse to a neighbouring state, and which we are
authorized to expect from an ally. Fully relying,
moreover, on the high sense of the English Cabinet,
we refrain from indicating in any way the measures
which it may see fit to take in order to comply with
this wish. We rest entirely upon it for estimating
the decisions which it shall deem best calculated to
attain the object."

There was little in this document to arouse the
susceptibilities of the nation ; and the Cabinet, sensible of the justice of some of the observations
contained in it, determined, without answering it
officially, to introduce a measure the effect of which
would be to make the crime of conspiracy to murder—
which had hitherto been treated as a misdemeanour

—a felony, punishable with penal servitude. Lord Palmerston's first idea was a measure to give power to the Secretary of State to send away any foreigner whom the Government might have good reason to suspect was plotting a scheme against the life of a foreign sovereign, the Government being bound to state the grounds upon which the person in question had been sent away, either to a secret committee of Parliament or to a committee composed of the three chiefs of the courts of law. This notion, however, was abandoned for the simpler form of Bill which would, it was believed, attain the object in view. The Bill, although strongly opposed, was read a first time by a majority of no less than two hundred. Meantime, however, events were occurring which rapidly altered the public tone. Addresses had been presented to the Emperor from members of the French army, which, while congratulating him on his escape, contained expressions and menaces but too well calculated to wound the pride and inflame the temper of the English people. Some of these " French colonels "—as they were popularly designated—spoke of the English as " protectors of assassins," and uttered threats to the effect that " the infamous haunt in which such infernal machinations were planned should be destroyed for ever."

These ridiculous effusions would have passed unnoticed, unless with contempt, had not some of them, unfortunately, been inserted in the ' Moniteur,' the official organ of the French Government. In vain did the ambassador, by order of his Government, express regret at their insertion and explain that it happened through inadvertence, owing to the number of addresses which, according to the usual custom, required such official notification : in vain did Lord Palmerston urge in the House that it would be unworthy of the nation to be turned from a course, otherwise proper, by the idle vapourings of irresponsible swashbucklers, and "upon any paltry feelings of offended dignity or of irritation at the expressions of three or four colonels of French regiments, to act the childish part of refusing an important measure on grounds so insignificant and trumpery." The nation's back was up. The House repented of its former vote, and the leader of the Opposition, who had spoken for the Bill on its first reading, joined with the other malcontents in giving it its death-blow, by supporting Mr. Milner Gibson's amendment to the question that it should be read a second time. This amendment was: " That this House cannot but regret that Her Majesty's Government, previously to inviting the House to amend the law of conspiracy at the present time, have not felt it to be their duty to reply to the important despatch received from the French Government, dated January 20."

Verbal answers, fitting both in substance and in tone, had been given to the French ambassador in London and, through Lord Cowley, to the French Cabinet at Paris; but an official despatch, in reply, had been deliberately postponed, under the conviction that in the actual temper of men's minds, no advantage, but only exasperation, would be the result of any answer which the English Foreign Office could consistently give.

Report said that Lord Derby, sitting under the gallery of the House of Commons and watching the progress of the debate, saw the turn of the tide with the quick eye of an old parliamentary tactician, and sent hasty word to his lieutenants that they should take it at the flood which led to office. Anyhow, Mr. Disraeli plunged into the stream, and, declaring that while, on the first reading, the question was between England and France, on this the second reading, by some strange metamorphosis, it had become one between the House of Commons and the English minister, he announced that he sided with the House. Mr. Gladstone also threw in his lot with the Opposition in a powerful speech; Lord John Russell joined the Radicals; and when a division was called, Lord Palmerston's Government found itself in a minority of nineteen.

This defeat was a complete surprise. Ministers, when they went down to the House of Commons on the afternoon of this 19th of February, did not even anticipate a narrow division, much less a crisis. There were unseen causes, however, which had been gradually sapping Lord Palmerston's ascendency over the House of Commons. Some injudicious appointments had alienated not a few of his supporters, and his manner lately had certainly, for some reason or other, become more brusque and dictatorial than was altogether pleasing to the members. Many, however, of those who voted in the majority did not wish to overthrow his Government, and had he thought fit to appeal to the House of Commons for a vote of confidence, it would probably have accorded it, and have remained satisfied with the reply already given by the public to the denunciations of the French army. But Lord Palmerston never showed any undue tenacity in the retention of office. He at once tendered his resignation to the Queen, and persisted, although Her Majesty at first declined to accept it.

Thus Lord Palmerston, after weathering many a turbulent storm, was overthrown by a gust, and Lord Derby, being sent for, reigned in his stead.

CHAPTER VI.

JUST before his resignation, Lord Palmerston had the satisfaction of being able to announce the capture of Canton and the successful issue of his China policy. He was thus quite content to retire awhile from the cares of office, convinced that the conduct of his Government in the matter of the attempt upon the French Emperor's life, though it involved him personally in a temporary banishment from power, had contributed to the preservation of that French alliance which it was one of his chief aims to maintain. Indeed, even after he had ceased to be responsible for the course of events, he still exerted his undoubted influence to smooth the path of his successors and to save them and the country from the consequences of a rupture with France. He writes on the 1st of March to Lord Clarendon :—

" I am told that Persigny says that if the Derby Government drop the Murder Bill he will be immediately recalled. It would be most unfortunate that the diplomatic relations of the two countries should be broken off on such a ground. Such a rupture would justly incense the British nation, would make any measure in the matter impossible, and would leave hardly any way for a reconciliation.

"It would be very desirable that you should convey, if you can, these considerations to Cowley, in order that he might, in case of need, press them upon the Emperor, and urge upon him strongly that his own personal interest as well as that of both countries would be very seriously injured by such a step as the recall of his ambassador."

We find him availing himself of his comparative leisure to serve on a committee about the pollution of the Thames, to preside at the Royal Literary Fund dinner, to see Rarey, the horse-tamer, perform on a mare called Surplice at the Duke of Wellington's Riding-school, and to make notes afterwards about his system of breaking and the pedigree of the animal. Such variety of employment must have been to him both new and refreshing.

In November he went over to Compiègne on a visit to the Emperor Napoleon, and with both horse and gun joined in the sports of the French Court, though, on the hunting days, a stag, and not a fox, was the quarry. He wrote to his brother-in-law: "They are all very civil and courteous, and the visits of the English to the Emperor serve as

links to maintain and strengthen English alliance."
I find a scrap of conversation recorded which is
amusing, as illustrating an odd bent of the French
mind. While the dancing was going on, Lord Palmerston and the Emperor walked up and down an
inner room, and the Imperial philosopher propounded
his idea of an improvement upon the existing system
of universal suffrage, namely, to limit the right of
voting to married men. He said that unmarried men
do not feel the same sentiments about their country
as those who have a family stake in it, and that such
a voting qualification would shut out both priests and
soldiers—classes which he would wish to see excluded.
Lord Palmerston could only answer that property of
some sort ought, in his opinion, to be the real basis for
the suffrage, and that while many bachelors might
own property, many a man with both wife and child
might have none.*

Lord Derby's ministry meanwhile was conducting
affairs in the face of a majority which did not show
much inclination to tolerate them for long. After
fulfilling the object of their call to power, namely,
writing an answer of some sort to Count Walewski's
despatch about the refugees, they had proceeded to
bring in and immediately to withdraw their India
Bill, and then to pass a different Bill, founded upon
resolutions of the House. They managed, how-

* During this conversation the Emperor also said that the Emperor
of Russia had told him that he would spend his last rouble, and
sacrifice his last man, to prevent the establishment of a Greek empire
at Constantinople.

ever, to struggle through the session by the aid of the self-sacrifice of one of their colleagues* and of the gladiatorial genius of their Chancellor of the Exchequer.

At the beginning of the session of 1859 a Reform Bill was introduced by the Government, one new feature of which was a franchise founded upon personal property. On the second reading, Lord John Russell moved an amendment condemnatory of its provisions, and Lord Palmerston spoke in support of Lord John's resolution; he chaffed the Ministry by assuring them that he did not want them to resign, but said to them, " As Voltaire said of some minister who had incurred his displeasure, ' I won't punish him; I won't send him to prison; I condemn him to keep his place.' " On a division in the House of 621 members, the Government were left in a minority of 39, and a few days later they announced their intention of dissolving Parliament.

Lord Palmerston was re-elected for Tiverton without opposition. Of course he had his usual tournament with the Radical butcher after he had finished his speech. In vain did Rowcliffe, from the middle of the crowd in front of the hustings, insist on a plain, straightforward answer to the questions he was about to put. He got what he asked for, but was left as much in the dark as ever.

---

* Lord Ellenborough resigned in consequence of an attack on the Government about the publication of his despatch censuring the Governor-General of India.

Yet it was all done so good-humouredly and with such an evident enjoyment of the fun of the thing, that the most exacting elector could not take it amiss.

"Mr. Rowcliffe said that as Lord Palmerston had talked a great deal about Lord Derby's Reform Bill, he hoped his lordship would favour the electors and non-electors with his views on Reform. He would ask his lordship whether he would vote for the ballot, and whether he was in favour of manhood suffrage, or £6 franchise, or rating franchise. He was once a member of the noble lord's committee, but finding his opinions in advance of his lordship's, he refused to remain a member any longer. (Laughter.) The noble lord also said a great deal about the Conspiracy Bill, but it was well known he was a pet of the Emperor of the French. (Continued laughter.) He believed that the noble lord was a downright Tory, and the best representative the Conservatives could possibly have. He hoped his lordship would answer his questions in a straightforward and honest manner."

"Lord Palmerston said he was delighted to find that his old friend, however far advanced in years, retained that youthful vigour which he possessed when first he knew him, and with his vigour he had retained also his prejudices and opinions. (Laughter, and a cry of 'No chaff.') His friend asked for a straightforward answer, and he would give him one. He totally disagreed with him in almost all his opinions. (Laughter.) He (the noble lord) thought the day would never come when he and his friend would agree in political faith. (Much laughter.) His friend asked him what he thought on many points. In the first place he would say he was opposed to the ballot. He was against manhood suffrage. [Rowcliffe: 'How far will you go with the franchise?'] He would give a straightforward answer to that. He would not tell him. (Laughter.) He held it was his duty, after the confidence they had reposed in him, to act according to his judgment in any measure relating to Reform. (Cheers.) He

hoped that the political difference of Mr. Rowcliffe and himself would not alter their private friendship. (Loud laughter.)
He was sorry to disagree with his friend, but no man could
agree with everybody. The man who did agree with everybody was not worth having anybody to agree with him.
(Cheers and laughter.)"

The elections were much influenced by the aspect
of foreign affairs. On New Year's Day the French
Emperor had electrified Europe by addressing the
Austrian ambassador, at the usual reception of the
diplomatic corps, in a manner which betokened an un-
pleasant feeling between the two countries. Whether
in so doing he was imitating his uncle, whose abrupt
remark to the English minister at Paris in 1803
immediately preceded the rupture of the peace of
Amiens, was a matter for curious speculation ; but the
parallel did not fail to excite general uneasiness.
The relations between Austria and Sardinia were
known to be strained, owing to the impatience of the
Italians at the continuance of Austrian predominance
in the Peninsula. Did these few words spoken at
the Tuileries import that France would join in the
fray should hostilities break out? This proved to be
their meaning, and, after a few months of suspense,
Austria fired the mine by a summons to Sardinia to
disarm. On her refusal war was declared, and French
troops began to pour into North Italy, as allies of
Victor Emmanuel. This was the moment of the
general election in England. Lord Derby's Government were, rightly or wrongly, suspected of leanings

towards Austria, while public feeling was strongly in favour of Italian independence. This sufficed to turn the scale wherever parties were evenly balanced, and so the dissolution failed to give the Conservative party a majority.

The Liberal party had meanwhile been engaged in preparing for the future by healing their dissensions and reconciling their leaders. Lord Palmerston and Lord John Russell had come to an agreement that whichever of the two was charged with the formation of a Government should receive the co-operation of the other. And at a meeting in Willis's Rooms, at which some of the Peelites were present, it was arranged that an immediate vote of want of confidence in ministers should be moved by Lord Hartington in the House of Commons. Accordingly, on the 10th of June, in a House of no less than 637 members, such a vote was carried by a majority of 13, in spite of Mr. Disraeli's amusing protest against the scene of Almack's, where dowagers and beauties formerly held sway, having been turned into an arena for the issuing of vouchers by political patrons.

Lord Granville, to the astonishment of everybody, was charged with the construction of a Ministry, the Queen feeling that " to make so marked a distinction as is implied in the choice of one or other as Prime Minister of two statesmen so full of years and honours as Lord Palmerston and Lord John Russell, would be a very invidious and unwelcome task." Lord Granville's failure to make a Government under the circumstances is worth noting, as an illustration of the working of our form of government, and of the fact that the House of Commons is the ultimate depositary of the power that makes, as well as unmakes, ministers.

Lord Palmerston consented to serve under Lord Granville for the reasons and under the limitations stated in the following paper :—

" 94, Piccadilly, June 11, 1859

" Viscount Palmerston presents his humble duty to Your Majesty, and has the honour of assuring Your Majesty that he will deem it his duty to afford Lord Granville his assistance and co-operation in forming' an administration in obedience to Your Majesty's commands. Viscount Palmerston considered himself to be promoting the public interest by taking an active part in the late proceedings in the House of Commons tending to the removal of Lord Derby's administration ; but he feels that it would have been inexcusable in him to have encouraged and organised those proceedings with a view to any personal objects or interests of his own. Those who unite to turn out an existing Government ought to be prepared to unite to form a stronger Government than that which is to be overthrown ; and it was in this spirit, and with a deep sense of what is due by public men to Your Majesty and to the country, that Viscount Palmerston and Lord John Russell, before they called the meeting at Willis's Rooms, came to an agreement to co-operate with each other in the formation of a new administration, whichever of the two might be called upon by Your Majesty to reconstruct Your Majesty's Government. That agreement did not extend to the case of any third person ; but Viscount Palmerston conceives that the same sense of public duty which had led him to enter into that engagement with Lord John Russell, should also lead him to give assistance to Lord Granville towards the execution of Your Majesty's commands. Viscount Palmerston's promise to Lord Granville has, however, been conditional. He thinks that it would be a great disappointment and an evil for the country if, on the overthrow of one administration by a deliberate vote of want of confidence by a recently elected House of Commons, the overthrowing majority should be so paralysed as not to be able to offer to Your Majesty a stronger administration than that which they have overthrown. But, on the other hand, it would be injurious to the interest of the Crown and of the nation, that on such an occasion an administration should be formed which, by the weakness of its personal elements, should be destitute of the inherent strength necessary to enable it to face and overcome the difficulties with which it must have to contend; and Viscount Palmerston deems himself bound by his duty to Your Majesty, and by a proper regard to what he owes to himself, to say that to an administration so composed he would feel it impossible to belong. The promise, therefore, which he has given to Lord Granville has been made conditional on Lord Granville's success in organising a Government so composed as to be calculated officially to carry on the public service and to command the confidence of Parliament and of the country."

This success did not attend Lord Granville's efforts. He found Lord John Russell reluctant to accept his leadership; and as he met with insuperable difficulties in the task which he had unwillingly undertaken, he resigned his commission. Lord Palmerston having been then sent for constructed a Ministry, with Lord John Russell at the Foreign Office and Mr. Gladstone at the Exchequer. He also offered the Board of Trade to Mr. Cobden, who declined it. Thus Lord Palmerston, in his seventy-fifth year, again became Prime Minister and leader of the House of Commons. The remainder of his course was to be comparatively smooth. For six years he was accepted by the country as the minister of the nation, and almost occupied a position removed from the chances of party strife. Whatever difficulties he had to contend with did not consist either in wars abroad or in parliamentary defeats at home. Such as they may have been, they were of a more hidden character. The events of this period are too recent to warrant either great detail in their history or absence of reserve on the part of the historian.

The war in North Italy was sharp and short. The victories of Magenta and Solferino drove the Austrians within their famous Quadrilateral, and the last week in July found the French and Sardinians pausing in view of these formidable defences. The Emperor Napoleon had previously learnt that Prussia was preparing to take the field and to march on Paris. He was anxious to make peace; and so it happened that, within a fortnight after accession to office, Lord Palmerston had to consider a proposal made to the British Cabinet that they should intervene between the belligerents, and propose an armistice upon terms which were laid before them by the French ambassador. In the following letter he gives his reasons for declining to place England in such a false position :—

" Piccadilly, July 6, 1859.

" MY DEAR JOHN RUSSELL,

"The more I think of Persigny's proposal the less I like it, and the more I incline to the opinion that we ought to be very careful not to involve ourselves, and not to commit ourselves by hastily adopting it. Those who propose to two belligerents on the point of fighting that they should agree to an armistice, in order to negotiate a peace, ought to have settled in their own minds the outline of such an arrangement as might be proposed to the belligerents with a chance of success; but we have no plan of our own, and we are asked to adopt as our own one sketched out by one of the belligerent parties out of three. It would be useless to propose an armistice to the Austrians unless we gave them an idea of the terms to be the subject of negotiation ;

but if we confine ourselves simply to the first condition, that Italy should be entirely given up to the
Italians, Austria would, of course, peremptorily
refuse. If we were to go farther, and communicate
the details of the Persigny scheme, we should identify
ourselves with it, and be committed to an approval
of it; but that I should be unwilling to do, though
if such an arrangement were to be worked out as the
result of the war, we should, of course, acquiesce in
it, and say that matters might have turned out worse.
It is to be observed that we are not told that this
scheme has the assent of the Sardinians nor of the
Italians generally. It would obviously fall far short
of the wishes and expectations of Italy; and if we
made it, we should be accused of having interposed
and stopped the allied armies in their career of victory, and of having either endeavoured or of having
succeeded to rivet on Italy a remnant of Austrian
shackles, and of having betrayed and disappointed
the Italians at the very moment when their prospects
were the brightest.

" The scheme proposes to give Venetia and Modena
to an Austrian archduke, as an independent Sovereign, by way of interposing some neutral state between Piedmont and Austria. But what would be
the result ? The same Austrian influences and interference which have been the bane of Tuscany would
soon afflict this new state. It would not be constitutional, and there would be worse neighbourhood
between it and constitutional Piedmont than there

would be between Venetia as part of Piedmont and Austria, because Venetia and Piedmont would be separated only by an imaginary line; whereas the Tyrol would be a buffer between Venetia and Austria. The freedom of Piedmont would excite the aspirations of the Venetians. Discontent and disturbance would arise. Austria would intervene, she could not see an archduke in trouble and not come and help him. She would again be brought into active interference in Italian affairs; and if Modena were added to Venetia, Austria would again take her place in Central Italy. Fresh quarrels would arise because the old grievances would spring up anew, and fresh wars would inevitably follow. If the scheme is the Emperor's own, it is suggested by jealousy of Sardinia and tenderness for the Pope; but we feel neither of these mental affections, and are not bound to adopt them. The scheme, moreover, throws wholly out of question the wishes of the Italians themselves, and we are asked to propose to the belligerents a parcelling out of the nations of Italy, as if we had any authority to dispose of them. I cannot be a party to Persigny's scheme.

"If the French Emperor is tired of his war, and finds the job tougher than he expected, let him make what proposals he pleases, and to whomsoever he pleases; but let them be made as from himself formally and officially, and let him not ask us to father his suggestions, and make ourselves answerable for them.

"Yours sincerely,

"PALMERSTON."

The French Emperor must have anticipated the refusal of England to become his cat's-paw. Anyhow, on the 5th of July, he acted for himself. On that day he sent General Fleury to the headquarters of the Emperor of Austria with a letter proposing an armistice. General Fleury arrived at a late hour, and the night was spent by the Emperor Francis Joseph in council with Count Rechberg, Prince Metternich, and Count Mensdorff. Next morning Napoleon received a reply accepting the armistice. An interview took place on the 8th between the two Emperors, and on the 11th, at Villafranca, a provisional treaty of peace was signed, containing as bases the creation of an Italian Confederation, under the presidency of the Pope, the cession of Lombardy to Sardinia, and the return of the Grand Dukes of Tuscany and Modena to their states. The Emperor Napoleon, however, obtained from the Austrian Emperor a verbal assurance that no force should be employed to restore the Grand Dukes. The definitive treaty was to be settled in a Conference at Zurich. Cavour withdrew from the Sardinian Ministry on the announcement of this peace. Lord Palmerston also lost no time in expressing his disappointment at the terms of the treaty.

" 94, Piccadilly, 13 juillet, 1859.

" Mon cher Persigny,

 " Si je comprends ce qui va être arrêté pour l'Italie, il est question d'une Confédération italienne où l'Autriche prendrait place en vertu de la Vénitie;

un tel arrangement serait funeste, et mettrait l'Italie au désespoir.

"La plus grande partie des maux de l'Italie, et l'esprit révolutionnaire qui s'y est montré, prennent leur source dans l'ingérence de l'Autriche dans les affaires des Etats au-delà du Pô. Jusqu'à présent cette ingérence n'a eu aucune base légitime, et un des buts que l'Empereur des Français se proposait d'atteindre était d'affranchir l'Italie de cette ingérence autrichienne en des pays ne faisant pas partie des possessions de l'Autriche.

"Mais une fois que l'Autriche devient membre d'une Confédération Italienne, toute l'Italie est livrée pieds et mains liés à l'Autriche. Jamais l'Angleterre ne pourra s'associer à un si mauvais arrangement. Au contraire, nous pourrions croire de notre devoir de protester hautement et en face de l'Europe contre un pareil asservissement des peuples de l'Italie. L'Autriche devrait au contraire être strictement exclue de toute ingérence politique ou militaire en dehors de ses frontières. Et si cela n'est pas fait, rien n'est fait, et tout sera à recommencer en fort peu de temps.

"Confédération politique des Etats italiens, oui ou non, c'est une question qui mérite examen. Il y a du pour et du contre. Le Pape, Naples, Toscane, Modena seraient toujours pour l'Absolutisme. Le Piémont seul pour un système liberal; comment on parviendrait à s'entendre reste à savoir.

"Union douanière de toute l'Italie avec un tarife

modéré et libéral encourageant le commerce, quant à cela il n'y aurait que du "pour" parmi les hommes intelligents. Mais même avec cette union, les relations de l'Autriche ne devraient être que celles d'un pays étranger faisant un pacte avec un corps dont il n'est pas membre.

"Soyez bien sûr que si l'Autriche n'est pas soigneusement exclue de toute ingérence, de toute espèce, dans les affaires de l'Italie, le sang français a été versé en vain, et la gloire de l'Empereur ne sera que de courte durée.

"Mille amitiés,

"PALMERSTON."

This scheme of an Italian Confederation was not proposed by Austria, but by Louis Napoleon. It had been floating in his mind for many years as a means of substituting Italian support of the Pope for the support of French and Austrian troops. The English Cabinet stated without delay, in a despatch to Paris, the objections to it, which they felt sure the French Government would, on consideration, recognise.

It further appeared likely that, in contravention of the verbal engagement given at Villafranca, and looking merely to the text of the provisional treaty, Austria might attempt to employ her troops in restoring the archdukes. An official remonstrance was therefore sent, in the month of August, by our Government to Vienna, which declared that "a provision for the employment of French or Austrian forces to put down the clearly expressed will of the people of Central Italy would, in the opinion of Her Majesty's Government, not be justifiable. Great Britain would feel it her duty to protest against a supplement to the treaty of Villafranca of that nature, if such were even contemplated." The Emperor Napoleon also was urged to remain firm on this point.

Naturally all this caused Lord Palmerston to be represented as very hostile to Austria, just as was the case in the former revolutionary years. He denies it.

"94, Piccadilly, August 22, 1859.

" My dear Cowley,

" I know that all the partisans of arbitrary government in Europe represent me as the bitter enemy of Austria, and I wish whenever you hear this to deny its truth. I am an enemy to bad government, to oppression and tyranny; and, unfortunately, the Austrian rule in Italy, as elsewhere, has been marked by those evils. I am an enemy, therefore, to the bad system of Austrian government, and heartily wish all Italians to be freed from the Austrian yoke. It would be better for Austria that this should be. It has been decided that Venetia shall still be a victim, but care ought to be taken that Austria be prevented, either as member of a Confederation, or in any other way, from interfering in the affairs of Italy beyond her own frontier. The Austrian Government is unfortunately hated in many Austrian provinces north of the Alps, and especially in Hungary and Galicia. I wish with all my heart she would change her system, and conciliate the good-will of her subjects; for I hold a great and powerful Austrian empire north of the Alps to be of the utmost importance for the general interests of Europe.

"Much is said at Paris of what are called the intrigues of Cavour—unjustly, I think. If it is meant that he has laboured for the enlargement of Piedmont and the freedom of Italy from foreign yoke and from Austrian rule, he will in history be called a patriot; but the means he has employed may be good or bad. I know not what they have been; but the end in view is, I am sure, the good of Italy. The people of the Duchies have as good a right to change their rulers as the people of England, France, Belgium, and Sweden; and the annexation of the Duchies to Piedmont would be an unmixed good for Italy, and for France, and for Europe. I hope Walewski will not sway the mind of the Emperor to make the enslaving of Italy the end of a drama, which opened with the declaration, 'Italy free from the Alps to the Adriatic,' and 'l'Italie rendue à elle même.'

"If the Italians are left to themselves all will go well; and when it is said that if the French garrison were drawn away from Rome, all the priests would be killed, the example of Bologna may be quoted, where the priests remain unmolested, and perfect order has been maintained.

" Yours sincerely,

" PALMERSTON."

When the French showed an evident leaning to Austria during the negotiations at Zurich, Lord Palmerston pithily said that this famous declaration, " l'Italie rendue à elle-même " was being turned into " l'Italie vendue à l'Autriche."

There was a dispute this year between Spain and Morocco, which, as affecting English interests, attracted Lord Palmerston's attention. Spain demanded a *rayon* of territory round her fortress of Ceuta on the African coast. This was agreed to by the Moors, but they could not come to a settlement as to what should be the boundary lines of the territory to be ceded.

" Broadlands, October 11, 1859.

" My dear John Russell,

 " It is plain that France aims, through Spain, at getting fortified points on each side of the Gut of Gibraltar, which, in the event of war between Spain and France on the one hand, and England on the other, would, by a cross fire, render that strait very difficult and dangerous to pass, and thus virtually to shut us out of the Mediterranean. The distance between part of the African coast and the Spanish coast is only eight miles. With a fortified port on each side, and guns that would carry three miles or more, a fleet of merchantmen or of transports would have some difficulty in keeping out of fire, especially if on each side there were a flotilla of gunboats, protected by the guns of the fortresses, firing from a certain distance out from these fortresses, and presenting but a small mark to any ships-of-war convoying the merchantmen or transports. As things now stand such vessels would be safe by keeping well over to the African coast, but they would no longer be so if that coast belonged to France or Spain.

" The French Minister of War or of Marine said the other day that Algeria never would be safe till France possessed a port on the Atlantic coast of Africa. Against whom would such a port make Algeria safe? Evidently only against England; and how could such a port help France against England? Only by tending to shut us out of the Mediterranean.

" I still think that the Spanish Government are determined to pick a quarrel with Morocco, and that their first act will be to take Tangier, and their *last* to evacuate it; and that the best way of preventing a serious difference between us and Spain would be to ask the Emperor of Morocco to request us to occupy Tangier in trust for him during hostilities with Spain, if war with Spain should break out.

" Yours sincerely,

" PALMERSTON."

War was declared a few days after this. It was intimated to the Spaniards that if Tangier were occupied by their troops, we could not permit the occupation to be prolonged after the close of the war.

The Spanish Foreign Minister promised that Spain " would not take possession of any point on the Straits the position of which would give her a superiority threatening the navigation." On this assurance being given, and the undertaking being observed, Great Britain remained neutral.

The next letter refers to the fortifications which were afterwards constructed. It was a subject much canvassed at the time, and on which Lord Palmerston was excessively anxious.

There would be no question which so thoroughly tested the patriotism of a British statesman, because the more it was successful the less likely it was to be popular.

The fact that we were placed in a state of adequate defence was precisely the fact that rendered any attack upon us unlikely; and if we were never attacked, it was sure to be said that our defences were uncalled for.

"94, Piccadilly, December 15, 1859.

" MY DEAR GLADSTONE;

" Sidney Herbert has asked me to summon a Cabinet for to-morrow, that we may come to a decision on a fortification question, and I am most anxious that the arrangement which he has proposed should be adopted.

" The main question is whether our naval arsenals and some other important points should be defended by fortifications or not; and I can hardly imagine two opinions on that question. It is quite clear that if, by a sudden attack by an army landed in strength, our dockyards were to be destroyed, our maritime power would for more than half a century be paralysed, and our colonies, our commerce, and the subsistence of a large part of our population would be at the mercy of our enemy, who would be sure to show us no mercy. We should be reduced to the rank of a third-rate power, if no worse happened to us.

" That such a landing is, in the present state of things, possible, must be manifest. No naval force of ours can effectually prevent it. Blockades of a hostile port are no longer possible, as of yore. The blockading squadron must be under sail, because there would be no means of supplying it with coals enough to be always steaming, while the outrushing fleet would come steaming on with great advantage, and might choose its moment when an on-shore wind had compelled the blockaders to haul off. One night is enough for the passage to our coast, and twenty thousand men might be landed at any point before our fleet knew that the enemy was out of harbour. There could be no security against the simultaneous landing of twenty thousand for Portsmouth, twenty thousand for Plymouth, and twenty thousand for Ireland. Our troops would necessarily be scattered about the United Kingdom; and with Portsmouth and Plymouth as they now are, those two dockyards and all they contain would be entered and burnt before twenty thousand men could be brought together to defend either of them.

" Then, again, suppose the manœuvre of the first Napoleon repeated, and a large French fleet, with troops on board, to start for the West Indies, what should we do? Would the nation be satisfied to see our fleet remain at anchor at Torbay or Portland, leaving our colonies to their fate? And if we pursued the French, they might be found to have doubled back, to have returned to the Channel, and for ten days or a fortnight to have the command of the narrow seas. Now the use of fortifications is to establish for a certain number of days (twenty-one to thirty) an equation between a smaller inside and a larger force outside, and this to give time for a relieving force to arrive. This in our case would just make the difference between safety and destruction. But if these defensive works are necessary, it is manifest that they ought to be made with the least possible delay; to spread their completion over twenty or thirty years would be folly, unless we could come to an agreement with a chivalrous antagonist not to molest us till we could inform him we were quite ready to repel his attack. We are told that these works might, if money were forthcoming, be finished possibly in three, or latest four years—long enough this to be kept in a state of imperfect defence.

" But how is the money, estimated in round numbers at ten or eleven millions, to be got? There are two ways : annual taxation, to raise for this purpose over and above all other expenses a third or a fourth of this sum, or the raising a loan for the whole amount, payable in three or four annual instalments, with interest, in twenty or thirty years. The first method would evidently be the best in principle, and the cheapest, but the burthen would be heavy, and the danger would be that after the first year the desire for financial relief might prevail over a provident sense of danger, and the annual grants would dwindle down to their present insufficiency ; and the works would thus remain indefinitely unfinished. The second course has the advantage of being financially as light, or nearly so, as the present system, because the annual repayment of principal and interest would be but little heavier than the present annual votes, while we should gain the same advantage of early completion of works which would be secured by the greater financial burthen of the first plan.

" Arrangements of this kind have been deemed, by the deliberate judgment and action of Parliament, wise and proper for private persons. Why should they not be so for a nation, in regard to outlays of the same nature as those for which private persons have been by law enabled to charge their estates ? The objection to borrowing for expenditure is stronger for individuals than for a nation.

" The individual, if he went on borrowing for annual expenses, would end by having no income left to live upon or to assign to a fresh lender. A nation would, perhaps, in the end come to the same standstill, but its power of increasing its income is greater than that of an individual; but still Parliament has encouraged and enabled private persons to borrow money for permanent improvement of their estates, the money so borrowed to be repaid in a limited number of years.

" If we do not ourselves propose such a measure to Parliament, it will infallibly be proposed by somebody else, and will be carried, not indeed against us, because I for one should vote with the proposer, whoever he might be, but with great discredit to the Government for allowing a measure of this kind, involving, one may say, the fate of the empire, to be taken out of their hands. People would say, and justly too, that we and the proposer ought to change places, and that he and his friends had shown themselves fitter than we were to assume the responsibility of taking care ' ne quid detrimenti respublica capiat.'

"Yours sincerely,

"PALMERSTON."

In accordance with these views he moved a resolution in the following session providing nine millions for the purpose of fortifying our dockyards and arsenals. His proposals were founded on the report of a Royal Commission which had inquired, during the preceding autumn, into our means of defence. The resolution was adopted by the House by a large majority, and the results of his action are seen in our existing forts and lines round Portsmouth, Plymouth, Chatham, and Cork.

CHAPTER VII.

France and the Italian Duchies—Syria—Emperor Napoleon's Schemes — Neutrality of Savoy—Attitude of France—The "Derby" of 1860—Conflict between Lords and Commons on Paper Duties—Discussion about the "Press."

WHATEVER may have been the previous differences which arose between Lord Palmerston and Lord Russell in the course of their long career, these two statesmen were, during the years which covered the second Palmerston administration, thoroughly united, both in their general views of policy and also as to the best manner of giving them effect.

In the year 1860, Italian affairs absorbed almost the whole interest of foreign events, and both ministers had for their one aim the speedy realisation of an independent and united Italy. In the following memorandum, drawn up by Lord Palmerston and circulated among his colleagues, we find sketched out the policy which, in agreement with the Foreign Secretary, he wished to pursue. We must, however, in order to appreciate it, recall the position of matters at the opening of the year.

The Congress which, by the Treaty of Zurich,

France and Austria had engaged themselves to summon had been postponed. The British Government had then come forward and proposed that France and Austria should agree not to interfere for the future by force in the internal affairs of Italy, that the French Emperor should concert with the Pope for the evacuation of Rome, and that Sardinia should not send troops into Central Italy until its several states had voted as to their future destiny, she being at liberty to do so as soon as a vote for annexation to her was passed. To these proposals France had instantly assented. Meanwhile the Duchies had preserved internal order, and had given unmistakable signs of their intention to declare for annexation to Sardinia if left to themselves. Lord Palmerston's memorandum was as follows:—

" Broadlands, January 5, 1860.

"The affairs of Italy are coming to a crisis, and it is indispensably necessary that the English Government should come without further delay to a decision as to the course which England is to pursue. But, in truth, that course has been already marked out. The English Government might have determined that, in regard to Italian affairs, England should abdicate its position as one of the great Powers of Europe. We might have said that we live in an island, and care not what may be done on the Continent; that we think only of making money, and of defending our own shores; and that we leave to others the task of settling as they like the affairs of the continent of Europe. But such has not been the policy of the wisest and greatest statesmen who have taken part in the government of this country. We might have deemed the present an exceptional case; we might have said the Emperor Napoleon has got into a scrape about Italian affairs; let him get out of it as he can: it is not our business to help him. But we rightly considered that what is at issue is not the interests of the Emperor Napoleon, but the interests of the people of Italy, and, through them, the welfare and peace of Europe. Therefore when a proposal was made that a Congress should meet to consider how best the independence and welfare of Italy could be secured, and when England was invited to be a party to that Congress, we accepted the invitation.

"But it would have been unworthy of the Government of a great Power like England to have accepted such an invitation without having decided upon the policy which we were to pursue when in the Congress. We had a policy, and we lost no time in making that policy known to the principal Powers invited to the Congress. That policy is in accordance with those principles which English statesmen in our times have professed and acted upon, and which are the foundation of public opinion in England. We declared that in going into Congress we should take our stand upon the principle that no force should be employed for the purpose of imposing upon the people of Italy any form of government or constitution, that is to say, that the people of Italy, and especially of Central Italy, should be left free to determine their own condition of political existence. We shall therefore go into Congress, if Congress there is to be, not as jurymen go into their box, discarding preconceived opinions and bound to be determined by what we hear in Congress, but like statesmen with a well-matured and deliberately formed policy, and with the intention of endeavouring to make that policy prevail. What is the best way of accomplishing this purpose? Why, obviously to persuade those Powers to agree with us, who are most able to sway the course of events in Italy and to bring them to the result we wish for.

"Which are those Powers? Obviously France and Sardinia. Austria, the Pope, and the King of Naples have views directly opposite to ours; and the other states to be represented in Congress are too far off to have the same influence as France and Sardinia on Italian affairs.

" It is demonstrable, therefore, that we ought to endeavour to come to an understanding with France and Sardinia, for the purpose of common and united action with them in regard to the matters to be treated of in Congress. We need take little trouble about Sardinia, because we know that her views tally with our own ; we can have little doubt as to the inclination of the Emperor Napoleon, because he has declared over and over again in manifestoes, in speeches, in letters and other communications that his object is to free Italy from foreign domination, to make Italy free from the Alps to the Adriatic, and to 'rendre l'Italie à elle-même.' There can be no reasonable doubt, therefore, that both France and Sardinia would unite with England in maintaining the principle that the Italians should be secured against foreign compulsion, and should be left free to determine, according to their own will, what shall be their future political condition. But what is the best time for endeavouring to establish this understanding. Shall we take steps now, or shall we wait till the Congress is assembled, and till some proposal is made by Austria or by the Pope, or by some other Power, which would be at variance with our views. Common sense seems to point out that if such an understanding is to be aimed at, we ought to endeavour to establish it without delay, and not to allow France and Sardinia to go into Congress ignorant whether England would or would not support efficiently the principles which she has theoretically declared. To put off endeavouring to establish an understanding with France and Sardinia till after the Congress had met and had begun its discussions, would be the most unbusinesslike proceeding that could well be imagined, and would, in all probability, expose us to deserved disappointment. Austria does not trust thus to the

chapter of accidents, but has been actively employed in
canvassing for support to her views.

" But what is the understanding or agreement which we
ought to establish with France and Sardinia ? Clearly a joint
determination to prevent any forcible interference by any
foreign Power in the affairs of Italy. This, it is said, would
be a league against Austria. No doubt it would be, as far as
regards the interference of Austria by force of arms in the
affairs of Italy; and such a triple league would better
deserve the title of holy alliance than the league which bore
that name.

" But such an engagement might lead us into war. War
with whom ? War with Austria. Well, suppose it did,
would that war be one of great effort and expense ? Clearly
not. France, Sardinia, and Central Italy would furnish
troops more than enough to repel any attempt which Austria
could make to coerce Sardinia or Central Italy. Our share
in such a war would be chiefly, if not wholly, naval ; and our
squadron in the Adriatic would probably be the utmost of
our contribution, unless we were asked to lend a couple of
regiments to garrison some point on the Adriatic, which,
however, we should probably not be asked to do, and if
asked, we might not consent to do. We ought not to be
frightened by words; we ought to examine things. But is
such a war likely ? On the contrary, it is in the highest
degree probable that such an engagement between England,
France, and Sardinia would be the most effectual means of
preventing a renewal of war in Italy. As long as England
keeps aloof, Austria may speculate upon our joining her in a
war between her on the one hand, and France and Sardinia
on the other. It is so natural that we should side with
France and Italy, that our holding back from doing so
would be looked upon by Austria as a proof that there was
some strong under-current which prevented us from doing
so; and the Austrian Government would not unnaturally
reckon that when the war had broken out, that under-

current would drive us to side with Austria against France; and this speculation would be a great encouragement to Austria to take a course leading to war. If, on the contrary, we made it publicly known that we engaged ourselves heartily on the side of France and Italy, it might be affirmed, as confidently as anything can be affirmed as to a future event, that there would be and could be no renewal of war in Italy, and the triple alliance, while it would be honourable to England (I might say, the only course that would be honourable to England), would secure the continuance of peace in Italy, and thereby avert one danger to the general peace of Europe.

"But it is said we cannot trust the Emperor Napoleon, and when we had entered into this triple alliance, he would throw us over and make some arrangement of his own without consulting us. It is no doubt true that such was the course pursued by Austria during the war which ended in 1815. Austria took our subsidies, bound herself by treaty not to make peace without our concurrence, sustained signal defeat in battle, and precipitately made peace without our concurrence. But on what occasion has the Emperor Napoleon so acted? On none. He differed with us about certain conditions and the interpretation of certain conditions of the treaty of peace with Russia, but the points in dispute were settled substantially in conformity with our views. There is no ground for imputing to him bad faith in his conduct towards us as allies. But it is said that he has not steadiness of purpose, and the agreement of Villafranca is a proof of this. That agreement was certainly much short of the declarations of intention with which he began the war, but he had great difficulties of many kinds to contend with in further carrying on the war; and though we, as lookers on, may think, and perhaps rightly, that if he had persevered those difficulties would have faded away, yet there can be no doubt that he thought them at the time real; and he is not the only instance of a sovereign or a general who has at the end of a war or a campaign accepted conditions of peace less full and complete than what he expected or demanded when hostilities began.

"But there is no ground for imputing to Napoleon unsteadiness of purpose in regard to his views about Italy. I have, during the last four or five years, had at different times opportunities of conversation with him upon many subjects, and, among others, upon the affairs of Italy, and I always found him strongly entertaining the same views and opinions which have filled his mind since January of last year, in regard to forcing Italy from Austrian domination, and curtailing the temporal sovereignty of the Pope. There seems, therefore, no reason to apprehend that if we came to an understanding with France and Sardinia, for the purpose of maintaining the principle that no force should be employed to coerce the free will of the Italians, the Emperor Napoleon would turn round and leave us in the lurch. There is every reason, on the contrary, to be confident that by such an agreement with France and Sardinia, we should without war complete a settlement of Italy highly honourable to the Powers who brought it about, and full of advantage, not to Italy alone, but to Europe in general.

"I have argued thus far on the supposition that the Congress will meet, and I think it most probable that it will meet. Austria and the Pope look to the Congress (mistakenly, I trust and believe, and mistakenly if the proposed concert with France and Sardinia is established) as the means by which the Archdukes are to be restored and Romagna brought back to obedience. These two Powers will not lightly let the Congress slip through their fingers. The Emperor Napoleon also wishes the Congress to meet, in order to relieve him from responsibility as to the settlement of Italy. The probability, therefore, is that the difficulty arising out of the pamphlet* will be got over, and that the Congress

* 'Le Pape et le Congrès,' by M. de la Gueronnière. Supposed to have been dictated by the Emperor himself. It advocated depriving

will meet. But if that difficulty should prove insurmountable, and the Congress should be given up, everything which I have said in this memorandum would equally apply; or rather, I should say, the necessity of coming to an agreement with France and Sardinia would be stronger still. In that case matters would have to be settled by diplomatic negotiation or by force of arms; and in either way an agreement between England, France, and Sardinia would carry into effect the objects which such an agreement might have in view.

"It is said, however, that although the course now recommended might in itself be right and proper, it would not be approved by the country nor by Parliament.

"My deliberate opinion is that it would be highly approved by the country, upon the double ground of its own merits, and of its tendency to avert a rupture with France, and to secure the continuance of peace with our neighbour. I am equally of opinion that it would be approved by Parliament; but if, by any combination of parties, an adverse decision were come to, it would, in my opinion, be the duty of the Government to appeal from Parliament to the country. My belief is that such an appeal would be eminently successful; but if it were not, I would far rather give up office for maintaining the principle on which the course which I recommend would be founded, than retain office by giving that principle up.

"Palmerston."

There was no need, however, of any formal league like this "triple alliance." The influence of the two Western Powers sufficed to restrain any forcible

---

the Pope of his temporal power except over the city of Rome. This pamphlet was the indirect cause of the failure of the Congress. Austria required from the French Government an undertaking not to support the measures advocated in it. France hesitating, Austria declined to appear at the Congress.

intervention, if such had been contemplated. In the month of March, Tuscany and Emilia declared by an immense majority in favour of annexation to Sardinia, and King Victor Emmanuel formally received them into the Piedmontese monarchy. Italy was already halfway on her road to unity.

The massacre of the Maronites by the Druses in the neighhourhood of Beyrout and Damascus led this year to the despatch of French troops to Syria, under the provisions of a convention between the five Powers and Turkey. Lord Palmerston consented, but unwillingly, to the expedition, fearing lest there would be much trouble in getting the French out again. This was, indeed, the case; for, although all danger of renewed violence had passed away by the time they arrived on the coast, it was not until the latter end of 1861 that they retired; and during this interval continuous representations to urge their departure were deemed necessary by the British Government.

Lord Palmerston had, no doubt, a personal partiality for Napoleon III., and fully acknowledged that his conduct had in many instances been that of an honourable ally, but he was not blinded to the tendency which this active-minded Prince, whose youth had been passed in schemes of personal ambition, had to the forming and nurturing of national projects which might be more or less inconvenient to his neighbours; and the English Government under Lord Palmerston, though very desirous to be friendly, would not in any emergency have been subservient to that of France.   A short note to our ambassador at Paris may serve as an illustration :—*

" John Russell has shown me his private letter to you.   I concur in all he says.   We must not take the language of Thouvenel or the Emperor as ordinances from the book of fate.   It is an old-established manœuvre to represent as settled and inevitable that which one desires to accomplish, and thus beforehand to deaden resistance by making people imagine it hopeless.

" The Emperor's mind seems as full of schemes as a warren is full of rabbits, and, like rabbits, his schemes go to ground for the moment to avoid notice or antagonism.

" We had no ground for war, and no sufficient reasons for war about Nice and Savoy, nor could we by any obvious means have prevented their annexation ; but other questions may arise in regard to which England could not be thus passive."

One, for instance, was the question of Genoa. When, later on, it was suspected that France was to be repaid for her acquiescence in Garibaldi's conquest of Sicily and Naples by the cession of Genoa or the Island of Sardinia, he let it be understood that the fleet of England would not be a passive witness of the transaction.   If any such intention existed—of

* To Lord Cowley, April, 1860.

which there is some evidence—his outspoken remonstrances acted as an effectual check to it.

He was not so successful in his efforts on behalf of Switzerland, whose position was greatly affected by the annexation of Savoy to France. The two districts of Chablais and Faucigny, bordering on the Lake of Geneva, had been declared by the treaties of 1815 to participate in the neutrality of Switzerland. It was at first hoped that the Emperor would consent to hand over these two northern districts of Savoy to the Swiss Confederation. When this expectation vanished, it was at any rate believed that France might be induced to cede a strip of territory, so as to leave the lake wholly to the Swiss, and to provide them with a strategic line on the frontier of the Valais. Lord Palmerston writes in this sense to the French ambassador, and appeals with great tact to those considerations of generosity which, on paper at any rate, have so much apparent influence with Frenchmen.

" 94, Piccadilly, 17 avril 1860.

" Mon cher Persigny,

" Soyez bien convaincu que nous souhaitons sincèrement de nous entendre avec la France sur cette question Savoyardo-Suisse, mais dans cette discussion la France et l'Angleterre ne partent pas du même point de départ ; chez nous, ici, l'habitude est de considérer les questions politiques d'après ce que nous croyons leur résultat pratique, et chez vous, en France, c'est trop l'habitude de traiter toutes les questions

politiques, non pas sur le terrain du résultat pratique,
mais sur le terrain de l'amour-propre national, et, si
vous me permettez de vous le dire, c'est surtout,
lorsque les arguments vous manquent, qu'on se place
à Paris le plus fortement sur le terrain de l'amour-
propre. Cependant ce n'est pas là la bonne manière
d'envisager les questions de haute politique ; mais le
vrai amour-propre national ne doit-il pas conseiller à
faire ce qui est juste et généreux et honorable ? et
n'est-ce pas que la justice, la générosité et l'honneur
conseilleraient à la France de satisfaire aux réclama-
tions légitimes de la Suisse ? La France a demandé
à la Sardaigne une frontière stratégique pour la
sûreté militaire de la France. Est-ce juste que la
France ôte à la Suisse la frontière stratégique que
l'Europe, la France elle-même incluse, avait donnée à
la Suisse pour la sûreté du territoire de la Confédération ? Tous les arguments dont la France s'est
servie pour justifier sa demande, soutiennent plus
encore la demande de la Suisse. Mais une grande
Puissance et un grand Souverain, en traitant avec un
voisin faible, devraient se montrer non-seulement
justes, mais généreux ; il n'est pas une faiblesse que
d'agir ainsi, c'est une preuve de la conscience de sa
force ; mais avec l'Empereur des Français ce n'est pas
seulement une question de générosité ; la reconnais-
sance y entre pour sa part. C'est en Suisse que
l'Empereur a fait ses premières études, et qu'il a
commencé à développer ce caractère qui lui a valu,
depuis, des succès si éclatants ; c'est en Suisse plus

tard, et dans des temps moins heureux que les der-
nières dix années, que l'Empereur a eu à se louer des
procédés de la Suisse à son égard : il est impossible
que l'Empereur ne sente pas de la bienveillance
envers la Suisse. On croit en Europe que l'Empereur a donné à espérer aux Suisses, qu'après que la
Savoie lui aurait été cédée par la Sardaigne, il donnerait à la Suisse les parties neutralisées ; ne serait-ce
pas inconséquent de leur refuser même la frontière
stratégique dont ils seraient contents ? Les bords du
Lac de Genève et la ligne stratégique, qui couvre le
Valais, paraissent essentiels pour la Suisse. Quant
aux bords du Lac, il est à remarquer que de toutes
les raisons stratégiques mises en avant par la France
pour appuyer la demande de la cession de la Savoie,
il n'y en a pas une qui s'applique aux bords du Lac
de Genève, tandis que toutes ces raisons s'appliquent à
la demande que fait la Suisse de ne pas avoir sur le
Lac un voisin aussi puissant que la France. Les
stipulations dont on parle, par lesquelles la France
s'engagerait à n'avoir aucun bâtiment armé sur le
Lac, et de ne construire aucune forteresse sur les bords,
ne pourraient guère être prises au sérieux : il y a
des invasions morales, tout comme des invasions militaires, et il est essentiel à l'intérêt commun de
l'Europe que la Suisse continue à rester Suisse ; il ne
s'agit pas dans cette affaire d'une question entre la
France et l'Angleterre : c'est un intérêt européen, et
non pas un intérêt anglais, dont il s'agit, et c'est à
l'Europe et non pas à l'Angleterre que la France doit

des égards à ce sujet. Pourquoi la France ne prendrait-elle pas l'initiative dans cette affaire ? pourquoi ne se ferait-elle pas un mérite de contenter spontanément les justes désirs de ses voisins en Suisse ? ne serait-ce pas agir en grand Seigneur, et cela sans rien sacrifier qui soit essentiel aux vrais intérêts de la France ?

"Soyez bien sûr que, dans les temps où nous vivons, la bonne opinion de l'Europe vaut tout autant qu'un petit bout de territoire.

"Mille amitiés,

"PALMERSTON.

"LE COMTE DE PERSIGNY."

All that was obtained, however, was an article in the Treaty of Cession declaring that the King of Sardinia could only transfer the neutralised parts of Savoy on the conditions upon which he himself possessed them.

There is no doubt that Lord Palmerston by this time had become really distrustful of the intentions of the Emperor Napoleon. His attitude about Savoy was coupled with the open avowals of some French officers that it was the intention of, and a necessity for, France to annex Geneva. Pamphlets supposed to be published by the Emperor's permission were appearing and advocating territorial changes. Ortéga, the martyr of the last Carlist rising, was reported to have declared that he had been encouraged in his enterprise by the Emperor; while the Portuguese minister in London stated it to be generally believed in the Peninsula that the Emperor of the French had agreed with Count Montemolin that if the Carlist attempt succeeded, the price of the acknowledgment and support of France was to have been the advance of the French frontier from the Pyrenees to the Ebro, or else the cession of the Balearic Islands, and that Spain was to have been assisted by France in conquering and annexing Portugal. Reports of the Emperor's conversation, derived from unimpeachable sources, contained expressions of opinion that it was necessary for France to obtain the Palatinate, and to acquire Saarbruck and Saarlouis, places which, indeed, became in 1870 the first point of his attack on Prussia. The general concurrence of many other such indications, some, no doubt, false, and each by itself perhaps trivial, gave strength to the distrust which Lord Palmerston had already felt at the end of the previous year, when he wrote to Lord John Russell.

" Broadlands, November 4, 1859.

" My dear John Russell,

" Till lately I had strong confidence in the fair intentions of Napoleon towards England, but of late I have begun to feel great distrust and to suspect that his formerly declared intention of avenging Waterloo has only lain dormant, and has not died away. He seems to have thought that he ought to lay his foundation by beating, with our aid, or with our concurrence or our neutrality, first Russia and then Austria, and, by dealing with them generously, to make them his friends in any subsequent quarrel with us. In this, however, he would, probably, find himself mistaken ; because with nations and governments resentments for former antagonism or gratitude for former benefits invariably give way to considerations of present and prospective interests ;* and Russia probably, and Austria certainly, would see no advantage in any great lowering of England for the augmentation of the preponderance of France. But this reasoning of mine may be wrong, and Russia, at least, might join France against us.

" Next, he has been assiduously labouring to increase his naval means, evidently for offensive as well as for defensive purposes; and latterly great pains have been taken to raise throughout France, and especially among the army and navy, hatred of England, and a disparaging feeling of our military and naval means. All this may be explained away, and may be accounted for by other causes than a deliberate purpose of hostility to England; but it would be unwise in any English Government to shut its eyes to all these symptoms, and not to make all due preparations for the gale which the

---

* " As to the romantic notion that nations or governments are much or permanently influenced by friendships and God knows what, I say that those who maintain those notions, and compare the intercourse of individuals to the intercourse of nations, are indulging a vain dream. The only thing which makes one Government follow the advice and yield to the counsel of another is the hope of benefit to accrue from adopting it, or the fear of consequences of opposing it."—*Speech of Lord Palmerston, House of Commons, March 1,* 1848.

political barometer thus indicates, though it may possibly pass away. Of course we should take as 'argent comptant' all their professions of 'alliance intime et durable,' as Walewski termed it in his China despatch; and the only expression we ought to give of anything like suspicion should be in the activity and the scale of our defensive arrangements. In regard to them, however, we must not be over-ruled by financial economy.

" Yours sincerely,

" PALMERSTON."

The incessant exertions which the French were making to place their navy upon the most complete and efficient footing did not tend to diminish the causes for anxiety. It was under these circumstances that Lord Palmerston urged forward our defensive preparations and the construction of fortifications, and encouraged the development of the Volunteer Rifle Movement. This was no mere " invasion panic." He felt that the salutary and restraining action of a great Power like England is not confined to the employment of physical force. If such a Power is known to be strong within itself, and capable of exertion when required, its diplomatic action will command attention, will often strongly influence the course of events, and, by dealing timely with begin-nings, may prevent proceedings which, if unchecked, would lead to great and disastrous international con-vulsions.

Lord Palmerston, however, also feared direct action against England if we remained unprepared. He says in a letter to the Duke of Somerset: "I have watched the French Emperor narrowly, and have studied his character and conduct. You may rely upon it that at the bottom of his heart there rankles a deep and inextinguishable desire to humble and punish England, and to avenge, if he can, the many humiliations, political, naval, and military, which, since the beginning of this century, England has, by herself and by her allies, inflicted upon France. He has sufficiently organised his military means; he is now stealthily but steadily organising his naval means; and, when all is ready, the overture will be played, the curtain will draw up, and we shall have a very disagreeable melodrama."

The following conversation with Count Flahault and the letter to Count Persigny are very characteristic. Lord Palmerston had an enviable power of telling hard truths under a sense of duty, while he avoided giving offence, owing to the frankness and geniality of his manner :—

"*Memorandum of a Conversation with Count Flahault on Tuesday, March* 27, 1860.

"Count Flahault came to me at a quarter after four, just as I was going down to the House of Commons. He said he was going to Paris next morning, and wished to know what he should say from me to the Emperor. I said I could not wait a minute, as I had to be in the House to answer a question, but that if he would go down with me in my brougham we might talk as we went along. To this he agreed. I then referred to what Lord John had said. He objected to that reference, saying that what had fallen from Lord John was personally offensive to the Emperor. I asked what part. He said not the latter part, which related to concert with other Powers; that was political, and could not be objected to; but Lord John had expressed distrust of the Emperor. I said distrust might be founded on either of two grounds: either upon the supposition of intentional deceit, or upon such a frequent change of purpose and of conduct as to show that no reliance could be placed upon the continuance of the intentions or policy of the moment, and Count Flahault must admit that, without imputing the first, there is ample ground for a feeling founded on the second consideration. Count Flahault said his great object was to prevent war between the two countries. I said that I feared the Emperor and Thouvenel had schemes and views which tended to bring about that result, and might array Europe against France. Count Flahault did not fear that, but was apprehensive that irritation on both sides might bring on war between England and France. I said that I was most anxious to prevent such a war; but if it was forced upon England, England would fearlessly accept it, whether in conjunction with a confederated alliance, or singly and by herself; that the nation would rise and rally as one man; although, speaking to a Frenchman, I ought perhaps not to say so, yet I could not refrain from observing that the examples of history led me to conclude that the result of a conflict between English and French, upon anything like equal terms, would not be unsatisfactory to the former.

"Count Flahault said that he had been at the battle of Waterloo, and knew what English troops are, but that the French army now is far superior to that which fought on that day. I said no doubt it is, and so is the present English army; but with regard to the excellence of the French army, I would remind Count Flahault of what passed between Marshal Tallard and the Duke of Marlborough, when the former was taken prisoner at the battle of Blenheim: 'Vous venez, milord,' said the Marshal, 'de battre les meilleures troupes de l'Europe.' 'Exceptez toujours,' replied Marlborough, 'celles qui les ont battues.' 'But,' said Count Flahault, 'what I fear is an invasion of this country, for which steam affords such facilities, and which would be disastrous to England.' I replied that steam tells both ways, for defence as well as for attack; and that as for invasion, though it would no doubt be a temporary evil, we are under no apprehension as to its results. That a war between England and France would doubtless be disastrous to both countries, but it is by no means certain which of the two would suffer the most.

"Arrived at the House of Commons, we took leave of each other. Count Flahault said he should not say anything to the Emperor calculated to increase the irritation which he expected to find, but would endeavour to calm. I said that of course Count Flahault would judge for himself what he should say, but he must have observed what is the state of public feeling and opinion in this country. The conversation was carried on in the most friendly manner, as between two private friends who had known each other for a long course of years."

"Broadlands, 18 octobre 1860.

" Mon cher Persigny,

"Borthwick s'est rendu ici il y a quelques jours, d'après votre désir, pour me donner communication de la conversation que vous avez eue avec lui.

"La substance de ce qu'il m'a raconté comme le résumé de ce que vous lui avez dit est à peu près que l'Empereur souhaite, aujourd'hui comme toujours, paix avec tous et alliance avec nous; mais que le maintien de cette alliance dépend beaucoup de nous. Vous avez dit que dans les masses en France il y a mauvais vouloir envers l'Angleterre ; que l'Empereur peut réprimer et contraindre ce sentiment, tant qu'il est aidé par une politique amicale de la part du Gouvernement anglais, et que ce qu'il faudrait de notre part, ce serait d'exprimer confiance en l'Empereur, et de nous abstenir de toute tentative d'organiser une coalition européenne contre la France. Que si nous devions poursuivre un autre et différent système, il y aurait danger de guerre entre les deux pays, chose que vous considéreriez comme déplorable pour les deux. Mais vous avez ajouté que dans l'état des préparatifs et des moyens guerriers sur terre et sur mer des deux pays, le résultat d'une telle guerre ne serait peut-être pas favorable pour nous ; qu'avec vos bâtiments blindés vous pourriez détruire nos chantiers, et que le résultat d'une telle lutte serait peut-être de mettre la France à la tête d'une coalition européenne dirigée contre l'Angleterre, isolée par sa politique autant que par la géographie, et finalement vous avez suggéré l'idée que, lorsque je vais à Leeds vers la fin du mois prochain, je pourrais utilement pour les deux pays profiter de l'occasion pour exprimer dans un discours notre confiance en les intentions pacifiques et désintéressées de l'Empereur.

" Eh bien ! je suis toujours bien aise d'apprendre, soit par les discours de l'Empereur, soit par ce qu'on nous rapporte de ses conversations, que la politique extérieure de la France est pacifique et désintéressée ;

et quant à la question de paix ou de guerre entre nos deux pays, vous pouvez être sûr qu'il n'y a personne en Angleterre qui voudrait la guerre, et qui ne désire pas la paix.

" Mais pour ce qui regarde la guerre, l'histoire du passé nous rassure quant aux chances de l'avenir. Il n'y a certainement pas de nation qui puisse se vanter d'être plus brave que la nation française, mais je crois que nos hommes ont quelques dix minutes de ténacité de plus que les vôtres ; et lorsque le courage est égal des deux côtés, c'est la ténacité qui décide du sort du combat. Pour ce qui regarde l'application de la science et des arts mécaniques à la guerre, je crois qu'il n'y a pas grande différence entre les deux pays, soit pour les opérations sur terre, soit pour celles sur mer ; mais nous avons plus de fer et de charbon que vous, et notre industrie en ces matières est plus développée que la vôtre.

" La grande différence entre les deux pays consiste en ceci, que tous nos préparatifs, soit militaires, soit navals, sont essentiellement défensifs, tandis que les vôtres ont du moins l'apparence d'être destinés pour des opérations offensives.

" Si par conséquent les autres gouvernements de l'Europe commencent, non pas à se coaliser pour attaquer la France, chose à laquelle la démence seule pourrait penser, mais pour s'entr'aider dans le cas où la France devenait agressive, ce sont les actes récents de la France et son attitude présente qui seuls en sont les causes. Mais ceci ne donne à la France

aucun juste sujet de plainte.   Il n'y a pas un homme
en Angleterre qui songerait à organiser une coalition
pour attaquer la France tranquille et paisible; mais
il n'y a pas un homme qui ne ferait son possible pour
organiser une coalition, pour restreindre la France
ambitieuse et envahissante.

"Il résulte de tout ceci, que l'Empereur a entre
ses mains les décisions de paix ou de guerre pour
l'Europe.   J'espère qu'il choisira la paix, et si cela
est, nous l'aiderons de tout notre cœur à la main-
tenir.

"Nous savons très-bien que, parmi les masses en
France, il y a mauvais vouloir envers l'Angleterre.
Il n'est pas surprenant que les passions haineuses
de nos guerres aient survécu plus longtemps en
France que chez nous.   Dans notre pays toute la
population est si activement occupée de la vie politique du présent, qu'elle oublie bien vite le passé,
et ne porte ses regards qu'à une petite distance dans
l'avenir.

"Chez vous en France, les masses ne prennent
que peu de part à la vie politique du présent, et par
conséquent elles retiennent beaucoup plus longtemps
les souvenirs du passé, et elles tournent leurs regards
plus activement vers l'avenir.   Mais pour vous dire
franchement la vérité, il nous revient de plusieurs
personnes que les agents du Gouvernement français
ne se montrent pas fâchés de voir ce mauvais vouloir
se propager, s'accroître et se perpétuer.

"Quant à Leeds, j'y vais pour rencontrer des

ouvriers, et pour leur parler ménage et éducation, et non pas pour faire un discours politique.

> " Mille amitiés,
>
> " PALMERSTON."

At the same time he acquaints the English ambassador at Paris with the correspondence that had taken place.

"Broadlands, November 2, 1860.

" MY DEAR COWLEY,

" As you say that Persigny has only sent extracts from my letter, I think it right to send you a full copy of it, which I wish you to show to Thouvenel, because the first part of the letter accounts for my having written at all, and for that which I did write.

" I could not consider Persigny's message, coming as he did straight from Paris, in any other light than as a sort of semi-official communication, and it was necessary for me to answer it civilly but firmly. I believe that I was not wrong in considering the communication as coming from superior authority at Paris, though possibly Persigny, in his zeal, may have added something of his own. He wrote me an answer, in which he pretty well admitted that Borthwick had faithfully rendered the substance of what had been said to him. I purposely omitted to allude to one thing which Persigny had said, which was that if I did not adopt a friendly course towards France, I should be turned out at the beginning of next session by a coalition of Tories and Radicals upon the cry of peace against what they would represent a policy calculated to bring about a war with France. Other things which I have heard satisfy me that Persigny spoke by order and according to orders, and, therefore, the Emperor and his ministers ought not to be hurt or offended at the answer which it was impossible for me not to give. If Persigny had been able to come down here, the dialogue would have been by word of mouth instead of by letter, and it would, therefore, have been less formal. But pray assure the Emperor that my great wish and that of all my colleagues is to maintain the closest relations of friendship and alliance with France, and that it will certainly not be our fault if things should take a different course. But they must know that confidence depends upon facts, and not upon words and things which have happened, and language which has been held for some time past could not fail to inspire distrust as to the future; but that distrust has not been accompanied by the slightest feeling of hostility to France, and is purely and entirely a feeling of a defensive character.

"The Emperor and those about him fancy we are making a coalition to attack France. We should be insane to do so. What would be the object of such an attack, and what possible hopes would any one have of success?

"France is an essential element in the balance of power in Europe, and, I may say, in the world.

All that we want is, that France should be content
with what she is, and should not take up the schemes
and policy of the first Napoleon, which many things
of late lead us to think she has an inclination to do.
Of course if that system were again to be acted upon,
it would be resisted now as it was before, but with
earlier success. The seizure of Savoy and Nice and
the breach of promise towards Switzerland about the
cession to the Swiss of the neutralised district are
matters which cannot be got over easily.

" Yours sincerely,
" Palmerston."

At Leeds he did not make a political speech, but
was there in October to open a mechanics' institute
and to converse familiarly, as he so well could, about
the everyday life of his hearers. When one of the
speakers, in a laboured oration, was enlarging on
every man having his own sphere, and that while the
mechanic would be out of place as Prime Minister, the
Premier would fail as a weaver, Lord Palmerston
quickly replied, amid general laughter, "Oh, my
business is not to weave, but to unravel!"

There was one confederacy of a totally different
kind from any that came across the path of his
official duties which baffled his "unravelling" powers
this year. When the much-coveted "blue riband"
of the turf seemed just within his grasp, his horse
Mainstone—third in the betting—unaccountably
broke down, with strong suspicion of foul play. The

entries in his list of interviews on the morning of Monday, the 21st of May, are striking by their variety :—

"John Day and Professor Spooner about Mainstone: settled he should run on Wednesday.—Shaftesbury about Church appointments.—Powell, to ask about Mainstone.—Sir Robert Peel, ditto.—Bernstorff to read me a despatch.—Sidney Herbert about his evidence to be given to-morrow before committee on army organisation.—Deputation from Manchester against intention of the House of Lords to throw out the repeal of the excise duty on paper."

The Derby day being the next but one, we may be sure that on this morning the trainer and the veterinary were received with even more interest than the Prussian ambassador and the deputation. In spite of the bad report from the stable, Lord Palmerston rode down to Epsom on Wednesday to see Thormanby win and his own horse only come in somewhere about tenth. It was a great disappointment to him. He had never been so near taking the great prize of the turf, and he was convinced that if his horse had been fairly dealt with, it would at any rate have made a good show to the front. Lord Palmerston's connection with the turf extended over a long period, commencing in 1815, with a filly called Mignonette, at Winchester, and only ending with his death. He seldom betted, but raced from innate love of sport and horses. He usually bred his animals himself, and named them after his farms. A visit to his three paddocks at Broadlands made his favourite Sunday afternoon walk. Changing his trainer after this affair, and feeling very much disgusted at the state of the turf, revealed, as he considered, by the treatment of Mainstone, he had no horse of any merit afterwards except Baldwin,* which he disposed of shortly before his death in the manner shown by the following letter :—

"94, Piccadilly, July 31, 1865.

" MY DEAR LORD NAAS,

" I have been obliged to throw my horse Baldwin out of training, in order to prevent his becoming regularly lame.

" I mean to devote the rest of his days to the production of good horses, and, if you like to accept him as a stallion for the Palmerstown breeding stud, I will gladly make him a present to that establishment, on the single condition that if at any time you found that he did not suit, he should be returned to me.

" Baldwin is a chestnut horse, rather more than fifteen hands three inches, and now five years old. He is by Rataplan, out of Austrey by Harkaway, and Austrey's dam was Zeila by Emilius. He is well-bred enough to get running horses, but I think his shape and make, his good action before and behind, his perfectly good temper, and his stoutness

---

* Baldwin was named by Lord Palmerston after Admiral Sir Baldwin Walker. The Admiralty had despatched a fast steamer to fetch Sir Baldwin back after he had sailed from Plymouth, but it could not catch him.

would make him a valuable sire for hunters and riding horses generally.

" If you take him, you should send some trusty person to Broadlands to take him over to Ireland, and the sooner the better.

" Yours sincerely,

" PALMERSTON."

The session of 1860 offered many occasions on which the tact and good humour of the leader of the House of Commons were required. Conspicuous among these was the dispute about the paper duties, which threatened to disturb the mutual relations of Lords and Commons. The Upper House had thrown out, by a large majority, the Bill for the repeal of the excise duty on paper, and, by so doing, they undoubtedly usurped a power which, by the spirit of the Constitution, whatever might be its letter, rested solely with the Lower House. Lord Palmerston was not inclined to allow the misunderstanding to grow into a quarrel. He moved for a committee to inquire into precedents, and, on its report, proposed three resolutions which affirmed that the right of granting aids and supplies is in the Commons alone, and that although the Lords had exercised on some occasions the power of rejecting Bills relating to taxation by negativing the whole, the House viewed such acts with peculiar jealousy, and reserved in their own hands the power so to frame Bills of Supply as to maintain their rights inviolate. He urged these reso-

lutions on the acceptance of the House with great
dexterity and, as it proved, with entire success. His
position was difficult. There was indeed no case for
a resolution at all ; but while he wished to build a
bridge for the retreat of the Lords, he had two colleagues in his Cabinet who were committed far too
deeply by their expressions of wrath at what they
termed an outrageous invasion of the liberties of the
people to permit of their passing the matter over in
silence. So he had, as a wise and moderate coun-
sellor, to vindicate in his speech the rights of the
Commons while sparing the susceptibilities of the
Lords. The resolutions were adopted, the question
rested for the remainder of this session, and the Bill
passed the Upper House in the next.

Another matter of smaller moment served to
illustrate his happy art of putting things. Mr.
Horsman had raised a discussion which involved
allusions to the connection between the Government and the press, and insinuated that the social
influences of Cambridge House · helped to sway the
political leanings of one of the chief organs of
public opinion. Lord Palmerston answered him as
follows :—

"My right honourable friend has stated that he did
not know what the influence was which drew one of the
editors or managers of the 'Times,' to me; and if by that
statement he means to imply a wish on my part to exercise
any influence over the line of conduct which is pursued in
the case of that journal, I can only say in answer to that
charge, in the words of Mrs. Malaprop, that I should be but

too glad to plead guilty to the soft impeachment, and to know that the insinuation which it involves was really founded on fact. If there are influences which, as the right honourable gentleman says, have fortunately led Mr. Delane to me, they are none other than the influences of society. My right honourable friend has observed, in that glowing address which he has just delivered, that the contributors to the press are the favourites and the ornaments of the social circles into which they enter. In that opinion he is, it seems to me, perfectly correct. The gentlemen to whom he refers are, generally speaking, persons of great attainments and information. It is, then, but natural that their society should be agreeable. My acquaintance with Mr. Delane is exactly of that character. I have had the pleasure of meeting him frequently in society, and he has occasionally done me the honour to join in society under my roof; that society was, I may add, composed of persons of all shades of politics and of various pursuits. I need hardly say I feel proud when persons so honour me without undertaking any other engagement than that which Mr. Delane always makes good—of making themselves agreeable during the time of their stay."

A tribute paid by the Lord Chancellor to Lord Palmerston's conduct of public affairs during this session is so forcible and compendious that I here insert it. Lord Westbury writes to him in the month of August: "I cannot close this note without expressing to you, with the most unfeigned sincerity, my admiration of your masterly leadership during this most difficult session. Great knowledge, great judgment, great temper and forbearance, infinite skill and tact, matchless courtesy, and great oratorical talent, rising with each important occasion, have in a most eminent degree marked your conduct of the

Government and your leadership of the House of Commons. Those who know the secrets of the Cabinet must feel that none but you could have kept it together. But what I esteem most is that happy quality you possess by which, whilst you receive the admiration, you at the same time win the affection of all around you."

We must remember that during all these years the Liberal party had only a small nominal majority of twenty in the House of Commons, and that the Cabinet, containing statesmen of marked individual importance, contained also strong elements of divergence. Lord Westbury was right in thinking that none but a minister possessing peculiar talent for reconciling, cementing, and commanding diverse idiosyncrasies could have overcome such obvious difficulties.

CHAPTER VIII.

State of Parties—Lord Wardenship of the Cinque Ports—Civil
War in America—Cotton Supply—Turkish Finances—Visit to
Harrow—Father Daly—Death of Prince Consort — 'Trent'
Affair—National Expenditure—Church Patronage.

POLITICAL parties were in a singular jumble at the
period which we have now reached. The Conservatives, alarmed at the "advanced" tendencies of the
Chancellor of the Exchequer, promised to refrain
from all attempts to turn out the Liberal Premier, if
only he would resist "democratic" budgets, and keep
his hands from any violent action against Austria.
Needless to say that Lord Palmerston was too loyal
to enter into any such secret understanding. The
Radicals, on the other hand, hopeless of any effective
pressure on their part, and impatient of the laggard
steps of the Whig Cabinet, offered to help the Tories
to turn out the existing Government, and to give the
administration which would succeed a two years'
lease of power. They anticipated that by that time
the country would be ready for such a Government
and such a Reform Bill as they would themselves
desire. Needless to say that the Conservatives were

not so shortsighted as to accept such an alliance.
The upshot was that Lord Palmerston, although
with a small nominal majority, continued to hold
an unassailable position both in the House and the
country.

The very ancient and dignified office of Lord
Warden of the Cinque Ports becoming vacant by the
death of Lord Dalhousie in the spring of 1861, the
dignity was conferred by Her Majesty upon Lord
Palmerston. It was at first intended that the post
should not be filled up; but, on representations being
made of the historical traditions which attached to it,
and of the long line of illustrious men who had filled
it, including during this century both Pitt and Wellington, the Premier rightly considered that, unless
for some good reason, a link with the past so interesting in its character should not be lightly broken.
The ancient residence of Walmer Castle still remained to the Lord Warden, although his emoluments, save a few droits of Admiralty, had disap-
peared. Lord Palmerston's installation took place at
Dover with pomp and circumstance. Under the anti-
quarian care of the town-clerk all the old traditions
had been unearthed and rusty ceremonies refur-
bished, and the new Lord Warden was conducted to
the Bredenstone with due solemnity to take the
oaths of office at a grand Court of Shepway. Lord
Palmerston entered into the thing with proper
spirit, and made an appropriate speech at the in-
augural banquet, in which reminiscences of the past

mingled with exhortations to the practice of modern patriotism.

But another penalty attached to the acceptance of the Lord Wardenship. It was a "place of profit" (though of small profit) "under the Crown." So during the Easter recess he had to vacate his seat in Parliament, and was compelled to enjoy what the newspapers of the day called his "favourite relaxation, when he had nothing else particular to do "— namely, the being returned for Tiverton. Of course the redoubtable Rowcliffe was on the watch, and from an open window near the hustings upbraided the Premier for his lukewarmness about reform. "You come to Tiverton to gull the people, but you don't gull me. I have given the Whigs a long trial, but now I throw them over. Go back to Downing Street, and bring in an honest Reform Bill, and let us have no more double shuffle." At the sound of the well-known accents Lord Palmerston came up smiling to the front, and, amid the cheers and laughter of the crowd, turned his tormentor inside out, and then went down and shook hands with him. This Tiverton butcher was a vulgar specimen, eager for notoriety; yet the spectacle of a Prime minister, at the height of his power and popularity, giving himself as much pains to answer these taunts as if they had come from the Leader of the Opposition had its moral. In some countries the man would have been ejected, or at least hustled; but in England his rights as an elector were recognised both by the mob and the minister.

The great event of this year was, undoubtedly, the outbreak of the civil war in America. The English Government, though it recognised the Southerners as belligerents, proclaimed its neutrality ; and the sentiments which inspired the Cabinet may be gathered from the tone of the following short note, which I insert as contradicting the generally received impression of Lord Palmerston's hostility to the American Republic. It is quite true that he entertained a feeling of contempt, and even of dislike, for many of the men who from time to time occupied public positions in connection with the United States Government. He thought them deficient in honesty and offensive in tone—in short, not "gentlemen," in the sense which is independent of birth and depends solely upon character; but for the American people, apart from its politicians, he had that admiration and regard which his truly English nature would necessarily feel for a free and kindred nation. To his correspondent who had been urging proposals for our mediation he writes :—

"94, Piccadilly, May 5, 1861.

" My dear Ellice,*

" The day on which we could succeed in putting an end to this unnatural war between the two sections of our North American cousins would be one of the happiest of our lives, and all that is wanting to induce us to take steps for that purpose is a belief that any such steps would lead towards the accom-

---

* Right Hon. Edward Ellice, M.P.

plishment of that purpose, and would not do more harm than good. The danger is that, in the excited state of men's minds in America, the offer of any one to interpose to arrest their action, and disappoint them of their expected triumph, might be resented by both sides; and that jealousy of European, especially of English, interference in their internal affairs might make them still more prone to reject our offer as impertinent.

" There would, moreover, be great difficulty in suggesting any basis of arrangement to which both parties could agree, and which it would not be repugnant to English feelings and principles to propose. *We* could not well mix ourselves up with the acknowledgment of slavery and the principle that a slave escaping to a free soil State should be followed, claimed, and recovered, like a horse or an ox. We might possibly propose that the North and South should separate amicably; that they should make some boundary line, to be agreed upon, the line of separation between them; and that each confederation should be free to make for its own internal affairs and concerns such laws as it might think fit—the two confederations entering, however, into certain mutual arrangements as to trade and commerce with each other.

" Do you think the time is come for any arrangement of such a kind? or is it not in the nature of things and in human nature that the wiry edge must be taken off this craving appetite for conflict in arms before any real and widespread desire for peace by mutual concession can be looked for ?

" Yours sincerely,

" PALMERSTON."

For those who looked ahead the civil war threatened an early blow to English interests in the shape of the loss of our cotton supply. Lord Palmerston writes to the President of the Board of Trade, to see if he could provide in any manner for the expected deficiency :—

" 94, Piccadilly, June 7, 1861.

" MY DEAR MILNER GIBSON,

"It is wise when the weather is fine to put one's house in wind and water-tight condition against the time when foul weather may come on. The reports from our manufacturing districts are at present good ; the mills are all working, and the people are in full employment. But we must expect a change towards the end of next autumn, and during the winter and the spring of next year. The civil war in America must infallibly diminish to a great degree our supply of cotton, unless, indeed, England and France should, as suggested by M. Mercier, the French minister at Washington, compel the Northern States to let the cotton come to Europe from the South ; but this would almost be tantamount to a war with the North, although not perhaps a very formidable thing for England and France combined. But even then this year's crop must be less plentiful than

that of last year. Well, then, has the Board of Trade,
or has any other department of the Government any
means of procuring or of helping to procure any-
where in the wide world a subsidiary supply of
cotton? As to our manufacturers themselves, they
will do nothing unless directed and pushed on. They
are some of the most helpless and shortsighted of
men. They are like the people who held out their
dishes and prayed that it might rain plum-puddings.
They think it is enough to open their mill-gates, and
that cotton will come of its own accord. They say
they have for years been looking to India as a source
of supply; but their looks seem to have had only the
first effect of the eyes of the rattlesnake, viz., to para-
lyse the objects looked at, and as yet it has shown no
signs of falling into their jaws. The western coast
of Africa, the eastern coast of Africa, India, Australia,
the Fiji Islands, Syria, and Egypt, all grow great
quantities of cotton, not to mention China, and probably Japan. If active measures were taken in time
to draw from these places such quantities of cotton
as might be procured, some portion at least of the
probable falling off of this next year might be made
good, and our demand this year would make a better
supply spring up for future years. I do not know
whether you can do anything in this matter;
but it is an important one, and deserves early attention.

" Yours sincerely,

" PALMERSTON."

With his care for the preservation of the rights of
the Ottoman Porte, Lord Palmerston had, of course,
never ceased to keep a watchful eye on the proceedings of the French in Syria.   He now writes to the
British ambassador at Constantinople, and bases on
the success of his endeavours in that quarter an
exhortation to the new Sultan to abandon the
architects and builders of Abdul Mejid for nobler
agents and objects more worthy of an enlightened
ruler.   The years which have since elapsed have
sufficiently shown how vain were the hopes of any
such change.

" 94, Piccadilly, June 26, 1861.

" My dear Bulwer,

          " I am heartily glad we have got the French
out of Syria, and a hard job it was to do so.   The
arrangement made for the future government of the
Lebanon will, I dare say, work sufficiently well to
prevent the French from having any pretext for returning thither.   But the death of the late Sultan
and the accession of the present one are the great
and important events of the day, as bearing upon
Eastern affairs.   Abdul Mejid was a good-hearted
and weak-headed man who was running two horses
to the goal of perdition—his own life, and that of his
empire.   Luckily for the empire, his own life won the
race.   If the accounts we have heard of the new Sultan
are true, we may hope that he will restore Turkey to
its proper position among the Powers of Europe.   If
he will continue the system of Liberal toleration and

progressive internal improvement established by his predecessor on paper, and in some cases and places carried into execution, and if he will apply to his empire the well-regulated economy with which he is said to have managed his own private affairs, he may be able to rescue his country from the downfall with which it has lately seemed to be threatened.

" You will, of course, encourage him to follow such a course, and the present Grand Vizier will be a useful instrument for such a policy. But the Sultan must begin by clearing out the Harem, dismissing his architects and builders, and turning off his robber ministers. The natural resources of the empire, intellectual, physical, and material, are great; and, if properly brought out and turned to account, would render Turkey a powerful and important state.

" Yours sincerely,

" PALMERSTON."

Lord Palmerston always entertained a great affection for Harrow, the place of his early education. Many a time did he ride down in the course of his life to revisit the old scenes, and this year he was present at an interesting ceremony, for he undertook to lay the foundation stone of the School Library, erected in honour of Dr. Vaughan, who had recently retired from the head-mastership. In spite of the pouring rain he went down on horseback, and was received by the assembled boys with great enthusiasm. He reminded them, in his speech, that the strength of a nation consists not so much in the number of the people as in the character of the men ; and then, turning the rain to account, went on :—

" We ought to pay due respect to those who form the character of the rising generation; who instruct them that self-control is better than indulgence; who tell them that labour is to be preferred to pleasure ; and that whereas mere amusements may be compared to the southern breezes, which, though pleasant to be enjoyed, yet pass away and leave no trace behind them, honourable exertion, on the contrary, may be compared to the fertilizing shower which, though it may, as you all know at the present moment, not be agreeable to those who are exposed to it (laughter), yet nevertheless leaves, by enriching and improving the soil on which it falls, solid marks behind it by the ample and abundant harvest which it helps to create. I must, as a Harrow man, be permitted to say that Harrow has held its place in public estimation and public service by furnishing men distinguished the most in all the careers which they may have chosen for their future life. We have named the most distinguished in arms. We are proud of one name—a poet, Lord Byron— who here imbibed the first elements of that classical attainment which afterwards led to his high fame. We may boast —I speak now as a Harrow boy—that in the present century four Harrow boys* have attained the post which I now have the honour to hold, and I trust that there are many other four Harrow boys who are destined to become distinguished men like those to whom I allude."

After this he rode back in the rain to pass the rest of the day and night on the Treasury bench ;

* Goderich, Peel, Aberdeen, Palmerston.

being at the time close upon seventy-seven years of age.

The manner in which from his place on that bench he, this session, countermined the workings of an unscrupulous intriguer deserves notice as illustrative of his readiness of resource and knowledge of human nature. The Government had announced the withdrawal of a grant given by the Derby administration towards the maintenance of a mail-packet service between the port of Galway and the United States. Great indignation was excited by this withdrawal in those parts of Ireland which had expected to profit by the scheme; and a certain Father Daly, armed with credentials from influential quarters, came over to England, with the avowed design, by means of the Irish vote, to put the Government in a minority should it refuse to give way. He had an interview with Lord Palmerston, and threatened him with this party defection on the forthcoming Budget. Lord Palmerston merely replied, that he should go straight down to the House of Commons and relate exactly what had just passed between them. He did so in a manner both frank and amusing, and with such effect, that the Irish Liberals, even had they secretly nursed any thoughts of playing traitor to their party for the sake of local emoluments, became ashamed to appear as dancing to the wire-pulling of an Irish priest, and the Budget was saved.

Some of Lord Palmerston's views about contemporary Italian and American affairs are given in the following letter :—

"Broadlands, October 18, 1861.

" MY DEAR RUSSELL,

"Your letter of yesterday furnishes, as you say, ample food for reflection, and treats of matters of the highest importance and beset with great difficulties. Any opinion given upon your lucubrations must therefore be taken with grains of allowance and be deemed liable to reconsideration.

" First, as to Rome, I believe you are right in not instructing Cowley to make, at present at least, any suggestion to the Emperor as to a final arrangement of the question about the Pope. We could not suggest any arrangement which was not founded on the basis that Rome and its whole territory should be evacuated by the French; that the Pope should have no temporal dominion over any part of the people of Italy, and that the city of Rome should be the capital of the Italian kingdom. But the first of these conditions would at once stop the discussion of the other two. Notwithstanding the affected regret of the Emperor at having been led to occupy Rome, it is, I think, pretty clear that he clings to the occupation of that central part of Italy, as affording him great military and political advantage which he is fully determined not at present to give up. He is ready there with his army of twenty-five thousand men, capable of being increased to any amount, either to take advantage of any successful disturbance in the Neapolitan territory, or to turn the flank of the Austrians in Venetia, or to pass over to Dalmatia, whenever it may suit him to quarrel with Austria —and he may very possibly do so next spring. But at all events his occupation of Rome, and the protection which he thus affords to Antonelli, the Pope, and King Francis in their intrigues, retards the consolidation of the unity of Italy and holds out to him a still glimmering ray of hope that he may succeed in his own scheme of an Italian confederation instead of an united kingdom. The course of events will settle the Papal question. Peter's pence will at last begin to fail; and if the Pope will only put forth a few more allocutions, even good Catholics will become reconciled to the cessation of his temporal power. I think you are right in believing that the Emperor will turn Austria out of Venetia before he turns himself out of Rome; and there can be little doubt that he remains in Rome for the purpose of being more easily able to turn Austria out of Venetia.

" The arrangement you suggest by which Turkey would sell Herzegovina to Italy, and Italy would give it to Austria in exchange for Venetia, would be a very good one, but it would be hard to accomplish. Turkey would not easily be persuaded to sell Herzegovina, and Austria would not be more disposed to take that province in exchange for Venetia, to which she foolishly attaches great military importance. I suspect that Austria will not give up Venetia till compelled to do so for nothing by defeat in war. It might be worth considering whether parties concerned might be sounded about some such plan—Turkey first, because the first cession would be made by her.

"As to North America, our best and true policy seems to be to go on as we have begun, and to keep quite clear of the conflict between North and South. It is true, as you say, that there have been cases in Europe in which allied Powers have said to fighting parties, like the man in the 'Critic,' 'In the Queen's name I bid you to drop your swords;' but those cases are rare and peculiar. The love of quarrelling and fighting is inherent in man, and to prevent its indulgence is to impose restraints on natural liberty. A state may so shackle its own subjects; but it is an infringement on national independence to restrain other nations. The only excuse would be the danger to the interfering parties if the conflict went on ; but in the American case this cannot be pleaded by the Powers of Europe.

"I quite agree with you that the want of cotton would not justify such a proceeding, unless, indeed, the distress created by that want was far more serious than it is likely to be. The probability is that some cotton will find its way to us from America, and that we shall get a greater supply than usual from other quarters.

"The only thing to do seems to be to lie on our oars and to give no pretext to the Washingtonians

to quarrel with us, while, on the other hand, we
maintain our rights and those of our fellow-countrymen.

> " Yours sincerely,
> " PALMERSTON."

Towards the end of the year 1861 two events,
very different in their nature, but alike sudden
and startling, highly excited the public mind. I
refer to the illness and death of the Prince Consort
and the seizure of the Confederate envoys on board
the British mail-steamer 'Trent,' which brought us
to the verge of a war with the United States. During
the simultaneous interval of suspense, Lord Palmerston
was laid up with an attack of gout, the worst of his
whole life. No doubt his symptoms were aggravated
by the anxieties of the moment ; and I remember that
both his hands and both his feet were completely
crippled, and that he was unable for a fortnight even
to open a letter for himself. Yet he never abandoned his post. Daily communications with the
physicians in attendance at Windsor, urging, perhaps
with unnecessary precaution, the summoning of additional advice, daily communications and interviews
with those charged with the duties of negotiation or
of preparation for war, showed that the spirit was
not daunted by the pain and prostration of body.
He felt the death of the Prince Consort most acutely,
and looked upon it as an irreparable loss. As to the
dispute with America, he regarded the despatch of

the Guards and other troops to Canada before the arrival of a reply to our demand for a surrender of the captives as the best means of averting war, and so it proved. Although by certain organs of the peace party it was denounced as an irritating measure, it was no such thing, but the one way of showing, without offence to the United States Cabinet, that England was in earnest. It was only by extraordinary exertions that the troop-ships were enabled to reach the St. Lawrence before the river navigation was closed by ice.

During these years there was constant friction at work between the two wings of the Liberal party about the national expenditure; both parties apparently agreeing as to the ends to be attained, but differing as to the necessary means. In 1862 Mr. Stansfeld, as spokesman of the one section, moved a resolution in the House that the national expenditure was capable of reduction without compromising the safety or the legitimate influence of the country. Lord Palmerston met this by a counter-resolution, by which the House, acknowledging the obligations of economy, declined to bind themselves to any declaration beyond a trust that such further reductions might be made as the future state of things might warrant. An amendment of Mr. Walpole's Lord Palmerston checkmated by treating it as a vote of want of confidence. The two following letters refer to this question of outlay on the army and navy, and to his disinclination to rest upon shifts and chances when the position of England was concerned :—

"94, Piccadilly, January 8, 1862.

" MY DEAR MR. COBDEN,

" I have many apologies to make to you for not having sooner acknowledged the memorandum* which you sent me some time ago suggesting an understanding and agreement between the Governments of England and France about the number of ships of war which each of the two countries should maintain. It would be very delightful if your Utopia could be realized, and if the nations of the earth would think of nothing but peace and commerce, and would give up quarrelling and fighting altogether. But unfortunately man is a fighting and quarrelling animal; and that this is human nature is proved by the fact that republics, where the masses govern, are far more quarrelsome, and more addicted to fighting, than monarchies, which are governed by comparatively few persons. But so long as other nations are animated by these human passions, a country like England, wealthy and exposed to attack, must by necessity be provided with the means of defence, and however expensive these means may be, they are infinitely cheaper than the war which they tend to keep off.

" Yours sincerely,

" PALMERSTON."

---

* See Appendix V.

"94, Piccadilly, April 29, 1862.

" My dear Gladstone,

"I read with much interest, as I came up yester-day by the railway, your able and eloquent speeches at Manchester; but I wish to submit to you some observations upon the financial part of the second speech. You seem in that speech to make it a re-proach to the nation at large that it has forced, as you say it has, on the Parliament and the Govern-ment the high amount of expenditure which we have at present to provide for. Now I do not quite agree with you as to the fact; but admitting it to be as you state, it seems to me to be rather a proof of the superior sagacity of the nation than a subject for reproach.

" The main sources of increased expenditure have been army, navy, and education. As to education, the increase has arisen from the working of a self-acting system. We may not have had the full value of our money, but we have derived great advantage from the outlay.

" Now as to the augmentation of our military and naval means of defence, I cannot give to the nation, as contradistinguished from Parliament and Govern-ment, the exclusive merit of having demanded them. It appears to me that the merit, as I call it, is equally to be shared by the nation, Parliament, and Govern-ment. Successive Governments have taken the lead by proposing to Parliaments such estimates as, acting upon their responsibility, they thought needful for the public service; successive Parliaments have sanctioned those estimates, and the nation has ratified those acts by their approval. It is, therefore, a mistake to say that this scale of expenditure has been forced upon Parliament or upon the Government ; and it is a still greater mistake to accuse the nation, as Cobden does, of having rushed headlong into extravagance under the impulse of panic. Panic there has been none on the part of anybody. There was for a long time an apathetic blindness on the part of the governed and the governors as to the defensive means of the country compared with the offensive means acquired and acquiring by other Powers. The country at last awoke from its lethargy, not indeed to rush into extravagance and uncalled-for exertions, but to make up gradually for former omissions, and so far, no doubt, to throw upon a shorter period of time expenses which earlier foresight might have spread over a greater length of time. The Government, the Parliament, and the nation acted in harmonious concert ; and if any proof were wanting that the nation has been inspired by a deliberate and sagacious appreciation of its position with respect to other Powers, that proof has been afforded by the long-continued and well-sustained sacrifices of time and money which have been made by the 160,000 Volunteers, and by those who have contributed to supply them with requisite funds.

"But have the Government, or rather have both Liberal and Conservative Governments, have the Parliament and the nation been wrong, and have Bright and Cobden been right? I venture to think that the Government, the Parliament, and the nation have taken the juster view of what the state of things required.

"We have on the other side of the Channel a people who, say what they may, hate us as a nation from the bottom of their hearts, and would make any sacrifice to inflict a deep humiliation upon . England.

"It is natural that this should be. They are eminently vain, and their passion is glory in war. They cannot forget or forgive Aboukir, Trafalgar, the Peninsula, Waterloo, and St. Helena.

"Increased commercial intercourse may add to the links of mutual interest between us and them; but commercial interest is a link that snaps under the pressure of national passions. Witness the bitter enmity to England lately freely vented, and now with difficulty suppressed, by those Northern States of America with whom we have had a most extensive commercial intercourse. Well, then, at the head of this neighbouring nation, who would like nothing so well as a retaliatory blow upon England, we see an able, active, wary, counsel-keeping, but ever planning sovereign; and we see this sovereign organising an army which, including his reserve, is more than six times greater in amount than the whole of our regular forces in our two islands, and at the same time labouring hard to create a navy equal to, if not superior to ours. Give him a cause of quarrel, which any foreign Power may at any time invent or create, if so minded ; give him the command of the Channel, which permanent or accidental naval superiority might afford him, and then calculate if you can— for it would pass my reckoning power to do so—the disastrous consequences to the British nation which a landing of an army of from one to two hundred thousand men would bring with it. Surely even a large yearly expenditure for army and navy is an economical insurance against such a catastrophe.

" Yours sincerely,
" PALMERSTON."

To the argument that, ample financial means being necessary for national defence, we should devote our principal attention during peace to the husbanding of our resources, he used to reply, that if a war should suddenly come, as it might have come, with France about Tahiti, or with America about the ' Trent,' the want of ships, troops, guns, and dock-yard defences would be ill made up for by the fact that some hundreds of merchants and manufacturers had made large fortunes; for that this " would only be offering to the butcher a well-fatted calf instead of a well-armed bull's head." When it was urged that our measures of preparation made the French angry, he answered that it was so only because these preparations rendered us secure against the effects of

French anger. "The anger of a Power no stronger than ourselves may be borne, with regret no doubt, but without alarm. The anger of a Power greatly and decidedly stronger must cause apprehension, and is likely to lead to humiliation or disaster."

He was also very watchful at this time for the security of our Canadian frontier, in presence of the strife in the United States, and insisted on an increase to our regular force in Canada, in order, by so doing, to "keep the United States Government in check, to give spirit and confidence to our own people in the provinces, and to take the best chance for the continuance of peace.*

The Church patronage which Lord Palmerston administered during his two premierships was so large, that the principle on which he declared himself to act, and on which, indeed, he consistently did act, is worth reading in his own words. I can certainly of my own knowledge assert, that the one way in which a clergyman could make it certain that he would not get preferment was to commence his letter of application by a statement of his political opinions, thus making them a ground of claim. Lord Palmerston writes to Lord Carlisle, then Lord-Lieutenant of Ireland† :—"I have never considered ecclesiastical appointments as patronage to be given away for grace and favour, or for personal or political objects. The choice to be made of persons to fill

---

* To Duke of Newcastle, September 1, 1861.
† Walmer Castle, August 17, 1862.

dignities in the Church must have a great influence on many important matters ; and I have always endeavoured, in making such appointments, to choose the best man I could find, without any regard to the wishes of those who may have recommended candidates for choice. I hope, therefore, you will see that, if I have not on this occasion adopted your advice, it has not arisen from any want of consideration for you either in your personal or your official condition."

I conclude this chapter with a short but suggestive note about Slavery and the Board of Admiralty :—

"August 13, 1862.

" MY DEAR RUSSELL,

" No First Lord and no Board of Admiralty have ever felt any interest in the suppression of the slave trade, or taken of their own free will any steps towards its accomplishment, and whatever they have done in compliance with the wishes of others they have done grudgingly and imperfectly. If there was a particularly old, slow-going tub in the navy, she was sure to be sent to the coast of Africa to try to catch the fast-sailing American clippers ; and if there was an officer notoriously addicted to drinking, he was sent to a station where rum is a deadly poison.

" Things go on better now ; but still there is at the Admiralty an invincible aversion to the measures necessary for putting down the slave trade. These prejudices are so strong with the naval officers of the

Board, that the First Lord can hardly be expected
not to be swayed by them.

" Yours sincerely,

" PALMERSTON."

For nothing will Lord Palmerston be more honourably remembered than for his long and successful
efforts for the suppression of the slave trade and the
discouragement of slavery. From the moment that he
was called to the Foreign Office in 1830, he entered
warmly into the subject, and with his whole heart
laboured for their extinction. He sought to engage
all maritime states in one great network of treaties
for the combined annihilation of this nefarious traffic
in human beings, and to a large extent he succeeded.
Some of the Spanish and other diplomatists used to
be quite surprised at what they thought his craze,
and were fain to humour him on, what they considered, so insignificant a matter. When action succeeded to negotiation—as, for instance, in the decisive
blow dealt in 1840 at the Portuguese slave dealers
by the destruction of their barracoons on the West
Coast of Africa—he never allowed any consideration
for the susceptibilities or anger of foreign Governments to induce him to halt in his course. On the
contrary, when the country, sick with deferred hopes
and aghast at the expense of the necessary squadrons,
seemed, at one moment, disposed to flinch, his earnest
language, conveying lofty aspirations, maintained its
spirit and strengthened it for renewed efforts.

CHAPTER IX.

As Premier, Lord Palmerston kept a watchful eye
over the proceedings of all the departments of his
Government, and was an unwearied attendant on the
sittings of the House of Commons, ready at any
moment to smooth a difficulty or avert a storm.
But he was very chary of speech; and when there
was nothing particular to say he did not attempt to
say it. The session of 1863 was entirely deficient
of any subject of debate, domestic or foreign, which
could call for any lengthened interposition on his
part, with the exception of the question of Poland;
and while this was being discussed he was kept away
by an attack of his old enemy the gout.

The immediate cause of the Polish outbreak was a
seizure by the Russian Government of all the young
men in the cities whom they had reason to believe
were disaffected, and their enrolment in the ranks of
the army under the name of a conscription, or " partial

recruiting." In fact, to use the words of our ambassador at Petersburg, it was " a simple plan, by a clean sweep of the revolutionary youth of Poland, to kidnap the opposition and to carry it off to Siberia or the Caucasus." No wonder that this produced resistance. Those who escaped took to the woods and organized themselves in armed bands.

Lord Palmerston writes to " condole" with the Russian ambassador :—

" 4 février 1863.

" MON CHER BRUNNOW,

" Je regrette beaucoup les insurrections qui ont éclaté en Pologne et en plusieurs des provinces de la Russie, parce que ces mouvements produiront de grands malheurs dans le pays, et parce que beaucoup d'hommes qui devraient se rendre utiles à leur patrie payeront de leur sang, ou par l'exil, la révolte dont ils ont été coupables.

" Mais, quant au Gouvernement russe, je considère ces insurrections comme une juste punition du Ciel, pour les menées dont ce Gouvernement a été coupable, pour préparer pour le printemps des révoltes et des insurrections dans la Moldo-Wallachie, en Servie et en Bosnie, contre le Sultan.

. . . . . . " ' Non lex est justior ulla,
Quam necis artifices arte perire sua.'

" Il est vrai que ces insurrections, ou éclatées, ou préparées, ne menacent de mort ni l'Empire russe ni l'Empire ottoman ; la Russie saura mettre ordre dans les provinces et la Porte saura apprendre à Couza, au Prince de Servie et aux Bosniacs, qu'il est mieux de rester fidèle à son Souverain que d'écouter les conseils subversifs d'un voisin ambitieux.

" Mais, pour le moment, la Russie souffre dans son intérieur le mal qu'elle a l'intention d'infliger à un voisin inoffensif. Vous concevez bien que je parle maintenant des cent mille et plus de fusils que le Gouvernement russe a envoyés en Servie et en Bosnie par des chemins détournés, et avec toutes les précautions pour cacher, autant que possible, ce que l'on faisait, et je fais allusion aussi à cette nuée d'agents provocateurs qui, venant de la Russie, abondent et travaillent dans les provinces Européennes de la Turquie. Si le Prince Gortschakoff était ami autant à moi comme vous l'êtes, je me serais adressé à lui au lieu de vous écrire, mais j'aimerais beaucoup qu'il sût l'impression que sa politique a faite sur nous.

" Mille amitiés,

" PALMERSTON."

General disgust had been excited throughout Europe by the Prussian Government having entered into a convention with Russia whereby the troops of either were authorized to cross the frontier, and pursue the Polish insurgents into the territory of the other. The following extract from a letter to the King of the Belgians shows that, however much Lord Palmerston disapproved of this active assistance being given by Prussia to one of the two contending parties, he was not going in consequence to allow England to become the cat's-paw of an ambitious neighbour :—*

" Your Majesty will have learnt that we declined to fall into the trap which the Emperor of the French laid for us by his scheme for a violent identical note to be presented to the Government of Prussia.

" It was evidently intended that the demands of such a note being refused, or evaded, a pretence would thereby have been afforded to France for an occupation of the Prussian Rhenish provinces, and the French Government have shown much ill-humour at the failure of that scheme. But the danger to Prussia and to other States is not over. If the Polish Revolution goes on, and Prussia is led to take an active part in any way against the Poles, the Emperor of the French is sure, sooner or later, and upon some pretext or other, to enter the Rhenish provinces as a means of coercing Prussia to be neutral. Your Majesty would render an essential service to Prussia and to Europe if you could exert your influence with the King of Prussia to abstain from any action of any kind whatever beyond the frontiers of his own territory."

During the ensuing months the British and Russian Governments were engaged in a long correspondence. Lord Russell proposed a suspension of arms, and a conference of the eight Powers to settle the affairs of Poland, on the basis of national repre-

* To the King of the Belgians, March 13, 1863.

sentation, liberty of conscience, establishment of a legal system of recruiting, and Polish administration of the country. The communications which were exchanged were couched in friendly, though very frank terms, but they yielded no visible fruit, Russia declining to accede to the English proposals. The feeling, however, which the reports of Russian misdeeds in Poland, whether exaggerated or not, had excited in the public mind, compelled the organ of the British Government to put on record such observations as he considered himself entitled to make, England having been a party to the Treaty of Vienna whereby Poland was secured to Russia.

In the spring of this year Lord Palmerston went to Scotland to deliver an address on being installed as Lord Rector of the University of Glasgow. He also visited Edinburgh, where he received the freedom of the city and an honorary degree at the University. He was received everywhere with marked enthusiasm. As he went down the Clyde in a small steamer to Greenock, both banks of the river were lined with thousands of workmen, who had left their work to catch a glimpse of the Premier on the paddlebox, and to cheer him as he passed. The captain of the guard-ship, anxious to do honour to the occasion, was hindered by the fact that a Prime Minister was not recognised in the code of naval salutes; but he found an escape from his dilemma in the discovery that Lord Palmerston was not only First Lord of the Treasury, but also Lord Warden of the Cinque Ports, for which great officer a salute of nineteen guns was prescribed—an apt instance of the minor anomalies of the Constitution under which we live.

Before the end of the Glasgow visit an incident occurred which illustrates the fun and simplicity that characterised Lord Palmerston to the end of his life. A number of gentlemen had confederated themselves together under the title of the "Gaiter" Club, with power to add to their number. This club had no local habitation, but only a name. Its objects, beyond a mild pedestrianism, were left undefined, but embraced all that could be comprised under the mysterious, yet far-reaching head of "gaiterdom." This body was about to entertain at a breakfast one of their number on his return from China, namely, that distinguished officer Admiral Sir James Hope, and they determined to profit by the opportunity to invite Lord Palmerston to become a "Gaiter." He entered with becoming zest into the Scotch humour of the thing, and in acknowledging the honour conferred upon him spoke without rising (every Gaiter being bound to speak sitting), and with appropriate brevity, " that whether the gaiters which the members wore were long or short, of which he was ignorant, of this he was quite sure, that his memory of that day would be as long as they could possibly desire." It had devolved upon Dr. Norman M'Leod, one of the Queen's chaplains, and also chaplain to the club, to propose that the new member should be received. Those who remember his rich vein of humour,

and the solemn fun which he kept ready for appropriate occasions, can picture for themselves the manner
in which he spoke as follows: That he had been
lately staying at Balmoral; that he had taken the
opportunity of informing Her Majesty that it was
contemplated by the gentlemen he now had the
honour of addressing to make Lord Palmerston a
" Gaiter;" and that it was only due to Her Majesty
that, before so grave a step was taken, she should
be asked for Her gracious permission.   That Her
Majesty had, after much consideration, replied, that
although, no doubt, it was a dangerous thing for any
subject to be both Prime Minister and a " Gaiter,"
still, considering Lord Palmerston's great services,
and, above all, his age and experience, which would
preserve him from any abuse of the power conferred
upon him, she would, in his favour, waive her objections.   The party had broken up laughing, when it
was discovered that a ' Times' reporter had been
present the whole time, and it was feared that he
might, perhaps, be a Scotchman who had neither
undergone operation by a surgeon, nor milder treatment by a " Gaiter," in order to admit the joke.
Dr. M'Leod had really just come from Balmoral, and
in panic terror lest all he had said might appear in
the next day's ' Times,' he rushed from the room,
called a cab, and hurried to the railway in time to
catch the reporter before his parcel left.   No doubt
the precaution was unnecessary, but the witty chaplain's agony of mind was none the less diverting.

At Edinburgh Lord Palmerston climbed to the top of Arthur's Seat, and wrote to his brother-in-law that he really felt very little more difficulty in so doing than when he used to mount it daily sixty years before. The past was also recalled to him by a visit which he paid to an old woman named Peggie Forbes, who had been servant at Dugald Stewart's when he was studying there in 1801. She produced an old box of tools, which she had preserved all these years because it had been the property of " young Maister Henry."

The French Emperor now sent letters to the different sovereigns of Europe, proposing the assembling of a Congress, and suggesting Paris as the place of meeting. "It is on the Treaty of Vienna," he said, " that now reposes the political edifice of Europe, and yet it is crumbling away on all sides." The British Government declined the invitation. Some of Lord Palmerston's remarks upon it are contained in the following letter :—

" 94, Piccadilly, November 15, 1863.

" SIRE,

"The subject to which Your Majesty's letter relates is one of very great importance and deserving of mature consideration. Our answer to the Emperor's proposal has been, in substance, that we do not admit that the Treaties of Vienna have ceased to be in force, inasmuch as, on the contrary, they are still the basis of the existing arrangements of Europe;

that, with regard to the proposed Congress, before we can come to any decision about it, we should like to know what subjects it is to discuss, and what power it is to possess to give effect to its decisions.

" To this inquiry Drouyn has replied that he can give no answer till he has seen the Emperor, and that he cannot do so till the 17th, when he is invited to go to Compiègne. This does not show much empressement about the Conference. Drouyn, however, intimated that the Emperor would probably say that to specify the subjects for discussion would be to anticipate the decisions of the Congress, which, if assembled, would determine for itself what subjects should be considered. But this is an evasive answer, or else it leaves a dangerously wide margin of deliberation to the proposed Congress. The argument, moreover, is unsound, because when members of Parliament fix beforehand what are the motions and what the subjects for discussion on each day, they in no degree whatever prejudge the decision which the House may come to upon the specified matters.

" My own impression is that the Congress will never meet, and that the Emperor has no expectation that it should meet.

" The truth is that the assembling of a Congress is not a measure applicable to the present state of Europe.

" In 1815 a Congress was a necessity. France had overrun all Europe, had overthrown almost all the former territorial arrangements, and had established a new order of things. Then came the returning tide of the Allied Armies overturning everything which France had created, and establishing, for the moment, military occupation of the greater part of Europe. It was absolutely necessary to determine to whom, and in what portions, and on what conditions, the vast regions reconquered from France should be thenceforward possessed. The Powers whose armies had made this reconquest were the natural and indeed the only arbiters; and they had, by their armies, the means of carrying their decisions into effect.

" Nothing of the kind exists in the present state of Europe. There are no doubts as to who is the owner of any piece of territory, and there are not even any boundary questions in dispute.

" The functions of a Congress, if now to be assembled, might be twofold, and would bear either on the past or on the future, or on both. Drouyn says that the Congress might take up the treaties of 1815, go through them article by article, strike out whatever has been repealed or set aside, and re-enact the remainder as the Treaty of 1863–64, the name of which would be less disagreeable to France than that of the Treaty of 1815, which brings to mind Waterloo and St. Helena. This may be a natural feeling for France; but it is no good reason why all the rest of Europe should meet round a table to please the French nation; and those who hold their estates under a good title, now nearly half a century old, might not be particularly desirous of having it brought under discussion with all the alterations which good-natured neighbours might wish to suggest in their boundaries.

" No doubt there have been some not unimportant changes made in the territorial arrangements of Europe established by the Treaty of 1815 ; but some of these were made regularly by treaty at the time, and the others, not so made, some of the parties to the Congress might not like to sanction by treaty acknowledgment.

" Chief among the first class is the separation of Belgium from Holland ; but. that was solemnly sanctioned by negotiations the length of which I cannot easily forget, and by a treaty between the five Powers and Holland and the German Diet. That transaction requires no confirmation.. Chief among the second class was the absorption of Cracow by Austria without any treaty sanction; and to that transaction the British Government, which protested against it at the time, would not be greatly desirous of giving retrospective sanction by treaty now. Then come the cession of Lombardy to Italy, and of Savoy and Nice to France. These were legally made by the rightful owners of the ceded territory, and no confirmation can be required. There was indeed, in the case of Savoy, an omission to attach to the territory as conveyed to France the condition of neutrality as to Chablais and Faucigny, subject to which the King of Sardinia held Savoy; but it may be doubted whether France would consent to undertake that condition ; and its real value, either for Switzerland or Italy, might, after all, be trifling. Then comes the absorption into the kingdom of Italy of Tuscany, Parma, Modena, Emilia, Naples, and Sicily. These were all violations of the Treaty of Vienna, done without treaty sanction ; but they were the will of the people of those countries. Those transactions have been virtually sanctioned by all the Powers who have acknowledged the King of Italy ; and if Victor Emmanuel is wise, he would be content with leaving those matters as they are, the more especially because if a new European treaty were to describe the kingdom of Italy as it now is, that treaty would be a virtual renunciation by the King of Italy to any claim to Venetia and Rome. On the other hand, Austria and the Pope would hardly be prepared to give their formal sanction to the acquisitions made by the Italian kingdom.

" As to the past, therefore, the functions of the Congress would either be unnecessary or barred by insurmountable difficulties.

" But then as to the future ? Would the Congress have to range over the wide and almost endless extent of proposed and possible changes, or would it have to confine itself to questions now practically pending ? There are but two such questions: the one relating to Poland ; the other to the difference between the German Confederation and Denmark about Holstein and Lauenburg and about Sleswig.

As to Poland, would Russia be more likely to yield in a Congress than she has shown herself to be in a negotiation? I much doubt it. And as to the question between Germany and Denmark, a smaller machinery than a European Congress might surely be sufficient to solve that question.

"But if the Congress were to enter upon the wide field of proposed and possible changes of territory, what squabbles and animosities would ensue! Russia would ask to get back all she lost by the Treaty of Paris; Italy would ask for Venetia and Rome; France would plead geography for the frontier of the Rhine; Austria would show how advantageous it would be to Turkey to transfer to Austria Bosnia or Moldo-Wallachia; Greece would have a word to say about Thessaly and Epirus; Spain would wonder how England could think of retaining Gibraltar; Denmark would say that Sleswig is geographically part of Jutland, and that, as Jutland is an integral part of Denmark, so ought Sleswig to be so too; Sweden would claim Finland; and some of the greater German states would strongly urge the expediency of mediatizing a score of the smaller Princes.

"If the members of the Congress should be unanimous in agreeing to any of these proposals, of course there would be no difficulty in carrying a unanimous decision into effect; but if a majority were one way, and a minority, however small, the other way, that minority, including the party by which a concession was to be made, is it intended that force should be used, or is the Congress to remain powerless to execute its own decrees?

"In the face of all these difficulties, my humble opinion is that no Congress will meet; and I shall be glad to think that the Emperor will have mended his position at home by making the proposal, while its failure will have saved Europe from some danger and much embarrassment.

"Lady Palmerston desires me to tender to Your Majesty her sincere thanks for your condescending message; and we both are greatly delighted at the prospect which Your Majesty's letter holds out to us of the possibility of having, in the course of the winter, the honour of receiving Your Majesty at Broadlands.

"I have the honour to be, Sire,

"Your Majesty's

"Most obedient and humble Servant,

"PALMERSTON.

"His Majesty The KING OF THE BELGIANS."

And a fortnight later he writes to Lord Russell:—*

"The state of Europe in 1815 was wholly different from what it is now. At that time the success of French arms had swept away most of the territorial boundaries and separate sovereignties which existed before 1792. The tide of conquest which at first ran from west to east, then returned back from

---

* December 2, 1863.

east to west, and swept away almost all that
France had established. Europe was a political
waste, and required the action of a body of in-
closure commissioners to allot the lands, and to
give holding titles. This was done at Vienna in
1814 and 1815. But nothing of the kind exists in
1863, and nobody wants an improved title to any
possession except those who ought not to get it;
as, for instance, Russia to the kingdom of Poland,
Austria to Cracow, France to Savoy without neutrality, and the Pope to what he holds and as much
as he could get back. It is quite certain that the
deliberations of a Congress would consist of demands
and pretensions put forward by some and resolutely
resisted by others, and that, there being no supreme
authority in such an assembly to enforce the opinions
or decisions of the majority, the Congress would separate leaving many of the members on worse terms
with each other than when they met.

" I think it seems pretty clear that, among
other schemes which the Emperor had for the
Congress, there was a proposal that there should be
given to the Pope a European guarantee for his unmolested possession of the territory now held for him
by the French troops, which then might have been
withdrawn. France and all the Catholic Powers
would willingly have joined in such an arrangement,
and Russia might have done so out of complaisance
to France. Italy would have been embarrassed, but
might have been overruled. We should have been

placed in a disagreeable dilemma, having either to refuse and to take openly a position hostile to the Pope and distasteful to our Catholic fellow-subjects, or to give our formal sanction and guarantee to the permanence of the temporal power of the Pope, against which we have not hesitated to declare our opinion.

" This, however, was probably only one of the traps laid by Napoleon for the silly birds he was trying to lure into his decoy."

Several of the other great Powers also declining the Congress, the project fell through.

An account of the intricate proceedings connected with the Sleswig-Holstein question cannot come within either the scope or the space of this book; but the part which Lord Palmerston's Government took in the matter must be briefly narrated.

The real dispute between Denmark and Germany dated from the year 1848, when an insurrectionary party in the former appealed to Germany for aid in establishing the union of Holstein and Sleswig with a constitutional existence separate from the rest of the monarchy. Germany assisted the insurrection, and at the peace of Berlin in 1850, although nothing was stipulated, it was understood that the Danish Monarchy was to be reconstructed with a view to satisfying the wishes of the Sleswig-Holsteiners. Negotiations followed, which, as far as Sleswig was concerned, were of an international character, and

not merely between Denmark and the Germanic Diet.
It was on the interpretation and fulfilment of the
engagements contracted by Denmark as the result of
these negotiations that the dispute with Germany
turned, which, while at its height, assumed a new
and more complicated aspect by the sudden death
of the King of Denmark. In conformity with the
Treaty of London, 1852, Prince Christian ascended
the Danish throne, including that of the Duchies, as
King Christian IX.; but the Duke of Augustenburg,
although his father had renounced for himself and
his family, insisted on being recognised as Duke of
Sleswig-Holstein. Some of the smaller German states,
in spite of the treaty to which many of them had
acceded, were disposed to go with him on the ground
that the treaty of 1852 was not binding unless the
other engagements alleged to have been entered into
by the Crown of Denmark at an antecedent time and
upon another subject were also fulfilled. To state
such a proposition was to refute it; and the British
Government had common sense and common justice
on their side when they urged that every consideration of honour and good faith demanded the acknowledgment of King Christian as King Duke of all
the territories which were under the sway of his predecessor, and that there would then be a responsible
sovereign from whom might be claimed the fulfilment of any and every engagement taken by the late
King and not made good. The German Diet, however, decreed a federal execution in Holstein—that

is to say, an administration of the Government by commissioners—and, though this was nominally done only in the interests of the Holsteiners, it was undisguised intervention in behalf of the Duke of Augustenburg, who made his appearance at Kiel, and was greeted as the rightful Duke. The close of the year saw the Danish and German troops confronting one another on the opposite banks of the Eider.

Austria and Prussia were at first inclined firmly to abide by the Treaty of London ; but the pressure of the Diet acting upon their mutual jealousies, and the fear of each lest it should jeopardise its position in Germany, combined to drive them along the path of aggression. The first to suffer was the Diet itself; for the matter was taken out of their control, and a combined Austrian and Prussian force advanced through Holstein into Sleswig. On the 2nd of February the Danes evacuated the Dannewerke, on which so much reliance had been placed, and fell back upon Düppel. Meanwhile, as might have been expected, there had sprung up in England a strong feeling of indignation at the violence offered to little Denmark by the two great military powers. It was suggested that France and Great Britain should offer their mediation on the basis of the integrity of the Danish monarchy and the engagements of 1851-52 ; and that, if such mediation were refused by Austria and Prussia, England should despatch a squadron to Copenhagen, and France a corps d'armée to the Rhenish frontier of Prussia. The following letter shows what Lord Palmerston said about this proposal :—

"94, Piccadilly, February 13, 1864.

" My dear Russell,

"I share fully your indignation. The conduct of Austria and Prussia is discreditably bad, and one or both of them will suffer for it before these matters are settled. I rather doubt, however, the expediency of taking at the present moment the steps proposed. The French Government would probably decline it, unless tempted by the suggestion that they should place an armed force on the Rhenish frontier in the event of a refusal by Austria and Prussia—which refusal we ought to reckon upon as nearly certain.

"The objections which might be urged against the measures suggested as the consequences of the refusal of Austria and Prussia may be stated to be : First, that we could not for many weeks to come send a squadron to the Baltic ; and that such a step would not have much effect upon the Germans unless it were understood to be a first step towards something more ; and I doubt whether the Cabinet or the country are as yet prepared for active interference. The truth is, that to enter into a military conflict with all Germany on continental ground would be a serious undertaking. If Sweden and Denmark were actively co-operating with us, our 20,000 men might do a good deal ; but Austria and Prussia could bring 200,000 or 300,000 into the field, and would be joined by the smaller German States.

" Secondly, though it is very useful to remind the Austrians and the Prussians privately of the danger they are running at home—Austria in Italy, Hungary and Gallicia ; Prussia in her Rhenish provinces—yet it might not be advisable nor for our own interest to suggest to France an attack upon the Prussian Rhenish territory. It would serve Prussia right if such an attack were made ; and if Prussia remains in the wrong we could not take part with her against France. But the conquest of that territory by France would be an evil for us, and would seriously affect the position of Holland and Belgium. On the whole, I should say that it would be best for us to wait awhile before taking any strong step in these matters.

" Yours sincerely,

" PALMERSTON."

The English Government was, in fact, not only hampered, but fettered by the refusal of Russia and France to join heartily with her. Russia acted, it may be supposed, from the same motives which have hitherto always kept her from breaking with Prussia ; France partly, no doubt, from pique at our refusal the previous year to agree to her Congress. It might, of course, have been very different could England have consented to French conquest on the Rhine as the price to be paid for French assistance.

Lord Palmerston, however, was anxious to do all he could for Denmark within the bounds of what was statesmanlike and possible. He wrote to the First

Lord of the Admiralty :* "I own I quite agree with Russell, that our squadron ought to go to Copenhagen as soon as the season will permit, and that it ought to have orders to prevent any invasion of, or attack upon Zealand and Copenhagen. It is not unlikely that Austria and Prussia, reckoning upon our passive attitude, contemplate the occupation of Copenhagen, and think to imitate what the first Napoleon did at Vienna and Berlin, and mean to dictate at the Danish capital their own terms of peace. We should be laughed at if we stood by and allowed this to be done."

The Prussians took Düppel in April, and soon after a solitary gleam of sunshine for the Danes broke the monotonous gloom of their reverses, and they gained a naval success against the Austrians off Heligoland. The two following letters tell Lord Palmerston's intended action in case of the Austrian Government proposing to reinforce their fleet in the Baltic :—

" 94, Piccadilly, May 1, 1864.

" MY DEAR RUSSELL,

"I felt so little satisfied with the decision of the Cabinet on Saturday, that I determined to make a notch off my own bat, and accordingly I wrote this morning to Apponyi, asking him to come here and give me half an hour's conversation. He came accordingly. I said I wished to have some friendly and

* To Duke of Somerset, February 20, 1864.

T 2

unreserved conversation with him, not as between an English minister and the Austrian ambassador, but as between Palmerston and Apponyi ; that what I was going to say related to serious matters; but I begged that nothing I might say should be looked upon as a threat, but only as a frank explanation between friends on matters which might lead to disagreements, and with regard to which, unless timely explanation were given as to possible consequences of certain things, a reproach might afterwards be made that timely explanation might have averted disagreeable results. I said that we have from the beginning taken a deep interest in favour of Denmark—not from family ties, which have little influence on English policy, and sometimes act unfavourably—but, first, that we have thought from the beginning that Denmark has been harshly and unjustly treated ; and, secondly, we deem the integrity and independence of the State which commands the entrance to the Baltic objects of interest to England. That we abstained from taking the field in defence of Denmark for many reasons—from the season of the year; from the smallness of our army, and the great risk of failure in a struggle with all Germany by land. That with regard to operations by sea, the positions would be reversed: we are strong, Germany is weak; and the German ports in the Baltic, North Sea, and Adriatic would be greatly at our command. Speaking for myself personally, and for nobody else, I must frankly tell him that, if an Austrian squadron were to pass along our coasts and ports, and go into the Baltic to help in any way the German operations against Denmark, I should look upon it as an affront and insult to England. That I could not, and would not stand such a thing; and that, unless in such case a superior British squadron were to follow, with such orders for acting as the case might require, I would not continue to hold my present position; and such a case would probably lead to collision—that is, war; and in my opinion Germany, and especially Austria, would be the sufferer in such a war. I should deeply regret such a result, because it is the wish of England to be well with Austria; but I am confident that I should be borne out by public opinion. I again begged that he would not consider this communication as a threat, but simply as a friendly reminder of consequences which might follow a possible course of action.

" Apponyi, having listened with great attention to what I said, replied that the considerations which I had pointed out were not new to his mind; that they had been forcibly dwelt upon, among other persons, by the King of the Belgians. That he was quite aware that, if the Austrian ships entered the Baltic, an English squadron would follow them; that in all probability one of two things would happen— either that the Austrian squadron would be destroyed, or that it would be compelled by orders from the English admiral to leave the Baltic. Thus they would run the risk of a catastrophe or a humiliation, and they did not wish for either.   That, therefore, whatever may have been said by Rechberg in his note, we might be sure that the Austrian squadron will not enter the Baltic.   This is satisfactory, as far as Apponyi may be considered the organ of the Austrian Government; but I think we ought to have something more positive in writing than we have got.

" I shall state to the Cabinet to-morrow the substance of my conversation with Apponyi.

" Yours sincerely,

" PALMERSTON."

At the same time he wrote to the First Lord of the Admiralty :—

" May 4, 1864.

" MY DEAR SOMERSET,

" It seems to me that we ought to insist that no Austrian ships of war shall at any time, or under any circumstances during the war, enter the Baltic. We have never declared ourselves neutral in this war : we have declined, for reasons of our own, to take a part in it; but we have done our best to help the Danes by diplomatic interference.

" The reasons which opposed military interference on our part do not apply to naval aid ; and, so far as forbidding the Austrians to enter the Baltic at any time during the war, we are rendering valuable aid to the Danes, without any great effort to ourselves.

I should be much disposed to allow the Danes to have their ironclad.   I am satisfied that a manifestation of good-will on our part towards the Danes must

contribute much to make the Germans more reasonable in negotiation. They have been encouraged
hitherto by a belief that nothing would induce us to
interfere ; and this belief has been much strengthened,
unfortunately, by letters and language received from
England.

" Yours sincerely,

" PALMERSTON.

" The DUKE OF SOMERSET."

In the meantime the British Government were
making active exertions, by a conference of the Great
Powers, to put a stop to the further prosecution of
the war; and after much trouble they persuaded
the belligerents to come into such a conference
to be held in London. It met on the 25th April,
and, after proclaiming an armistice, proceeded to
business. But no agreement could be arrived at as to
the future frontier between Denmark and the Duchies.
The victorious Germans were exacting ; the desperate
Danes were obstinate ; and after sitting for two
months the conference broke up without any result of
their labours. Hostilities were renewed at the end of
June, and Denmark was compelled to sign a peace at
Vienna, by which she finally surrendered to Germany
the Duchies of Sleswig, Holstein, and Lauenburg.

Parliament now intervened to call Ministers to
account for their conduct of these affairs. During
the whole of the session there had been frequent
interpellations and fragmentary debates upon this
Dano-German question ; but in the beginning of July

a simultaneous attack was made in both Houses upon the policy of the Government. In the House of Lords the resolution moved by Lord Malmesbury was carried by a majority of nine, and in the House of Commons Mr. Disraeli proposed a similar resolution. He asked the House to join with him in expressing the opinion that the course pursued by Her Majesty's Government had " lowered the just influence of this country in the Councils of Europe, and thereby diminished the securities for peace." This was a distinct vote of censure, and was accepted as such. The debate, which lasted for four nights, aroused much public interest, because the strength of parties was pretty nearly equal, and on the result of the vote depended the continuance or retirement of Lord Palmerston's administration. Each afternoon, as Lord Palmerston went down to the House, he was cheered by the crowd assembled in Palace Yard. He spoke on the last night. As the successful winding up of a great party debate, involving the fate of a Ministry, his speech on this occasion was his last triumph, and showed that though he spoke at the end of a night of long and weary sitting, his old vigour and cunning of fence had not deserted him. He had, in truth, a difficult task. There had been a conspicuous failure ; of that much there could be no doubt. Allies, colleagues, and circumstances had proved adverse ; yet the excuses for failure could not be laid on any of them. So, with the exception of a dexterous allusion to the words of the resolution as " a gratuitous libel upon the country by a great party who hoped to rule it," he did not detain the House for long on the points immediately at issue, but, dropping, the Danish matter altogether, went straight into a history of the financial triumphs of his Government. What has this to do with the question? asked impatient Tories. But it had all to do with the party question, for it decided the votes of doubting men, who, caring little about Sleswig-Holstein, cared a great deal about English finance. Anyhow it commanded success, for the Government got a majority of eighteen, and thus renewed their lease of power. Both inside the House of Commons and outside in Westminster Hall the excitement and cheering about the result was immense.

To the King of the Belgians Lord Palmerston shortly afterwards opens his mind:—

"94, Piccadilly, August 28, 1864.

" SIRE,

"I have many apologies to make to your Majesty for not having sooner thanked you for your letter of the 15th June. We were at that time in the midst of an engrossing session of Parliament, and the unequal contest between Denmark and Germany was still undecided, though with little hope that right could prevail over might. The Danish Government, both under the late and under the present King, undoubtedly committed many mistakes, both of commission and omission, and they showed throughout these affairs, from beginning to end, that inaptitude to deal with great concerns which might, perhaps, have been expected from a nation shut up in a remote corner of Europe, and not mixed up or practised with the general politics of the world. It was, however, an unworthy abuse of power by Austria and Prussia to take advantage of their superior enlightenment and strength to crush an antagonist utterly incapable of successful resistance; and the events of this Danish war do not form a page in German history which any honourable or generous German hereafter will look back upon without a blush. I wish that France and Russia had consented to join with us in giving a different direction to those affairs; and I am convinced that words from three such Powers would have been sufficient without a recourse to blows. One consequence is clear and certain, namely, that if our good friend and neighbour at Paris were to take it into his head to deprive Prussia of her Rhenish provinces, not a finger in England would be stirred, nor a voice raised, nor a man nor a shilling voted to resist such retribution upon the Prussian monarch; and when France and Italy shall be prepared to deliver Venetia from the Austrian yoke, the joy with which the success of such an undertaking will be hailed throughout England will be doubled by the recollection of Holstein, Lauenburg, Sleswig and Jutland.

"I have the honour to be, Sire,

"Your Majesty's most obedient humble Servant,

"Palmerston."

He went to the north after the session, visiting Bradford, where he had a very cordial reception, and afterwards proceeding to Hereford, to uncover the statue erected in memory of Sir George Lewis. And in reply to a note of congratulation from the Foreign Secretary, writes as follows :*

" Many thanks for what you say about my August peregrinations; they were not sought for by me, but they were successful, not simply as regards myself, but as relates to the Government; and I may safely affirm that our general conduct has been approved by the country, and especially the management of our foreign affairs, notwithstanding the run made against us on that point in Parliament. You say that with less timidity around us we might probably have kept Austria quiet in the Danish affair. Perhaps we might; but then we had no equal pull upon Prussia, and she would have rallied all the smaller German Powers round her, and we should equally have failed in saving Denmark.

" As to Cabinets, if we had colleagues like those who sat in Pitt's Cabinet, such as Westmoreland and others, or such men as those who were with Peel, like Goulburne and Hardinge, you and I might have our own way on most things; but when, as is now the case, able men fill every department, such men will have opinions, and hold to them; but unfortunately they are often too busy with their own

* To Lord Russell, September 11, 1864.

department to follow up foreign questions so as to be fully masters of them, and their conclusions are generally on the timid side of what might be the best."

Before going to Bradford he went with Lady Palmerston to visit her estates in Northamptonshire, and to assist her at Towcester to cut the first sod of a railway from Northampton to Stratford-on-Avon. Of course he was well received; and the county member,* in his speech at the banquet, very happily hit off the popular sentiment about the Premier, illustrating as follows the way in which his personal nfluence buoyed up the Ministry, and the exceptional position which he held with all parties in the state :—

"The noble lord and his Ministry seem to be always engaged in the game of chuck-farthing, and it is invariably with 'Heads I win, tails you lose.' (Cheers and laughter.) Whenever it comes up 'head,' the noble Viscount very properly has all the credit; when it comes up 'tail,' the rest of the ministers get the blame. I do not mean to say that the noble Viscount is guilty of unfair play, but the people, it is evident, are determined to give him all the halfpence, and the rest of the Ministry all the kicks. (Great laughter.)"

His own speech on this occasion is an instance of how genially he could touch the veriest commonplace. It was after dinner, and his topic was the advantages of railways. Instead of giving a laboured dissertation on steam and civilisation, he brought home to the country squires, in the following words, what they would gain by a new railroad :—

* Mr., now Sir Rainald, Knightley.

" In former times a gentleman asked his friend in London
to come down to him in the country, and the friend came
with things to last him a fortnight or three weeks, and he
took, perhaps, a week on the journey. Now, if a friend meets
another in St. James's Street and says, 'I shall have some
good shooting next week; will you come down to me and
spend a few days?' the friend says, 'Oh, by all means; I
shall be charmed. What is the nearest station to your house?'
'Well,' the friend says, 'I am not very well off at present
with regard to railway communication; the nearest station is
sixteen miles from my house; but it is a good road: you will
get a nice fly, and you will come very well.' Upon which
the invited guest says, 'Did you say it was Tuesday you
asked me for?' 'Yes,' says the countryman; 'and I think
you told me that you were free on that day.' Upon which
the other replies, 'I have a very bad memory. Upon my
word, I am very sorry, but I have a particular engagement
on that day. Some other time I shall be happy to come
down to you.' (Laughter.) Then he offers himself as a visitor
to some other friend, who has a station within one or two
miles of his house. (Cheers and laughter.)"

This autumn Lord Palmerston became eighty
years old. Traits of physical vigour at such an
advanced period of life are always interesting and
generally instructive, as teaching us how best to
preserve and enjoy those bodily faculties which we
receive at our birth. Lord Palmerston was endowed
with an excellent constitution, and was very tem-
perate both in eating and drinking; but he maintained his freshness, both of mind and body, to a
great degree by the exercise of his will. He never
gave anything up on the score of age. At any rate,
he never owned to that as a reason. He used to go

out partridge-shooting long after his eyesight was too dim to take a correct aim, and persevered in his other outdoor pursuits. Twice during this year, starting at nine o'clock and not getting back till two, he rode over from Broadlands to the training stables at Littleton, to see his horses take a gallop on Winchester racecourse. He rode down in June to Harrow speeches, and timed himself to trot the distance from Piccadilly to the head master's door, nearly twelve miles, within the hour, and accomplished it. On his eightieth birthday, in October, he started at half-past eight from Broadlands, taking his horses by train to Fareham, was met by Engineer officers, and rode along the Portsdown and Hilsea lines of forts, getting off his horse and inspecting some of them, crossing over to Anglesey forts and Gosport, and not reaching home till six in the evening—an instance of such combined energy both of mind and body as cannot in the nature of things be very common at fourscore.

Lunacy, when pleaded as an excuse for crime, has been frequently handled as a subject for discussion. Lord Palmerston had at any rate distinct notions as to how he should meet it, as is seen in the following extract of a letter to the Home Secretary. The occasion that elicited this letter was the reprieve of Victor Townley, who had murdered Miss Goodwin because she had broken off her engagement with him. Neither the presiding judge nor the Commissioners of Lunacy reported to the Home Office in terms sufficient to justify an exercise of the prerogative of the Crown, but three justices and two medical men obtaining access to the condemned man, sent in a certificate to the effect that he was insane. This certificate had been prepared in conformity with an Act of Parliament, which, when thus put in force, Sir George Grey conceived he had no alternative but to comply with. The convict was accordingly respited. Lord Palmerston, after saying that the statute could never have been intended to act in this way, and that it ought to be altered, went on :*

" For my part I never have had but one opinion upon the manner of dealing with murderers said to be insane. It seems to me that if a man is sufficiently in possession of his reasoning faculties to be able to take care of himself, and not to maim or attempt to kill himself, he is, and ought to be, made to answer for taking away the life of another person.

" The object of punishment is not vengeance on the criminal, but deterring example to others. Madmen are proverbially cunning, and are perfectly able to calculate consequences, and can be swayed like other people by the fear of evil to themselves resulting from violence committed upon others. The doctrine set up in the Townley case seems to me most dangerous to the general interests of society. Here is a man who, after much deliberation, commits a barbarous murder, having gone about and mixed in

* To Sir George Grey.

society without being reputed insane, and he is rescued from the hands of justice, and from the sentence of the law, because four gentlemen choose to say that he has imperfect notions of the distinction between right and wrong, and because he chose to maintain that he had a right to put his victim to death. Why what murderer would not, *after* condemnation, and in order to save his own life, make a similar declaration ? And what an encouragement it is to murder to let it be known that by such means a man may escape the penalty of the law. Again, the doctrine of these benevolence-mongers is that the more atrocious the deed, the more should be the impunity to the doer ; because, the greater the enormity of the crime, the more certain it must be that the criminal was out of his mind, for no man in his right senses would be guilty of such a crime.

" What is called in such cases mercy to the guilty is, in fact, cruelty to the nation at large, by taking away some of the restraints which the laws impose on the bad and violent passions of mankind. The true test, as it appears to me, is not whether the culprit, after condemnation, chooses to say that he does not admit the difference between right and wrong, but whether, at the time of committing the crime, he knew that by the law punishment would follow."

The following letter to our minister at Madrid is applicable to the present day, in so far as Spain still holds in bondage the blacks in Cuba, who must by this time have all been imported after the trade was forbidden, and are therefore entitled to their freedom under treaty engagements with this country.

"February 17, 1864.

" DEAR SIR JOHN CRAMPTON,

"I have been reading your account of your representation to the Spanish minister about the slave trade, carried on for the supply of Cuba. Your arguments are perfectly just, and your statements are all borne out by facts. If you have occasion to talk with him again on these matters, you may say, as a proof that the feeling against the slave trade is not confined in England to enthusiasts and West Indian proprietors, that there are no two men in England more determined enemies of the slave trade than Lord Russell and myself, and certainly we are neither of us bigoted enthusiasts nor West Indian proprietors, but we have both laboured assiduously and with much success for the extirpation of that abominable crime.

"During the many years that I was at the Foreign Office, there was no subject that more constantly or more intensely occupied my thoughts, or constituted the aim of my labours; and though I may boast of having succeeded in accomplishing many good works —and among them materially assisting the Spaniards to get rid of their tyrannical dynasty, and to establish Parliamentary Government — yet the achievement which I look back to with the greatest and the purest pleasure was the forcing the Brazilians to give up their slave trade, by bringing into operation the Aberdeen Act of 1845. The result, moreover, has been greatly advantageous to the Brazilians, not only by freeing them from a grievous crime, but by very much improving their general condition.

"I am sure that no Spaniard can reflect without a blush upon the long-continued and systematic violation in this respect of the treaty engagements of the Spanish Crown; and as long as this state of things is allowed to continue, Spain never can, in the opinion of the British nation, take or hold her proper and natural position among the Powers of Europe, and from time to time things will necessarily be said about Spain, in our two Houses of Parliament, to which may be applied by the Spaniards the lines,

> "' . . . . pudet hæc opprobria nobis
> Et dici potuisse, et non potuisse refelli.'

> "Yours sincerely,
> "PALMERSTON."

The sympathy which Lord Palmerston's Government had shown for Italian unity—the realisation of which was most hateful to the Papacy—had deprived it to a great extent of the Liberal Irish vote. Lord Palmerston speaks of this in the following letter to the Irish Secretary :—

> "September 10, 1864.

"MY DEAR FORTESCUE,

"I should, of course, be very glad to have the support of the Catholic body in Ireland; but as their political action is regulated by the orders they receive from time to time from Rome, and as the Papal Government is pleased to deem us its enemy, because we are of opinion that Italian unity would be a good thing, nothing that we could do with propriety in Ireland would have the slightest influence upon the Irish Catholics. If they were in any degree capable of political gratitude they would have supported the Whig Government; but two Monsignores from Rome, and a ' Grandis Epistola' from the Vatican, array in hostility to us men in the House of Commons who call themselves Liberals, but who are ready to vote as Tories in obedience to foreign injunctions. This, it is true, was foretold by the opponents of the Catholic Emancipation, and we who supported that measure derided the prediction. But though I am sorry to have been in this respect a false prophet, I do not the less rejoice at that act of sound policy and strict justice.

" Yours sincerely,

" PALMERSTON."

And two days later he says to the same :* " We have invariably endeavoured to deal with equal impartiality between Protestant and Catholic, but there is no shutting our eyes to the fact that in Ireland, as elsewhere, the Catholic priesthood—and through them a portion of the laity—while professing a desire for religious equality, aim at nothing less than political domination, and strive to transfer the source and

---

* To Mr. Chichester Fortescue, September 12, 1864.

directing centre of that domination to a foreign authority."

Closely connected with this subject was that of Catholic Colleges—a matter which has already caused much debate, and may cause much more. His view of the matter is thus conveyed to the Lord Lieutenant of Ireland :—

"July 28, 1865.

"My dear Wodehouse, ∴

"The new arrangement to be made about the Catholic College will require much circumspection. What is required is that young men brought up in that establishment should have the means of being examined for a Degree. What the Irish Catholics want to accomplish under cover of this reasonable purpose, is to substitute their Sectarian College entirely for the Queen's Colleges, which are founded on the principle of mixed education. This is an aim which we must not allow them to accomplish. Their scheme of affiliation, plausibly recommended, tends to that end. My opinion, on the contrary, is that the aggregate University body of the Queen's Colleges should examine for Degrees all comers, wheresoever educated. It is said that this would not give any security for moral character, but that might be required from the instructors of each candidate; and it may safely be inferred that a young man, who by study and application has qualified himself for a Degree, must be possessed of sufficient self-control to

prove him to be a well-conducted young man. What
the Catholic priesthood want is that this Catholic College should be the only place of education for the
young Irish Catholics, and that it should be, like May-
nooth, a place where young men should be brought
up to be bigoted in religion, to feel for Protestants
theological hatred, and to feel political hatred for
England. It is proposed to put a number of lay
Catholics into the council of the aggregate University.
This would be quite right, but would be little check
upon the priests and bishops. How could such men
as O'Hagan and Monsell be expected to stand up
against Cullen and others upon any important religious matter ? They might make a good fight about
Euclid and algebra, or chemistry or astronomy, but
upon all questions involving the real objects of the
Catholic priesthood they would give way. The conclusion I come to is, that we ought to give the stu-
dents of the Catholic College the means of obtaining
Degrees, if they are sufficiently instructed to pass
examination ; but that we ought not to give to the
Catholic College a University condition of existence.
Therefore, if it should be necessary to give that College
a charter of incorporation, such charter should be
limited to the usual capacities of suing and being
sued, but should not convey the power of holding
lands, either by purchase, grant, or bequest, and of
course should not give power to confer Degrees. The
result of the elections is indeed highly satisfactory ;
not merely with reference to the greater strength we

have acquired, but also with reference to the number of bores and troublesome men who have been thrown out.

" Yours sincerely,

" PALMERSTON."

Clerical rule he regarded as very objectionable, in whatever communion it might be found; and he writes to the Home Secretary about Convocation :—

"May 24, 1865.

" MY DEAR GREY,

" I see that Convocation have been very active, and are proposing to draw up a Reform Bill for themselves. My opinion is that, unless kept very tight and within the narrowest bounds, Convocation would become a nuisance, and I should not be disposed to consent to any alterations which would tend to give them a more real and practical existence. Might not some hint be given them to check their exuberant activity? I remember that Aberdeen, who was not addicted to unnecessary vigour of action, sent them about their business one time when they were beginning to be meddlesome.

" Yours sincerely,

" PALMERSTON."

His last two letters about foreign affairs will, I think, be found interesting :—

" September 3, 1865.

" MY DEAR COWLEY,

" The Duke of Somerset writes me word that the French were surprised, during the recent meeting at Portsmouth, to find how real the cordiality was with which they were received. If this should happen to be mentioned or observed upon to you by any of the French ministers, it might not be amiss that you should explain to them that we Englishmen see two distinct entities in France, the nation and the Government. Towards the French nation we all feel that cordial friendship which was expressed by words and deeds during the late meetings; all old sentiments of rivalship and antagonism as between Englishmen and Frenchmen are, on our part, extinguished. But with regard to the French Government, we see, from time to time, measures taken and schemes put forward which, whether framed or not in hostility to England, are, in our opinion, calculated to be injurious to our national interests. Such schemes, therefore, we do our best to oppose and to defeat; not, as some French agents endeavour to make out, from hatred to France and to everything French, but solely from that watchful care of the interests of our country which it is the duty of every Government to exert. The result is that, on the one hand, the French nation ought not to see in our occasional opposition to the schemes of their Government anything inconsistent with the friendly feelings manifested in the late meetings of the two navies; and, on the other hand, the French Government should not infer, from the friendliness of our reception of their fleet, that we shall be more likely to give way upon any

matters in which the interests of England are concerned.

" Yours sincerely,
" PALMERSTON."

" September 13, 1865.

" MY DEAR RUSSELL,

" It was dishonest and unjust to deprive Denmark of Sleswig and Holstein. It is another question how those two Duchies, when separated from
Denmark, can be disposed of best for the interests
of Europe. I should say that, with that view, it is
better that they should go to increase the power of
Prussia than that they should form another little
state to be added to the cluster of small bodies politic
which encumber Germany, and render it of less
force than it ought to be in the general balance of
power in the world. Prussia is too weak as she now
is ever to be honest or independent in her action;
and, with a view to the future, it is desirable that
Germany, in the aggregate, should be strong, in
order to control those two ambitious and aggressive
powers, France and Russia, that press upon her
west and east. As to France, we know how restless
and aggressive she is, and how ready to break loose
for Belgium, for the Rhine, for anything she would
be likely to get without too great an exertion. As
to Russia, she will, in due time, become a power
almost as great as the old Roman Empire. She can
become mistress of all Asia, except British India,

whenever she chooses to take it; and when enlightened arrangements shall have made her revenue
proportioned to her territory, and railways shall
have abridged distances, her command of men will
become enormous, her pecuniary means gigantic, and
her power of transporting armies over great distances most formidable. Germany ought to be strong
in order to resist Russian aggression, and a strong
Prussia is essential to German strength. Therefore,
though I heartily condemn the whole of the proceedings of Austria and Prussia about the Duchies, I own
that I should rather see them incorporated with
Prussia than converted into an additional asteroid in
the system of Europe.

" Yours sincerely,
" PALMERSTON."　　　

In July, 1865, Parliament having nearly reached
its full term of existence, had been dissolved. There
was a contest at Tiverton, and Lord Palmerston
went down there for the last time, and was re-elected,
although his Liberal colleague lost his seat. The
general result of the elections was very favourable
to the Ministry.

During the latter part of the preceding session
Lord Palmerston had suffered continuously from gout
and disturbed sleep. He never abandoned his duties
as leader of the House; but without doubt they were,
under the circumstances, a matter of much physical
difficulty for him, and greatly aggravated his dis-

order.   Immediately after the Tiverton election he retired to Brocket in Hertfordshire—the place Lady Palmerston had inherited from her brother, Lord Melbourne—selecting this in preference to Broadlands, as being more within reach of medical advice. The gout had flown to the bladder, owing to his having ridden on horseback before he was sufficiently recovered ; and, although all his bodily organs were sound, and there was no reason why, with proper care, he should not have lived for several years longer, those around him could not fail to feel anxiety about his evident state of weakness, not only for the moment, but at the prospect of his again meeting Parliament as Prime Minister. That he himself felt the same anxiety for the future was clear; and one morning, about a fortnight before he died, I witnessed an incident which was both evidence of this and also very characteristic of the man. There were some high railings immediately opposite the front door, and Lord Palmerston, coming out of the house without his hat, went straight up to them after casting a look all round to see that no one was looking. He then climbed deliberately over the top rail down to the ground on the other side, turned round, climbed back again, and then went indoors. It was clear that he had come out to test his strength and to find out for himself in a practical way how far he was gaining or losing ground. Not that he had any excessive dread of death, for, as he put it one day, in homely fashion, to his doctor, when pressing for a frank opinion as to his state, "When a man's time is up there is no use in repining." The most touching and characteristic feature of his bearing at this time was his solicitude to avoid adding to Lady Palmerston's anxiety, and the cheerfulness which he assumed in her presence. Indeed consideration for others was, as in life so in death, one of his finest qualities. I remember that, only a few days before his end, when, so far as the aspect of his face could betoken illness, he appeared as ill as a man could be when about and at work, Lady Palmerston, at breakfast, alluded to the cattle plague, which was then making great havoc in England. He at once remarked that all the symptoms of the disorder were described by Virgil, and repeated to me some eight lines out of the Georgics descriptive of the disease. He then told us a story of a scrape he got into at Harrow, for throwing stones; and the excess of laughter, which he was unable to restrain, with which he recalled the incident, was the only token that could have betrayed to Lady Palmerston how weak he was.

A chill caught while out driving brought on inflammation of the kidneys; and on the 18th of October, 1865, within two days of completing his eighty-first year, he closed his earthly career. The half-opened cabinet-box on his table, and the unfinished letter on his desk, testified that he was at his post to the last.

I here quote a letter written very shortly before

his death, as it shows him, instead of being engrossed in his own state of health, solicitous and active about the health of a subordinate. On Sir Arthur Helps, as Clerk of the Council, had come a great influx of business, owing to the outbreak of rinderpest, and Lord Palmerston had already volunteered to help him by undertaking some of the work :—

" Brocket, October 3, 1865.

" My dear Gladstone,

"I have this morning received the enclosed from an eminent physician of Southampton. The report he makes of the health of Helps and of the state of the Council Office Establishment seems to me to require immediate and effective action. I have, therefore, written to Helps positively to forbid his going to Balmoral; and, as it seems that his second in command, Harrison, is also knocked down by excessive work, and as the limited establishment of the Council Office is already too small and weak for the daily work pouring in upon it by reason of these cattle, sheep, and pig diseases, together with a threatening of extension to horses, I have written to Waddington to request him to send some Home Office clerk to Balmoral to officiate at the Council.

I have also told Helps that, as head of the Government, I authorize him to take, without any delay, such steps as may be necessary to procure additional assistance for his office which this great influx of daily business continues to press upon it. I have told him that I will write to you to ask you to give the necessary directions for an official sanction to the arrangement; but I have said that he ought not to delay taking the necessary steps for obtaining relief by additional assistance.

" Yours sincerely,
" PALMERSTON."

That, in spite of the depressing influence of his illness, he was also fully alive to any new emergencies which might arise is shown by the next letter, of the same date, to the Home Secretary, about the Fenian movement in Ireland :—

" Brocket, October 3, 1865.

" MY DEAR GREY,

" I am clearly for sending to Ireland a regiment of cavalry to take the place of the one which it seems was lately brought away from Ireland, and whether Rose* is for such a reinforcement or against it. If the question was reversed, and we were considering whether a regiment could be spared from Ireland, we could not properly decide to diminish the Irish force without the full assent of the general commanding; but the question being whether we could add to the existing force, though it is highly satisfactory to find that Sir Hugh Rose does not consider any addition necessary, we ought nevertheless to send it. Sir Hugh Rose has been accustomed to walk over everything and everybody opposed to him ; but in this case final success is not the only thing to

* Commander-in-Chief in Ireland.

be provided for. If there is any outbreak it will begin by partial risings in scattered places, and in small numbers, but yet numbers sufficient, if there should be no protecting force, to murder, burn, and lay waste particular villages and landlord residences. A small regular force, capable of rapid movement, would do what would be necessary in such cases, and cavalry would be well fitted for the purpose. The Fenians, moreover, may have arms for infantry, and may, by possibility, have guns, though that is unlikely, but cavalry they cannot have; and a Fenian put suddenly on horseback, even if they could so fit out some of their men, would not be a cavalry soldier. Then, upon the general principle, we should be inspiring confidence in the loyal, and be giving a useful warning to the Fenians by showing that we could, if needed, add to the regular force now in Ireland.

"Yours sincerely,

"Palmerston."

The same week he is writing to the Secretary of State for War to suggest heavier armaments for the works round Quebec, and to inquire into the provision of arms and ammunition in Canada.

Thus indefatigable to the last, in his care of the interests committed to his charge, did Lord Palmerston complete his work, which had lasted through a longer term of public service than is easily paralleled in official annals.

In one life he summed up the political honours of several generations, for he was a member of every Government from 1807 to 1865, except those of Sir Robert Peel and Lord Derby. He sat in sixteen Parliaments, and was elected to sit in the seventeenth. During the later years of his life a detractor might have been driven to say of him what the sarcastic Archbishop Sheldon said of his ancestor, Sir John Temple, " He has the curse of the Gospel, for all men speak well of him." He died full of years and honours, and free from fears or unmanly regrets. Over his grave might well be written the words, " Felix etiam opportunitate mortis," for he suffered neither long nor painfully, died at work, and quitted the scene with undimmed reputation, before any failing on his part had made the audience impatient. He bequeathed his Party to his successor, newly strengthened and consolidated by a general election, fought and won under his name ; while to the Party itself he left as a noble legacy the example of a long and honourable career, spent indeed within their ranks, but devoted, even in the closing hours, to the service of the whole country. The national voice decreed for his remains the tribute of a public funeral and a grave in Westminster Abbey.

The foregoing pages do not profess to give a " history of the times " during which Lord Palmerston was successively at the Foreign Office, at the Home Office, and at the head of the Treasury, but only those events and incidents in which he individually took a marked share. A very rapid retrospect of a more general character may not be out of place.

The years of his last administration of the Foreign Office have this peculiar feature about them, that they form the last period of active intervention by England in the affairs of other countries. We appear to be removed from that epoch by a vast interval. It seems difficult for us now to imagine the despatch of a British legion to assist a sovereign against a portion of his subjects, to realise a Quadruple Alliance in which England should join to secure the succession to a continental throne, or even to believe in the advance of a British fleet to protect a weak neighbour from wrong. In the first place, such a foreign policy requires a man like Lord Palmerston to carry it out successfully, and such men are rare. It demands, further, such circumstances of comparative freedom to act without check or interference as can hardly be the lot of any minister, however able, now-a-days, when foreign matters are made as familiar to the peasant, if he can only read, as aforetime to the prince. The doctrine of " non-intervention " and the penny press have rapidly and simultaneously grown into favour with the British public; and the activity which characterised the Foreign Office under the Palmerstonian régime is a thing of the past. Yet the fruits which Lord Palmerston was able to show as the results of his energy and determination were well worth some risk and trouble in the cultivation. Peace between nations was preserved right through an era of revolutions, constitutional government was planted in a great part of Europe, and, meanwhile, England was known, respected, and dreaded wherever the name of Palmerston had penetrated; and that was—everywhere.

Of course the enemies of such a policy became countless. Disturbers of the peace must dislike the constable; neither despots nor their friends relish constitutions; bullies, whether high or low, hate those who keep them in order; and the selfish or apathetic at home grow weary of being constantly called upon for exertions in behalf of objects which, however just, do not affect their immediate interests. These combined antipathies, foiled in 1850, made a renewed attack the following year, and, as they hoped and believed, succeeded in crushing Lord Palmerston. Had he been a mere partisan, relying for his position solely on his connection with a great party, the blow might perhaps have proved as fatal as it was intended to be; but his strength lay, as he well knew, in the country itself, which saw in him a statesman, not indeed without blemish, but who maintained the honour of England, extricated her from innumerable difficulties without drawing the sword, and extended abroad those principles of civil and political liberty which are dear to Englishmen.

During the greater part of Lord Palmerston's next term of office questions relating to Turkey and the Crimean war filled the foreground of politics. We have seen that, from the first, he foresaw that Russia was so bent on an aggressive movement, that ordinary diplomatic remonstrances would not suffice to check her, and that nothing would stop her in time except a conviction that she would have to face an active Anglo-French alliance. The success with which, when called to the head of affairs, he finished the war and settled the terms of peace greatly consolidated his power.

The short interval which separated his first from his second Premiership sufficed to enable him to renew and cement his political association with those whom diplomatic and parliamentary disasters consequent on the war had temporarily removed from his side; and he was thus, in 1859, in a position to form a very strong administration.

The relations between England and France were at this moment somewhat strained, Lord Derby's cabinet having shown scant sympathy towards the French Emperor's action for the liberation of Italy. Lord Palmerston's Government not only quickly established a good feeling with France, but, by its influence, greatly aided the Italian people to become a nation, and, in so doing, they were undoubtedly acting in harmony with the general feeling of the English people.

Although Louis Napoleon had taken the French

army to fight for Italy, he was in no way desirous of seeing Italian unity such as it exists to-day. He wished for a Northern and Southern Italy, with a Papal sovereignty between them; and this was the secret of his persistent retention of French troops at Rome. He kept a large force there in order to hold for the Pope what remained to him, and in the hope also of being able to set up some nominee of his own as King of Naples if Ferdinand became impossible. Italy would thus have been divided into three portions, each too weak to resist his influence. But the march of events was too strong for him; and although the frank and urgent representations which Lord Palmerston used to make against the continued occupation of Rome failed of effect, his Government was of signal service to the Italian cause, both when there was a question of restoring the Grand Dukes after the peace of Villafranca, and later on, when Garibaldi was helping to crown the edifice. So sensible were the Italians of this that, after the annexation of Naples, addresses of thanks poured in to Lord Palmerston from all parts of Italy.

One of the earliest and most beneficial results of the accession to power of a Liberal Ministry was the conclusion of a commercial treaty with France, which was ratified at home in spite of strong re-sistance from the Conservative Opposition. The treaty was signed in January 1860; and to Mr. Cobden, its distinguished negotiator, Lord Palmerston offered, as an acknowledgment, in the name of the Queen, the choice of a baronetcy or a seat at the Privy Council; but Mr. Cobden declined to receive any titular distinction.

The general financial achievements of Lord Palmerston's Government, with Mr. Gladstone as Chancellor of the Exchequer, cannot be forgotten, embracing as they did extensive relief to trade, industry, and labour by the remission of taxation, simplification of the tariff, and reduction of debt. Notwithstanding the cotton famine and the war in America, the nation, during this period, made great progress in wealth and prosperity.

In the early part of 1860, the Imperial Court of China having shown its determination still to evade its treaty engagements, a second Chinese war was undertaken in conjunction with the French. Lord Elgin was sent out from this country to co-operate with Baron Gros; and, finally, the success of the allied forces enabled us at last to obtain regular diplomatic intercourse with the Court of Pekin.

During the civil war between the Northern and Southern States of America, Lord Palmerston's Government maintained a strict neutrality, in spite of many temptations and frequent solicitations to take a different course. They showed themselves, however, firm in demanding the surrender of Messrs. Mason and Slidell, when these two Confederate envoys were forcibly removed from the British mail-steamer 'Trent' by the crew of the United States war-steamer 'San Jacinto.' The prisoners were released, and war was thus avoided.

Overtures were made to this country by France, the object of which was to persuade us to assist them in obtaining some compensation, if possible, for the losses sustained by the holders of Mexican bonds, and to restore peace to Mexico, long distracted by chronic revolution. The Palmerston Ministry, though consenting to aid in operations at Vera Cruz, where the proceeds of the customs were seized, wisely declined to join in any further intervention. The discomfiture of the French and the sad fate of the Archduke Maximilian, who had accepted the Imperial crown of Mexico, showed how fully justified the British Government were in their refusal.

Greece, through the bad government of King Otho, became the scene of revolution, and was for some time in a state of anarchy. At last our Government and that of France determined on a friendly intervention, and had to find a new king for the Greeks, who wanted an English prince. Any member of the English, French, or Russian Royal families was, however, excluded by a mutual agreement to that effect, and finally, after much fruitless search for a fit man, Prince George of Denmark accepted the crown, and the Ionian Islands were handed over by England to the reconstituted kingdom.

We have seen how the Polish rising began, and also the attack on Denmark by Germany. In both

these cases Lord Palmerston could easily have stirred
up a cry for war. English feeling was much excited
on either question; but it was felt that neither the
English interests involved, nor our available means
of offence, were sufficient to justify an appeal to
national sentiment.

CHAPTER X.

Character—Characteristics of Style of Writing and Speaking.

LORD PALMERSTON'S character has been so frequently discussed—its many-sidedness offering to such various dispositions some point or other of attraction—that it may seem superfluous in me to attempt a repetition of a similar kind. Yet, in closing this history, I cannot resist the desire to put, however imperfectly, on record the impressions made upon me by seven years of close intercourse, both private and official. Biographers are proverbially partial; and it is, on the whole, to their credit that they should be so. Retrospect should rather fasten on the good than the evil. But, on the other hand, indiscriminate and extravagant praise is as unreal as it is unsatisfactory; and whoever undertakes to inform his fellow-countrymen is bound to bring his judgment as well as his affection into play.

Lord Palmerston, then, was a great man chiefly in the sense that he was so complete a man. His character deserves our attention more from its unusual combination of good qualities than from the marked presence of any one great quality or attribute. He had about him neither the glories nor the follies of a genius; but he possessed, in rare harmony, characteristics which are generally in antagonism. He had great pluck, combined with remarkable tact; unfailing good-temper, associated with firmness amounting almost to obstinacy. He was a strict disciplinarian, and yet ready above most men to make allowance for the weakness and shortcomings of others. He loved hard work in all its details, and yet took a keen delight in many kinds of sport and amusement. He believed in England as the best and greatest country in the world, while he had not confined his observation to her affairs, but knew and cared more about foreign nations than any other public man. He had little or no vanity in his composition, and, as is seen in several of his letters to his brother, he claimed but a modest value for his own abilities; yet no man had a better opinion of his own judgment, or was more full of self-confidence. It was amusing to notice the good-natured pity with which he quite unconsciously regarded those who differed from him in questions whereon he had made up his mind. He never doubted for an instant in such a case that he was right, and that they were wrong.

This gave him great tenacity of purpose, and helped him through many difficulties, and even mistakes, which would have swamped a weaker man. He seems almost to be describing himself when, writing to Sir Stratford Canning in December 1850

about the Turkish ministers, he says : " I believe
weakness and irresolution are, on the whole, the worst
faults that statesmen can have. A man of energy
may make a wrong decision, but, like a strong horse
that carries you rashly into a quagmire, he brings
you by his sturdiness out on the other side." During
the critical moment before the breaking out of the
Franco-Austrian war in 1859, Monsieur Drouyn de
Lhuys, talking to Lord Clarendon, used the same
simile. " I sigh," he said, " for one hour of Palmerston. No one knows better than I do his faults. I
have often suffered by them, and so has England, and
so has Europe. But his merits, his sagacity, his
courage, his trustworthiness, are invaluable when you
want

" 'A daring pilot in extremity :'

with whom one feels as if one was mounted on a first-
rate hunter, who pulls, indeed, and rears and kicks,
but never swerves, never starts, and carries you over
everything as long as you give him his head."

He liked office and the possession of power, but no
statesman showed more indifference to its trappings,
or so cordially detested the flatteries which it not
unfrequently attracts. Perhaps his strongest abhor-
rence was affectation of any sort. He could not abide
it in others, and never even dreamt of it for himself.

He was, for instance, always above the timid and
feeble tone of those who think it necessary to affect
coyness with respect to office, and who can talk of
nothing else but the sacrifice they made to duty on

the last occasion of accepting it. His language was always frankly to the effect that office is the natural and proper object of a public man's ambition, as the sphere in which he can most freely use his powers for the interest and advantage of his country. Lord Palmerston never pretended to dislike it.

Who, again, at a social party ever saw him retire into a corner with a colleague or a diplomat, in order by mysterious looks and enigmatical gestures to rouse an admiring curiosity among the bystanders? Many an ambassador of the old school must have felt chagrin at his own discomfiture, but he was indeed a clever man who could " buttonhole " Lord Palmerston at an evening party unless he really had something very pressing to say. She also was a clever woman who could at dinner draw him on to politics, with a view to impress the other guests with the high range of the conversation at the head of the table. The easy interchange of familiar talk on social subjects being the appropriate coin for the payment of what is due to society, Lord Palmerston was too downright a gentleman to allow a fraud on society for the sake of effect.

Men of one strong dominant idea are those that usually come most rapidly to the front, whether they succeed or not in afterwards retaining their foremost position. The tardiness with which Lord Palmerston reached political prominence, though no doubt owing to a variety of circumstances, may in part have had its origin in this very conflict of qualities by which his sympathies were held in suspense, and he himself misunderstood. His manner, arising from an instinctive horror of pomposity or affectation, created a belief in his levity; his good-humour and forbearance, a belief in his indifference; his reticence, a belief in his paucity of ideas. A passage from " Greville's Memoirs," under the date of August 7, 1836, shows however that, whatever was the judgment of the public, his talents were early recognised by competent judges :—

" It is surprising to hear how Palmerston is spoken of by those who know him officially. Lady Granville, a woman expert in judging, thinks his capacity first-rate; that it approaches to greatness from his enlarged views, disdain of trivialities, resolution, decision, confidence, and above all, his contempt of clamour and abuse. She told me that Madame de Flahault had a letter written by Talleyrand soon after his first arrival in England, in which he talked with great contempt of the ministers generally, Lord Grey included, and said there was but one statesman among them, and that was Palmerston. His ordinary conversation exhibits no such superiority ; but when he takes his pen in his hand his intellect seems to have full play, and probably when engaged exclusively in business."

Perhaps the most valuable quality for a commander, whether in the field or the Cabinet, is " knowledge of character." To be able to choose fit instruments is often a battle half won ; to be able to test reports that are brought in is often a defeat half saved. For both these purposes knowledge of character is indispensable —knowledge gleaned not from laborious investigations, for which there is seldom time, but from that instinctive judgment which is a .gift in itself, and which only requires for its exercise a few moments' conversation with the person whose character is to be learned. This gift Lord Palmerston had in a large degree. The consciousness of its possession led him, no doubt, on some rare occasions to be over-hasty in condemnation; but distrust of a new-comer is for a minister a safer fault than blind confidence.

At the time when the Greeks were being urgently pressed to satisfy certain English claims, M. Eynard, the banker, came to Lord Normanby and said that Coletti had, without any warning, drawn upon him for 500,000 francs in favour of the British Government, the Greeks availing themselves of an outstanding offer on his part; that it would cost him 80,000 francs to provide the money at once, and that he wished to make a request to the British Government to wait for a few months, so as to spare him this loss. The English ambassador, in a letter home, recapitulated the ingenuous statements of the financier, and was evidently moved by his appeal. Not so Lord Palmerston :—

" C. G., August 15, 1847.

"MY DEAR NORMANBY,

    "I have received your letter giving an account of your interview with Eynard. I rather think he what Lowther used to call *débuted* in London many years ago as an amateur actor; and he seems, according to what you say, not by any means to have trained off in his powers of performance in that line. He did his part throughout the whole scene admirably, and the only pity was that there were no spectators to crown him with applause. But, as the report of the best-acted scene never can produce the same effect as the seeing and hearing would, just as the best speech is tame without the ' os habitumque hominis,' so I am concerned to say neither Mr. Eynard's generosity, nor his impending loss of 80,000 francs, nor his desertion by Guizot, nor his European reputation, nor his Philhellenic enthusiasm, can light one spark of sympathy in my cold and gloomy mind, and I feel as stone-hearted as Shylock himself, even after reading your letter to an end. I don't know Eynard as well as you do, and therefore, perhaps, I know him better. Rely upon it that in all these matters he is simply an instrument of humbug in the hands of other persons. But we are too old birds to be caught by such chaff. Pray, therefore, tell Eynard, in such civil terms as you think best, that we have nothing to do with him in this matter, and can enter into no communication with him on the subject. Our business is with the Government of Greece, and not with the banker of that Government. We mean to settle our affairs with Greece with the Greek Government, and he will, of course, settle his affairs with Greece with the

Greek Government also; but we cannot settle our affairs with Greece with him, nor allow him to settle his affairs with Greece with us. Depend upon it, the money will not come from his pocket, but from the till of Louis Philippe, and Guizot and Co., and they sent him to you to endeavour to bamboozle us. But, even if this were not so, and he was the good-natured, soft enthusiast he represents himself to be, the only result would be that Greece would have to pay him the 80,000 francs which he *says* he is going to lose, if that assertion is true. All this is nothing to us, and we have nothing whatever to do with the matter. It is a question entirely between the Greek Government and Eynard.

" Yours sincerely,

" PALMERSTON."

He was the most steadfast and loyal of chiefs to those who served under him. " There is the devoted friend who stands or falls by one, like the noble Lord." So spoke, satirically, the leader of the Opposition, referring to Lord Palmerston, in the debate of the 16th June, 1855. But the party sneer contained an acknowledged truth whose universal acceptance did Lord Palmerston both honour and good service during his long career. He was served with zeal because the absent knew that he would shirk no difficulties in their defence, and that he would listen to no depreciatory tales against them, unless accompanied by substantial proofs.

Lord Howden, British minister at Madrid, begs him not to attend to private and slanderous reports about him. The reply is as follows:—

" Broadlands, September 7, 1850.

" My dear Howden,

"I have received your letter of the 25th of last month, and beg you not to trouble yourself about the matters to which it relates. If I had not full confidence in you I should not have recommended you to the Queen for the post you occupy; and when I have confidence in a man I do not allow that confidence to be shaken by the tales of intriguers and backbiters, even if such should reach my ears, which in your case they have not and probably will not. I say will not, because the commercial principle that supply follows demand extends to other matters besides trade; and when certain supplies are known to be discouraged and rejected, they are apt to be withheld. In fact, the usual effect of underhand attempts to injure a man is, with me, to make me more disposed to take his part. I have some little experience in my own proper person of the way in which falsehood is enlisted into the service of personal pique or unfounded resentment.

" Yours sincerely,

" Palmerston."

This is a letter which deserves to be remembered on account of the truth which it contains. Talebearers found no market for their goods in Lord

Palmerston's study, and so did not attempt to smuggle them in.

Nor was he more willing to yield to the open efforts of those in high places who sought to persuade him to sacrifice his agents abroad to their prejudices or dislikes. "Pray make him clearly comprehend," he writes to an English minister abroad, "that I will never sacrifice any British diplomatic officer, high or low, to the whims and caprices of any foreign prince or potentate." *

When the Greek Court used its personal influence with our Court at home to bring pressure upon the Foreign Office for the removal of Lord Lyons from Athens, he writes to Lord John Russell :—

" Broadlands, August 20, 1847.

" Otho's dislike to Lyons is not personal but political. It is not that Lyons is disagreeable in himself, but that the political advice which he has been always instructed to give, and the political principles and party which he has been instructed to support, are odious to Otho, and he hates Lyons upon the same principle that a dog snaps at a stick. You would not alter the feeling by changing the stick. It is the established formula of proceeding in such matters to run down the man as an easier method than combating his policy, or, rather, the policy of which he is the organ. I think it is very unwise

---

* To Sir J. Milbanke, January 31, 1848, when the Bavarian Government asked for the removal of the English secretary of Legation at Athens.

to give way to an intrigue; to do so is a proof either of great blindness or of weakness of character; and when people once find out that by bringing a certain amount of combined intrigue to bear against a given individual, or upon a given object, they can carry their point, either by imposing upon belief or by tiring out resistance, their system of political tactics is reduced to the same certainty with which a general can tell you the precise number of days which it will take him to capture a fortress."

Where a public servant is molested abroad he speaks out plainly, and sends a direct message to the responsible authority :—

"Broadlands, October 29, 1849.

" MY DEAR MONCORVO,*

" I am sorry to say that the last Lisbon mail brings me another correspondence which has taken place between Mr. Howard and Count Tojal upon the subject of another act of petty vexation on the part of Dr. Moacho, the Guarda Mor of the Health Department at Belem, towards Mr. Philipps, our Vice-Consul. I confess I am astonished that the Portuguese Government should permit one of their inferior officers to continue to carry on this system of malicious annoyance; but pray make Count Tojal clearly understand (which you will best do by sending him this note) that it is quite impossible for me to permit a deserving servant of the British Crown to be the victim of the low rancour and vulgar malig-

* Portuguese minister in London.

nity of any Guarda, whether he be ' Mor' or not; and I do intreat the Portuguese Government not to allow this ill-conditioned Doctor to bring on a quarrel between England and Portugal.

> " Yours sincerely,
> " Palmerston."

> "F. O., March 10, 1851.

" Dear Gordon,[*]

"I have received your letter about the attacks made upon Sir E. Lyons, and I request you will tell Baron Sterngeld in plain terms that I will not stand a continuance or renewal in Sweden of those base intrigues which were got up against Sir E. Lyons at Athens. We have chosen for the Queen's representative at Stockholm an able and distinguished diplomatist, and a brave and honourable naval officer. We expect and require that he shall be received at Stockholm with all the courtesy which is due to his personal merits, and to the respect which is owing to the Government and country which he represents; and if the Swedish Government attaches any value to the maintenance of its friendly relations with England, it will take proper care that we shall have no just cause of complaint on that score. Pray read this letter to Baron Sterngeld.

> " Yours sincerely,
> " Palmerston."

Not that he omitted to convey privately to his agents very plain expressions of his opinion if in

---

[*] British minister at Stockholm.

any respect he considered that they had failed in judgment or energy; but such rebukes created no ill-feeling when the motive was not to shift blame but to discharge a duty. In the case of minor errors he managed to intimate his opinion without giving offence. " But we must suspend our judgment and decision," he writes to Lord Normanby, " till we know exactly what has happened; and if a friend of mine had done so in his communications on these matters with the French Government, he would not have found himself worse placed thereby in subsequent discussions." *

I have already alluded to his thoughtfulness about others. With this was combined that attention to details which alone makes such thoughtfulness of any practical utility. To the Commander-in-Chief he suggests that the Guards should be relieved of some of the weight of their headgear : —

" There is another subject which seems deserving of your Royal Highness's attention. When your Royal Highness, or any other sportsman, goes out shooting, whether in winter or summer, carrying no other load than a double-barrelled gun weighing about eight pounds, and intending to walk leisurely only a few hours, the lightest possible wideawake is put upon the head, and a loose jacket and trousers leave the limbs as free as possible; but when a soldier of the Guards is ordered upon a long and

* To Lord Normanby, May 10, 1850.

fatiguing march, or has to make all the bodily exertion required on the field of battle, as if his tight clothing and his musket, knapsack, ammunition, and other things, weighing probably about sixty pounds, were not sufficient restraints upon muscular exertion, he has to carry on his head a great bearskin cap, weighing, it is said, about two pounds four ounces, whereas a far lighter headgear, even if made of bearskin, would answer every purpose, and relieve his head and brain from the heat and pressure of the present head-dress. I would venture to submit for your Royal Highness's consideration that a very light cap, partly bearskin, if that must be, but smaller and lower than the Artillery busby, would be a great relief to the men of the Guards; and that after such an improved head-dress had come into use everybody would wonder that the present high and heavy cap had ever been worn." *

When, for the purpose of preparing papers for Parliament, or from any other cause of pressure, the hours of work in some department of the Foreign Office were unusually prolonged, he used to send for a list of the clerks who had been so detained, and would convey to them individually his thanks and his appreciation of their work. I find notes put away docketed, " Names of Foreign Office Clerks who sat up " for such and such a purpose. It is not every chief who, in the middle of all his engrossing

* To Duke of Cambridge, November 12, 1861.

employments, would trouble himself about the share which each individual under him had taken in the general work.

During a fit of the gout he hears that a colleague is also laid up. Straightway, thinking of his friend's health, and not absorbed only in his own, he sends him the following letter :—

" Piccadilly, May 22, 1857.

" MY DEAR CLARENDON,

" Sympathy between colleagues is a good thing, but it may be carried too far, and I am sorry to hear that you have pushed it to the point of joining me in a touch of gout.

" Peel said that no man should give advice till he is called in, and you have not called me in; but I am called in by the interest which we all take in your health. What, then, would be your objection to the following suggestion ?

" You want more air and exercise. Much you cannot have, a little you might have, and every mickle makes a muckle, and a little every day tells in the course of the year. Why should you not provide yourself with a steady hack, with good action, who would give you no trouble when on him, and not prevent you from thinking over the draft you are next going to write ? Why should not the aforesaid quadruped be at your door every morning just as you finish your breakfast, and why should you not ride him to the end of Hyde Park and back again, or down to the Office, making a slight deviation by the way? It would take you only half an hour, but you would soon find the advantage of that half-hour, if daily taken.

> " Yours sincerely,
>
> " Palmerston."

He himself practised what he preached. His groom relates that often in his early days the horses were kept waiting at the door of the Foreign Office up to ten or eleven o'clock at night, so that, at any rate, Lord Palmerston might ride home, and so observe his rule of daily exercise on horseback. He was fond of saying that " Every other abstinence will not make up for abstinence from exercise.

Although, perhaps, almost too hard in his language during the combat, he was, after it was over, entirely free from petty malice or lasting rancour. There was always a desire to forgive and forget within the bounds of what was just. This won him at length the attachment even of his political foes. " He was always a very generous enemy," said Cobden, on his death-bed.

He had a wonderful faculty of dismissing from his mind any matter, however anxious, when, for the time, it was disposed of, and his disposition allowed him to feel perfect confidence in his subordinates so long as they had done nothing to forfeit it. These two qualities were mighty aids to him in his work, as they not only assisted his power of concentration, which was already naturally strong, but freed him from that perpetual head-worry which has worn out so many busy men. It is almost needless to add that, in spite of his long official habits, he never succumbed to that infirmity of small minds which is well described and well understood by the term " red-tapism."

Fearless truthfulness was one of his distinctive characteristics, which, while it made him some enemies, in the long run won him more friends. In his intercourse with foreign ministers, however, it sometimes served a purpose which he at the time little anticipated. I have heard him say that he occasionally found that they had been deceived by the open manner in which he told them the truth. When he had laid before them the exact state of the case, and announced his own intentions, they went away convinced that so skilful and experienced a diplomatist could not possibly be so frank as he appeared, and imagining some deep design in his words, acted on their own ideas of what he really meant, and so misled their ownselves.

A distinguished author of an essay on the working of the English Constitution lays down that a statesman who aspires to be a leader must also be an unflinching partisan. This appears to be so far true that it would, perhaps, be impossible to name any other man than Lord Palmerston whose life has been an illustration of the contrary; but he never seemed to take much interest in purely party politics, and party spirit influenced few of his acts. It used to be said of an eloquent Conservative leader that he led the Opposition with the spirit and keenness of a jockey riding a race; every nerve was strained, and every legitimate means resorted to, to "dish" his opponents. Lord Palmerston, on the contrary, once owned, in a letter to his brother, that he was not fit to be a leader of Opposition, because, as he said, "I have not faction enough in my composition."

But if in public life he was genial, straightforward, and considerate, in his private life these qualities were equally marked. As an English country gentleman — that type of landed proprietor which foreigners recognise as peculiar to this country, and by which so many of our best qualities are fostered — he took a keen interest and a personal share in all rural pursuits and business. Sports or meetings, farmers' dinners or agricultural shows, village schools, where he sometimes himself examined the children, or labourers' teas, when he always had a cheery word ready, and friendly advice mingled with fun — as on one occasion, when handing to a man a prize of twenty-five shillings, given for the tidiest couple, he added: "Scripture says that a virtuous woman is a crown to her husband; but in your case, you see, she is five crowns" — into each and all he threw himself with unaffected zest and enjoyment; for intercourse with his fellow-creatures, of whatever degree, was a positive pleasure to him, and in this Lady Palmerston resembled him. Her memory, cherished by his private friends, should not be less preserved in connection with his public career. Her assemblies—neutral ground where distinguished persons of all parties, whether foreign or domestic, met for social intercourse, forgetting for the moment their political differences—were a powerful aid to him as head of a Government. The manner in which she performed what Lord Palmerston, in reply to a complimentary letter from the American minister, once termed "her portion of our joint duties," sufficiently proved that to the refinement and kindliness of a " grande dame " she joined the genial and sympathetic nature of her husband. Both host and hostess succeeded in pleasing because they were pleased themselves; for age had not blunted their delight in the society of their fellow-men, or their pleasure in seeing others happy. By a natural law these hospitable efforts strengthened their influence in the political world, for the very reason that such was not the sole object they had in view when they threw open their doors, not grudgingly or of necessity, but because they liked it.

Let two instances suffice to illustrate Lord Palmerston's considerate kindness to those round him in the country :—One day Lady Palmerston brought him home word that during her drive she had heard of one of his tenants having met with a serious accident. Although it was late, and the hour for his daily work in his library, he instantly ordered his horse, left his despatches, and within half an hour was by the side of what proved to be a dying man. Again, when, in 1859, he presented the parish clergyman, Mr. Moore of Romsey, to the living of Sutterton, knowing that Mrs. Moore had indifferent health, and was anxious about the quality of the water in her future home, he directed specimens of it to be sent to him out of Lincolnshire, and himself fowarding them for analysis to the Royal College of Chemistry, obtained a satisfactory report, which he handed to Mr. Moore.

Lord Palmerston's style of writing illustrates his character, and may be studied with advantage. Let it be borne in mind that the letters which have been given in these volumes were for the most part written hastily, amid the press of business, and always without erasure or correction. Great simplicity, fun, and clearness convey the true impression of a straightforward correspondent whose object in writing is not a display either of wit or of erudition, but the communication of what he has to impart in as short and as easy, but in as effective a manner as possible. As a pompous and reserved statesman too often gets, among the vulgar, the credit of wisdom, so a dark and heavy writer is supposed to be profound. If he is clear and light-hearted, he is often regarded as shallow. No greater mistake. Lord Palmerston's letters survive as a protest against any such false judgment.

He wants a reform both in the manner and substance of a young diplomatist's reports; so he says to Lord Normanby,* "Your new man sends a long bavardage in an illegible hand. Pray tell him that his reports are of no use if they cannot be read, and that unless he encloses a couple of spare half-hours with each report he had better keep them to himself. The F. O. is not a spelling school. He should write a larger hand, throw over his reflections, and state his facts concisely like a table of contents." He is tormented by the difficulty of reading the faded colour of the Vienna despatches, so through Lord Ponsonby he takes the mission to task: "Your attachés put me out of all patience by the paleness of the ink in which they write out your despatches. Pray give them my compliments, and say I have put them all at the bottom of their respective lists, and if they do not mend their ways I shall be obliged to send you in their stead another set who will pay more attention to writing that which can be read." †

His own language being simple and accurate, he was apt to speak out when he came across sentences of a different quality. "Lord Palmerston desires me," writes his secretary, ‡ "to hint to you privately that he has great objection to the introduction of any Gallicism into a despatch which may have to be laid before Parliament. He observes, for instance, that you use the word *adhesion*, which he says is not an English word in the sense in which you use it; and he considers the same remark applicable to the

---

* March 7, 1849.   † To Lord Ponsonby, February 8, 1849.
‡ Sir G. Shee to Mr. Morier, April 22, 1834.

phrase, *It may be permitted to doubt,* which is also employed." *

To the Home Secretary he conveys a common-sense view about the supposed claims of civic functionaries to marks of royal favour :—

"November 18, 1862.
" My dear Grey,

"It seems to me that there are strong objections to giving Baronetcies to Mayors and Lord Mayors. In the first place, it would be opening a door without being able to say how many would have to enter by it; for if once you begin, it would be difficult to draw a line of distinction between cases to be accepted and cases to be refused. But in fact it would be handing over to municipal corporations the power of disposing of dignities granted by the Crown; and no wonder that all the magistrates of Edinburgh express a wish that they may be allowed to make a Baronet.

"Municipal corporations exercise their own pre-

* So, also, once in a speech in the House of Commons, he raised his voice against a common error of expression :—" We have heard the term ally and allies rung in our ears by those who either must be ignorant of the slipslop expression they were using, or, who, through what I must admit to have been its general acceptation, forgot that they were using a totally unmeaning term. Why, what is an ally? An ally is a Power allied by treaty engagements in carrying on some active operation, political or otherwise. But to call a country an ally merely because it is in a state of friendship with you is to use an expression that has no meaning whatever, because it is applicable to every other Power in the world with whom you may happen not to be in a state of war."—*July* 21, 1849.

rogative in conferring upon one of their members the dignity of Mayor; and the Crown exercises its prerogative in conferring upon those whom it deems worthy of it the dignity of Baronet.

" But each party should keep within its own bounds; and corporations should not try to make Baronets, any more than the Crown should try to make Mayors.

" Yours sincerely,
" PALMERSTON."

He declines to forward an oft-repeated recommendation from the Lord-Lieutenant of Ireland, in a note which is quite a model of brevity, because though curt it is civil :—

" Broadlands, April 24, 1862.

" MY DEAR CARLISLE,

" I have received your letter of the 19th. I remember a sarcastic critic exclaiming, ' Here comes Dudley Stuart with his eternal Poles.' I shall parody the exclamation by saying, here comes Carlisle with his eternal X——; but I think the Poles better entitled to their freedom than X—— is to the Commandership, and so let us adjourn the debate.

" Yours sincerely,
" PALMERSTON."

He was often very happy in the phrases with which he described a man's failings. Of a diplomatist who would obstinately stick to his own idea in spite of instructions from home, and for whom he was meditating a rebuke, he says, "S—— is like a bad retriever, that will not let go his game till he gets a rap on the nose." Of another, whose charity was not so large as his egotism : " I wish B——'s letters were not so full of backbiting : however, he makes up for his disparagement of others by his praises of himself." There is a whole type of diplomatists described .in the following sketch of a foreign ambassador: " Colloredo is agreeable in private society, but diplomatically he is a very unsatisfactory man to deal with. He seems always in a fright lest he should say anything that would commit him ; he is ever on the defensive, and there is no discussing any matter on equal terms with him. He ends a long conversation by saying, ' Mais souvenez vous que je ne vous ai rien dit,' and while he is talking seems to fancy that there is a short-hand writer behind the screen taking down what he says.*

"What energy," he once said, speaking of the Turks, " can be expected of a people with no heels to their shoes ?" And when a message was sent to him from a foreign sovereign, asking that a baronetcy might be conferred on an Englishman for whom that sovereign professed an attachment, the only remark he made was that while titles and honours were said to be the cheap rewards bestowed by princes, they certainly were cheapest of all when borrowed from a neighbour. .

Sir John Bligh, our minister at Hanover, writes to complain that the King will persist in giving balls

* To Lord Ponsonby, October 19, 1849.

on Sunday, and asks for Lord Palmerston's approval
if he leaves the palace when the band strikes up.
The Foreign Secretary, in reply, sanctions the conduct of the English minister, but so words his communication as to check any disposition that might
exist to make too grave a matter of the affair :—" It
is certainly somewhat singular that the King of
Hanover, who lays so much stress upon religion,
should choose Sunday of all days in the week for his
ball-night, and in this respect he seems to be the
reverse of Lord Fitzhardinge, who said to somebody,
that, to be sure, he had not much religion, but that
what little he had was of the best quality.   The
King of Hanover professes to have a great deal ; but
its quality seems rather indifferent, and I should think
that his friends in England would not be much edified
by hearing of his Sunday-evening polkas.   However,
I think you are quite right in making your bow at
these parties, and in then going away." *

His illustrations, often homely, generally went to
the root of the matter, as, for instance when discussing the policy of insisting on reciprocity from
France before throwing our markets open to her, he
thus condemned the notion :—" I look on the tariffs
of the two countries as if they were two turnpikes,
one on each side of a river dividing two counties,
both of which require payment from all passing
across. Who would not laugh at county A. if it
were to insist on continuing to pay the turnpike on

* Foreign Office, October 26, 1847.

its own side, unless it were also relieved from paying the turnpike on the B. side of the river? But high custom duties are like turnpike tolls, a charge making passage more expensive for everything that comes in."

As a public speaker, Lord Palmerston's success was very great, and surely results are good tests of merit in the art of persuasion. He certainly never aspired to the lofty rank of a great orator nor to the magic wand of a great master of phrases; but in the power of conveying abundant knowledge in an apt, logical, and convincing form, he yielded the palm to none. I find traces of careful preparation for the speeches of his earlier years; but during the latter half of his life he made little or none. The great changes in the constitution of the House of Commons which successive Reform Bills have made must never be forgotten by those who would compare the Parliamentary speakers of the present with those of a former generation. The House of Commons of the nineteenth century, for a variety of reasons, all perhaps excellent, gives no encouragement to oratory. A man may succeed in spite of it if he possesses knowledge of details sufficient to redeem his defect; but if he cherishes the models studied by Pitt and Fox he bears about him rather a burden than a source of power.

Shortly after Lord Palmerston's death there appeared a short criticism on his public speaking which is so good, as far as it goes, that I here insert it. It is taken from the columns of a newspaper * which, as a Radical organ, had been very hostile to him. The tribute to his powers is all the more impartial :—

"Lord Palmerston was successful chiefly because he always made it his business to understand the temper of his audience, and accommodate himself to it. He was not an orator in any critical sense of the word. He never made the slightest attempt to rival such men as Pitt and Fox, as Gladstone and Bright, in eloquence. But few men were ever more successful in effecting, by means of public speaking, the objects at which they aimed. Lord Palmerston never indulged in any attempts at fine language. He studied nothing of elocution except the art of speaking distinctly out. His action was generally monotonous. Although fluent, he had a fashion—perhaps an affectation—of interjecting occasionally a sort of guttural sound between his words, which must necessarily have been fatal to anything like true oratorical effect, but which somehow seemed to enhance the peculiar effectiveness of his unprepared, easy, colloquial style. Certainly the occasional hesitation, real or affected, often did much to increase the humour of some of the jocular hits in which Lord Palmerston so commonly delighted. The joke seemed to be so entirely unpremeditated; the audience were kept for a moment in such amusing suspense, while the speaker was apparently turning over the best way to give the hit, that when at last it came it was enjoyed with the keener relish. His jokes were always suited to the present capacity of those whom he happened to address. If the House seemed in a humour for mere nonsense, then Lord Palmerston revelled in mere nonsense. He had the happy art of making commonplaces seem effective. He never rose above his audience; he never vexed their intellect by difficult propositions or entangled

* The late 'Morning Star.'

arguments. Unless where he purposely chose to be vague or unintelligible, he always went straight to the mark, and talked in homely, vigorous, Saxon English. He never talked too long ; he never by any chance wearied his audience. He always knew, as if instinctively, what style of argument would best at any given moment tell upon the House. He brought to bear upon every debate an unsurpassed tact, and a memory hardly rivalled. He could reply with telling effect, and point by point, to a lengthened attack from an enemy, without the use of a note or memorandum of any kind. When argument failed, he employed broad, rough English satire. He was never dull; he was never ineffective; he was never uninteresting. One of his rough and ready speeches helped to carry many a division, when Burke would have turned friends into foes from sheer impatience, and when brilliant eloquence of any kind might have been as dangerous to play with as lightning." *

But whatever his merits as a speaker, it was to the general confidence felt in his judgment, motives, and character that Lord Palmerston owed the great

---

* As a chance illustration of his after-dinner speeches let me give an extract from one of the last he made, namely, at the banquet of the Fishmongers' Company in 1864. He followed another minister who descanted learnedly on the blessings of the British Constitution. Lord Palmerston spoke more appropriately of the blessings of fish :—" I believe that one of the functions of this ancient corporation is particularly connected with the position of the country to which it belongs, because in an island country it is natural that one of the first functions of an efficient civic corporation should be to regulate the immigration of the vast multitude of the inhabitants of the ocean that come in contact with the population (laughter). That duty has been from time to time most worthily performed by this corporation ; and I am told that to this day the inhabitants of this great metropolis are weekly and daily indebted to its guardian care ; for that there are multitudes of immigrants that come here. from the depths of the ocean unfitted to mix with the population of this island, and being unable to obtain the necessary passport are refused an entrance through the vigilance of this ancient corporation (laughter)."

position which he latterly occupied in the country. Public confidence is, for a statesman in a free community, one of the first requisites for success; and if this be wanting no amount of brilliancy in speaking will long supply such a capital defect. There have, no doubt, been temporary exceptions; but leaders of party in England, and above all, leaders of the Liberal party, must command the moral trust as well as the intellectual homage of thinking men. I find among his papers the following passage, copied out by himself from some essay which he had been reading about De Witt, Grand Pensionary of Holland. It may serve as an appropriate ending to this story of his career :—

"The statesman who, in treading the slippery path of politics, is sustained and guided only by the hope of fame or the desire of a lofty reputation, will not only find himself beset with incessant temptations to turn aside from the line of strict integrity, but the disappointment he is sure to meet with will probably drive him to misanthropy, perhaps even irritate him to tarnish by vindictive treachery a virtue founded upon no solid or enduring principle. But the statesman who looks in the simple performance of his duty for consolation and support amid all the toils and sufferings which that duty may call him to encounter, who aims not at popularity, because he is conscious that continued popularity rarely accompanies systematic and unyielding integrity; who, as he is urged to no questionable measures by the hope of fame, so is deterred from none that are just by the fear of censure, such a man may steer a steady course through the shoals and breakers of the stormiest sea; and whether he meet with the hatred or gratitude of his countrymen is to him a consideration of minor moment, for his reward is otherwise sure. He has laboured with constancy for great objects; he has conferred signal benefits upon his fellow-men; nobler occupation man cannot aspire to; greater reward it would be very difficult to obtain."

This extract bears date 1843. Did Lord Palmerston make these maxims his own? His public life, I venture to think, proves that he did.

APPENDIX.

<hr>

I.

LETTER FROM LORD SHAFTESBURY ABOUT LORD
PALMERSTON'S CHARACTER.

"January 6, 1876.

" My dear Evelyn,

"You have asked me to commit to paper a few notes founded on my experience of Lord Palmerston's public and private character. Much that I could tell you must of necessity be suppressed, for many of his cotemporaries are still alive, and the sovereign whom he served is still on the throne. The reminiscences, moreover, of his great decision and remarkable exercise of individual responsibility might raise some displeasure in the minds of those who had felt their power.

" When I first entered Parliament, in 1826, he was Secretary at War, as he had been for many years. He passed, so far as I could then judge, for a handy, clever man, who moved his estimates very well, appeared to care but little about public affairs in general, went a good deal into society, and never attracted any other remark than one of wonder, which I often heard, that he had been so long in the same office.

" I doubt whether, at that time, he had much personal

ambition. It was not, indeed, until his retirement along with Mr. Huskisson and others, that, having become one of a small but compact party, he began to feel his individual importance, and resolved to manifest his power of debate. The great and dominant study of his life—the foreign policy of England—was at once displayed; and in able and consecutive speeches on the Greek Question (far more elaborate than those of his later life), he raised himself to so high a level, that Lord Grey, when summoned to form a Cabinet, offered him the department of Foreign Affairs.

"His light and jaunty manner did him great disservice in his earlier years; and I recollect perfectly well that, on our first acquaintance, I could see nothing in him of the statesman, but a good deal of the dandy.

"This manner attended him throughout life in all the intercourse of society, even when engaged, heart and soul, in the most arduous and important matters. It was not assumed; it was perfectly natural and easy; for, whether at home or abroad, he seemed to be always disposed to take a light-humoured view of all and everything that came under his notice.

"But this was simply the efflorescence of certain great principles fermenting within. I do not hesitate to say that the two great objects of his heart—one, the institution of a true and vigorous foreign policy, suited to the honour and position of the kingdom of England; the other, the extinction of the slave trade—were founded, not only on his personal love of freedom (which was intense), but on his deep and unalterable conviction that civil liberty all over the world would be good for the human race, and specially so for the British people.

" His ardour to abolish the traffic in slaves was stimulated constantly by the atrocities of the system, for he could feel very keenly the wrongs of others. And though, doubtless, many will criticise him unsparingly for his efforts at constitutions in foreign countries, he would reply, I know (were he alive), that representative government, with all its abuses, is the best, on the whole, for the safety, honour, and improvement of mankind; and that he had not flinched, and that he would never flinch, from any legitimate opportunity to urge its advancement.

" Such vigorous assertion of his own principles, in the face of very hostile and sensitive powers, was often misconstrued as a readiness for war; nay, even as a recklessness on the question. It is not necessary for me to defend or to censure many things that he did. The world must judge him by the aggregate of his actions, and their results. From war, as war, I believe he shrank with horror; but he was inflexibly of opinion that the best way to avoid it was to speak out boldly, and ever be prepared to meet the emergency.

" In his day he was oftentimes twitted with love of office. He never denied his predilection for it. He ever maintained that the pursuit of it was, to some persons, almost a duty. He did not think himself single in this view; for he said to me one day, 'I have never known any public men who after a certain tenure of office did not pray to be quit of it; nor any who having been turned out of office did not wish, after a very short time, to get back to it again.' Unquestionably he was born for a bureau; the thing and its whole surroundings were a part of his existence. It amounted to a complete absorption of the man in his devotion to the special duties; he then scarcely gave a thought to other matters.

And I could adduce some remarkable instances, during times when the pressure of foreign affairs was urgent and heavy, of his almost absolute ignorance of what was passing in the world, the House of Commons, and even in the Cabinet.

" When charged with selfish change of opinion for the sake of office, he barely comprehended what people meant; for while he felt that he stood firm to his own foreign policy, he never conceived that he had changed anything at all.

" I was always struck by his generous bearing towards meritorious persons, and his desire to recognise real public service. I do not speak of his hospitality and personal kindness to such men, for that was overflowing; nor of his liberality in the matter of money; I speak of the use he made of the patronage and honours of the state. Any one of desert who had been overlooked was sure, on application to him, to obtain redress, if redress were possible. Many could I name who 'appealed to Cæsar,' and obtained justice. And he did not pause for an instant in praying Her Majesty to confer the rank of Baronet on Mr. Crossley, of Halifax, and Mr. Baxter, of Dundee, in acknowledgment of their magnificent liberality towards the people of their respective cities.

" This action of generous sentiment was seen in less conspicuous instances; he would never abandon a public officer who had conscientiously endeavoured to serve him well. He regretted the mistakes into which his agent had fallen, and he felt the difficulties inflicted on himself; but if he saw diligence and sincerity in the man, he would make the best of the job, and stand by his officer to the very last.

" This principle shone out in his higher appointments. He

had much solicitude for the honour and efficiency of the episcopal office. He ever sought for good and proper men; and he discarded, in the search, all considerations of mere politics, or attention to personal requests. 'If the man is a good man,' he often said, 'I don't care what his political opinions are. Certainly I had rather not name a bishop who would make party speeches and attacks on the Government in the House of Lords; but short of that, let him do as he likes.' 'I am a very lucky man,' he remarked to me; 'luckier than most ministers. I have no sons, grandsons, or nephews to stuff into the Church; and, so far as all that is concerned, I can do what I think right.' An instance of his disinterestedness occurred to myself. I had ventured to suggest to him the name of a very learned but comparatively unknown man for a high professorship. 'I must state,' I added, 'that he is a person of no social account, and has no friends to endorse him.' 'What does that signify?' he replied: 'is he a proper man?' 'Yes; a very proper man.' 'Then he shall be appointed.' And he was so appointed.

" I must add here that a part of his definition of a 'good and proper man' for the Episcopal Bench, was one who would go on well with the nonconformists. He had a very special dislike of every form of clerical assumption.

"On matters where he fully believed that he was master of the subject his conclusions were very decided and positively unchangeable. This was the case, for example, as to his foreign policy; and yet no one will say that, either in public debate or private conversation, he maintained his opinions offensively; and, in truth, on these points he was too well satisfied with himself to be angry. Those who then differed from him he regarded with something like compassion; and I am sure that the sentiment, though he did not utter it, was often in his mind, 'Poor things! they know no better!'

"He had no care, so far as I ever saw, for posthumous fame. Certainly he was not indifferent, when alive, to public reputation; but about his credit with future generations he never seemed to entertain a thought. He gave no instructions about the publication of his papers; and laboured defences were, in his estimation, useless. As I once heard Lord Melbourne say, 'Why in such a hurry to answer letters?—most letters answer themselves in about a fortnight:' so Palmerston believed that a man's character, if it was a good one, would sooner or later come right, without any special bother on the subject.

"This calmness of spirit was a grand ingredient of his mental and moral composition. It enabled him to endure much labour and face many responsibilities. Once only, so your grandmother used to say, had she known him in a state of disturbance and anxiety—I mean as to public matters. The source of this trouble was the great motion to be made in the House of Commons on foreign affairs in general, and specially on the case of Don Pacifico. Though fully confident in himself, he felt, as he said, that the existence of the Ministry depended on his success. He was deeply and seriously disquieted. Success having attended his efforts, he returned to his ordinary composure. He received no end of congratulations in his good-humoured, easy way; and the next day he had as much set aside the whole thing as though it had never happened.

"It is said of Dr. Johnson that he had the power of concentrating suddenly all his faculties, and even the strength of his memory, on any matter under discussion. Lord Palmerston had much of the same power. Lord Granville gave me, on the authority of Lord Ossington, who was at that time Speaker of the House of Commons, an instance of his coolness and self-possession. Mr. Disraeli had made a very vigorous and telling speech, to which Lord Palmerston was to reply. Mr. Disraeli having finished, the Speaker quitted the chair for a few minutes, having called on Lord Palmerston to occupy the House. On his return, he found Lord Palmerston so little in anxiety that he was fast asleep. He was roused, and went, so the Speaker said, through the whole question, taking up and answering every point, and all without a single note or reference on paper. He was indeed, in that respect, very fanciful; for he always maintained that any use whatever of notes by a speaker invariably spoiled the effects of the oration.

"Both in private and in public life he was of a very placable spirit. There might be, but very rarely, now and then little bursts of irritation, but they soon passed away. Of public resentments he had no memory at all; and I never heard him speak but of one man as so bad in his estimation that he had rather have nothing to do with him. On one occasion he had decided to name a certain clergyman to a vacant bishopric. A day or two afterwards he wrote to me to say that since he had made up his mind for Dr. ——, he had received a letter from Lord Russell, with a request that a friend of his might be appointed to the see. 'If,' he continued, 'Russell's man be a good and proper man, I should wish to appoint him, because you know Russell once treated me in a very rough way, and I desire to show him that I have quite forgotten it.'

" In all my experience I have not seen any man so kind to all alike; so delicate, tender, and considerate in all the relations of domestic life. The loss of his sisters very deeply affected him; and his correspondence with his brother exhibits very much the private character of the man. His attentions to Lady Palmerston when they, both of them, were well stricken in years were those of a perpetual courtship. The sentiment was reciprocal; and I have frequently seen them go out on a morning to plant some trees, almost believing that they would live to eat the fruit, or sit together under their shade. For a long time he seemed scarcely aware of the progress of age, and never but once, in my hearing, did he make any allusion to it, and that once was simply, ' I who am no chicken.'

" But nature at length began to assert her reign, and the greater part of his last session in the House of Commons, and the few months which followed down to his decease, were, I am satisfied, a period of terrible toil and suffering. His eyesight had become exceedingly weak, and he read, even when aided by strong glasses—an infirmity he was very desirous to conceal—with great pain and difficulty. His bodily vigour was giving way, symptoms to which he was wholly unused had appeared, and he saw for the first time that he must succumb like other men. His resolution, however, so long as he retained his post, was to work, without care of himself, for the service of the state. He retained it from principle and patriotism. Ambition and the love of office had entirely vanished. He seemed to be more than usually thoughtful on coming events. Not long before his death, when I was alone with him one evening, he said, ' When I am gone, and some other shall have got my place,

there will be many changes, with much anxiety and confusion in the country.' People will judge of this sentiment
according to their particular politics. I quote it only to
show how the belief had affected his own mind, and brought
him (so contrary to his habit) to leave the present, and speak
seriously of the future.

"It is a wonderful fact in the physiological history of
public men that he should have been able to undertake,
at more than threescore years and ten, and carry on, up
to and beyond eighty years of age, the responsible and
overwhelming offices of Prime Minister and Leader of the
House of Commons—a terrific strain on the moral and physical powers of those even in the prime of life. He never
quitted the House till the hour of its adjournment; and he
invariably maintained that his constant attendance was one
main cause of his success; and that by being ever on the
spot, he prevented a hundred things that might otherwise
have burst out in debates, motions, and deputations. His
nervous system was singularly well balanced; his digestive
organs seemed never at fault; and at whatever hour he retired
to bed, he could fall asleep at once, and take, what he invariably insisted on, eight hours of repose.

"The time was well appointed for his departure; to within
ten days of his death he was still in a green old age, and
with all his faculties about him. England enjoyed to the
last the full service of his noblest qualities; his infirmities
affected only himself, with which most of us must sympathise,
because we, most of us, share them.

"The testimony that I bear is, perhaps, of little value, as
being that of a man who had ever received from him the
look, the voice, and the action of kindness. But take

the testimony of Sir R. Peel, a political antagonist. Sir Robert, when addressing the House of Commons, at the close of Palmerston's great speech on the foreign policy of the Government, exclaimed, with unrestrained admiration, ' We may have many differences of opinion with the noble lord, but the country is proud of him.'

"And as the country was then, so is the country now.

" Yours affectionately,

" SHAFTESBURY.

" Hon. EVELYN ASHLEY."

II.

VIEWS ABOUT THE SUEZ CANAL SCHEME.

LORD PALMERSTON did not favour the Suez Canal scheme. On that everybody seems agreed; but there are many versions of the reasons which induced him to withhold his support. The following letter indicates why, under the actual circumstances, he thought that the English Government should stand aloof from Monsieur Lesseps and his project. Even with the light of later experience we can see that he was not so far wrong. There were political objects inconvenient to England clearly connected with this canalisation at the time when France was under an imperial régime; and as to the financial question, when the funds and labour provided by the Khedive come to be added to the expense incurred by the company itself, besides the amount of interest lost during construction, and the further outlay which the maintenance of the navigation will soon demand, Lord Palmerston's views as to the probable money return may not appear very wide of the mark :—

"94, Piccadilly, December 8, 1861.

"MY DEAR RUSSELL,

"The proposal of a French, English, and Austrian commission to inquire into the practicability of the Suez Canal sounds fair and plausible, but would be a dangerous measure.

"There are three aspects under which this scheme may be looked at. First, as to the commercial advantage of it, if completed; secondly, as to the engineering and financial practicability of executing; thirdly, as to the political effect of the canal, if completed.

" Now, we cannot deny that, if no objection could be urged against the scheme on the second and third heads, no valid objection could be made to it on the first. Looking at the matter purely with reference to the commerce of Europe, any great work which would shorten considerably the voyage to India, would be advantageous to all nations trading by sea to Asia. Even on this ground, however, there is something to be said against the scheme, because it was demonstrated by a Dutch engineer that, owing to difficulties of navigating the Red Sea, in consequence of coral reefs, prevailing winds, and intense heat, the navigation round the Cape would, except with regard to very powerful steamers, be cheaper and shorter than through the canal.

" But the second point hardly admits of a doubt. The Lesseps Company have now been ostensibly at work for nearly ten years at a canal that is to be a hundred feet wide and thirty feet deep from sea to sea, with ports for sea-going ships on the Mediterranean and Red Sea ends; and yet up to this moment, though a very large part of their nominal capital has been spent, not one single spadeful has been turned up for the construction of this canal. Lesseps has begun what he calls his ' rigole,' a boat canal twelve feet wide and four feet deep, of which one-third, beginning from the north, has been finished; a second third may be completed in the next spring or early summer, and the remaining third would be more easily finished by letting the water of the Red Sea into a salt marsh some way to the north of Suez. Lesseps is eager about this, because he thinks his shares would rise in the market at Paris if he could show that he had actually floated a boat from sea to sea. But he will not tell his shareholders what is nevertheless the fact, that this boat canal, or ' rigole,' is not to form any part whatever of the ship canal; the ship canal is to be dug in a line parallel to this boat canal, and the boat canal is only to be used like a railway, for the easier conveyance of workmen, provisions, and materials as the great work goes on. I understand that there is scarcely one among the French engineers employed who would not, if he told the truth, acknowledge that the ship canal could not be made without an amount of money and a period of time far exceeding all the calculations hitherto made, and that, if accomplished, it never could be made to pay interest on the cost incurred. It may safely be said, therefore, that, as a commercial undertaking, it is a bubble scheme, which has been taken up on political grounds, and in antagonism to English interests and English policy.

"Well, then, we come to the last point, namely, the political objects of the enterprise; and these are hostility to England in every possible modification of the scheme.

"It requires only a glance at the map of the world to see how great would be the naval and military advantage to France in a war with England to have such a short cut to the Indian seas, while we should be obliged to send ships and troops round the Cape. Thouvenel proposes, indeed, that the passage of ships-of-war should be forbidden as at the Dardanelles, but I presume he does not expect us to receive such a proposal except with a decently suppressed smile. Of course the first week of a war between France and England would see 15,000 or 20,000 Frenchmen in possession of the canal, to keep it open for them and shut for us. But then, moreover, so strong a military barrier between Syria and Egypt would greatly add to the means of the Pacha for the time being to declare himself independent of Turkey, which would mean his being a dependent of France; and lastly, if the canal should never be made, the French company are to have a large grant of land in the centre of Egypt, and would establish in Egypt a colony whose complaints against the Egyptian Government, well or ill-founded, would give the French Government pretences for interfering in all the internal affairs of the country.

"I should say, therefore, on the whole, that it would be best for the French and English Governments to leave this scheme as a commercial and engineering question to be settled by the result of experience and the money markets of Europe; and that, as regards the political question, all we ask of the French Government is not to interfere in the matter, but to let all questions between the Sultan and the Pacha be settled according to the mutual rights and reciprocal obligations of those two parties.

"Yours sincerely,
"PALMERSTON."

III.

LETTER ABOUT MUTUAL RELATIONS OF MEMBERS OF A CABINET.

To a member of Parliament who inquired of Lord Palmerston what was the constitutional view of the relations of the members of the Cabinet to one another and to the First Lord of the Treasury, he wrote as follows:—

"Broadlands, January 13, 1852.

"MY DEAR SIR,

"In answer to your question, I should say that, strictly and technically, each minister at the head of a department is primarily responsible for all things done in the department over which he presides, and not for anything done in any other department; and thus the First Lord of the Treasury, in his capacity as such, is answerable only for things done by and in his own department. But then established practice modifies this abstract principle.

"As all the principal members of the Executive Government meet from time to time in Cabinet councils, to consider and to determine upon all the important measures to be executed by the several departments, all the members of the Cabinet must be considered as concurring in every important step taken separately by each in his own department; and thus all the members of the Government are answerable for what is done of an important nature in each department. And then, in regard to financial arrangements and questions of expenditure, the Treasury being the department which

2 A 2

brings forward the Budget, and which proposes to Parliament the amount of taxation for the year, it is reasonable and proper that the First Lord of the Treasury should have a control over the whole of that expenditure, for which he, or his assistant, the Chancellor of the Exchequer, is to propose to Parliament to provide the necessary ways and means, because otherwise the Treasury might be asking Parliament to continue or to impose taxes to cover expenses which a more efficient control on the part of the Treasury might have prevented.

"Then again, in regard to the tenure of office by the several members of the Government, the sovereign, when a new administration is to be formed, sends generally for some one person, who is commissioned to form an administration. That person recommends to the Crown the men whom he thinks best for the several offices to be filled; and as that person, who is the Prime Minister, recommends the other ministers, when they are appointed he is also fully entitled, at any future time, to recommend to the Crown any changes or removals which he may deem proper. Of course, the exercise of all these functions must be subject to discussion in Parliament, the Prime Minister, the Treasury, and the heads of departments being all liable to be called upon to account to Parliament for the manner in which they have exercised the powers which law and practice have entrusted them with.

"My dear Sir,

"Yours faithfully,

"PALMERSTON."

IV.

CORRESPONDENCE WITH SIR GEORGE LEWIS ON "PREVENTION
BETTER THAN CURE."

SIR GEORGE LEWIS was a man to whom Lord Palmerston
was much attached, and a politician in whose judgment he
had the greatest confidence. The following letters are interesting, as illustrations of their different modes of thought and
of the frank nature of their mutual intercourse. The question of how far evils should be anticipated by steps taken to
prevent their occurrence, is treated by the man of action and
by the philosophic statesman from different points of view:—

"November 22, 1860.
" MY DEAR LEWIS,

" You broached yesterday evening what seems to me
a political heresy, which I hope was only a conversational
paradox, and not a deliberately adopted theory. You said
you dissented from the maxim that prevention is better than
cure, and that you thought that, instead of trying to prevent
an evil, we ought to wait till it had happened, and should
then apply the proper remedy. Now I beg to submit that
the prevention of evil is the proper function of statesmen
and diplomatists; and that the correction of evil calls forth
the action of generals and admirals. Evils are prevented
by the pen, but are corrected by the sword. They are pre-

vented by ink-shed, but can be corrected only by blood-shed. The first is an operation of peace; the second, the action of war.

"It seems to me to be no valid argument to say that measures taken to prevent an evil may by possibility lead to war, when it can be shown to be far more probable that the evil, if it happens, will lead to that result.

"There are endless instances of serious conflicts which might have been prevented by timely vigour and negotiation, and an equal number of cases in which timely vigour and activity have averted dangerous consequences. If the Duke of Wellington's Government, in 1830, had not been swayed by the same timidity which prevailed in the Cabinet yesterday, the French would not now have had Algeria—a possession which, whenever we have a war with France, will give us trouble and cause us much annoyance. If Lord Aberdeen's Government had shown less timidity when the Russians prepared to invade the Danube Principalities, it is pretty certain that we should not have had the Russian war; but it is needless to multiply examples to prove what appear to me to be self-evident propositions.

"Yours sincerely,

"PALMERSTON."

"Kent House, November 23, 1860.

"MY DEAR LORD PALMERSTON,

"As a medical maxim, it is true universally that prevention is better than cure; but it seems to me that this maxim must be applied with discretion in political, especially in foreign, politics. If the evil is proximate and certain, or highly probable, no doubt a wise statesman will, if he can, prevent it. But with respect to remote and uncertain evils, the system of insurance may be carried too far. Our foreign relations are so numerous and so intricate, that if we insure against every danger which ingenuity can devise there will be no end of our insurances. Even in private life it is found profitable for those who carry on operations on a large scale not to insure. One thing, according to the received though not very precise saying, insures another. A man who has one or two ships, or one or two farmhouses, insures. But a man who has many ships, and many farmhouses, often does not insure.

" We keep in every country of the world a paid agent, often of great activity and intelligence, whose time in general is only half employed, and whose business it is to frighten his own Government with respect to the ambitions and encroaching designs of foreign Governments. I am not seeking to undervalue the services of diplomatic and consular agents. I know that, on the whole, they are of great benefit to the country which employs them; but it is natural and proper that they should keep a sharp look-out for the machinations of foreign Governments, and that their imagination should sometimes be stronger than their reason. If their advice was listened to, we should be perpetually taking expensive precautions against remote and problematical risks.

" Generally, I think that our foreign policy is too timorous; that we are apt to be scared by bugbears, and to underrate the power of England, and the fear of it entertained by foreign nations. I do not believe that the possession of Algeria by France is any real disadvantage to us. It acts as a constant drain on the military and financial resources of France, and in the event of a war would necessarily fall into our hands, if we were able to obtain and maintain the empire of the sea. The possession of Egypt and Malta did nothing for France in the late war.

" If an evil is certain and proximate, and can be averted by diplomacy, then undoubtedly prevention is better than cure. But if the evil is remote and uncertain, then I think it better not to resort to preventive measures, which insure a proximate and certain mischief. The evil may probably never occur ; the cure may perhaps be simple and inexpensive, and may not imply hostilities. It seems to me that our foreign relations are on too vast a scale to render it wise for us to insure systematically against all risks; and if we do not insure systematically, we do nothing.

> " Believe me,
> > " Yours very sincerely,
> > > " G. C. Lewis."

V.

MEMORANDUM BY MR. COBDEN ON "MUTUAL DIS-ARMAMENT."

THIS memorandum, sent to Lord Palmerston by Mr. Cobden in 1862, is interesting, and, whatever opinions might have been held as to the practicability of the proposal, it was highly honourable to Mr. Cobden's character and consistent with his persevering efforts in the cause of peace.*

" The present peculiar and exceptional state of the English and French navies, the result of scientific progress in maritime armaments, offers an opportunity for a reciprocal arrangement between the two Governments of the highest interest to both countries.

" During the last century, and down almost to the present day, the relative naval strength of the two countries has been measured by the number of their line-of-battle ships. But, owing to the recent improvements in explosive shells and other combustible missiles, and in the modes of projecting them, these large vessels have been pronounced, by competent judges, no longer suited for maritime warfare; and warning voices have even proclaimed that they will henceforth prove only a snare to those who employ them.

* See page 221.

" This opinion has found utterance in several emphatic phrases.

" ' Wooden ships of the line,' says one, ' will, in a future naval war, be nothing but human slaughter-houses.'

" ' They will be blown to lucifer matches,' says another.

" A third authority tells us that in case of a collision between two such vessels, at close quarters, the only words of command for which there will be time will be, ' Fire, and lower your boats !'

" Whilst a fourth declares that ' any Government that should send such a vessel into action against an iron-plated ship would deserve to be impeached.'

" It hardly required such a weight of evidence to convince us that to crowd nearly a thousand men upon a huge wooden target, with thirty or forty tons of gunpowder at their feet, and expose them to a bombardment with detonating shells and other combustible projectiles must be a very suicidal proceeding.

" The Governments of the great maritime states have shown that they share this opinion by abandoning the further construction of line-of-battle ships.

" America, several years since, gave the preference to long low vessels possessing the utmost possible speed and being capable of carrying the largest guns. France was the next to cease building ships of the line. The British Government have come to the same decision, and they gave a pledge last session, with the approval of Parliament, that they will not complete the vessels of this class which were unfinished on the stocks.

" It is under these circumstances that the two countries find themselves in possession of about one hundred wooden ships of the line with screw propellers. England has between sixty and seventy, and France between thirty and forty of these vessels, the greater part of them in commission ; and their maintenance constitutes the principal item in the naval

expenditure of the two countries. It will be admitted that
if these vessels did not exist, they would not now be constructed. It is equally indisputable that they have been
built by the two Governments with a view to preserve a
certain relative force towards each other. In proof that this
rivalry has been confined exclusively to England and France,
it may be stated, on the authority of the official representative of the Admiralty in the House of Commons, that Spain
has only three, Russia nine, and Italy one, of this class of
ships. America has only one.

" These circumstances suggest, as an obvious course to the
two Governments, that they should endeavour to come to an
amicable agreement by which the greater portion of these
ships might be withdrawn and so disposed of as to be rendered
incapable of being again employed for warlike purposes.
This might be effected by an arrangement which should
preserve to each country precisely the same relative strength
after the reduction as before. For instance, assuming, merely
for the sake of argument, England to possess sixty-five and
France thirty-five, then for every seven withdrawn by France
England should withdraw thirteen; and thus, to whatever
extent the reduction was carried, provided this proportion
were preserved, the two countries would still possess the same
relative force. The first point on which an understanding
should be come to is as to the number of ships of the line
actually possessed by each; a very simple question, inasmuch
as it is not complicated with the comparison of vessels in
different stages of construction. Then the other main point
is to agree upon a plan for making a fair selection, ship for
ship, so that the withdrawals on both sides may be as nearly
as possible of corresponding size or value. If the principle
of a proportionate reduction be agreed to, far fewer difficulties will be found in carrying out the details than must
have been encountered in arranging the plans of co-operation
in the Crimean and Chinese wars, or in settling the details
of the Commercial Treaty.

"And is this principle of reciprocity in the adjustment of the naval forces of the two countries an innovation? On the contrary, it would be easy to cite the declarations of the leading statesmen on both sides of the Channel, during the last twenty years, to prove that they have always been in the habit of regulating the amount of their navies by a reference to each other's armaments. True, this has been invariably done to justify an increase of expenditure. But why should not the same principle be also available in the interest of economy, and for the benefit of the taxpayers? A nation suffers no greater loss of dignity from surrendering its independence of action in regulating its armaments, whether the object be to meet a diminution or an increase of its neighbour's forces.

"Although this reduction of the obsolete ships of the line presents a case of the easiest solution, and should, therefore, in the first place, be treated as a separate measure, it could hardly fail to pave the way for an amicable arrangement for putting some limit to those new armaments which are springing out of the present transition state of the two navies.

"The application of iron plates to ship-building, which has rendered the reconstruction of the navies necessary, must be regarded as the commencement of a series of indefinite changes; and, looking to the great variety of experiments now making, both in ships and artillery, and to the new projects which inventors are almost daily forcing upon the attention of the two Governments, it is not improbable that a few years hence, when England and France shall have renewed their naval armaments, they will be again rendered obsolete by new scientific discoveries. In the meantime neither country adds to its relative strength by this waste of national wealth; for, as both Governments aim at only a proportionate increase of their forces, it is not contemplated that either should derive any exclusive advantage from the augmentation. An escape from this dilemma is not to be sought in the attempt to arrest the march of improvement, or to discourage the efforts of inventive genius. A remedy for the evil can only be found in a more frank understanding between the two Governments. If they will discard the old and utterly futile theory of secrecy—a theory on which an individual manufacturer or merchant no longer founds his hopes of successful competition with a foreign rival—they may be enabled, by the timely exchange of explanations and assurances, to prevent what ought to be restricted to mere experimental trials from growing into formidable preparations for war. If the secret thoughts of those who are responsible for the naval administration of the two countries were disclosed, it would probably be found that they are appalled at the prospect of a rivalry which, whilst it can satisfy neither the reason nor the ambition of either party, offers a boundless field of expenditure to both.

" Nor should it be forgotten that the financial pressure caused by these rival armaments is a source of constant irritation to the populations of the two countries. The British taxpayers believe, on the authority of their leading statesmen, that the increased burden to which they are subjected is caused by the armaments on the other side of the Channel. The people of France are probably taught to feel similarly aggrieved towards England. The feelings of mutual animosity produced by this sacrifice of substantial interests are not to be allayed by the exchange of occasional demonstrations of friendship between the two Governments. On the contrary, their inconsistent policy in incessantly arming against each other at home whilst uniting for common objects abroad, if it do not impair public confidence in their sincerity, tends at least to destroy all faith in an identity fo interests between the rulers and the ruled, by showing how little advantage the peoples derive from the friendship of their Governments. But the greatest evil connected with these rival armaments is that they destroy the strongest motives for peace. When two great neighbouring nations find themselves permanently subjected to a war expenditure without the compensation of its usual excitements and honours, the danger to be apprehended is, that if an accident should occur to inflame their hostile passions—and we know how certain these accidents are, at intervals, to arise—their latent and pent-up sense of suffering and wrong may reconcile them to a rupture as the only means of eventual escape from their intolerable burdens and anxieties.

"Circumstances appeal strongly to the two Governments, at the present juncture, in favour of a measure of wise and safe economy. In consequence of the deplorable events in America, and the partial failure of the harvests of Europe, the commerce and manufactures of both countries are exposed to an ordeal of great suffering. Were the proposed naval reduction carried into effect, it would ameliorate the financial position of the Governments and afford the means for alleviating the fiscal burdens of the peoples. But the moral effects of such a measure would be still more important. It should be remembered that, although these large vessels have lost their value in the eyes of professional men, they preserve their traditional terrors for the world at large ; and when they move about in fleets, on neighbouring coasts, they excite apprehension in the public mind, and tend to check the spirit of commercial enterprise. Were such an amicable arrangement as has been suggested accomplished, it would be everywhere accepted as a pledge of peace, and, by inspiring a confidence in the future, would help to reanimate the great centres of trade and industry, not only in France and England, but throughout Europe.

" Will not the two Governments, then, eagerly embrace this opportunity of giving effect to a policy which, whilst involving no risk, or sacrifice of honour, or diminution of relative power, will tend to promote the present prosperity and future harmony of the two countries, and offer an example of wisdom and moderation worthy of this civilized age and honourable to the fame of the two foremost nations of the earth?"

THE END.

LONDON: PRINTED BY WILLIAM CLOWES AND SONS, STAMFORD STREET AND CHARING CROSS.

A

CATALOGUE

OF

New and Standard Works

PUBLISHED BY

RICHARD BENTLEY & SON,

Publishers in Ordinary to Her Majesty,

And to the Palestine Exploration Fund.

LONDON: NEW BURLINGTON STREET, W.

FEBRUARY 1876.

A LIST OF WORKS

PUBLISHED BY

RICHARD BENTLEY & SON,

NOW IN PRINT.

ADYE'S MUSICAL NOTES.
By Willett Adye. Small crown. 3/6

ANECDOTES OF ANIMALS.
With Eight spirited Illustrations by Wolff. Gilt edges. 5/-

ANDROMACHE OF EURIPIDES:
With Copious Grammatical and Critical Notes ; also with a Brief
Introductory Account of the Greek Drama, Dialects, and principal
Tragic Metres. By the Rev. J. Edwards, M.A., and the Rev.
C. Hawkins, B.C.L. Used at Eton, post 8vo., 4/6.

ANNE HEREFORD.
By Mrs. Henry Wood, Authoress of "The Channings," &c. In
crown 8vo, cloth. 6/-

ASTRONOMY, WORKS ON,
See 'Guillemin,' 'Marvels of the Heavens,' &c.

ARGOSY MAGAZINE (The).
6d. Monthly (the December Number, 1/-) Volumes 5/- Cases 1/6

AT ODDS!
By the Baroness Tautphœus, Authoress of "The Initials," &c.
With two Illustrations. In crown 8vo, cloth. 6/-
   "A work that will give pleasure to many."—*Spectator*
   "A pretty story prettily told."—*Saturday Review.*
   "An entirely original story. The descriptions of scenery and
characters are excellent."—*Observer.*

AUMALE'S (Duc d') LIVES OF THE PRINCES
OF THE HOUSE OF CONDÉ. Translated under His Royal
Highness's Supervision by the Rev. R. Brown-Borthwick. 2 vols.
8vo. With two fine Portraits. 30/-

AUSTEN'S (Miss Jane) NOVELS. (Bentley's edition).

The only complete edition. In Six Volumes, Crown 8vo., 6/- each. *See* List of Favourite Novels on back page, or each one under its name.

AUSTIN'S POETRY OF THE PERIOD.

By ALFRED AUSTIN, Author of " Madonna's Child," &c. Reprinted from the "Temple Bar" Magazine. Crown 8vo. 7/6

ARHAM (Life of the Rev. Richard Harris),

Author of the "Ingoldsby Legends," including his Correspondence and Unpublished Poetical Miscellanies. By his Son. 2 vols., large crown 8vo. With Portrait. 21/-

BATH ARCHIVES, THE,

A further Selection from the Letters and Diaries of SIR GEORGE JACKSON, K.G.H. from 1809 to 1816. Edited by LADY JACKSON. In 2 vols, 8vo. Price 30/- [*See* Jackson]

"The 'Bath Archives' abound in interest."—*Times.*

BENTLEY BALLADS (The).

Edited by JOHN SHEEHAN. In crown 8vo. Roxburghe binding. 6/-

BENTLEY'S BURLINGTON LIBRARY.

Each Volume to be had separately in crown 8vo., cloth, price 6/- The volumes with an asterisk attached (*) are in Roxburghe binding, gilt tops, same price.

> *Guizot's Life of Oliver Cromwell.
> *Mignet's Life of Mary Queen of Scots.
> The Day after Death.
> *McCausland's Sermons in Stones.
> McCausland's Adam and the Adamite.
> McCausland's Builders of Babel.
> *Lord Dalling and Bulwer's Historical Characters.
> *Timbs' Lives of Painters.
> *Timbs' Lives of Statesmen.
> *Timbs' Wits and Humourists. 2 vols. 12/-
> *Timbs' Later Wits and Humourists. 2 vols. 12/-
> Timbs' Doctors and Patients.
> *Bentley Ballads.
> Doran's Table Traits, with Something on Them.
> South Sea Bubbles. By the Earl and the Doctor.
> Wilkie Collins' Rambles beyond Railways.
> Guillemin's The Sun.
> *Earl Dundonald's Autobiography of a Seaman.
> Besant and Palmer's History of Jerusalem.
> Crowest's The Great Tone Poets.

For further particulars, each of these Books will be found in its Alphabetical position in this Catalogue.

BENTLEY'S FAVOURITE NOVELS.

Each volume can be obtained separately at any booksellers in Crown 8vo, price 6/- bound in cloth. *See* Complete List on the back page of this Catalogue, or each one separately under its name.

BESANT AND PALMER'S HISTORY OF JERU-
SALEM: THE CITY OF HEROD AND SALADIN. By
WALTER BESANT, M.A., and E. H. PALMER, M.A., Arabic Fellow
of St. John's, Cambridge. Crown 8vo. 6/-

BESANT'S FRENCH HUMOURISTS, FROM THE
TWELFTH TO THE NINETEENTH CENTURY. By WALTER
BESANT, M.A., Christ's Coll., Cam., Author of "Stu ies in Early
French Poetry," &c. 8vo. 15/-

BESSY RANE.
By Mrs. HENRY WOOD, Authoress of "East Lynne," &c. With one
Illustration. Crown 8vo, cloth. 6/-

BROUGHTON'S (Miss) NOVELS.
Price 6/- each, in Crown 8vo., cloth. *See* List on back page of this
Catalogue, or each separately under its name.

BUCKLAND'S (Frank) CURIOSITIES OF NATU-
RAL HISTORY. The PEOPLE'S EDITION, with Illustrations. All
volumes together, 14/- or separately as follows :—

> 1st Series. — Rats, Serpents, Fishes, Frogs, Monkeys, &c.
> Small 8vo. 3/6
> 2nd Series.—Fossils, Bears, Wolves, Cats, Eagles, Hedge-
> hogs, Eels, Herrings, Whales. Small 8vo. 3/6
> 3rd Series.—Wild Ducks, Fishing, Lions, Tigers, Foxes, Por-
> poises. Small 8vo. 3/6
> 4th Series.—Giants, Mummies, Mermaids, Wonderful People,
> Salmon, &c. Small 8vo. 3/6

> "These most fascinating works on Natural History."—*Morning Post.*

BULWER'S (the late Lord Dalling and Bulwer)
HISTORICAL CHARACTERS.—Talleyrand, Mackintosh, Cobbett,
Canning, Peel. By the Right Hon. LORD DALLING AND BULWER,
G.C.B. Fifth Edition. In crown 8vo., Roxburghe binding. 6/-

———————— LIFE OF SIR ROBERT PEEL. A Memoir. In
demy 8vo. 7/6

BURGOYNE, Field Marshal Sir John: his LIFE
and CORRESPONDENCE. Including Extracts from his Journals
during the Peninsular and Crimean Wars. Edited by Lieut.-Col. the
Hon. GEORGE WROTTESLEY, R.E. Two vols. 8vo., with Portrait, 30/-

BY-GONE DAYS IN DEVONSHIRE & CORN-
WALL. By Mrs. HENRY PENNELL WHITCOMBE. With
Notes of Existing Superstitions and Customs. Crown 8vo. 7/6

**AMPAIGN OF 1870-71.**
Reprinted from the 'Times,' by permission. Crown 8vo, with
Maps. 10/6

CAPTIVES (The).
From the Latin of Plautus. By H. A. STRONG, M.A. Limp Cloth. 4/-

CARACCIOLO, MEMOIRS OF THE PRINCESS
HENRIETTA, EX-BENEDICTINE NUN; or, The Mysteries of
the Neapolitan Cloister. New Edition, in small crown 8vo, boards, 2/-

CHANNINGS (The). Twenty-Fifth Thousand.
By Mrs. HENRY WOOD, Authoress of "East Lynne," &c. With
two Illustrations. Crown 8vo, cloth. 6/-

"'The Channings' will probably be read over and over again, and
it can never be read too often."—*Athenæum.*

CHESTERFIELD'S (Lord) WIT AND WISDOM.
Edited, with brief Notes, by ERNST BROWNING. Small demy 8vo. 7/6

CHORLEY'S (Henry Fothergill) AUTOBIOGRAPHY,
MEMOIR and LETTERS. Edited by HENRY G. HEWLETT. 2 vols.,
crown 8vo, with Portrait. 21/-

COOKERY.
See "Francatelli," "What to do with Cold Mutton," "Everybody's
Pudding Book," "Tibs' Tit-Bits," &c.

COMETH UP AS A FLOWER.
By RHODA BROUGHTON, Authoress of "Red as a Rose is She," &c.
Crown 8vo. cloth. 6/-

"A strikingly clever and original tale, the chief merits of which
consist in the powerful, vigorous manner of its telling, in the exceeding
beauty and poetry of its sketches of scenery, and in the soliloquies,
sometimes quaintly humorous, sometimes cynically bitter, sometimes
plaintive and melancholy, which are uttered by the heroine."—*The
Times.*

COMIN' THRO' THE RYE.
By HELEN B. MATHERS. Third Edition, in crown 8vo., cloth. 6/-

CONSTANCE SHERWOOD.
By LADY GEORGIANA FULLERTON. Crown 8vo. cloth. 6/.

COURT OF LONDON, from 1819 to 1825.
By RICHARD RUSH, United States' Minister in London during that
Period. Edited by his Son, BENJAMIN RUSH. In 1 vol. demy 8vo. 16/-

COWTAN'S MEMORIES OF THE BRITISH
MUSEUM. By ROBERT COWTAN. 8vo., with Frontispiece. 14/-

CREASY'S (Sir Edward) WORKS.
THE FIFTEEN DECISIVE BATTLES OF THE WORLD:
from Marathon to Waterloo. Twenty-first Edition, with Plans. Crown
8vo. 6/-

Also a LIBRARY EDITION. In 8vo, with Plans, price 10/6

———— HISTORY OF THE RISE AND PROGRESS OF THE
ENGLISH CONSTITUTION. A popular Account of the Primary
Principles, the Formation and Development of the English Constitu-
tion, avoiding all Party Politics. Twelfth Edition. Post 8vo. 7/6

CROWEST'S GREAT TONE POETS.

Being Short Memoirs of the Greater Musical Composers—Bach, Handel, Gluck, Haydn, Spohr, Beethoven, Weber, Rossini, Schubert, Mendelssohn, Schumann, &c, &c. By FREDERICK CROWEST. Second Edition, in Roxburghe binding. Crown 8vo. 6/-

CUMMING'S (Rev. John, D.D.) WORKS.

THE FALL OF BABYLON FORESHADOWED in her Teaching, in History, and in Prophecy. Crown 8vo. 5/-

———— THE GREAT TRIBULATION COMING ON THE EARTH. Crown 8vo. 5/- Fourteenth thousand.

———— REDEMPTION DRAWETH NIGH; or, the Great Preparation. Crown 8vo. 5/- Seventh thousand.

———— THE MILLENIAL REST; or, the World as it will be. 8vo. 5/- Fourth thousand.

———— READINGS ON THE PROPHET ISAIAH. Fcap. 8vo. 5/-

CURTIUS' HISTORY OF GREECE.

FROM THE EARLIEST TIMES DOWN TO 337 B.C. From the German of PROFESSOR ERNST CURTIUS, by A. W. WARD, M.A. Five vols., demy 8vo., 84/-; or separately, Vols. 1 and 2, each 15/- Vols. 3 and 4, each 18/- Vol. 5, with Index, 18/-

"A History known to scholars as one of the profoundest, most original and most instructive of modern times."—*Globe.*

CYRILLA.

By the BARONESS TAUTPHŒUS, Authoress of "At Odds!" &c. Crown 8vo., cloth. 6/-

"A book of much merit, with many clever and lively scenes, and good pictures of life and manners in Germany. Cyrilla is a charming heroine."—*Graphic.*

AY AFTER DEATH; or, the Future Life Revealed by Science. By LOUIS FIGUIER, Author of "The World before the Deluge." A New Edition in crown 8vo, with Illustrations. 6/-

DEAD CITIES OF THE ZUYDER ZEE.

From the French of M. HENRI HAVARD by MISS ANNIE WOOD. In 8vo., with ten Illustrations. 14/-

"A fresh and charming work. M. Havard has discovered a *terra incognita* in the centre of Europe, and has caught, just as it was disappearing, a phase of life highly picturesque and pleasant for the artist's eye. M. Havard has gone among the sleepy cities of the Zuyder Zee with a loving eye. He is a keen and thoughtful observer, and it is apparent on every page of his bright, sparkling narrative, that he really likes the people and their ancient ways, and the consequence is that he inspires his readers with the same feeling."—*Observer.*

"M. Havard's interesting account of these towns, which, once prosperous, have now fallen into decay, seems to have been published at the very nick of time. Not much cared for by the Dutch, they are, as M. Havard points out, absolutely unknown to the other nations of Europe; while attention is now being directed to them by the project just formed for draining the Zuyder Zee, on whose shores they stand."—*Pall Mall Gazette.*

DENE HOLLOW.
By Mrs. HENRY WOOD, Authoress of "Verner's Pride," &c. With an Illustration. Crown 8vo., cloth. 6/-

"Novel readers wishing to be entertained, and deeply interested in character and incident, will find their curiosity wholesomely gratified by the graphic pages of 'Dene Hollow.'"—*Morning Post.*

DENISON'S (The late Edward) LETTERS AND CORRESPONDENCE. People's Edition, in·luding several Letters, now printed for the first time. Tauchnitz size. 3/6

DOBELL'S (Sydney) THE ROMAN: A Dramatic Poem. Post 8vo. 5/-

DORAN'S (Dr.) LADY OF THE LAST CENTURY. Mrs. ELIZABETH MONTAGU. Including Letters of Mrs. Montagu never before published. By DR. DORAN, F.S.A., Author of 'The Queens of England of the House of Hanover.' Second Edition. 8vo. 14/-

——— LIVES OF THE QUEENS OF ENGLAND OF THE HOUSE OF HANOVER. By DR. DORAN, F.S.A., Author of "Table Traits and Something on Them," &c. 2 vols. 8vo. 25/-

——— "MANN" AND MANNERS AT THE COURT OF FLORENCE; 1740-1786. Founded on the Letters of Sir Horace Mann to Horace Walpole. By DR. DORAN, F.S.A. In 2 vols., 8vo. 30/-

"Sir Horace Mann's letters are delightful reading. They sparkle with anecdote and entertaining Court gossip, contain numerous life-like portraits of celebrated persons, and from beginning to end of the 900 pages to which they extend have hardly a single dull or uninterest-ing one."—*Standard.*

"Those who have already some knowledge of the eighteenth century, and are desirous of adding fresh links to previous facts, and following up old acquaintances in new climates, will here find no mean entertainment, and will not fail to thank Dr. Doran for his successful labour."—*Athenæum.*

"It is almost superfluous to do more than announce that a book is by Dr. Doran, in order to insure its eager welcome in every reading household. Assuredly expectation will not be diminished when he treats of so stirring a time and so interesting a city."—*Morning Post.*

——— TABLE TRAITS AND SOMETHING ON THEM. Post. 6/-

"The best thing I have seen for many a day. It would make the fortune of a diner-out to get it by heart."—SHIRLEY BROOKS.

DUNDONALD'S (Earl) AUTOBIOGRAPHY OF A SEAMAN. Popular Edition. With Portrait and Four Charts. In crown 8vo. Roxburghe binding. 6/-

"Full of brilliant adventures, described with a dash that well befits the deeds."—*Times.*

"It ought to be a classic in every library afloat or ashore."—*Daily News.*

——— THE LIFE OF ADMIRAL LORD COCHRANE, TENTH EARL OF. (Concluding "The Autobiography of a Seaman.") By his SON, the Eleventh Earl. 2 vols. 8vo, 30/-

EAST LYNNE.
Sixty-fifth Thousand. By Mrs. HENRY WOOD, Authoress of "The Channings," &c. With one Illustration. Crown 8vo., cloth. 6/-

"'East Lynne' is a first-rate novel. It exhibits very great skill, both in characterization and construction, and is found by all its readers to be highly entertaining."—*The Times.*

ELLENBOROUGH (Lord). HISTORY OF HIS
ADMINISTRATION IN INDIA. Containing his Letters to Her Majesty the Queen, and Letters to 'and from the Duke of Wellington. Edited by LORD COLCHESTER. In one vol., 8vo. 18/-

ELSTER'S FOLLY.
By Mrs. HENRY WOOD, Authoress of "The Channings," &c. Crown 8vo., cloth. 6/-

EMMA.
By JANE AUSTEN, Authoress of "Pride and Prejudice," &c. Crown 8vo., cloth. 6/-

"Shakespeare has neither equal nor second. But among the writers who have approached nearest to the manner of the great master we have no hesitation in placing Jane Austen, a woman of whom England is ustly proud."—*Macaulay's Essays.*

ENGLAND: Literary and Social, from a German
POINT OF VIEW. BY JULIUS RODENBERG. In 8vo. 14/-

"A very excellent book on England, alike instructive and amusing, has left the German Press, by Julius Rodenberg. It is a worthy sequel to the various similar publications by which the author has endeavoured to make his countrymen know and love England. Literary essays of uncommon merit are relieved in these teeming pages by historical sketches and descriptions of men and scenery. The book is so full of valuable matter, and so well-written withal, that when translated, it is certain to be an interesting addition to English literature."—*Times.*

EVERY-BODY'S PUDDING BOOK. Fcap. 8vo. 1/6

EYRE, LIFE OF GOVERNOR.
In crown 8vo., cloth. 6/-

EYRE'S (Miss) OVER THE PYRENEES INTO
SPAIN. Crown 8vo. 12/-

————— WALKS IN THE SOUTH OF FRANCE. Second Edition. Crown 8vo. 12/-

**AIR LUSITANIA: A Portuguese Sketch-Book**
By LADY JACKSON, Editor of "Bath Archives." In super royal 8vo, with Twenty very beautiful full-page Illustrations, engraved from Photographs by George Pearson, 21/-

FLETCHER'S (Col.) HISTORY OF THE AMERI-
CAN CIVIL WAR. In 3 vols. 8vo. Price 18/- each.

FONBLANQUE, LIFE AND LABOURS OF
ALBANY. Including his contributions to "The Examiner." Edited by E. B. DE FONBLANQUE. In 8vo. 16/-

"Lord Lytton scarcely exaggerated when he compared Fonblanque with Swift. We are sure the contents of this volume will be read again and again by those who appreciate wit and wisdom. Journalists and political writers, can scarcely find a more brilliant model in close and vigorous reasoning, terse and lucid expression, and an almost unrivalled wealth of apposite information."—*Times.*

FOURFOLD MESSAGE OF ADVENT (The).

Four Sermons preached at Chiswick. Fcap., cloth. 2/6

FRANCATELLI'S "MODERN COOK."

By CHARLES ELMÉ FRANCATELLI, late *Maitre-d'hôtel* to Her Majesty. In 8vo. Twenty-third Edition. Containing 1500 Recipes and sixty Illustrations. 12/- ·

FRANCATELLI'S "COOK'S GUIDE."

By the Author of the 'Modern Cook.' 41st thousand. In small 8vo. Containing 1000 Recipes and forty Illustrations. 5/-

"An admirable manual for every household."—*Times*.

FRENCH DIALOGUES.

By RICHARD and QUÉTIN. 32mo. 1/6. READER. By BRETTE and MASSON. Fcap. 8vo. 2/-

FRENCH SOCIETY FROM THE FRONDE TO THE GREAT REVOLUTION. By HENRY BARTON BAKER.

2 vols. crown 8vo. 21/-

GEORGE CANTERBURY'S WILL.

By Mrs. HENRY WOOD, Authoress of "East Lynne," &c. Crown 8vo., cloth. 6/-

GOOD-BYE, SWEETHEART!

By RHODA BROUGHTON, Authoress of "Cometh up as a Flower," &c. With a fine Illustration on Steel. Crown 8vo., cloth. 6/-

"Miss Broughton writes from the very bottom of her heart. There is a terrible realism about her."—*Echo*.

GREGORY THE SEVENTH, THE LIFE OF. By M. VILLEMAIN, of the French Academy. Translated by JAMES BABER BROCKLEY. In 2 vols. 8vo. 26/-

GUILLEMIN'S THE HEAVENS.

An illustrated Handbook of Popular Astronomy. By AMÉDÉE GUILLEMIN. Edited by J. Norman Lockyer, F.R.A.S. An entirely New and Revised Edition, embodying all the latest discoveries in Astronomical Science. Demy 8vo., with nearly 200 Illustrations. 10/6

————————— THE SUN.

By AMÉDÉE GUILLEMIN, Author of 'The Heavens.' Translated by Dr. Phipson. With fifty Illustrations. Crown 8vo. 6/-

GUIZOT'S (M.) LIFE OF OLIVER CROMWELL.

Crown 8vo., in Roxburghe binding, with four Portraits. 6/-

HAUNTED HOUSE (The).

Translated from the "Mostellaria" of Plautus, by H. A. STRONG, M.A. Limp cloth. 4/-

HECKETHORN'S HISTORY OF SECRET SO-CIETIES OF ALL AGES AND COUNTRIES. By CHARLES W. HECKETHORN. In 2 vols. crown 8vo. 21/-

"No one could propose to himself a more fascinating study than the History of Secret Societies."—*Pall Mall Gazette*.

"A most interesting and instructing work."—*Standard*.

HERBERT'S (Lady) WORKS,

———— ———— DOROTHEA WALDEGRAVE. From the German of the Countess HAHN-HAHN. 2 vols. Crown 8vo. 21/-

———— ———— GERONIMO. A True Story. In fcap., with Frontispiece. 4/-

———— ———— LIFE OF ST. MONICA, THE MOTHER OF ST. AUGUSTINE. Fcap. 8vo., red edges. 2/6

———— ———— —— LOVE, OR SELF-SACRIFICE. Crown 8vo. 10/6

———— ———— MISSION OF ST. FRANCIS OF SALES IN THE CHABLAIS. In post 8vo. 6/-

———— ———— SEARCH AFTER SUNSHINE: A Visit to Algeria in 1871. Square 8vo. with Sixteen Illustrations engraved by George Pearson. 16/-

HOLBEIN AND HIS TIME.
From the German of Dr. ALFRED WOLTMANN, by F. E. BUNNÉTT. 1 vol. small 4to, with Sixty beautiful Illustrations from the Chief Works of Holbein. 21/-

HOOK'S (Dean) LIVES of the ARCHBISHOPS
of CANTERBURY, from St. Augustine to Juxon. 11 vols., demy 8vo., £8 4/- or sold separately as follows:—Vol. 1, 15/-; Vol. 2, 15/-; Vols. 3 and 4, 30/-; Vol. 5, 15/-; Vols. 6 and 7, 30/-; Vol. 8, 15/-; Vol. 9, 15/- Vol. 10, 14/- Vol. 11, 15/- The Second Series commences with Vol. 6.

Vol. I. Anglo-Saxon Period, 597-1070.—Augustine, Laurentius, Mellitus, Justus, Honorius, Deusdedit, Theodorus, Brihtwald, Tatwine, Nothelm, Cuthbert, Bregwin, Jaenbert, Ethelhard, Wulfred, Feologild, Ceolnoth, Ethelred, Plegmund, Athelm, Wulfhelm, Odo, Dunstan, Ethelgar, Siric, Elfric, Elphege, Limig, Ethelnoth, Eadsige, Robert, Stigand.

Vol. II. Anglo-Norman Period, 1070-1229.—Lanfranc, Anselm, Ralph of Escures, William of Corbeuil, Theobald, Thomas à Becket, Richard the Norman, Baldwin, Reginald Fitzjocelin, Hubert Walter, Stephen Langton.

Vol III. Mediæval Period, 1229-1333.—Richard Grant, Edmund Rich, Boniface, Robert Kilwardby, John Peckham, Robert Winchelsey, Walter Reynolds, Simon Mapeham.

Vol. IV. Same Period, 1333-1408. John Stratford, Thomas Bradwardine, Simon Islip, Simon Langham, William Whittlesey, Simon Sudbury, William Courtenay, Thomas Arundel.

Vol. V. Same Period, 1408-1503.—Henry Chicheley, John Stafford, John Kemp, Thomas Bouchier, John Morton, Henry Dean.

The New Series commences here.

Vols. VI. and VII. Reformation Period, 1503-1556.—William Warham, Thomas Cranmer.

Vol. VIII. Same Period, 1556-1558.—Reginald, Cardinal Pole.

Vol. IX. Same Period, 1558-1575.—Matthew Parker.

Vol. X: Same Period, 1575-1633.—Edmund Grindal, John Whitgift, Richard Bancroft, George Abbott.

Vol. XI. Same Period, 1633-1663.—William Laud, William Juxon.

" The most impartial, the most instructive, and the most interesting of histories."—*Athenæum.*

HYMNS AND ANTHEMS.
Edited by the Rev. Dr. TREMLETT.   Crown 8vo., cloth.   1/-

 **NGOLDSBY LEGENDS, or, Mirth & Marvels.**
THE ILLUSTRATED EDITION.   With Sixty beautiful Illustrations by Cruikshank, Leech, and Tenniel; and a magnificent emblematic cover, designed by John Leighton, F.S.A.   Printed on Toned Paper.   Crown 4to, cloth, bevelled boards, gilt edges.   21/-, or bound in morocco, price 42/-

"A series of humourous legends, illustrated by three such men as Cruikshank, Leech, and Tenniel—what can be more tempting?"—*The Times.*

"Abundant in humour, observation, fancy; in extensive knowledge of books and men; in palpable hits of character, exquisite grave irony, and the most whimsical indulgence in point of epigram.   We cannot open a page that is not sparkling with its wit and humour, that is not ringing with its strokes of pleasantry and satire."—*Examiner.*

———— THE ANNOTATED EDITION.   A Library Edition, with a History of each Legend, and other Notes, and some original Legends now first published.   In 2 vols. demy 8vo, handsomely printed, with an Original Frontispiece by George Cruikshank; and all the Illustrations by Cruikshank and Leech, including two new ones by the latter artist.   Edited by the Rev. RICHARD DALTON BARHAM.   24/-

———— THE BURLINGTON EDITION.   AN ENTIRELY NEW EDITION printed in LARGE clear type, in 3 vols., fcap. 8vo.   10/6

"Yet another edition of Barham's immortal work, beautifully printed and chastely bound."—*The World.*

———— THE CARMINE EDITION.   In crown 8vo.   With 17 Illustrations by Cruikshank and Leech, with gilt edges and bevelled boards.   10/6

———— THE POPULAR EDITION.   Crown 8vo.   Plain edges, 5/-; gilt edges, with three Illustrations, 6/-

———— THE 'VICTORIA' EDITION.   In fcap. 8vo.   2/6.

———— THE JACKDAW OF RHEIMS.   An Edition of this celebrated Legend in 4to, with Twelve highly coloured Illustrations, extra cloth, gilt edges, 7/6.

INITIALS (The).
By the Baroness TAUTPHŒUS, Authoress of "Quits!" &c.   With two Illustrations.   Crown 8vo, cloth.   6/-

 **ACKSON'S (Sir Geo.) DIARIES & LETTERS**
From the Peace of Amiens to the Battle of Talavera.   Edited by Lady JACKSON.   Two vols. 8vo.   30/-   [*See* also "The Bath Archives."]

JAMES' NAVAL HISTORY OF GREAT BRITAIN.
From the Declaration of war by France, in 1793, to the accession of George the IV.   By WILLIAM JAMES.   With a continuation of the history down to the Battle of Navarino, by Captain CHAMIER.   Embellished with portraits of Lord Nelson, Sir Thomas Troubridge, Earl St. Vincent, Lord Duncan, Sir Hyde Parker, and Sir Nesbit Willoughby.   Six volumes, crown 8vo., 36/-   [*Reprinting*

JAPAN AND THE JAPANESE. By Aime Hum-
BERT, Envoy Extraordinary of the Swiss Confederation. From the
French by MRS. CASHEL HOEY, and Edited by W. H. BATES,
Assist.-Sec. to the Geographical Society. Illustrated by 207 Drawings
and Sketches from Photographs. In royal 4to, handsomely bound, 21/-
published at 42/-

JESSE'S MEMOIRS OF CELEBRATED ETO-
NIANS, including Fielding, Gray the Poet, Horace Walpole, William
Pitt, Earl of Chatham, Lord Bute, Lord North, Horne Tooke, Lord
Lyttleton, Earl Temple, Admiral Lord Howe, &c. By JOHN HENEAGE
JESSE, Author of " Memoirs of the Reign of George III.," "Memoirs
of the Court of the Stuarts," &c. In 2 vols. 8vo. 28/-

"Mr. Jesse's volumes are charmingly fresh, and are full of delightful snatches of anecdote and political gossip. The author's power
of character-sketching seems to us remarkably noteworthy."—*Daily
Telegraph.*

JOHNNY LUDLOW. The New and Popular
EDITION. Crown 8vo. cloth. 6/-

" We regard these stories as almost perfect of their kind."—*Spectator.*

ADYBIRD.
By Lady GEORGIANA FULLERTON, Authoress of "Too Strange
not to be True." With two Illustrations, in crown 8vo. cloth. 6/-

LADY ADELAIDE.
By MRS. HENRY WOOD, Authoress of "The Channings," &c. In
crown 8vo., cloth. 6/-

LADY SUSAN and THE WATSONS.
By JANE AUSTEN, Authoress of "Emma," &c. With a Memoir and
Portrait of the Authoress, in crown 8vo. cloth. 6/-

"Miss Austen's life as well as her talent seems to us unique among
the lives of authoresses of fiction."—*Quarterly Review.*

LAMARTINE'S (Alphonse de) **MEMOIRS OF**
REMARKABLE CHARACTERS.—Nelson, Bossuet, Milton, Oliver
Cromwell, &c. Crown 8vo. Roxburghe binding, 6/- (*Reprinting.*

LAST OF THE CAVALIERS (The).
With two Illustrations. Crown 8vo, cloth. 6/-

" A novel of considerable power, which will become popular amongst
all readers."—*Observer.*

" A work exceedingly similar to some of Sir Walter Scott's best
efforts. It is one of the best historical novels we have read for many
years."—*Morning Chronicle.*

LEECH'S PORTRAITS OF THE CHILDREN OF
THE MOBILITY. Drawn from Nature by JOHN LEECH. With a fine
Portrait of Leech, and a Prefatory Letter by JOHN RUSKIN. Repro-
duced from the Original Sketches by the Autotype Process. 4to. 10/6

LEONARD MORRIS.   A Tale by Father Ignatius.
Crown 8vo. 6/-

LESSONS OF THE FRENCH REVOLUTION,
1789-1872. By the Rt. Hon. Lord Ormathwaite. 8vo. 10/6

LIFE AMONG THE MODOCS.
By Joaquin Miller, Author of "Songs of the Sierras." In 8vo. 14/-

"No fresher or more entertaining work has appeared for a generation."—*Globe.*

LIFE'S SECRET (A).
By Mrs. Henry Wood, Authoress of "East Lynne," &c. Crown 8vo, cloth, 6/-

LORD OAKBURN'S DAUGHTERS.
By Mrs. Henry Wood, Authoress of "Verner's Pride," &c. With two Illustrations. Crown 8vo, cloth. 6/-

"This story is admirably told."—*Spectator.*

LYTTON   (Lord)   MISCELLANEOUS   PROSE
WORKS OF EDWARD BULWER LYTTON. Now first collected, including Charles Lamb—The Reign of Terror—Gray—Goldsmith—Pitt and Fox—Sir Thomas Browne—Schiller, &c., &c., &c.
In 3 vols. 8vo. 36/-

MANSFIELD PARK.
By Jane Austen, Authoress of "Pride and Prejudice," &c.
Crown 8vo, cloth. 6/-

"Miss Austen has a talent for describing the involvements and characters of ordinary life, which is to me the most wonderful I ever met with. Her exquisite touch, which renders commonplace things and characters interesting from the truth of the description and the sentiment, is denied to me."—*Sir Walter Scott.*

MARTYRS OF CARTHAGE.
See Webb.

MASTER OF GREYLANDS.
By Mrs. Henry Wood, Authoress of "East Lynne," "The Channings," &c. Crown 8vo, Cloth. 6/-

"A book by Mrs. Wood is sure to be a good one, and no one who opens 'The Master of Greylands' in anticipation of an intellectual treat will be disappointed. The keen analysis of character, and the admirable management of the plot, alike attest the clever novelist."—*John Bull.*

MARVELS OF THE HEAVENS.
From the French of Flammarion. By Mrs. Lockyer, Translator of "The Heavens." Crown 8vo. With 48 Illustrations. 5/-

MAULE, EARLY LIFE OF SIR WILLIAM.
By His Niece, Emma Leathley. Crown 8vo. 7/6

McCAUSLAND'S (The Late Dr.), WORKS,

ADAM AND THE ADAMITE; or the Harmony of Scripture and Ethnology. With Map, 6/- [*Reprinting*

"Interesting, attractive, and useful."—*Notes and Queries.*

——————— BUILDERS OF BABEL; OR, THE CONFUSION OF LANGUAGES. A New Edition in crown 8vo. 6/-

——————— SERMONS IN STONES; or, Scripture confirmed by Geology. A New Edition, with a Memoir of the Author, in Roxburghe binding, with 19 Illustrations. 6/-

MEMORIALS OF THE SOUTH SAXON SEE AND

CATHEDRAL OF CHICHESTER. From original sources, by the Rev. Prebendary STEPHENS, Author of "The Life and Times of St. John Chrysostom," &c. In 8vo. with Illustrations.

MIGNET'S LIFE OF MARY QUEEN OF SCOTS.

In Roxburghe binding, with Two Portraits, crown 8vo. 6/-
"The standard authority on the subject."—*Daily News.*
"A good service done to historical accuracy."—*Morning Post.*

MILDRED ARKELL.

By Mrs. HENRY WOOD, Authoress of "Mrs. Halliburton's Troubles," &c. Crown 8vo, cloth. 6/-

MIRAMION (Mde. de).

Life of Madame de Beauharnais de Miramion, 1629-1696. By M. ALFRED BONNEAU. Translated by the Baroness de Montaignac. Edited by Lady Herbert. Large crown 8vo. 10/6

MITFORD'S (Mary Russell) LIFE.

Told by Herself in Letters to her Friends. With Sketches and Anecdotes of her most celebrated Contemporaries. Edited by the Rev. A. G. L'ESTRANGE. With an Introductory Memoir, &c., by the late Rev. WILLIAM HARNESS, her Literary Executor. In 3 vols. post 8vo. 31/6. Second Series, Edited by Henry Chorley. 2 vols. 21/-

MOMMSEN'S (Dr. Theodore) HISTORY OF ROME

FROM THE EARLIEST TIME TO THE PERIOD OF ITS DECLINE. By Dr. THEODOR MOMMSEN. Translated with the Author's sanction, and Additions, by the Rev. W. P. Dickson. With an Introduction by Dr. Schmitz. 4 vols. crown 8vo. 51/6; or sold separately, Vols. 1 and 2, 21/-; Vol. 3, 10/6; Vol. 4, in 2 parts, with Index, 20/- The Index separately, 3/6

Also a LIBRARY EDITION, in 4 vols. demy 8vo. 75/- With Index. These volumes not sold separately. The Index separately 3/6

*** *In ordering the Index, the* SIZE *of the Edition must be given.*

"A work of the very highest merit; its learning is exact and profound; its narrative full of genius and skill; its description of men are admirably vivid. We wish to place on record our opinion that Dr. Mommsen's is by far the best history of the Decline and Fall of the Roman Commonwealth."—*Times.*

"Taking the author's complete mastery of his subject, the variety of his gifts and acquirements, his graphic power in the delineation of natural and individual character, and the vivid interest which he inspires in every portion of his book, he is without an equal in his own sphere."—*Edinburgh Review.*

MONTGOMERY'S (Florence) STORIES. The Uni-
FORM EDITION.

——————— MISUNDERSTOOD. Fifteenth Thousand. Crown 8vo. 5/-

——————— THE TOWN-CRIER, &c. Fourth Thousand. Post 8vo. 5/-

——————— THROWN TOGETHER. Crown 8vo, 6/-

——————— THWARTED. Fifth Thousand. Crown 8vo. 5/-

——————— WILD MIKE. Fourth Thousand. Post 8vo. 3/6

Also

——————— MISUNDERSTOOD. The Illustrated Edition, with 8 full-
page Illustrations by George Du Maurier. Fcap. 4to. 7/6

MONTH AT GASTEIN, A.
In crown 8vo, cloth, with woodcuts, 6/-

MOORSOM'S (Capt.) RECORD OF THE 52nd
REGIMENT. In 8vo, with coloured Plans. 31/6

MRS. GERALD'S NIECE.
By LADY GEORGIANA FULLERTON, Authoress of " Ladybird," &c.
Crown 8vo, cloth, 6/-

MRS. HALLIBURTON'S TROUBLES.
By MRS. HENRY WOOD, Authoress of " The Channings," &c. With
two illustrations. Crown 8vo. cloth. 6/-

" It is long since the novel-reading world has had reason so thoroughly to congratulate itself upon the appearance of a new work as in
the instance of 'Mrs. Halliburton's Troubles.' It is a fine work; a
great and artistic picture."—*Morning Post.*

MY LIFE, AND WHAT I LEARNT IN IT.
An Autobiography. By GIUSEPPE MARIA CAMPANELLA. 8vo. 14/-

" A most remarkable volume, well worthy of perusal."—*Rock.*

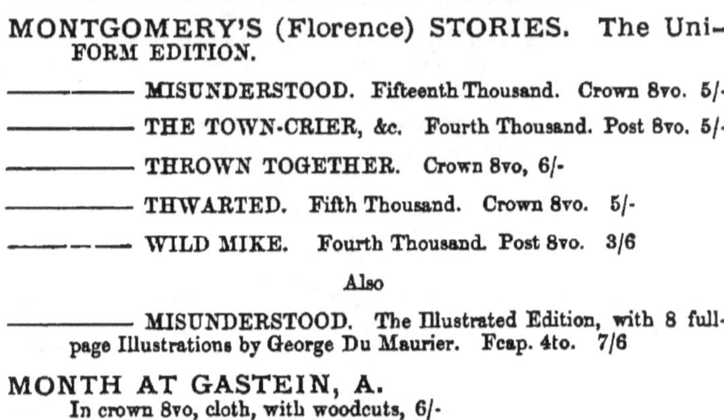

ANCY.
By RHODA BROUGHTON, Authoress of " Cometh up as a Flower,"
" Red as a Rose is She," &c. With an Illustration on Steel.
Crown 8vo. cloth. 6/-

" If unwearied brilliancy of style, picturesque description, humorous
and original dialogue, and a keen insight into human nature can make
a novel popular, there is no doubt whatever that 'Nancy' will take a
higher place than anything which Miss Broughton has yet written. It
is admirable from first to last."—*Standard.*

NEVILLE'S THE STAGE: Its Past and Present in
RELATION TO FINE ART. By HENRY NEVILLE. Demy 8vo.
96 pp. 5/-

NORTHANGER ABBEY.
By JANE AUSTEN, Authoress of " Pride and Prejudice," &c. Crown
8vo, cloth. 6/-

NOTES ON NOSES.
By Eden Warwick. Fcap. 8vo. 2/6

NOT WISELY BUT TOO WELL.
By Rhoda Broughton. Authoress of "Nancy," &c. In crown 8vo., cloth. 6/-

GIER'S FORTUNATE ISLES; OR, THE
ARCHIPELAGO OF THE CANARIES. By M. Pegot-Ogier. Translated by Frances Locock. 2 vols. crown 8vo. 21/-

OLD NEW ZEALAND.
By An Old Pakeha Maori. With a Preface by the Earl of Pembroke. In 8vo.

OSWALD CRAY.
By Mrs. Henry Wood, Authoress of "East Lynne," &c. With an Illustration. Crown 8vo, cloth. 6/-

OUGHT WE TO VISIT HER?
By Mrs. Annie Edwardes, Authoress of "Archie Lovell," &c. With an Illustration on Steel. Crown 8vo, cloth. 6/-

" To this novel the epithets spirited, original of design, and vigorous in working it out, may be applied without let or hindrance. In short, in all that goes to make up at once an amusing and interesting story, it is in every way a success."—*Morning Post.*

ALESTINE FUND STATEMENTS.
Published Quarterly by the Palestine Exploration Fund as under. Old Series: Nos. 1*, 2*, 3*, 4, 5, 6, 7*, One Shilling each. New Series: January, April*, July*, October 1871, January*, April, July, October, 1872; January, April, July, October, 1873; January*, April, 1874; One Shilling each. July, October*, 1874; January, April*, July, October, 1875; January 1876; 2/6 each. Continued Quarterly at 2/6. The Numbers to which an asterisk (*) is affixed are out of print.

PALESTINE, OUR WORK IN. A History of
the Researches conducted in Jerusalem and the Holy Land by Captains Wilson, Anderson, Warren, &c. (Issued by the Committee of the Palestine Exploration Fund.) Fcap. 8vo. Illustrated by upwards of 50 Woodcuts and Plans. 3/6.

PALMERSTON (The Life of Viscount.)
With Selections from his Diaries and Correspondence. By the late Lord Dalling and Bulwer. Fourth thousand. In 2 vols. 8vo., (1784-1841) with fine Portrait, 30/- Volume the Third (1835-1847) edited by the Hon. Evelyn Ashley, M.P., 8vo, 15/-

PALMERSTON (The Life of Viscount) 1847–1865.
By the Hon. Evelyn Ashley, M.P. 2 vols. 8vo., with two Portraits. 30/-

PALMERSTON'S (Viscount) SELECTIONS FROM
TWO TOURS TO PARIS IN 1815 AND 1810. 8vo. Limp cloth. 60 pp. 2/6

PEACOCK'S (Thomas Love) COLLECTED WORKS

Including his Novels, Fugitive Pieces, Poems, Criticisms, &c. Edited by Sir HENRY COLE, K.C.B., with Preface by LORD HOUGHTON. With a Biographical Sketch by his Grand-Daughter. In 3 vols. crown 8vo, with Portrait. 31/6

PRIDE AND PREJUDICE.

By JANE AUSTEN, Authoress of "Sense and Sensibility," &c. Crown 8vo, cloth. 6/-

"'Pride and Prejudice,' by Jane Austen, is the perfect type of a novel of common life; the story is so concisely and dramatically told, the language so simple, the shades of human character so clearly presented, and the operation of various motives so delicately traced, at·est this gifted woman to have been the perfect mistress of her art."—*Arnold's English Literature.*

QUITS!

By the Baroness TAUTPHŒUS, Authoress of "The Initials," &c. With two Illustrations. Crown 8vo, cloth. 6/-

"A most interesting novel."—*Times.*

"Witty, sentious, graphic, full of brilliant pictures of life and manners, it is positively one of the best of modern stories, and may be read with delightful interest from cover to cover."—*Morning Post.*
"Interesting in the highest degree."—*Observer.*

RAIKES' HISTORICAL RECORDS OF THE FIRST REGIMENT OF MILITIA; or Third West York Light

Infantry. By Captain G. A. RAIKES, 3rd West York Light Infantry, Lieut. Instructor of Musketry, Hon. Artillery Company, &c. With Eight full-page Illustrations. In 8vo., price 21/-

RAMBLES BEYOND RAILWAYS; or, Notes

taken Afoot in Cornwall; to which is added a Visit to the Scilly Isles. By WILKIE COLLINS, Author of "The Woman in White." In crown 8vo. 6/-
"A very pleasant book."—*Times.*

READE'S (Charles) DRAMAS.

Edited by TOM TAYLOR. I. Masks and Faces. II. Two Loves and a Life.* III. The King's Rival. IV. Poverty and Pride. 1/6 each.
* Out of Print.

RED AS A ROSE IS SHE.

By RHODA BROUGHTON, Authoress of "Good-bye, Sweetheart," &c. With an Illustration on Steel. Crown 8vo, cloth. 6/-
"There are few who will not be fascinated by this tale."—*Times.*

RED COURT FARM.

By Mrs. HENRY WOOD, Authoress of "Verner's Pride," &c. Crown 8vo, cloth. 6/-

RECOVERY OF JERUSALEM.

An Account of the Recent Excavations and Discoveries in the Holy City. By Captain WILSON, R.E., and Captain WARREN, R.E. With an Introductory Chapter by DEAN STANLEY. Third thousand. Demy 8vo. With 50 Illustrations. 21/-

ROCK INSCRIPTIONS IN THE PENINSULA

OF SINAI. By GEORGE BENTLEY, F.R.G.S. 1/-

ROLAND YORKE. A Sequel to " The Channings,"

By Mrs. HENRY WOOD, Authoress of " East Lynne," &c. With
an Illustration. Crown 8vo, cloth. 6/-

"In all respects worthy of the hand that wrote 'The Channings'
and 'East Lynne.' There is no lack of excitement to wile the reader
on, and from the first to the last a well-planned story is sustained with
admirable spirit and in a masterly style."—*Daily News.*

ROMANCE OF THE ENGLISH STAGE.

By PERCY FITZGERALD, M.A., F.S.A., Author of "The "Life of
Garrick," &c. In 2 vols. demy 8vo 24/-

ROME, HISTORY OF.

See MOMMSEN.

ROOTS: A Plea for Tolerance.

Reprinted from the "Temple Bar Magazine," with an additional
chapter. In 1 vol. demy 8vo. 6/-

AUNDERS' EVENINGS WITH THE SACRED

POETS. By FREDERICK SAUNDERS. Post 8vo., gilt edges. 10/6

SCAMPER TO SEBASTOPOL AND JERUSALEM.

By JAMES CREAGH. 8vo. 15/-

SENSE AND SENSIBILITY.

By JANE AUSTEN, Authoress of "EMMA," &c. Crown 8vo, cloth. 6/-

SHADOW OF ASHLYDYAT.

By Mrs. HENRY WOOD, Authoress of " East Lynne," &c. With two
Illustrations. Crown 8vo, cloth. 6/-

"The best novel that Mrs. Wood has written. It has not the
painful interest of 'East Lynne,' but it is a better constructed story,
and for steadily accumulating interest we do not know a novel of the
present day to be compared to it."—*Athenæum.*
"Very clever. The interest never flags."—*Spectator.*

SISTER'S STORY (A).

By Mrs. AUGUSTUS CRAVEN. Crown 8vo, cloth. 6/-

"A book which took all France and all England by storm."—*Black-
wood's Magazine.*
"Written in a charming, natural, and touching manner, and full of
life-like pictures of society."—*Morning Post.*

SITANA: A Mountain Campaign on the Borders

OF AFGHANISTAN IN 1863. By COLONEL JOHN ADYE, C.B,
Royal Artillery. 8vo. with Maps and Illustrations. 6/-

SOUTH SEA BUBBLES. By the Earl and the

DOCTOR. Library Edition, 8vo, 14/- Popular Edition, Crown 8vo, 6/-

STEVEN LAWRENCE: YEOMAN.

By MRS. EDWARDES, Authoress of "Leah: a Woman of Fashion." In crown 8vo., cloth, with an Illustration on Steel. 6/-

ST. MARTIN'S EVE.

By Mrs. HENRY WOOD, Authoress of "Roland Yorke," &c. Crown 8vo, cloth. 6/-

STRANGE, MASTERPIECES OF SIR ROBERT,

A Selection of Twenty of his most important Engravings reproduced in Permanent Photography. With a Memoir of Sir Robert Strange, By FRANCIS WOODWARD. Folio. 42/-

STRANGFORD (Viscount) SELECTIONS FROM

THE WRITINGS OF, on Social, Political, and Geographical Subjects. Edited by the VISCOUNTESS STRANGFORD. 2 vols. crown 8vo. with Portrait of Lord Strangford, and map. 21/-

———— ANGELA PISANI. 3 vols. crown 8vo. 31/6

SUMMER DAYS IN AUVERGNE.

By H. DE K. In crown 8vo., with 5 full-page Illustrations. 5/-

SUSAN FIELDING.

By Mrs. ANNIE EDWARDES, Authoress of "Ought we to Visit Her?' &c. With a fine Illustration on Steel. Crown 8vo, cloth. 6/-

"One has not to read far into 'Susan Fielding' before one feels that the writer is by no means a common person. In the very best sense of the term she is a true artist. The story itself is intensely interesting, keeping the reader's attention alive from the first page to the very last."—*Globe.*

TALES FOR CHRISTMAS-EVE.

By RHODA BROUGHTON, Author of "Cometh up as a Flower," &c. Crown 8vo, bevelled boards. 2/6

TEN YEARS OF MY LIFE.

By the Princess FELIX SALM-SALM. In 2 vols. crown 8vo., with a Portrait of the Princess. 21/-

"The Princess Felix Salm-Salm is one of those persons who cannot be accused of mistaking their vocation when they take to writing their personal memoirs. Many of the Princess's recollections are really valuable as contributions to history, while all her experiences and adventures are told so as to make them very agreeable reading."— *Saturday Review.*

"A copious and interesting narrative of facts."—*The World.*

TERESINA IN AMERICA.

By THERÈSE YELVERTON, Lady AVONMORE, Author of "Teresina Peregrina." In 2 vols., crown 8vo. 21/-

"Readers of Teresina's books will not need to be told that these volumes are throughout lively and entertaining. Teresina has travelled twenty thousand miles through the most important districts of America, and a glance at her table of contents is alone sufficient to show that she has done the country pretty thoroughly. Some people appear destined to meet with romantic adventures, and in these Teresina's tour was rich to abundance."—*Pall Mall Gazette.*

TERESINA PEREGRINA; or, Fifty Thousand MILES OF TRAVEL ROUND THE WORLD. By THERESA YELVERTON, LADY AVONMORE. 2 vols, crown 8vo. 21/-

THE THREE CLERKS. By Anthony Trollope. Crown 8vo. cloth. 6/- With an Illustration.

> "A really brilliant tale, full of life and character."—*Times.*

THIERS' (M.) HISTORY of the GREAT FRENCH REVOLUTION, from 1789 to 1801. By ADOLPHE THIERS, and translated by FREDERICK SHOBERL. With forty-one fine Engravings and Portraits by Greatbach. In 5 vols, small 8vo. 30/- (*Reprinting*)

THORVALDSEN, THE LIFE AND WORK OF. By EUGÈNE PLON. From the French by Mrs. CASHEL HOEY. In imperial 8vo, with numerous Illustrations. 25/-

TIB'S TIT-BITS. Two Hundred and thirty Recipes, for soups, made dishes, fish, sauces, pickles, pies, vegetables, preserves, eggs, puddings, sweet dishes, pastry. cakes, beverages, &c. Edited by FRANCES FREELING BRODERIP. With Preface by TOM HOOD. Fcap. 8vo., cloth 1/6

TIMBS' (John) LIVES OF STATESMEN. Burke and Chatham Crown 8vo, Roxburghe binding. 6/-

———— DOCTORS AND PATIENTS. A New and Revised Edition in one Volume, crown 8vo 6/-

———— LIVES OF PAINTERS:—Hogarth, Sir Joshua Reynolds, Gainsborough, Fuseli, Sir Thomas Lawrence, Turner. Crown 8vo, Roxburghe binding. 6/-

———— LIVES OF WITS AND HUMOURISTS:—Swift, Steele, Foote, Goldsmith, the Colmans, Sheridan, Porson, Sydney Smith, Theodore Hook, &c., &c. In 2 vols., crown 8vo, Roxburghe binding, with Portraits. 12/-

———— LIVES OF THE LATER WITS AND HUMOURISTS:— Canning, Captain Morris, Curran, Coleridge, Lamb, Charles Mathews, Talleyrand, Jerrold, Albert Smith, Rogers, Hood, Thackeray, Dickens, Poole, Leigh Hunt. 2 vols., crown 8vo. Roxburghe binding. 12/-

TOO STRANGE NOT TO BE TRUE. By Lady GEORGIANA FULLERTON, Authoress of "Ladybird," &c. With two Illustrations, crown 8vo, cloth. 6/-

> "This story is wonderful and full of interest."—*The Times.*
> "One of the most fascinating and delightful works I ever had the good fortune to meet with."—'*Einonach*' *in Notes and Queries.*

TREASURY OF FRENCH COOKERY. By MRS. TOOGOOD. Crown 8vo. 5/-

TRAVELS IN THE AIR.

A Popular Account of Balloon Voyages and Ventures; with Recent attempts to accomplish the Navigation of the Air. By J Glaisher, of the Royal Observatory, Greenwich. Second Edition, with 138 Illustrations, royal 8vo. 25/-

*** Containing also the account of Mr. Glaisher's ascent of *seven* miles from the earth.

TRENCH'S (F. M. T.) JOURNAL ABROAD IN
1868. In post 8vo. 7/6

TREVLYN HOLD.

By Mrs. Henry Wood, Authoress of "The Channings," &c. Crown 8vo. cloth. 6/-

"We cannot read a page of this work without discovering a force of delineation which it would not be easy to surpass."—*Daily News.*

TURNING POINTS IN LIFE.

By the Rev. Frederick Arnold. Two vols. crown 8vo. 10/6

"A book intended for and especially suited to young men entering on life. It is extremely readable, with well chosen examples and a great amount of excellent information and advice."—*Daily Review.*

VERNER'S PRIDE.

By Mrs. Henry Wood, Authoress of "East Lynne," &c. Crown 8vo, cloth. 6/-

"A first-rate novel in its breadth of outline and brilliancy of description. Its exciting events, its spirited scenes, its vivid details, all contribute to its triumph."—*The Sun.*

WANDERINGS IN WAR-TIME:

Being Notes of Two Journies taken in France and Germany in the Autumn of 1870 and the Spring of 1871. By Samuel James Capper. Crown 8vo. 6/-

WAR, A HISTORY OF THE ART OF, from the
EARLIEST TIMES. By Colonel Graham. In post 8vo., with Diagrams. 5/-

WEBB'S (Mrs. J. B.) MARTYRS OF CARTHAGE.

A Tale of the Times of Old. In fcap. 8vo, gilt edges. 3/6

WESTERN WANDERINGS.

A RECORD OF TRAVEL IN THE LAND OF THE SETTING SUN. By J. W. Boddam-Whetham. With 12 full-page Illustrations, engraved by Whymper. Demy 8vo, 15/-

WHAT TO DO WITH THE COLD MUTTON.

Fcap. 8vo. 2/-

WHICH SHALL IT BE?

By Mrs. Alexander, Authoress of "The Wooing o't," &c. In crown 8vo., cloth. 6/-

WICKHAM'S (Rt. Hon. W.) CONFIDENTIAL
CORRESPONDENCE. 2 vols., 8vo, with portraits. 30/-

WIGRAM'S TWELVE WONDROUS TALES.
By W. Knox Wigram, Barrister-at-Law. With Comic Illustrations. Crown 8vo, 6/-

WILKINS' ART IMPRESSIONS OF DRESDEN,
BERLIN AND ANTWERP. By William Noy Wilkins. In post 8vo, 3/6

WITHIN THE MAZE.
By Mrs. Henry Wood, Authoress of "Verner's Pride," &c. With an Illustration. Crown 8vo, cloth. 6/-

"A very clever novel; interesting from the first page to the last"—*Daily Telegraph.*

"The decided novelty and ingenuity of the plot of 'Within the Maze' renders it, in our eyes, one of Mrs. Henry Wood's best novels. It is excellently developed, and the interest hardly flags for a moment."—*The Graphic.*

WOOD'S (Mrs. Henry) NOVELS.
All the Popular Novels of this favourite Writer. Each work can be had separately at any Booksellers, price 6/- bound in cloth.

A complete List of Mrs. Wood's Novels will be found on the back page of this Catalogue, or each one separately under its name.

WOOING O'T (The).
By Mrs. Alexander. Crown 8vo, cloth. 6/-

"The whole character of Maggie is very tenderly touched, and very clearly conceived. Simple and self-respecting, loving and firm, she is of the best type of English girls, and one that we have not met for a long time in the pages of a novel."—*Saturday Review.*

"Singularly interesting, while the easiness and flow of the style, the naturalness of the conversations, and the dealing with individual character are such that the reader is charmed from the beginning to the very end."—*Morning Post.*

"A charming story with a charming heroine."—*Vanity Fair.*

WORD-SKETCHES IN THE SWEET SOUTH.
By Mary Catherine Jackson. Demy 8vo. 10/6

YONGE'S (Professor) WORKS.
ENGLISH-LATIN AND LATIN-ENGLISH DICTIONARY. Used at Eton, Harrow, Winchester, and Rugby.

This Work has undergone careful revision, and the whole work (1070 pages) is reduced to 7/6. The English-Latin alone sells for 6/-, and the Latin-English alone for 6/-

"It is the best—we were going to say the only really useful—Anglo-Latin Dictionary we ever met with."—*Spectator.*

———— VIRGIL. With copious English Notes. Used at Eton, Harrow, Winchester, and Rugby. Post 8vo, strongly bound, 6/-